HAWK

THE QUIET PROFESSIONALS | BOOK 2

RONIE KENDIG

SHILOH RUN PRESS
An Imprint of Barbour Publishing, Inc.

Scripture taken from the New American Standard Bible, © 1960, 1962, 1963, 1968, 1971, 1972, 1973, 1975, 1977, 1995 by The Lockman Foundation. Used by permission.

Additional scripture taken from the HOLY BIBLE, NEW INTERNATIONAL VERSION®. NIV®. Copyright © 1973, 1978, 1984, 2011 by Biblica, Inc.™ Used by permission. All rights reserved worldwide.

This book is a work of fiction. Names, characters, places, and incidents are either products of the author's imagination or used fictitiously. Any similarity to actual people, organizations, and/or events is purely coincidental.

For more information about Ronie Kendig, please access the author's website at the following Internet address: www.roniekendig.com.

Cover Design: Kirk DouPonce, DogEared Design

Published by Shiloh Run Press, an imprint of Barbour Publishing, Inc., P.O. Box 719, Uhrichsville, Ohio 44683, www.shilohrunpress.com

Our mission is to publish and distribute inspirational products offering exceptional value and biblical encouragement to the masses.

ecpa Member of the
Evangelical Christian
Publishers Association

Printed in the United States of America.

DEDICATION

Narelle Mollet—Steadfast, loyal, beautiful,
encouraging—you are a light in my life! Thank you!
XOXOX

ACKNOWLEDGMENTS

Special thanks to:

To my family—Brian, Ciara, Keighley, Ryan & Reagan—thank you for
enduring on-your-own meals as I race toward deadlines and for loving
me through the zombielike states after all-nighters spent writing!

Julee Schwarzburg—thank you for the countless hours you've spent on
my many manuscsripts. I am very grateful!

Tom Dean, David Dean, and Troy McNear—thank you for your time
and help to make the thread against the super-secure network plausible
and yet protecting not only me but our men and women in uniform by
not supplying too much information.

Steve Laube—thank you, Agent-Man, for your steadfast support and
encouragement.

Narelle Mollet, Dineen Miller, Carla Laureano, Shannon McNear, and
Sarah Penner—thank you for your steady encouragement, laughter,
and friendship!

Thank you, Barbour Fiction Team—Annie Tipton, Shalyn Sattler,
Becky Germany, Kelsey McConaha, Elizabeth Shrider, Linda Hang,
and Mary Burns, for making this book happen! You're awesome!

Ironmance Team: Rachel Hauck, Lynette Eason, Katie Ganshert, Dani
Pettrey, and Becky Wade—Wow! What would I do without you ladies,
your prayers, and your support?! Thank you!

Rapid-Fire Fiction Task Force—You are absolutely awesome! Thank
you for your help, encouragement, and loyalty!

LITERARY LICENSE

In writing about unique settings, specific locations, and invariably the people residing there, a certain level of risk is involved, including the possibility of dishonoring the very people an author intends to honor. With that in mind, I have taken some literary license in Hawk, including renaming some bases within the U.S. military establishment, creating sites/ entities that do not otherwise exist, and other aspects of team movement/integration. Also, some elements of the story are pure entertainment and, as with any work of fiction, demand a level of suspension of disbelief. Writing about a potential threat to our American military personnel can be tricky, and those experts within that field cannot divulge too much information. Therefore, to protect our heroes, some elements of the story about the cyber-security threat have been left intentionally and paritally vague. I have done this so the book and/or my writing will not negatively reflect on our military community and its heroes. With the quickly changing landscape of the combat theater, this seemed imperative and prudent.

GLOSSARY OF TERMS/ACRONYMS

AHOD—All Hands On Deck
ANA—Afghan National Army
CID—Criminal Investigations Department
DIA—Defense Intelligence Agency
Glock—A semiautomatic handgun
HK416—Military assault rifle
IED—Improvised Explosive Device
Klick—Military slang for *kilometer*
M4, M4A1, M16—Military assault rifles
MRAP—Mine-Resistant Ambush-Protected vehicle
MWD—Military War Dog
OIC—Officer In Charge
OPSEC—Operational Security
QBZ-95—Chinese assault rifle
RPG—Rocket-Propelled Grenade
RTB—Return To Base
SAS—Special Air Service (Foreign Special Operations Team)
SCIF—Secure computer used by the military
SFOC—Special Forces Operational Command
SOCOM—Special Operations Command
STK—Shoot To Kill
UAV—Unmanned Aerial Vehicle
WO1—Warrant Officer, 1st Class

CHARACTER LIST

Boris Kolceki—expert computer hacker

Brian "Hawk" Bledsoe (Staff Sergeant)—Raptor team member; coms specialist

Cassandra Walker (Lieutenant)—works for DIA's National Military Joint Intelligence Center

Dean "Raptor Six" Watters (Captain)—Raptor team commander

Eamon "Titanis" Straider (SAS Corporal)—Raptor team member; Australian; engineering specialty

Fekiria Haidary (a.k.a., Second Lieutenant Rhmani)—ANA helicopter pilot; Zahrah Zarrick's cousin

Kiew Tang—executive assistant to Daniel Jin

Lance Burnett (General)—Raptor's commanding officer; attached to Defense Intelligence Agency

Meng-Li Jin /Daniel Jin—Chinese businessman

Mitchell "Harrier" Black (Sergeant First Class)—Raptor team member; combat medic

Mitra—Fekiria's friend; runs a secret girls' school

Mitra's "girls"—Aadela, Hadassah (Mitra's daughter), Jamilah, Sheevah, Wajmah

Salvatore "Falcon" Russo (Warrant Officer)—Raptor team member; aka team "daddy"; expert in ops/intel

Sandor Ripley (Captain)—U.S. Air Force pilot; Fekiria's flight advisor

Todd "Eagle" Archer (Staff Sergeant)—Raptor team member; weapons expert; team sniper

Zahrah Zarrick—Fekiria's cousin; Dean's girlfriend; missionary teacher

SUNDRY CHARACTERS

Adam Brennan (Sergeant)—soldier stationed at Bagram Airfield
Adeeb Haidary—Fekiria's older brother
Baktash and Belourine—married couple who help Mitra
Brie Hastings (Lieutenant)—General Burnett's administrative officer
Chris Riordan (Lieutenant Colonel)—Navy SEAL officer
Ddrake—military war dog
Garret Slusarski (Major)—officer stationed at Bagram Airfield
Grant Knight (Sergeant)—Ddrake's handler
Jack Bledsoe—Brian's grandfather
Kitty Bledsoe—Brian's grandmother
Mahmoud (Colonel)—ANA officer
Mason (Captain)—female officer at Bagram Airfield
Mike Sanderson (Specialist)—soldier at Bagram Airfield
Sajjan Takkar—CEO of Takkar Corp.
Tony "Candyman" VanAllen—former Green Beret on Dean Watters's team
Zmaray/"The Lion"—assassin, terrorist

SPECIAL FORCES CREED

I am an American Special Forces soldier. A professional!
I will do all that my nation requires of me.
I am a volunteer, knowing well the hazards of my profession.
I serve with the memory of those who have gone before me:
Roger's Rangers,
Francis Marion, Mosby's Rangers, the first Special Service Forces
and Ranger Battalions of World War II,
the Airborne Ranger Companies of Korea.
I pledge to uphold the honor and integrity of all I am—in all I do.
I am a professional soldier.
I will teach and fight wherever my nation requires.
I will strive always, to excel in every art and artifice of war.
I know that I will be called upon to perform tasks in isolation,
far from familiar faces
and voices, with the help and guidance of my God.
I will keep my mind and body clean, alert and strong,
for this is my debt
to those who depend upon me.
I will not fail those with whom I serve.
I will not bring shame upon myself or the forces.
I will maintain myself, my arms, and my equipment
in an immaculate state
as befits a Special Forces soldier.
I will never surrender though I be the last.
If I am taken, I pray that I may have the
strength to spit upon my enemy.
My goal is to succeed in any mission—and live to succeed again.
I am a member of my nation's chosen soldiery.
God grant that I may not be found wanting,
that I will not fail this sacred trust.

"De Oppresso Liber"

CHAPTER 1

Hindu Kush, Afghanistan
17 December—0915 Hours

Grip of death. The icy maw of winter in the Hindu Kush crushed breath from lungs with hammering winds. Bone-numbing iciness. Snowdrifts that could bury an entire mountain face as quickly as it could a person. Bitter and cruel, winter in Afghanistan held nothing back. Much like the insurgents trying to stop Raptor from seeing Christmas. Between deadly crevasses and IED-laden roads, the mountain range was a veritable kill zone.

Staff Sergeant Brian "Hawk" Bledsoe scrambled for cover. Shoulder to the hill, he ignored the rocks digging into his joint. "What'd you see?" he shouted ahead.

Captain Dean Watters went to a knee three yards up, a small cleft the only protection against the rounds of the Taliban they'd happened upon. "Eight, maybe ten fighters," the commander called over his shoulder.

As the communications sergeant of Raptor team, Brian was responsible for establishing and maintaining tactical and operational communications. He'd really like to communicate as much death to these death-loving Taliban as possible. "Mockingbird, this is Hawk. Raptor team is taking fire. Request air support."

"Hawk, this is Mockingbird. Sorry, but negative on the air support."

Brian's gut tightened. "Mockingbird, I repeat—need *immediate* assist."

"Raptor, your location is designated no-fly at this time."

"What the—?"

"Raptor, advise you disengage and RTB. Mockingbird out."

"Return to base," Brian muttered. "If we could do that—"

Rock and dirt spat at him.

Brian buried his chin, hunching against the barrage of weapons' fire. "If we die," he shouted into the coms, "it's your butt!" Snapping up his weapon, he cursed.

And immediately felt the disapproval of the team captain. Brian slid his gaze in that direction. Sure enough—a scowl. "We're on our own," Brian bit out as he shifted around and aimed his M4 over the limb of a snow-draped shrub. Scanning the hill above them, he groaned. Insurgents had the high ground. Meant they had the advantage, too.

Which meant Raptor had to find the dogs and rout them.

He threw himself up the footpath and behind a bramble of shrubs. In position, he eased his weapon through the icy tundra and again checked the hillside. A patch of tan—smooth and consistent—peeked out.

Brian eased back the trigger. Nice and easy. Three-round burst.

A body tumbled from a ledge.

Hooah. One down, too many to go. He reacquired the location. Scanned left with his pulse whooshing in his ears. Two days. Two lousy days left before some R & R, and *now* they step into this mess? He continued searching for the terrorists. Rocks. Debris. A defiant sprig of green.

Gray!

Brian fired—and saw the small explosion of muzzle flash seconds before he felt the searing across his arm. With a hiss, he dropped back against the hill, rocks and twigs digging into his back as someone on Raptor returned fire.

"You okay?" Mitchell "Harrier" Black shouted.

"Fine." Brian glanced down at his arm, the trail of blood small. "Just made me a little madder."

"Pity the guy," Harrier quipped.

"Nah," Eamon Straider, the Australian SAS corporal they'd dubbed Titanis, said. "I just delivered him to his seventy-two virgins."

"Hooah," the captain murmured.

Falcon elbowed out of the rocky alcove in which he'd taken cover and started forward. "Let's finish this. I'm ready to head home."

Home. The guys all had somewhere to go, someone to spend the holidays with. Lucky ducks had—

"Hawk, your six!"

As the shouts of his call sign registered, so did the crunching of rocks behind him. Brian spun, coming up just in time to see something—

someone—dropping on him. Adrenaline jacked, he knew this was fight or die! He lifted his arms.

Too late!

His head thudded against the rocks. Teeth clattered.

Weapon!

Brian grabbed the top end of the Talib's AK-47 and jerked it forward, yanking his enemy with it—right into his fist. A solid crack sent the insurgent stumbling backward. Brian leapt after him. The guy had come to kill him. If he let him get away, the terrorist would find a way to finish the job. So Brian had to finish him first. He landed on the guy, skidding across the downsloping path. With a swift draw of his Cold Steel SRK, Brian ended the terrorist's life.

Adrenaline spiked, he verified the man was dead before climbing off. Pops and cracks of weapons' fire continued behind him. Adjusting his M4, he sized up the enemy positions. Where Raptor was pinned down. If they didn't get to high ground, they'd be *ground* meat.

Grabbing a crevice with both hands, he hauled himself up. This was where his upper body strength, the way he worked off steam and frustration, benefitted him. He might not be as fast as Salvatore "Falcon" Russo, their team sergeant/daddy, but he had the strength to take down the worst of their enemies.

"Hawk!" Captain Watters's shout chased him up the hillside. "Hawk, no!"

Too late. He was halfway up and angrier than ever. These terrorists screamed and demanded honor but fought without it. The way they hid like cowards and picked off his team, men who worked hard to help make Afghanistan successful and peaceful in its own right, ticked him off. "And what do we get," he grunted as he dragged himself up the last stretch. "Shot!"

Hidden in a deep crevasse that gave him a sweet line of sight on the three shooters, he went to a knee. Propped himself up so he wouldn't fall. Wind howled over his ears, despite the hat and helmet, as seconds clicked off, waiting for someone to fire at Raptor again so he could spot them.

Crack.

Brian flicked his weapon's reticle back to the left. Sighted the first one. Bravado would be the man's fall—literally. He'd chosen a ledge that exposed him to Brian. *Adios!* He fired. The guy slumped as a crimson stain spread over the rocky edifice.

It took a second to locate the next shooter who'd taken cover, Brian imagined, when his friend went to hang with the virgins. He almost smiled. At least the guy wasn't making it *too* easy for him. Evening his breathing, Brian took aim and eased back the trigger. The fighter twitched, lost his balance, and fell from his hiding spot.

Now, the third.

Thwack!

Snow and rock dribbled onto Brian's forehead. With a curse, he took cover. Slipped down the crevasse. He scrabbled for traction. Caught himself with a toe in a small indention. His breath puffed before him. "Easy, easy," he whispered. Controlled breathing wasn't easy with his heart pumping twice its normal rate, but Brian focused. He eased down, propping himself forward, weapon trained out. Snow now dusted his muzzle.

More camouflage, he hoped. He slowed his breathing as he traced the rocks. The shrubs. More rocks. *Come out, come out, wherever you—*

Gotcha.

Brian fired.

Shrieking, the man tumbled forward. The rocky ledge broke.

Pulse rapid-firing, Brian drew back. Stared. In a split-second recon, he saw what was coming. "Oh crap!" A dark line spread across the cleft.

Crack!

The ledge gave way.

"Go, go!" Brian shouted as he twisted around and leaned back, sliding down the treacherous incline. "Avalanche!"

A meaty roar preempted the terror that gripped him. Snow and rock exploded, and with it came the rumbling of a mountain. As if bemoaning the deaths of the insurgents.

Brian threw himself downward, shuffle-sliding down the loose rock and debris. *Keep moving, keep moving.* Like he needed to think it. He had to stay upright and ahead of the deadly elements. His calves burned as rocks and branches tore at his pants and scraped his flesh. Something punched the side of his face. He blinked and bit down hard as pain reverberated through his neck and back. But he didn't stop.

Finally found traction. Grabbed the ledge and launched himself into the path of Raptor. His body pitched forward. A yank on his drag strap snapped him upright. He sprinted with Falcon, his heart thundering through his ears louder than the wind.

As the rumbling faded and the rocks settled, Brian glanced back. He slowed, his heart rate decelerating. A laugh escaped, disbelieving. He could've been buried alive. Once again, he'd cheated death.

"You stupid, insane idiot!" Falcon's shout ripped through the sudden calm.

Brian ignored the team sergeant.

"What were you thinking?" This time it was Captain Watters. "I told you to *stay*."

"Stay?" Brian warned himself to calm down as he walked toward their armored vehicle. "They were picking us off like dogs! If I hadn't done something, we'd still be up there, and who knows what wounds and bodies we'd be carrying back."

The captain's eyes blazed. "It wasn't your call!" Anger lurked behind the normally stoic gaze. "I need to know—"

"—pinned down and taking fire!" crackled through the coms, stunning them into silence. "Repeat: pinned down and taking fire. Request immediate assist!"

Chin tucked, Captain Watters's gaze shifted down as he listened to the radio chatter.

Brian stilled at the shouted panic erupting through the coms.

"Unidentified caller, this is a U.S. military station. What is your location and designation?"

The captain snapped a finger toward him.

"On it." Brian snatched out his military-grade GPS.

"Echo Company," came the shrill voice of someone who identified himself as a private and provided the location.

"Dude." Brian angled himself around, orienting the GPS. "They're less than five klicks from us." He stabbed a finger toward the east. "Over there."

"Too far. Can't see anything." Captain Watters peered through his binoculars.

A strangled scream came through the coms. A string of expletives seared the communication. "They just killed the sergeant!" Whimpering. "Oh man. Oh man. I'm in charge now."

"What? Is this place crawling with those demons?" Falcon hissed.

"We'll need a medevac," Harrier said, glancing in the direction of the attack.

The captain lifted his head but not his gaze. "Eagle—how are we on weapons?"

Staff Sergeant Todd Archer didn't flinch. Weapons were his responsibility, and he had a finger on the ammo pulse. "Enough to engage but not for anything sustained."

"Enough to get in and get out?"

"Won't know till we try."

"Help!" the voice exploded through the coms. "They just killed two more—oh God, help us!" All-out crying. "Only four of us left. And two are wounded."

Captain Watters twisted, his face dark and shadowed.

Brian tensed, knowing the captain's personal story of being ambushed in a convoy and spending months as a POW years ago, tortured and watching his team raped and murdered in front of him. But seriously? "What are we waiting for?"

"We need immediate evac! *Please!*" The team leader under attack provided his coordinates once again.

"That's the village we were warned to stay out of," Falcon said. "We go in there. . .even if we get them out alive, we're dead meat back at SOCOM."

"What was a team doing there in the first place?" Titanis gave a single shake of his head. "Sorry, mates. This doesn't feel right."

"When *does* combat feel right?" Brian tucked back his frustration and focused on the captain. The one who made the decisions. "We got some of our own in harm's way. We don't go in there, and they die. . .?"

"Hawk's right. We're wasting time and lives," Captain Watters finally announced. "Let's move!" As the captain keyed his mic, Falcon revved the engine and tore across the rugged terrain. "Mockingbird, this is Raptor Six Actual. We are en route to provide backup and aid to Echo Company."

"Copy that Raptor Six Actual. I've notified Overlook and have been cleared to deploy Glory One. ETA in twelve."

"Roger that, Mockingbird. Ready those birds for triage."

Even as the MRAP trounced over the desertlike terrain, Brian felt his gut climb into his throat. Brothers-in-arms were in trouble. Taking heavy fire. He craned his neck and peered out the front armored windows, searching the monochromatic landscape for signs of the attack.

He didn't need nocs to see the armored vehicle spewing fire and smoke into the sky. "IED," Brian muttered, wanting to curse the savages who laid in wait like the cowards they were.

"Stop," Eagle shouted. "Lemme out." With his sniper rifle slung over his shoulder, he flung himself out the back door. For a guy with as much bulk as Brian, he moved fast. Spine bent parallel to the ground, head down, he raced to the side. Scurried up a tree then threw himself onto a rock outcropping. Sweet spot, Eagle called it—a location that gave him a bird's-eye view. Close enough to be lethal but far enough out for protection.

"Eagle in position," Todd's slightly labored breath came through their coms.

"What do you see?" the captain asked as they navigated the wicked, messed-up land. Potholes, big holes, and more holes gouged this arid region worse than the Grand Canyon. They waited for his response, their vehicle bounding from one spot to another over the uneven fields.

Brian glanced at Titanis, who shrugged.

"Eagle, report."

"I. . .I got nothing, Captain."

"Come again?"

"Nothing. It's. . .the village is em—wait."

Brian held a breath as their sniper ordered.

"No. It's clear. Using thermals—nothing's there, Captain. The place is deserted."

"We got those coordinates wrong?"

Brian glanced down at the numbers he'd jotted in his coms notebook. Verified it on his GPS. "Negative." He checked the village. "That's the place."

As their vehicle eased up to the hard-packed road that led into the grape huts and plaster structures, tension thickened the air.

"Eyes out," Captain Watters said as Falcon cut the engine and let the truck roll behind a small structure, providing cover.

What Brian heard in the captain's voice mirrored what Brian felt deep in his gut. Cheek against his weapon, he emerged into the bitter elements, his fingers aching against the cold. He walked carefully in strategic formation with the others. Falcon and Titanis cleared the first juncture, which turned out to be the only road with buildings straddling it on either side.

"Not good," Brian said in a low voice as he eased around the cover, his spine to the frozen plaster and eyes out. "It's a ghost town."

Buildings were missing more walls than they had. Windows were half blown. A few fluttering rags once served as curtain doors.

"Eagle, you got anything yet?" Captain Watters walked slowly, peering around the eerily silent compound.

"Negative."

The captain keyed his mic again. "Mockingbird, this is Raptor Six Actual."

"Go ahead, Raptor Six Actual."

"We're at the given coordinates but this place is deserted," the commander said, his gaze tracking the holes and piles of rubble.

Brian walked over the debris littering the ground, verifying each room, each house, each structure didn't have a trap or bomb.

"Can you radio Echo and have them confirm the coordinates?"

"Roger that, Raptor. Give me a minute."

Crunch-pop!

Brian's heart tripped over what should be an innocuous noise, but even the sound of rocks beneath his boots sounded and felt like a punch to the gut. *This isn't right.*

"Captain? Thoughts?" Falcon trudged toward their team leader, having made his rounds in the abandoned village.

"This place has some bad mojo." Brian couldn't escape the creepy chill sliding down his spine. The howling wind carried the eerie voices of the past that once occupied this place and tickled the hairs on the back of his neck. "This is straight out of some thriller flick or something. I don't like it."

"Agreed." The captain looked ticked, his lips tight and his brow knotted.

"Um. . .Raptor, Mockingbird Actual advises you RTB."

Brian cocked his head. "That sounded a whole lot like general speak for 'Run for your lives.'"

Finger pressed to his ear mic, Captain Watters stopped at the MRAP. "What's going on, Mockingbird?"

"Sir, I'm not sure how to say this, but. . .Echo is here."

Brian stopped short, staring at the captain. "Do *what*?"

"Come again?" He scowled.

"Sir, Echo company is here. At the base. Have been for the last two days."

"Then who the heck radioed for immediate assist?"

"Working on—"

"Raptor, get out of there!" boomed the voice of General Lance Burnett. "Now!"

Sprinting back to their vehicle, Brian felt the icy ghosts of this village chasing them. Taunting them. He cleared the corner.

"Go, go, go!" the captain shouted.

The howling wind surrendered to a shrieking of superheated air. Behind him, a white-hot light exploded.

Brian flung forward, knocked by an invisible hand. His feet flew up. A tree raced toward him. His helmet thunked against the bark. He dropped hard. Cold became hot. Loud, deafeningly quiet.

White went black.

CHAPTER 2

Mazar-e Sharif, Afghanistan
17 December—1045 Hours

Exhilaration zipped through her veins as she marched in formation with her peers. Head cocooned in the black hijab set her apart almost more than her curves in this army of mostly male soldiers. She drew in a breath of elation, keeping her face stonelike and her drill perfect.

At parade rest, Afghan Air Force Second Lieutenant Rhmani stood proud among the other dozen soldiers during their Undergraduate Pilot Training ceremony. Of the twelve, four were Afghan males and seven American males.

She the only female.

Another thrill-induced breath drew raggedly through her. If it were not for Niloofar Rhmani, the first female pilot, she would not have had this opportunity. Her chin lifted. As their flight instructors stood before them with their flight-wing pins, she felt a squeeze in her stomach. *I wish* Madar *could be here!*

But of course, that was impossible.

"You have completed the UPT, consisting of 145.5 flying hours trained on the MD 530..."

Her mind wandered the skies. The hours spent among the heavens. So close to God. So free from...*everything*. All the torments. All the restrictions.

The shuttering of a camera made her stiffen. She hoped the hijab and uniform concealed her identity enough. But the continuous clattering of cameras made her wish for her wide sunglasses.

"Well done, Lieutenant," came the soft, firm voice of her flight advisor, Captain Sandor Ripley of the 438th Air Expeditionary Advisory Group. Had she been a male, he would've pinned her. Instead, for custom and propriety, he handed the pin to a female officer, who fastened it above her left breast.

"Thank you, sir."

"I expect to see you in advanced training next month."

"Of course, sir." She drew in another spurt of excitement.

With a salute, he stepped back. The words from the stage blurred in her mind. What would her cousin think? Would she be shocked and angry? So many lies got Fekiria to this point. She couldn't imagine anyone would be happy for her.

But that did not matter. *She* was happy. For the first time in her life.

"Dismissed!"

She flinched but then tucked her chin and hurried toward a side door.

"Lieutenant Rhmani," a male voice called.

Her heart sped. She couldn't talk to anyone. Not now. She had worked so hard for so long. . . Her feet scurried faster.

"Hey! Wait—I just wanted to invite you."

Around the corner, she felt her arm tugged. Her eyes closed as she stopped her flight. She turned, surprise squirreling through her. "Captain."

He released her, his brow tangled in consternation. "You okay?"

Inclining her head, she made sure photographers hadn't followed them. "Never better."

His gray experienced eyes took her in. "Okay," he said, obviously not convinced but unwilling to argue with her. "There's a group of us going out tonight to celebrate UPT graduation. Since you're a graduate," he said, his smile kind, "it makes sense you should come."

"I–I'm sorry, Captain." She swallowed, very much wanting to accept his offer, but that would create questions. More questions she couldn't answer. More lies she'd have to tell. "I can't. But thank you for the consideration."

Disappointment slid through his handsome, dark features. "Celebrating with your family?"

She smiled. "Of course. They are thrilled for me, though they could not come today."

"I understand." He nodded then tugged something from his pocket. "I was going to give this to you there."

Glancing at the paper in his hand, she hesitated.

He chuckled. "Don't worry. It's not a love letter, though I did try my hand at one."

She took a step back.

Captain Ripley really laughed this time. "Kidding! I'm only kidding." He wagged the paper at her. "It's your acceptance letter for the advanced-training program."

She widened her eyes then took the paper.

"Well, take care—I'll see you." Captain Ripley stepped back with a faint salute to her. "Proud of you, Lieutenant. You're going to take the skies by storm."

His praise exploded through her. She fought the tears. "Thank you."

He considered her and nodded.

Voices erupted at the other end of the hall, sending him around the corner. She turned and headed for the gate. She checked out and climbed into her car. After making the 2.8-kilometer trip to the local café, she parked. Retrieved her bag from the trunk and entered the small structure. The warm, heady scent of coffee beans and hookah wafted through the cramped space. Weaving in and around tables, she made her way to the back restroom. There, she hung the bag on the hook, locked the door, and removed the flight uniform.

Careful to keep the wrinkles out, to show it the respect it deserved for setting her wings free, she set it in the bottom of the large tote. Removed her boots. Slipped into the sage-green long tunic and pants. She wrapped a floral silk hijab around her black one. Tucking on her sunglasses, she lifted the bag from the hook.

Back in the café, she ordered a black tea and sipped it. Along with some naan and honey. Comfort food. Stomach full, though the bread had done nothing to soothe her nerves, she removed herself to the street. Drew in a breath and drove herself home. Eased into a slot in front of the apartment building.

Nerves tangled, she made her way up to the apartment and let herself in.

Laughter from the kitchen snapped her out of the numbness that had swarmed her.

"Ah, Cousin! You're just in time to celebrate."

Her heart spasmed as she met Zahrah's brown-eyed gaze. How had she found out?

"Director Kohistani just received a large grant to build a real school!" Her half-American cousin came out of the kitchen with a tray of baklava. "Can you believe it? Say you will come back. I miss you there."

"No." She hated the snip in her voice, but they'd been over this a thousand times. She stalked past her cousin, ignoring the delicious pastries.

"I put chocolate in them—the way you like them!"

"I'm not hungry."

"Fekiria! What is wrong with you?"

"Nothing." She spun and faced her cousin in the door to her room. "In fact, I've never been better." Defiance streaked through her—that is, until she saw the hurt on her cousin's face.

"You've been so strange since I. . ." Zahrah wilted. "Please. . .please tell me you don't still blame yourself."

"No." But she did. A lot. If she had been there instead of running off getting more training, Zahrah might not have been taken. "Please. I am just tired. It was a long day."

Zahrah slid the plate of baklava onto the small table by the chairs. "Will you ever shed this secrecy and tell me what's happening in your life?"

Guilt strangled her response.

"I miss our talks. Once we were like sisters."

"Bickering and fighting."

Zahrah smiled. "Yes—what else do sisters do?"

She loved her cousin's laugh, her smile, her bright spirit. But the lies, the. . .secrets created this vast cavern between them. One that Zahrah was blind to and Fekiria could never cross. Unless she wanted her parents to find out. Then she'd be whipped. Beaten. Maybe even killed. An honor killing, *Baba* would say.

Zahrah moved forward.

The terror that somehow her secrets would come crashing down made her sick. Angry. "I can't help it if you spend all your time with your American soldier." Fekiria pivoted and slammed the bedroom door, shutting out her cousin's niceties. The guilt—no. She couldn't shut that out no matter how hard she tried.

—᠅—

Five Klicks Outside Mazar-e Sharif, Afghanistan
17 December—1135 Hours

"Hawk!"

Something struck his shoulder. Brian blinked. Adrenaline shot through him, recalling the explosion. Must've knocked him out. He scrambled up and to cover. Captain Watters and Falcon were whispering . . .wait. No—not whispering. Shouting!

Brian stuck a finger in his ear to unplug it and felt a warm stickiness. "Great." One glance at his bloodied finger told him his eardrum might've ruptured. As his mind reconnected the dots that left him on the ground, he looked to the crumbling village. It now stood less one building.

In the warbling vacuum that was his hearing, he heard *"Move!"* loud and clear. He propelled himself toward their vehicle. As he ran, he saw Titanis and Harrier moving swiftly and precisely, weapons trained on possible fire traps. A slap to his shoulder made him jerk.

The massive Aussie didn't seem fazed as he stood, weapon up and scanning.

Folding himself into the vehicle, Brian shook his head in the eerie, vacuous silence that had engulfed him. Shook it harde r. He didn't need to hear to know they had to clear out. Now.

In their MRAP, he noticed the emptiness of sound even more. He grabbed the rag from his neck and wiped the blood. Falcon leapt behind the wheel, and they tore away from the village.

In the relative safety of the vehicle, Brian gave himself a mental pat down for injuries. Checked the team. A line of blood traced the side of Falcon's face. The captain didn't need the cut across his nose and cheek to look ticked—he did that fine on his own.

After that near-death experience, it wasn't surprising Falcon kept vigilant, driving only in the middle of the road and sometimes off-road to ensure they didn't attract the fatal effects of an improvised-explosive device. Nothing could guarantee their safety, but the more precautions taken, the more chances of surviving increased.

They hit a rut in the road. The vehicle dipped to the left then rammed against a rock as it returned to even ground. The jolt freed Brian's ear with a painful *pop!* He hunched his shoulders against the pain but gritted through it.

". . .of nowhere. I want to talk with Echo's team leader." The captain held his coms mic, head craned to the side as he listened. "Negative, sir."

Only then did Brian realize his coms piece must've broken. He couldn't hear anything through it. He removed it and grunted at the split casing and blood around it. Swiping the side of his face confirmed he was bleeding in more places than one.

"Sir." Captain Watters bit out the term of respect, his jaw muscle popping. He slid a glance to Falcon, who shook his head.

"What's going on?" Brian leaned forward in his seat. "My coms broke."

"Nothing." The captain rammed his elbow against the window. "Ramsey's blocking me from talking with Echo Company's team leader."

"What the—*why*?" That didn't make any sense. The team needed to rout whoever had made that call. If it was someone within Echo, they had to find that out before more trouble hatched.

"DIA and CID are checking into it. For now, we have a mission."

"What mission?" Falcon objected. "We have been sent on more drug and weapons cache raids in the last three months than all combined missions. What are they trying to keep us from?"

"The truth," Brian snapped.

"No," the captain said, looking over his shoulder at Brian. "I think this is about them having no idea what's happening. They're scared, so they're trying to keep tight control on assets."

Okay, now that was an interesting scenario. And for Brian, one that finally made sense. "So, you think—"

"We need to talk to Burnett."

Brian found himself nodding along with the captain as they returned to the sub-base command center. The main door opened as the team climbed out. A group of soldiers emerged, hovering. Waiting.

Brian's fists balled as he saw the familiar faces. SEALs. The same ones who'd been a pain in their butts.

Captain Watters slowed as he removed his helmet.

"Captain." At five-ten, the guy stood a few inches shorter than Raptor's team leader, but there was no difference in power wielded.

"Commander Riordan." Watters drew up and planted his hand on his tactical belt. "What can I do for you?"

Riordan, jaw tight and gaze fierce, shot a glance to Brian and the others. Then he lowered his gaze, as if second-guessing his purpose here. He let out a breath then lifted his head. "The team and I are heading to Aazam's tonight."

Hookah bar? Was the dude serious? "We're in the middle of a freakin' war." Though Brian would like to have some downtime, he never had gotten into the hookah thing.

The captain held up his hand to Brian without looking at him. To

Riordan, he said, "I hope you gentlemen have a good time."

"If you change your mind, we'll be there—2100."

Hand on the door, Captain Watters hesitated. Met the commander's eyes. Then gave a quick nod as he tugged the door open. Falcon stepped through, and Brian moved around the SEALs to enter when one of the frogmen stepped into his path.

Brian's shoulder collided with the guy.

Old instincts flared. He snapped a hand up.

Watters's hand on Brian's chest slowed the fire. "Good day, gentlemen."

Heart hammering, Brian aimed himself into the building. Fists balled, teeth clenched, he dialed down the punch of adrenaline that demanded he make that SEAL eat his bullying.

As sunlight was snapped out by the closing door, a vise clamped onto Brian's shoulder. "Work on that, Hawk." Watters patted him then stepped ahead.

Disappointment chugged through Brian. No matter how hard he *did* try, those impulses erupted on their own. Just when he thought they were under his control, some punk SEAL stepped into his face. But why did it always have to happen in front of Captain Watters, the one soldier he wanted to prove himself to?

And why was the captain's approval so important?

"General Burnett, this is Dean Watters. . ."

Incident chunked, Brian zeroed in on the team hunkered in the corner by the captain's desk. "Put it on speaker," Brian said.

"Sir?" Captain Watters frowned. And man, when that guy looked ticked, people ran.

Brian's bid to hear the conversation vanished. This didn't sound good, so maybe he didn't want to hear after all.

Leaning forward, the captain cradled his forehead with his fingertips. "Sir, I respectfully—" Silence clapped through the room. "Yessir. . .understood, sir. . .no, sir." He shook his head. Staring at the phone, he slowly lowered it to the cradle.

"So?" Falcon asked, his thick arms folded over his chest.

"We lay low."

"Till when?" Falcon's question—and the look in his brown eyes—read more like a challenge than a question.

The captain pushed out of his chair. He looked each of them in the eye. "Let's shower up and grab some grub."

Brian choked back a laugh. "You're kidding, right?" He held out his hands. "Just pretend someone out there didn't just try to kill us."

Captain Watters snapped him a glare.

Right. Anger... Brian drew back. Tempered the storm in his gut. "Fine." The commander knew something. And he wasn't telling them. Which... Was there a reason, or was he being Burnett's puppet again?

Brian left the building and showered. Tended the cuts and scrapes, grateful there didn't appear to be any permanent damage to his eardrum. He grabbed a bowl of Mongolian beef and rice from one of the restaurants and headed back to his desk at the sub-base. The captain may not have the know-how to do some light *investigating* via their Internet, but Brian did.

He logged in and worked his way through the protocol series, digging deeper and deeper. With each mouthful of food, with each hour and layer of security, his tension rose. *If I get caught...*

Once into the base's main server, he gained access. It'd take a few hours to find what he needed, but the journey had to start somewhere. He'd need the names of Echo Company to verify their locations at the time of the incident and cross-check that with video surveillance. Troll radio-chatter transcripts.

"Hawk."

Something in the chatter transcripts tugged at the back of his mind, but he couldn't figure out what. "Yeah." He glanced over his shoulder and froze. Oh crap.

CHAPTER 3

Captain Watters strode toward him, his brow knotted.

Brian slumped back against his chair.

"What are you doing?"

"Research."

Towering over him, the captain frowned. "What kind of research?"

"The kind that protects us out there when someone's trying to blow us up."

Lips flat, the captain stared him down. He breathed in. Out. "Even after I told you to leave it."

"You didn't, actually." Not that he was being facetious or smart-alecky. "You told us to shower. Grab some food. I did"—he dropped the Styrofoam carton in the trash—"then I did my job. Communications."

"You knew full well what I meant, what was implied. You sorry. . ." The captain drew in a ragged breath and let it out slowly. "You'd better pray you didn't just bury us. Or so help me—" He pivoted and started for the door. "Let's go."

Brian rose to his feet. Glanced at the clock. Do what—2000 hours already? "Where?"

"Move!"

Moonlight streamed through the curtain and beamed onto her bed. Fekiria lay staring up at the sky, her flight-wing pin between her hands. The stars. If she closed her eyes, she was there. Among them. Among the stars and not down here. Not with the trouble and ridicule and disapproval. Their ancient customs and patriarchal fury.

She lifted the pin into the light and smiled. *I did it!*

Advanced training. If she wanted to fly something bigger and faster …she'd have to head south to Kandahar Airfield. Away from her family. Away from everything she knew. It wouldn't be as if she'd go alone. As part of the ANA, she would be on the base among other soldiers. It wouldn't be improper.

But it still wouldn't be acceptable. Not to Baba. Nothing she did was acceptable to him.

And why was it improper for a woman to live alone?

She could do more than most men. Had outscored and outflown nearly every one of her fellow pilot candidates. Now she had the capability to drop bombs on men like those who had killed the children. Nearly killed her cousin.

But if she went. . .she could never come back. Baba and Madar would not understand. Zahrah would never talk to her again because much of what she believed about Fekiria right now was based on lies.

Her phone buzzed. She lifted it from the small table beside her bed and glanced at the text. A smile riffled through her. Sandor Ripley. She opened it and found his message. BORING HERE WITHOUT YOU. Her flight advisor had encouraged her. Probably more than he should have. She was not so blind that she missed his attraction to her. But he was American.

Yes. An American who taught you how to fly.

To fulfill a dream. One Baba said could not happen. Perhaps she was a hypocrite. Captain Ripley was not the only American soldier who had been nice to her. There had been plenty, in truth. But there had been one. . .one she could not especially stand. The friend of Zahrah's Captain Dean. The one who had come to little Ara's funeral. Who had kept her busy so she could not interrupt Zahrah's conversation. She did not trust Americans. And he made it worse.

They'd called him Sergeant Brian. Gray-green eyes. Light hair. Too much attitude. He had openly flirted with her.

Captain Ripley had shown her respect. Admiration.

Fekiria pulled herself from the bed. Still dressed, she lifted the hijab she'd worn earlier. No. The pale pink one. She lifted it from a drawer then quietly slipped out of her room. Darkness shrouded the apartment. A crack of light sneaked beneath Zahrah's bedroom door and slid across the vinyl floor to Fekiria. She hurried to the front door and let herself out. As she scampered down the stairs, she heard a door above open.

Heart in her throat, Fekiria shoved back against the stairwell. She could not let Zahrah see her. Pure and perfect, Zahrah would try to convince her—again—of the error of her ways. Her cousin presumed she was doing things a woman of morals and virtue would not do. Perhaps that was true, but not in the way everyone assumed. Not in a way that damaged her worth. Yet if they found out, she'd be flailed for the lies, the secreting out, the half-truths. What she had accomplished, what she had earned, would not matter. Only the lies.

Bah! Irritated, Fekiria continued down. Cruised the perimeter, plaster cold against her fingers as she scurried in the darkness.

"Fekiria!" came a hushed whisper-shout from the top.

Sucking in a breath, she reached the ground level. Shoved herself across the foyer and out the door. Staying close to the exterior wall, she secured her hijab then stuffed her arms through her coat. It took only fifteen minutes to make it to the bar. Nightlife in Mazar-e was not like what one saw in Western cities.

At the hookah bar, she waited till a group of girls entered and quickly fell into step with them. Entering alone would draw attention and risk word getting out to her family. She'd be fine once she met up with her fellow soldiers. Inside, the low lighting made it difficult to see through the haze of smoke. A rumble of laughter burst from the side.

Gray eyes met hers at almost the same time. Captain Ripley came to his feet with a smile and no small amount of surprise.

His reaction gave her pleasure that pushed her through the crowds to the seating area where the UPT graduates lounged. Captain Ripley motioned to the cushioned sofa. "I didn't think you were coming."

"Nor did I." She tucked herself onto the cushioned settee. When he assumed the spot next to her, she stiffened but told herself she was being foolish. If she had not come to see him, then why *had* she come? She must relax. Stop worrying.

"Lieutenant Rhmani!" One of the other pilots spotted her. "Awesome flying out there."

She inclined her head. "As with you, Lieutenant Atwood."

He grinned, his gaze bouncing between her and Captain Ripley for a second, but long enough to make her uncomfortable, then he was pulled into a conversation.

"How was your celebration with your family?"

Fekiria shot the captain a glance, her stomach clenching. "Fine." She barely remembered to smile. "These things are not as important here." So tired of the lies, she searched for a way to divert the conversation. "Kandahar..."

He bent forward, elbows on his knees, his shoulder almost touching hers. "Advanced training." Brown hair cut high and tight, he was handsome. And nice. "Please tell me you've decided to go."

Fekiria nodded before she could change her mind.

"Awesome!" He touched her shoulder, his enthusiasm waning a bit. "What about your family?"

Her family had long ago lost the right to have a voice in her life. "What of them?"

"Won't they miss you? I thought you said—"

"I must make this decision for myself. I am of age, and..." She drew in a steadying breath. "I want to do this."

He nodded with another smile. "I'm glad. I'd hoped you would."

What did he mean by that? The sparkle in his eyes bespoke something more than his happiness that she would continue her pilot training down in Kandahar. Away from him. If he was so excited to see her go, he couldn't like her that much.

When he didn't stop grinning at her, she finally gave in. "What? You have something in your eyes."

He dipped his head sheepishly. "One of the instructors is heading back to the States. They offered me the position." His gray eyes held hers. "My orders came through about ten minutes ago. They're sending me to Kandahar."

She should be thrilled. He was one of the finest instructors in the training program. He was patient, nice, and—though a bit older than she'd prefer—good looking. And he held a world of expectation in his gaze and words. Maybe that is why her stomach squirmed. She just found her wings, in more ways than one, and she wasn't sure she wanted them clipped by being tethered to a man.

"So, you're going."

"I am."

Fekiria should enjoy his attention. He wasn't married. He didn't have another wife. He didn't have grandchildren like the man her parents had tried to match her with six months ago. Handsome, kind...

What is wrong with me?

"You're not happy I'm going."

"No—I mean, yes!" She laughed and used the moment to gather her nerves. "I'm not sure how to answer that question." Another laugh. "I am happy you're going. You have made all the difference in the world in my training. That you will be there, training me—"

"*Possibly* training you. There are no guarantees I'll be your flight advisor. But I will be there."

Fekiria beamed. "I am relieved I'll know someone there. That was one of my major concerns." She patted his arm. "It is good to have a friend, a friendly face in a new place."

"Friend."

Fekiria couldn't meet his eyes after the disappointment she heard in his voice. "You've been wanting this, too, haven't you? To work the advanced program."

"Been waiting years."

"Then see? It is good for all!"

"Hey, Captain." Someone slapped his knee. "Check it out."

Fekiria followed their gazes to where a group of men entered the bar. Their bearing screamed American military as much as if they wore uniforms. Dressed in all black and a serious attitude, the men stood at the entrance for a few minutes.

Then the tall one turned and looked her way.

Fekiria drew back. Captain Watters! Cold washed across her shoulders and spine. *What is he doing here?* If he was here, then. . . Almost on their own, her eyes searched the other four men huddled around him. The really big guy. The dark-haired one. A shorter one.

Oh thank goodness! He had not come.

The really big soldier craned his neck to the side, his gaze forward on the hazy room, as he seemed to listen to someone. Then with a smile, he shifted.

And she saw him—Sergeant Brian.

Fekiria hauled in a breath and straightened, pushing her gaze to the teal carpet. Panic swirled. If he saw her. . .

She started to turn to her left, but that would put her in a rather intimate position with Captain Ripley. What if Sergeant Brian saw that? She cut a quick glance to the side.

Green eyes met hers. He looked away.

Oh. He hadn't recognized her. She shouldn't be hurt. Relief. She should feel relief. Had he forgotten her so quickly? It was easier, didn't complicate things, if he forgot her.

His gaze flicked back to hers, recognition evident in his raised eyebrows and cocky grin.

Fekiria closed her eyes. Touched her fingers to her forehead.

"You okay?" Captain Ripley asked, his attention bouncing between her and the newcomers. "Know them?"

"Not really." The words were honest. But not entirely.

"One of them seems to know you."

"He. . . We were at the same funeral once."

Captain Ripley's eyebrows rose as his gaze seemed to follow someone. Then he stood. "Can I help you?"

Fekiria's heart pounded as another set of shoes appeared.

"No. I'm here to say hi to her."

Mustering her courage, Fekiria looked up. Wanted to pretend she didn't recognize him. But this close, he seemed. . .large. Powerful. When their eyes met, something in her warmed.

"Miss Hai—"

Her name! "Sergeant Brian." He knew her *real* name. She punched to her feet. "A surprise to see you here." She refused to glance back to the other Americans, terrified Zahrah's boyfriend would join them. But her body acted on its own. A dizzy flood of relief washed through her when she found the foyer empty—the others were gone.

"I could say the same for you." His taunting tone drew her gaze. His gray-green eyes were mere inches from her.

She pulled in a steadying breath, willing herself not to look away. Not to yield to the electrical storm surging between them. Curse the man! Why did he find everything so amusing? "I'm out with friends. Not so strange, is it?"

Something curious and penetrating flashed through his eyes. "I guess not." As he studied the UPT—One. At. A. Time.—he seemed to take in a lot of information with the way his eyes darted and processed. An intense awareness that this man could unravel the last two years of hard work became apparent as he angled his head toward her. "Just didn't realize you hung out with U.S. military. Last I recall, you had a particular dislike for my kind."

She lifted her chin. "Yes, *your* kind. That hasn't changed."

Green eyes locked on to her.

"Have we been introduced?"

Sergeant Brian smirked at Captain Ripley, who held out his hand. Then Sergeant Brian patted the captain's shoulder. "Good luck. You're going to need it."

Embarrassment heated her cheeks. "I—"

"Miss Haidary—my pleasure."

"It was only yours, Sergeant Brian."

His grin grew. "Yes, ma'am. I reckon it was." With that, he turned and navigated the thick throng, vanishing into the smoky back room like a ghost. One that could definitely haunt her if he told Captain Dean. Who would, no doubt, tell Zahrah. Beyond that, he'd used her name. Which meant this could come back to end her piloting career.

"Who is he?"

Fekiria started. Then smiled at Captain Ripley. "A soldier who helped my cousin."

"The one who was taken captive?"

Fekiria stilled. Met the gray eyes that bespoke confidence and intelligence. And a hint of romance. "How did you know that?"

"Don't worry about secrets. We all have them, Lieutenant Haidary."

BORIS

Unknown Location, Afghanistan

Invincible. Indestructible. I've laid below their radar for almost a year now. My programs are infecting their systems. My mastery evading their efforts. I've wreaked havoc against one of the most invincible cyber networks in existence.

And I'm still alive.

They haven't caught me. Nor are they even on my trail, thanks to Zmaray. Distracted by the lion, they don't see the panther hiding in their own systems. Because of their success against his effort and rescuing the girl, they're blinded by their own arrogance and have forgotten the thorn in their side.

A festering thorn. Creating a wound that will abscess and kill its host.

Almost too poetic, isn't it?

Almost too much for me to bear.

I said, *almost.*

After the fiasco six months ago, I thought my windfall had. . .well, *fallen.* Assets were locked. I had to vanish. And now, now it's their turn. They thought they'd squished this bug. Now, I'm back. Bigger and better.

I've relocated my home away from home to a different site. Really, it's insane how close I am to them. If I wanted I could step outside, hook up to their power box, and be up and running. (Okay, maybe that's a slight exaggeration.)

Except that I won't. That'd be stupid—like leading an electrical bread-crumb trail right to my metal cabin. They'd discover me before I got the door closed on the way back in. So, I'm playing it safe. Taking it slow.

Had a friend in high school who always said, "Fast is slow. Slow is fast." The guy had some serious OCD issues, but I see what he means. Take it slow and steady and you can make it. Rush, screw something up, and you're starting all over.

My phone rings and I glance at the caller ID. Compare the number against my codec. It's one of the dozens of contacts I'd made in the last few months trying to track down the special ops team who infiltrated the former factory, ripped the girl from Zmaray's hands, and destroyed a year of work.

So not letting that one go. They'll pay. Mightily, if I can swing it. You know what they say about payback.

"Salim, my friend." I put as much college-boy into my words as possible. "What can I do for you?"

"Those men you ask about?"

I pump my fist but restrain the excitement from my voice. "Yes?"

"Men just came into the bar. I am not sure if they are the ones you are looking for, but. . ."

"I'll be there." Excitement nearly chokes me as I shove to my feet. Then remember my manners. "Thank you."

"What of my money?"

"Of course. I'll have it." I grab a stack from the safe as I set up the security protocols to alert me if anyone so much as breathes on my little piece of heaven on earth. But then, why would they? The outside just looks like a run-down piece of junk. Which sucks considering the frigid temperatures said to be coming in.

For a second, I wonder if this tin can rusts. If the snow will make it hard to open doors. With a glance over the bank of monitors streaming the data, the codec flickering through security footage feeds with a facial-recognition software to find matches, I turn. It's the thought of payback that keeps me warm as I head into the oncoming storm to tag and bag them.

CHAPTER 4

Mazar-e Sharif, Afghanistan
17 December—2010 Hours

Distraction had never been so pretty—or annoying. Brian shifted to the edge of the chair he occupied in the corner of the hookah bar. Angled his body in the hopes his mind would get the message and home in on the convo. But that put him closer to the SEALs. They smelled like fish. Actually, everything in here smelled bad. A tickle at the back of his throat made him cough.

The SEAL next to him glared.

Dude. Get a grip, he mentally chided the frogman. Uptight, fish-out-of-water guys tended to get grumpy on land.

"So, it's connected to the SCIFs we were chasing all over creation five months ago."

Bent forward, elbows on his knees, Captain Watters looked primed to blow.

"Wait," Falcon said. "What's the proof on this?"

Commander Riordan swept a piece of thin bread around the hummus before tucking it in his mouth. He chewed, clearly savoring the fact that an SF team was waiting on him. "About a month ago, a team of Rangers went into a location. No sooner did they touch down than they were set upon. RPGs took out their vehicles."

No exit.

"Then snipers took them out, one by one. IEDs went off." Riordan, dark eyes probing the men gathered around him, seemed in his element. "Ramsey sends us in to bring them home. By the time we get there, nobody's alive."

"It was a calculated, systematic ambush," one of the SEALs—the one who constantly rammed his shoulder against Brian's—said. "Never seen anything like it."

"Then you"—Riordan pointed to Raptor team—"are lured into a location believing brothers-in-arms are under heavy fire."

Brian bit back the urge to defend their actions.

"The coms chatter," Falcon said.

"Anyone who heard it would make the same call." Brian nodded. "That's what was off with that chatter. It was perfect. Exactly what they knew it'd take to get us out there, against orders and alone."

Riordan was on the edge of his seat now. "Absolutely. And that's what they want."

"Who?" Brian asked simultaneously with Captain Watters.

"Whoever got into the system."

"They're in." The captain shook his head. "That's. . ."

His captain wanted to say it was impossible. That someone would've told them. In fact, Brian saw those thoughts in the eyes of his entire team—Harrier, Titanis, Eagle, and especially Captain Watters and Falcon.

"They've pulled back nearly every SOCOM team. Black ops have been ordered on high alert, even strongly advised to RTB." Riordan dumped back a glass of water.

"Why is Command keeping this under wraps?" the captain asked.

"Because if this leaks out that someone got in—we are screwed."

Churning in his gut pushed Brian to his feet. He wanted to punch someone. Hurt someone for this. Taking down the American military. The sheepdogs. "I'll be back." He headed to the restrooms, needing to move. Needing to walk off the frustration of feeling like a sitting duck. Or worse—a dog on a leash being led into trap after trap.

After he relieved himself, he scrubbed up, watching as water swirled down the sink. All their efforts, all the carefully negotiated alliances with Bedouins and farmers. Locals. What little trust they'd built, Raptor would now have to question. They'd have to vet who they *could* trust. SOCOM and JSOC would have to adjust protocols. Reel in their embedded operatives, if that hadn't already been done. But why. . .*why* didn't Burnett give it to them straight?

"You done?"

Brian blinked and caught the smirk of that SEAL in the mirror standing behind him. "If I was, I'd move." He again scrubbed his hands with soap. Patted water on his face. Grinned at the SEAL. Then ripped off a paper towel, dried his hands, and slammed the towel in the trash. Muscles taut, he waited—*expected*—the guy to shoulder-butt him again.

Only when he stepped into the hall, one that barely allowed a guy to breathe let alone walk, did Brian release that anticipation of a fight.

"Sergeant Brian."

The firm, sweet voice tugged him around. Brian pivoted, surprised—*pleasantly* surprised—when Fekiria Haidary emerged from the semidark corner near the exit.

"May I talk to you?"

He held out his hands—accidentally bumping someone. After a hurried apology to the bystander, he redirected his attention to her. "I'm all yours."

A half smile and a chin tuck either spoke of her timidity—heck no; there wasn't a timid bone in this woman's body—or frustration. "I must ask a favor of you, Sergeant Brian."

"Just Brian."

"I must ask that you. . ." She wet her full lips and her gaze slid to his right.

He glanced back to gauge the trajectory of her gaze and spotted Raptor and the SEAL team.

"I must ask that you not tell anyone you saw me here."

Brian folded his arms. Curiosity filled his mind with a bank of data and possibilities. But the one that bugged him the most made it past his lips. "Afraid someone will find out you're dating an American?" She'd been awfully cozy with the buzz-cut Airman who smelled of officer.

Irritation twitched her left cheek. "You know I would never do that." She lowered her eyes but couldn't hide the flash of anger from him. "I don't know why I thought I could trust you—"

"Whoa." He caught her arm as she tried to slide past. "Hold up there, chief. Don't question my character. If you don't want anyone to know, what's it to me?"

A flicker of a smile made it to her face as wide, wary eyes considered him. Slowly, the tension knots smoothed from between her eyebrows. "Thank you." Quietly, she eased around him.

Brian wouldn't let her off that easy though. "One condition."

Suspicion crowded her expression as she hesitated, waiting. But not speaking.

"Tell me what you're doing here with them."

"That's not your business."

"You're right, but this business that isn't any of mine—you're asking me to be secretive about. I need to know it's all legit, that you aren't getting into something that could hang my butt out to dry."

Her lip curled. "Just like an American—only worried about his own interests."

Man, the chick had some heated issues with Americans. "Hey, what *interests* me is you, and you're here. But you're afraid I'll say something." Brian glanced at the captain, knowing she feared somehow something would be said to the captain and it'd get back to her cousin. "I'm a guest in your country, but if I'm caught in some mess because of a promise I keep—and I will keep it—then you and I are going to have problems."

Fekiria closed the distance a bit. "If I swear on my life that this is nothing that will endanger you, is that enough?"

Cinnamon. Something else. She smelled like Thanksgiving dinner. And she looked good, even in this dim lighting. " 'fraid not."

Her chin lifted. How Muslims thought that a woman wearing a hijab kept them from tempting a man, Brian had no idea. Because the woman in front of him, her hair and neck concealed beneath the silky fabric, was doing a serious number on his memory. Like remembering local women were hands off. That Captain Watters would have *his* neck in a noose.

But he sure wasn't standing down because of a little competition. The wusses at the front of the bar had the look and smell of officers. He could take 'em.

Warning buzzed at the back of his mind. One more tangle and the captain might make good on his threat to bust Brian down a rank or two. Maybe discharge him. Was this girl worth it?

He didn't know anything about her except her name, a passing familiarity with her family, that her cousin was dating his captain, and she had killer eyes—and lips. Yet for all he knew, she could be plotting some serious scheme to take out Americans.

Nah. She might spew her American hatred easily, but he didn't see the darkness in her eyes necessary for such a campaign.

"Listen." After a glance back to the officer she'd left, Fekiria once again slipped into the shadows of the small hall, pulling Brian around so he had his back to the team. To danger. He just wanted to know if she had the hots for that guy. Was that what she wanted his help to cover up?

"What you must know—"

"Hawk!" A boisterous voice erupted from the side as someone

slapped him on the back.

Brian rounded, indignant when he met the gaze of the SEAL who'd ridden his case since they met in the motor pool.

"What do we have here, Sergeant?" The SEAL angled around and grinned broadly at Fekiria. "Whoa, soldier. You are going all out. This is one fine woman."

"Hey." *Keep cool, keep cool.* "Go on back to your frogmen, Schmidt." Fekiria shrank against the wall.

"I like this scenery better." He touched Fekiria's cheek. "Afraid of some competition, Hawk?"

At the touch, she jerked back with a quick intake of breath.

Heat spread across Brian's shoulders. "Stand down." He would not—*not*—get into a fight. Not here. Not right in front of Captain Watters.

"Easy there." Schmidt laughed. "You can't keep them all to yourself." He took her arm. "We're here to protect and serve, aren't we?" His smile turned into a sneer.

"No." Fekiria tugged back, trying to wrest free of the SEAL.

"Let her go." Brian tugged Fekiria out of Schmidt's grasp and stood between them, knowing his large frame shielded her. What ticked him off most was that this SEAL had been begging to pick a fight with him, and he chose to do it with Fekiria in the middle. Piece of dirt! "Beg off, Schmidt. Move on. Back to the group."

Challenge lit the guy's dark eyes. "You first, Gee-Bee. Isn't that your motto—you lead the way?"

Was the guy still in high school? That was the Ranger's motto. All this guy wanted was to goad Brian. Rather than make his point with a fist, Brian worked his jaw muscles, struggling against the storm brewing in his gut. No way would he walk away and leave Fekiria with this jerk. "We were having a conversation. It's not your concern."

"Hey, why don't you let the lady speak for herself. She might want me, a real man who can show her a good time." Schmidt crowded toward Fekiria.

Brian's blood boiled. "Hey! Enough." He nudged the SEAL's shoulder back.

"Hands off, Green Beret." The threat, the hunger for a fight, lurked in the words. Then that stupid, sloppy grin honed in on Fekiria again.

She took a step back, defiance clear but also no small amount of fear. "If I wanted you," Fekiria said, "would I be talking to him?"

The fear she exuded tipped things toward "bad" with Brian. No woman should feel threatened like that. "Guess you heard for yourself. She doesn't want someone wet behind the ears and inexperienced." Again, he angled in between them, feeling Fekiria's hands on his back. The position pinned her in a corner, but he'd rather have her there than within reach of the slimy webbed hands of the frogman.

"Warned you once: hands off." Jaw jutted, eyes narrowed, the challenge was clear. "You want a fight with me, fine. But grow a brain and leave her out of this."

A greedy gleam hit the man's brown eyes. "You want a fight?"

No. No. Any other day, he would've shown this punk his knuckles, up close and personal. But. . .Captain Watters. *He'll run you up the pole so fast. . .* "What is with you, man? How did you even make it past the psych team in BUD/S? Treating a lady like that, stepping in on a guy— you sure don't have honor."

The punch flew hard and true with a string of expletives that would singe the ears of more reputable sailors.

Brian's teeth rattled as his neck snapped back. Pain radiated through his head and neck. The weight of the punch threw him against Fekiria, who pressed her hands against his deltoids and whimpered.

Adrenaline spiraling, Brian lunged.

—⁓—

"Agreed." Dean Watters roughed a hand over his face. If what Riordan suggested tonight held true, they were in a deep vat of boiling water. "I'll do the same."

Riordan gave a crisp nod. "It's some kind of messed up when—"

Crack!

Dean pushed to his feet and pivoted as he glanced over his shoulder. A tangle of bodies broke a table. Glass shattered. Guests scattered amid screams and the telltale thuds of fists.

Sal Russo thumped a hand against Dean's shoulder.

No need. Dean saw the six-foot Hawk haul a shorter, wiry guy to his feet by the collar.

Riordan cursed. "Knew it."

Dean shoved forward as Hawk drove his fist into the SEAL's face, who responded by throwing one of his own then slamming his shoulder into Hawk's abdomen. The two went spiraling backward, Hawk's fist pounding.

Built like a linebacker, Hawk hammered the guy. The SEAL

somehow flipped Hawk. Pinned him and sliced a hand-blade against Hawk's side. With a howl of pain, the demon within Hawk roared to the surface. Lightning-fast reflexes—so fast Dean wasn't sure what happened—sent the SEAL flying.

Hawk dragged himself from the ground, holding his side, growling.

Titanis lunged, catching Hawk in a full nelson, giving Dean time to get in front of his guy. "Hawk! Stand down!"

Blood dribbling down his lip, right eye swelling, Hawk breathed hard but still struggled. The demon was blind to common sense. Only feeding off the fury within.

Dean got into his face. Eye to eye. "Stand down," he growled against the din behind them. "You with me, Hawk?"

Green eyes flickered, as if stepping from some nightmare to a calm mind. He gave a sharp nod, and Dean met Titanis's gaze with a signal to release him. "Get him out of here," Dean said to Titanis and Sal, who led Hawk out.

Dean searched the room, surprised—and yet not—to find the SEALs gone. The owner rushed to him, shouting in Farsi. At a loss, Dean held up his hands and nodded. Started for the door, praying they weren't looking to press charges or something. He turned at the door and handed the owner a card. Damages, if a claim was filed, would come straight out of Hawk's pay and backside.

The gesture seemed to appease the owner. Feeling released to leave, Dean glanced around. A couple of broken tables. Glasses. And a whole lot of military personnel. One man with a crew cut and stiff posture eyeballed Dean.

So much for a low-key night.

In the frigid evening, Dean stalked to the vehicles, where the team huddled. Harrier crouched over Hawk, who sat propped against the bumper. "Move," Dean snapped. What in blazes did Hawk think he was doing picking a fight with a SEAL in a hookah bar? Was the guy hell-bent on getting discharged?

Harrier straightened and stepped aside. "Think the SEAL broke a rib."

"He fought dirty." Hawk spit blood from his mouth.

Dean leaned into the vehicle and retrieved a zip strap. He pivoted and grabbed Hawk's hands, noticing the bloodied knuckles. Looking his guy in the face, he cuffed him.

"You're freakin' kidding me," Hawk growled.

"You're under arrest, Sergeant Bledsoe."

CHAPTER 5

Camp Marmal, Afghanistan
18 December—0945 Hours

Two MPs stood guard outside the hospital room as Brian carefully threaded his arms back into his T-shirt, feeling like he was breathing fire. Taking X-rays proved painful—and icy cold, especially against the throbbing in his side. In striking Brian's solar plexus and riddling him with agony, the SEAL also cracked a rib. Gingerly, he straightened and worked his way into the tactical shirt. The butterfly stitch over his brow pinched as he tugged down the shirt. Then another fiery stab in his side.

"Okay, Sergeant Bledsoe," the doctor said, entering with his clipboard, "your rib is fractured but not a full break. You'll be in pain for a while, so I encourage you to stay taped up for a week or so. No rigorous activity for a week, maybe two." Over his BCGs, the doc glared. Why anyone wore Army-issued glasses, he'd never understand. They earned the "birth-control glasses" moniker ardently. "But since you'll be reporting to the brig, you'll have time to heal before ending up with extra duties, if not more."

Brian bit his tongue. No good arguing with this officer. Digging his grave was a knack he didn't need to hone more.

The doctor stepped back out and nodded to the MPs. "He's all yours."

Handed his pride and career in one blow, Brian cradled his left side and made his way out of the curtained room. The MPs considered him, and one produced a set of handcuffs.

"Seriously?" Brian wanted to laugh at them. "Do I look like I'm going to do anything?"

The scrawny specialist swallowed. "Maybe not, sir, but you're trained to kill."

"We're soldiers," Brian said with a growl. "We all are. Trust me—I can't walk with this cracked rib if you cuff me. So, if you want steel on my wrists, you'll need to carry me."

"Pardon me for saying so, but you look like that after sparring with a SEAL. And I saw the condition you left that SEAL in, so. . ." Puny and scared spitless, the specialist nodded. "No trouble, sir?"

Shame, thick and heady, coated Brian's shoulders. He shook his head and sighed. "Let's. . ." He motioned with a finger. "Let's just go."

They made it across the base and to the detention facility with minimal jarring and exposure, but walking across that blacktop, past men he'd been in the trenches with—it was enough to humiliate the tar out of him. *You know better!*

Processed in, he stood in the space defined by bars and sterility. Dosed with four ibuprofen, Brian lay out on the thin gray mattress in the cell but still felt the pain of the cracked rib as if he'd been stabbed. He grappled with his future. If he had one. Captain Watters had vowed he'd put him out, strip him of his beret. For what?

A promise to a pretty woman.

The bugger of it all? He couldn't tell his captain what started it.

But if he didn't, his career was over.

Staring up at the ceiling, Brian groaned. Shouldn't be surprised that his two weaknesses—women and fighting—would combine to take him down. There had to be a way to defend himself.

Right. Because you're so innocent.

Behind bars was where he belonged. Just like his dad.

He thudded his head against the pillow as the light in his cell blinked out. Just like life—darkness. Cold darkness. How—*how*—did this stuff keep happening? Minding his own business, intent on keeping the code, keeping his word to the captain. . .and *this. This* was where he ended up.

Why did he even try?

He turned on his side, though it lit fire through his lungs. He needed the pain. Needed to remember this night. Figure out some way to stop this. Sleep tugged at him, but he resisted. Ignored the writhing demons that lay in wait for him to succumb.

Weightlessness lifted and carried him into the void of slumber. First the darkness. Then the howling wind that slowly morphed into screams. Suddenly the weightlessness deadened his limbs, making them thousand-pound weights he couldn't lift as he stood in that paneled hall.

Brian snapped himself awake, heart racing. Steadying his breathing did little to quiet the roaring in his head. The pain in his side throbbed. Easing onto his back, he once again stared up at the ceiling. Just one night—one uninterrupted night of sleep—was it too much to ask?

Arm over his eyes, he folded himself into a light sleep. Fighting hard to hold tightly to the conscious world's tether, not to fall so heavily into slumber that the memories would invade.

But it pulled him.

Pulled.

She was there. Waiting. Walls lined with oak, their home had become a prison among exquisite appointments, marble floors, antiques, and gilded mirrors. All reflecting the wealth his father had attained. The wealth that meant so little when it couldn't stop the unimaginable.

Blond hair matted with blood. Right arm grotesquely broken. Rivulets of crimson gliding down her neck and soaking her pale-pink nightgown. "Why? Why didn't you help me?"

"I...I couldn't."

"You were my only hope of getting out..."

"Why didn't you stop him?"

"You blame me?" Her sobs turned into wails. She lunged at him.

Brian snapped upright. Though logic said a fifteen-year-old couldn't do anything against a grown man, he always felt he'd failed his mother. His dad had never laid a hand on her, but the verbal abuse translated viciously in his dreams. Cruel words bludgeoned her confidence.

Excruciating pain exploded. Dots sprinkled his vision. "Augh!" He froze against the torrent of fire searing his lungs. Screwed his face tight as he steadied himself. With gritted teeth, he lowered himself back down. A chill twitched his flesh. *Cold. Why am I cold?* Sure, it was December, but—the place was heated. Only then did he realize sweat drenched him.

Dragging the back of his hand over his face, he hauled in a ragged breath as he remembered the very real nightmare that had become his life. All he'd wanted in life was to be the hero. To be someone respected. Someone people looked up to. All he found in life was trouble. Now, Captain Watters would make good on his promise to, at the very least, bust him down a rank, if not completely discharge him.

Ten years in the Army down the drain. He loved being a Special Forces soldier. Being a Green Beret. Being elite.

Now what? Where could he go? What would he do? He was on his own. No home, no parents, no friends. Not outside Raptor. They were his family, his friends, his home. Without them. . .what?

"You'll stay in here till I get back."

Brian flinched, startled to find Captain Watters standing outside his cell. Lights on in the hall. Soldiers moving about. Was it already morning? He struggled to his feet, grinding his teeth against the shards of pain digging into his muscles. He stood at ease. Then his mind bungeed the words his captain had said. "Wait—what? I thought—"

"No, I don't think you did, Sergeant." Sparks shot from the captain's eyes. "I gave you a warning. I told you what would happen next time you did something like this. For all the good it did, I might have well been talking to a wall." He paced then turned back to Brian with his hands on his belt.

That was when the dress uniform registered. Where was he headed?

The captain leaned in. "I don't get it. You are crazy-smart. Nobody can touch you with coms. You're a kick-butt shooter. Why do you think I handpicked you for the team?"

Brian blinked. "You did?" He thought those decisions went through Burnett.

"You made it. You made the team. There's nothing left to prove. And yet. . .*this* is what you do every time." He scratched his head. "You've tied my hands. This can't go unaddressed."

"I understand."

He cocked his head. "Do you? Because I sure don't. What happened out there?"

Brian shoved his gaze to his boots. Swallowed. Hated that he couldn't explain it, not without breaking a promise.

"Was it bravado? Had to demand more respect from someone beneath you?"

Brian snapped a look at the captain. Right. That's what he would expect. That's what Brian had done before. But not this time. And freak of it all—he couldn't say a thing.

"You know what?" A disbelieving laugh preceded the captain shaking his head. "Fine—don't tell me. In fact, I'm not sure I want to know. Not right now. I'm too ticked." Captain Watters scowled better than the best of them. "I have to go before Ramsey when I get back and explain why a member of my team was involved in a brawl with a

SEAL, damaging local property and injuring two innocent bystanders."
He sighed. "For now. I'll leave you to your demons."

The words nailed Brian between the eyes, haunting and torturing.
The last words his mom said to him.

"You're one of the best soldiers I've met, but your anger is jeop-
ardizing your future with SOCOM and with the Army." The captain
shifted, his boots scuffing on the vinyl floor. "What happened out
there? Help me understand. Convince me this wasn't just you blowing
off steam again."

Brian felt his breath heaving. Curse his luck. The one time it wasn't
his fault—and he couldn't clear his name. If only that stupid SEAL had
kept his mouth shut and hands to himself.

"Look at you—so mad even now, you're ready to fight *me*."

Awareness flooded Brian that his hands were fisted.

"You've had an excuse for every bloody or broken nose you've
handed out. I'm sick of them! A Special Forces soldier controls that fire,
aims that fire at the enemy but never at one of our own."

Insane! When goaded and baited, what man wouldn't fight? That
SEAL asked for it. Captain Watters just rode a little higher in the
saddle than most soldiers. It wasn't so bad—

"Count your lucky stars or whatever you believe in, Brian." The
captain shot him a glare. "And be *very* glad this review isn't happening
today because I'd sign on the dotted line for a dishonorable discharge."

MITCH

When are you coming home, Daddy?"

Ella's million-dollar question tugged at Mitch's heart. "Soon, baby girl. How are you doing in school?"

"Okay, but I don't like Henry Walters. He's mean and picks his boogers."

"Gross, nobody cares about that, Ella," Noah chided from behind her, and then he leaned in closer, edging his sister out. "Dad, I made the honor roll!"

"Hooah," Mitch said, his chest filling with pride. He held his fist toward the iPad's camera for a fist-bump. Noah did the same. "That's my boy!"

"You said if I did that, you'd take me to the range again."

"I did, didn't I?" Mitch laughed at his son's tenacity. He'd already taught both kids gun safety and proper handling of a weapon. He took the approach that it was better to teach them proper handling and respect of a weapon than to hide it and hope they never found it. Curiosity bred danger in that situation. "I'll get it worked out with Aunt Sienna."

Noah pumped both hands in the air. "Yes!" He went into a full end-zone touchdown dance.

Laughing, Sienna directed him away from the camera. "He's been bugging me to Skype so he could tell you that."

"I'm glad you called." And he was. Something about her and the kids set his day right.

"Daddy," came Ella's sweet voice as she returned with a book in hand. "Can I read you a bedtime story?"

It was morning in Afghanistan, but he'd never turn down hearing his daughter read to him. She had skills she wanted to show off. After climbing into Sienna's lap, Ella brushed her light brown hair from her face and opened the book. She held up a hand to Sienna. "Don't help me, Auntie Sie, I can do this."

With a smile, Sienna nodded, casting a look at the camera, at Mitch. "Okay, Ella. It's all you, sweetie."

Something knocked loose in Mitch's chest. He felt something he hadn't since Ellery's death. It both startled and worried him.

Focus on Ella. But his gaze lingered awhile longer on Sienna. She was dressed in jeans and a T-shirt, her auburn hair hanging loose and free. In the years since Ellery's death, her sister had stepped in and been a surrogate mother to Ella and Noah. She'd covered gaps when Mitch got deployed. Never complained. Always helped.

"Daddy?"

Mitch blinked. "Huh?" Had he been staring? "Did you fall asleep again?" Ella asked, exasperated.

"Well, it was a bedtime story, wasn't it?"

"For me, silly," Ella said with her adorable giggle. "Auntie Sie said it's morning there. You gotta work, Daddy."

"Oh, that's right."

"Okay, you two," Sienna said. "Say night to your daddy then go climb in bed. We have an early morning. I'll be there in a minute."

Ella's face grew large in the camera then blurred as a noisy kissing noise reverberated through the feed. "Night, Daddy. I love you!"

Mitch's throat constricted. "Love you, too, baby girl!"

"I'm not a baby. I'm six!"

"Yes, you are. Now, off to bed," he said, fighting the tears. He wanted to be there with them. Hold her and smell that strawberry shampoo in her hair.

"Night, Dad," Noah said, once again fist-bumping the camera.

Mitch returned it. "Proud of you, champ. Warrior on!"

"You, too. Night."

Choked up, Mitch turned away, pinching the bridge of his nose. *God, just get me home to them. Don't take me from them, too.*

"Hey." Sienna's silky soft voice eased out of the speaker. "They're doing good. You'd be proud of them."

"I *am* proud of them. Miss them like crazy. Sucks to be away from them."

"I know. And they miss you, too." She folded her arms on the table and bent forward. "Listen. . ."

"Uh-oh."

"Yeah," she said, bunching her shoulders. "Ella's teacher said something to my mom about me taking care of them."

He braced himself. "And they said something to you?"

"They did."

"They weren't happy."

"No."

"Why can't they just accept that I can love my kids and still be a soldier?" He grunted. "Sorry to drag you into this."

"Drag me into it? I'm their aunt. My sister and I might have had our differences, but those kids mean the world to me. I really gave my parents a piece of my mind at their accusations."

It was a salve to the wound her parents inflicted. "Wait. What accusations?"

Sienna winced. "They called you an absentee father, said you're injuring the children's emotional state."

"That's ludicrous!"

"I know—"

"It's my job. I have to work. If I don't work—"

"Mitch." Sienna leaned in to the camera. "You don't have to defend yourself with me. I calmed my parents down, told them to think about the kids. It worked."

"It makes me crazy and mad."

"Me, too."

At her words, he held her gaze, torn between the fury of his in-laws' meddling and Sienna's caring. "Thank you."

She nodded with a somber smile. "Hang in there, chief. We'll be here when you get back."

He liked that. Liked the way she dropped the *we* in that sentence instead of *they*. Mitch could only hope he was reading it right. "I look forward to seeing you, all of you."

Sienna held his gaze for three long, stirring moments. "Me, too." A slight smile. "Next time, Mitch."

"Next time, Sienna."

CHAPTER 6

Camp Marmal, Afghanistan
18 December—1205 Hours

What'd you find out?" General Lance Burnett closed his briefcase and punched the locks.

"He's not talking," Watters said as he folded his arms.

"What're you going to do?"

"Do I have a choice?"

"Always, son." Lance set the briefcase on the chair by the door and went for his lined jacket on the coatrack. "Bledsoe isn't the first soldier to have problems like this. Your job is to root out what's causing it and determine the appropriate disciplinary action. The law affords you room, choices—from extra duties to honorable discharge to other-than-honorable."

Watters hunched his shoulders. "I just want to throttle him."

"Of course you do. You picked him for a reason. You trust him with your life, but he's got an Achilles' heel. We all do, Watters." Lance grinned at the young captain. "Speaking of—how's Miss Zarrick?"

Watters's gaze darted around, as if searching for an appropriate response.

Lance chuckled. "You don't have to answer." A rap on the door drew his attention to the half window in the door with the open blinds. Russo stood at the door. Lance waved him in.

"Sir," Russo saluted.

"At ease. Got good news for you, Sergeant," Lance said as he returned to his desk. He lifted a manila envelope and passed it over to the Italian-Latino. "Your promotion came through. Effective immediately."

Russo straightened, his eyes widening. "Sir."

"You'll get your official recognition next week, but as of this moment, you're a warrant officer." Lance grinned at the guy who'd been a walking storm the last eight months. "How's it feel, *Warrant Officer* Russo?"

Russo skated a glance to Watters then back to Lance. "An honor, sir."

"You got that right. Raptor is one of the finest teams out there, and I'm dang proud of you guys."

"Thank you, sir."

Lance nodded. "Now, what is it you came in here for?"

"Two things—with Harrier heading Stateside for some time off with his kids, we're a man down. I'd like a replacement—"

"We're tight on personnel, but I'll look into it."

Russo nodded with tight lips. "I'd also like to ask about the attacks."

With a long expel of breath through puffed cheeks, Lance again nodded. "I need you and Watters to give me some time. I'm working on a few things, but—"

"Sir," Russo said. "No disrespect, but we were *ambushed*. No, worse— we were lured into that trap. Our communications are compromised. How can we—?"

"Stop right there." Lance tempered his words, careful of the edge creeping into his tone. He held up a hand. "I hear you. Believe you me, I hear you. But just as I trust you to make calls out there, you need to trust the calls I make here. You may not understand what I'm doing or why, but I need that trust."

Russo scowled. "Even if it means men die?"

Watters came to his feet. "Easy, Falcon."

"No." Russo's expression went hard as granite. "I don't think so. It's one thing to ask us to do our job with accurate intel, but to ask us to grope around in hostile territory not knowing what intel is accurate—"

"I understand your concerns."

Fire blazed through Russo's dark eyes. "Do you? Because last I recall, you sat here in—"

"Falcon." Watters stepped forward.

Heart thudding at the disrespectful tenor of Russo's words, Lance stared. "You'd be wise to listen to your captain. And to trust me. I can't tell you what I'm working on just yet, but you can be sure I won't be sending you out on fool's errands. Terrorists have taken enough of our boys."

Lips tight, he glared at the newly minted WO1 for a few long seconds then threaded his hands through his coat sleeves. "I'd be real careful of the accusations you throw around in your anger and zeal to protect your men. Remember, Russo—they're my men, too."

Lance lifted his briefcase, reminding himself to breathe. "If you gentlemen will excuse me..."

—⁂—

Mazar-e Sharif, Afghanistan
19 December—1120 Hours

Dread coiled in the pit of Fekiria's stomach as Captain Dean entered the apartment she shared—at least for one more day—with her cousin Zahrah. Had Sergeant Brian told him she was at the club? Had he seen her at the base? She tried to meet the tall captain's gaze. When she did, he gave her an acknowledging nod and hello but swiftly turned his attention to Zahrah. And his expression changed. Radically. The terse intensity that oozed out of the elite soldier softened as a small smile tugged at his clean-shaven face.

And though Fekiria hated to admit it, he looked handsome in his dress uniform.

"What's happening?" Concern filled Zahrah's question as she led him to the tan sofa.

"I have to head out for a week or two."

"Or two?" Zahrah's disappointment couldn't be hidden, but she weathered the news well, all the same.

Fekiria worked on layering the baklava, her cousin's favorite treat, as the two talked and she listened in.

Zahrah had always been strong. Brave. Fearless. Hands in her lap, she put on that tough exterior. "I will pray for you."

Captain Dean smiled. "Thank you." When he reached over and took Zahrah's hand, Fekiria ducked. Spread honey over the thin pastry and added another layer.

Even as Zahrah had lain in the hospital seven months ago with her hair butchered, Captain Dean had been there. Watched over her. Hovered. He wasn't an emotional person, but having seen him on several occasions, Fekiria noted the tenderness with which he approached her cousin. Zahrah still bore telltale scars of her captivity but none more than the ragged one on her cheekbone that turned bright pink every time she saw Captain Dean.

Nobody had ever treated Fekiria that way. And probably never would. She had too much fire in her belly.

"What's wrong?" Zahrah touched the side of his face. "You look upset."

He nodded. "One of my guys was in a fight."

Fekiria's hands slowed, remembering the incident at the club. Remembering Sergeant Brian.

"Is he okay?" Zahrah asked.

"Yeah—busted rib." He sighed heavily then shrugged. "Can't figure him out. He's facing disciplinary action but won't tell me what happened." Captain Dean rubbed his fingers over his knuckles, as if kneading dough.

"Is it that serious?"

Setting aside the first batch, Fekiria listened closely, her mouth dry. Sergeant Brian was getting in trouble? Because of her. But—he'd kept her secret. *Please have kept my secret.*

He nodded, his head dipping a little lower with the admission. "I don't want to put him out, but. . ."

"Put him out?"

Zahrah's head snapped up and her brown eyes met Fekiria's—and only then did Fekiria realize she'd actually spoken the question.

"Forgive me," Fekiria said, tucking her chin. She glanced at the baklava, but all she could see was Sergeant Brian's face. The frightening swiftness of his anger. Especially once the other man punched him. But not nearly as fierce as the expression when the man had made inappropriate advances on her. "It's not my concern."

"So, he's looking at an other-than-honorable discharge?"

Captain Dean steepled his fingers. "It's an option." He leaned back with a groan. "If he hadn't gotten into a couple of scraps already, I'd overlook it, but this was at a local place the other night. The owner wants us to cover damages, and two people were hurt."

As sticky and thick as the honey on her fingers, guilt spread over Fekiria's shoulders. Sergeant Brian would lose his career in the Army? *Because of me?* Her conscience thudded against the guilt.

At the hookah bar, he had been kind and attentive—in a bold, flirtatious way. But that other man—a shudder rippled through Fekiria at the memory—he'd been creepy. Forceful. When the punches started, she let her selfish fear of being discovered overcome her and slipped out the side door before anyone saw her.

"Fekiria." Zahrah sat up then looked back at the captain. "What night was this?"

"Two nights ago."

Zahrah looked back at her. "You were out the other night, right? Did you see anything?"

"No. Of course not." The lie stung. He'd defended her. Protected her. *And* kept his promise. "Mazar-e is not small. There are many bars."

Captain Dean sat forward, his sharp eyes narrowed. "I never said it was at a bar."

Panic stretched through her breast. She shrugged, her pulse racing. "That is where most of the American soldiers go, is it not?" Another shrug. "That is where I have seen them." They were still watching her. She lifted her hands. "Sorry. Need to clean up." She turned her back and held her hands under the hot water, frantic. What if they figured it out?

They could not. Her plans to go to Kandahar would be ruined.

And nothing—and no one—would ruin her escape from this city. From her parents.

MITCH

I want to ride the Superman!"

Mitchell Black glanced down at his sandy-haired daughter. At six years old, she was more ready for life and adventure than most teens. He grinned as he met the blue eyes, so like her mother's. She wasn't tall enough for the ride, and he knew telling her that would fire up that cauldron in her belly. "Ella, we already talked about this."

Her lower lip protruded.

Mitch felt his heart coil into a thousand knots. He wanted to give her everything. Let her have her way. Walk on the moon, if she wanted. But that wouldn't develop character. That wouldn't teach her anything but that she had her daddy wrapped around her little finger. But they were here. On vacation, something he hadn't managed to pull off since Ellery's death.

"We could ask—"

"Dad," eight-year-old Noah dragged out the vowel in the name, pleading. "You promised. Just you and me."

"He's my daddy, too!" Ella stamped her foot. "I want to ride Superman!"

Long, delicate fingers coiled around Ella's. Tanned legs bent as Sienna Leitner squatted beside his daughter. "Guess what?" Eyes alive, she surreptitiously turned Ella to face her. "I just saw Tweety heading toward the Looney Toons area."

Ella's eyes and mouth widened with a gasp. "Really?"

Breathing a sigh of relief at the save executed by the kids' aunt, Mitch felt the knots loosen. Ella had been waiting to see Tweety since they'd arrived two hours ago.

"Daddy, can I go with Aunt Sienna, please? *Please!*" Ardent and redirected, Ella would not be dissuaded.

"I don't know. . ." he teased.

"Oh come on," Sienna said, her long auburn hair tied back and the tennis visor shading her pretty brown eyes. "You guys can't be the only ones to have fun. We girls need our own time." She turned to Ella. "Right?"

Ella thrust a fist in the air. "Right!"

"Fine, fine." He held up his hands in surrender. "I give up. Go."

Squealing, Ella danced a jig.

Mitch caught Sienna's arm as they turned to leave. "Thanks."

She smiled, promised to meet him later, then headed off.

He watched them go, Ella and her aunt—the woman who had covered for him more times than he could count. She'd been a better friend to him and the kids than their own mother. Ellery hadn't been a bad person, but she'd been more concerned with her friends and parties. Mitch had struggled to strike a solid balance between being a father and being a soldier. Since Ellery hadn't held a job for long, he had to maintain an income. That meant time away from the kids. Too often. And her parents had given him no small amount of grief over it.

But then there was Sienna. Smart, funny, invested in her niece and nephew.

"Dad!"

Mitch turned to his son, embarrassed at the minutes he'd spent pondering their aunt. His sister-in-law. "Ready?"

"Yeah!" Noah raced ahead of him, forcing Mitch to jog to catch up. The thirty-minute line for the roller coaster would've been worse if they'd come on a weekend, but he'd managed to swing this time off for the kids.

As with any amusement park ride, the thrill lasted a few minutes— too short compared to the lengthy time spent in line.

"Can we do it again?" Noah asked.

Mitch glanced at his watch. "If the line's short."

With less than fifty people ahead of them, they climbed back into the queue. Adrenaline high and feeling good, Mitch couldn't believe his son would head into fourth grade this year.

"You excited about school starting back up?"

"Am I an alien?" Noah shot back, rolling his eyes.

Mitch could only smile. He remembered hating school—mostly out of boredom. "I sure hope not, or someone pulled a fast one on me when you were born."

As they snaked through the line, Mitch savored every second with his son. The sparkle of the eyes that were his own. The sandy-blond hair that hung loose and swept to the side. He'd wanted Noah to cut his hair, but he left the decision up to Noah. Unfortunately. "I might sneak into your room tonight with a razor."

Noah cocked his head. "You promised I could grow it out."

"Yes, but I didn't mean you should look like a girl."

Anger flashed through his son's face, warning Mitch to veer off. "I don't look like a girl."

Ruffling Noah's hair, he laughed. "You're right. You don't. You're growing into a fine young man."

A bell intoned from his phone. Mitch glanced down, expecting a "Where are you?" text from Sienna. Instead, his heart stopped at the message he saw. "AHOD."

Mitch wanted to curse. Not now. Not today.

Anger churned through him. He wanted to punch someone. Throw his phone away. But then he saw the faces of his team. His friends. The buddies who would rely on him, the team medic. "We have to go."

"What?"

Mitch bent under the cordoned-off rope and moved to the side. "There's only ten people ahead of us."

"Sorry, bud."

"Dad, no!"

Mitch was tempted to reprimand his son's outburst, but something in the kid's panicked tone concerned him. "We'll come back another—"

"Dad, please— You can't do this."

"Son, I have to." They navigated through the park to meet up with Sienna, Mitch texting as they moved. "You know that."

Noah swung around in front of him. "No. You can't." Ferocity struck like lightning. "I heard him, Dad. I heard him say they'd take us away if you left us again."

The world powered down as if caught in the vacuum of an explosion. "Who? Who said that?" But Mitch knew.

"Pawpaw." Noah's eyes were a mixture of panic and grief. "He told Meemaw that you didn't spend enough time with us, that your job in the Army was hurting us."

The boom of that explosion detonated in Mitch's chest. He ran a hand along the back of his neck and let out a painful breath. No, no. Will and Carol wouldn't do that to him. "They were probably just upset about something. I'm sure they didn't mean it." He wrapped an arm around Noah's shoulder. "C'mon. We need to find Ella and Aunt Sienna." She could tell them if this threat was real.

When they met up by a snack cart, Mitch's mind raced.

"Hey." Her smile faded into concern. "What's wrong?"

"We have to leave."

She deflated. And at first, he read it that she wanted to be with him, but in light of Noah's announcement, he wondered. . . "You got paged."

He held up his phone, watching her eyes. Her body language. Arms folded. She looked away and sighed before turning back and giving him a faint smile. "You go. I'll stay with the kids."

"Can I talk to you?" He stepped to the side, motioning for Noah to stay with Ella. Sienna joined him, frowning as she glanced back at the kids. "Noah told me something. Are your parents planning to take the kids from me?"

Sienna's eyebrows rose and she drew back. "Why would they do that?"

"Noah said he heard your dad say if I left the kids again, he'd take them away."

Covering her mouth, Sienna shook her head. "He hasn't told me that. . ."

"But?" There was a but at the end of that, wasn't there?

"He seems particularly critical of you," Sienna said softly, her eyes lowering. "I'm sorry. I think they just want what's best for Ella and Noah."

"*I* want what's best for my kids!" Mitch slapped a hand to his forehead. "Unbelievable." His phone buzzed again, prompting him to reply to the AHOD.

Sienna touched his arm. "Go, Mitch. I'll stay with the kids. They'll have a good time."

He shook his head. A good time with their aunt, but not with their dad. What kind of father abandoned his kids at an amusement park? Will Leitner would have a field day with this. He'd use this against Mitch.

"You were reporting back in five days anyway, right?"

He nodded, gauging her confidence. Her assuredness. He'd entrusted his most prized possessions—Ella and Noah—into her hands over the last few years. Why would now be any different?

Because of her parents.

She squeezed his arm. "My parents won't know. I'll keep Ella and Noah with me this week, then drop them off at school, and they'll go home with my parents just like usual."

It was deceitful. But he was desperate. "You're sure?"

"Completely."

CHAPTER 7

Camp Marmal, Afghanistan
20 December—1105 Hours

*D*on't preach at me, man." Brian spun away and paced in the small barred cell he'd spent the last few days in.

Eagle held his ground—in fact, he gained some when he took a step closer. "Get mad, if you want."

"Done." Brian shot him a challenging look.

With a throaty laugh—that wasn't a laugh—Eagle gave a shake of his head. "Hawk, you have a weapon inside you. But you're choosing to drink poison."

"Weapon? Poison?" Brian touched his fingertips to his temples and held out his hands. "Dude, have you lost it?"

"No, but you have. Brian, you need help."

"What I need is for my friends to treat me like a friend, not a therapy subject." The roar in his skull made it hard to think. To tame the flames of fury devouring him.

"All I'm saying is you can't do it on your own. You said you had gone to youth group."

"Girlfriend's church," Brian snapped. "Never met a more hypocritical bunch of people."

"Is that how you see Christians?"

"Yes."

"Even me?"

Brian shoved his gaze to the ground. "Just leave, Pops." Would he ever get used to calling the oldest member of Raptor by his designated call sign, Eagle? "I'm not. . . I'm no good." Man. Wasn't that the truth. "I'm not good—tonight."

"Here." Eagle slid a small book between the bars. "Might find some *good* in there."

"Tss." Brian shook his head. "You gotta be kidding me." But he took the pocket Bible. And pocketed it. Anything to get Eagle to leave.

Movement to the side turned them both in that direction.

A woman in a hijab and a facial veil stood there, only her eyes—wide green eyes—visible.

"Son of a biscuit." Brian closed his eyes and groaned. "I think God is punishing me."

Eagle grinned. "More like calling your number. Finally."

"Then why are you smiling?"

A bigger smile. "I can't wait to see this. If I know you, you aren't going down without a fight. I know what happened to a man who wrestled God." He nodded and pointed to the camo-clad Bible. "Read that. Find some answers. I'll be back."

With a heaving sigh, Brian pinched the bridge of his nose—and cringed at the prick of pain. A swirl of cinnamon and something else hit his nose—and he knew by his growling stomach that she stood before him. Could he just keep his eyes shut and she'd go away?

"I. . .I heard."

Guess not. "Kind of hard to hear when you aren't there." Brian finally looked at her, glaring.

She ducked. "I—I know. I. . .When the fight started, I got scared."

Those wide eyes. She shifted on her feet—nervous. Guilty.

I don't care. I don't care. I don't care. A million more times and he might get it into his head. "And you rabbited."

Confusion skidded across her face for a second.

"You made like a chicken. Left. Skedaddled. Fled." Though he tried to put disgust in his words, he couldn't. Not with the puppy eyes she was working on him. Ya know—the way a puppy does when he knows he's messed up and eaten your autographed Nolan Ryan baseball. Yeah. That look.

"I could not let anyone know I was there."

"And yet, here you are. If the captain or Falcon sees you—poof! Game over." He cocked his head, ignoring the way that blue satiny hijab made her skin look smooth and soft. This would be a good time for her to say she just couldn't stand for him to take the fall for her. Because she cares about him too much. It'd be all romantic and stuff. Right?

"Did you tell them?"

Brian snorted. He should've known better. Shook his head. He started to turn away but faced her again. "You do realize coming here risks your little secret?"

She lowered her head more. "It's why I wore the veil. And I. . .I didn't use my name on the register." Left shoulder pressed against her ear, she briefly met his gaze. "I just wanted—"

"I know what you wanted." Why had he ever promised he'd keep her secret? Now—now his career was flushed down the latrine with a hefty dose of antibacterial cleanser.

"Did you tell them? You can't tell them! You don't understand what I risk—"

Brian's blood boiled. "I gave my word," he bit out as he angled closer, ignoring the burn in his side.

"Yes, but your career—if you don't tell them—"

"I. Gave. My. Word." Brian's nostrils flared. "To you. Do you understand? I don't go back on that."

"No. Of course not." She tilted her head, shielding her face as an officer walked past them. "I am sorry. . .but I'm just worried. If you tell them—"

"Look. Maybe in your country a man's word doesn't mean anything—heck, we've got ANA shooting their friends, trainers, and allies in the back or blowing them to Kingdom Come. But me? I gave my word."

"You Americans are not all good." Defiance lifted her chin again. "I've seen what you have promised and what you have done. They are not the same thing."

"Guess y'all taught us well."

"How your word means nothing when a president wants to shift attention or when he needs reelection. And maybe next time—"

"Babe, there won't be another time." Brian gritted his teeth. "Because this—you and me—isn't happening again. When you walk out that door, I'll forget you exist. You'll never hear from me again, especially not another promise. Just go back to your soldier boy and forget this happened. Or wait. Are you going to stab him in the back, too?"

Her face reddened. She shot daggers out of those green eyes. Fekiria whipped around and hurried down the hall.

"I'll take that as a yes!"

—⁓—

Palm on the sergeant's desk, ballpoint pen in hand, Dean hesitated over the login book as his gaze followed the black-and-white images on the security monitor. The woman rushed out of view, and from the feed, and he could tell Hawk was saying something as she left. What was that about?

Dean slipped to the side door and pressed his shoulder against the wall. The woman scurried out the exit without a glance back.

But he didn't need to see her face to know it was Fekiria Hadairy. *Couldn't be.* What would she be doing here—and talking to Hawk? He knew her attitude toward Americans, so hanging out with them. . . And what would she want with an unruly one like Hawk? So maybe it wasn't her. Wouldn't make sense for her to be here.

"Specialist, everyone visiting signs in, right?"

"Yes, sir."

Back at the sign-in desk, Dean slid his pointer finger along the entry above his: Zahrah Zarrick. "Not even close," he mumbled as his brain zinged through the meaning. Zahrah had a certain level of autonomy and clearance on this base because of her father. *And me.*

Fekiria did not. But why would she use Zahrah's name? Did she use Z's name at the front gate, too?

What are you up to, Fekiria?

Two nights ago at the apartment, she'd stepped into his conversation with Z—Dean cocked his head to the side, looking out the door—about the disciplinary action. She mentioned the bar. When he hadn't. He thought she'd acted a little strange, but then again, Zahrah's cousin usually did act strange. She didn't like that her cousin was dating him, but she respected the relationship. As far as someone so strident in her views could, he supposed.

Dean stared at the camera that held the grainy image of Hawk. His mind sparred with the facts: Hawk. Fekiria. The fight. SEAL. Hawk's silence over what happened. Fekiria knowing too much. Showing up here.

"You okay, Captain?"

"Yeah. Thanks." Dean tossed the pen aside and strode down the hall to Hawk's cell. He rounded the corner, unsure what the game was with Brian, but the fights and outbursts had to stop.

Hawk lifted his booted feet to the mattress and was halfway down when his gaze slid into Dean's. Eye still swollen, it now had a garish purple hue. Butterfly stitches on his right cheekbone and temple bore testament to the SEAL's skilled punches. Hawk grunted. Swelling might be going down but his attitude wasn't.

"On your feet." He worked to say the words evenly. He might not have succeeded by the hesitancy that skidded through Hawk's battered face.

Hawk pulled himself to his feet. "Can't a guy get some rest?"

Sarcasm. Dean tightened the reins on his slipping anger. "Saw a woman here."

Hawk grinned. "D'you get her number? For me—I know you're tangled up with Double Z right now."

Dean stared. Hard. Kept his mouth closed, knowing he'd unleash on the guy.

Hawk said nothing. He swallowed.

"Want to tell me something about the woman wearing a hijab who just left in a hurry?"

The guy didn't need a dog—his eyes and body language barked his message. Ticked. And...something else, but Dean couldn't figure it out. Didn't care. Not this time. Brian Bledsoe wasn't going to be forthcoming so he'd pay the price for that. Just like he'd pay for his out-of-control actions at the hookah bar.

So be it. Dean gave a lopsided nod. "Once the doctor clears you, you'll return Stateside. A month, maybe two with your family might set your head right."

"Stateside? We have a killer who's hijacked our computers!"

"If or when you return, you'll have extra duties."

Hawk's mouth tightened.

"KP."

Hawk remained unmoved.

"And latrine duty."

His jaw muscle jounced—once.

"From there, you'll be assigned patrol. In Bagram."

"Bag—" Hawk clamped his mouth shut.

"You'll lose a stripe, but you'll stay in. Depending on your attitude during that time, you might regain your position with SOCOM—"

"Regain?" Hawk's brow knitted, darkening his intense eyes.

When he saw the punishment hit its mark, Dean stepped back. "Hope we see each other again. Good-bye, Sergeant Bledsoe."

"Wait—bye?" Hawk's arms spread. "Where—what about Raptor?"

"Raptor is not your concern, Sergeant."

"Are you freakin' kidding me?"

Rigid with anger and indignation, Dean slid closer to the bars that kept him from wringing Hawk's neck. "Right now, you should be counting your lucky stars that I consider you a *friend*. That I know enough about you to know that this behavior, this idiocy, isn't you. I am the only reason you're still wearing a uniform right now." His chest heaved with the effort to contain his anger. "Whatever storm is swelling inside you, Brian, calm it down. Or get out."

Hawk stood as if a steel rod had slammed down his spine.

He was through here. Hawk understood the situation. Understood the ledge he stood on now. It'd be up to him to scramble to safety or jump off. There was nothing more Dean could do. So he backed up a step, gave a curt nod, then strode down the hall, the weight of justice served pushing down on him as if an entire courthouse had dropped on him.

"So, what?" The rattle of bars and Hawk's shout chased Dean to the exit. "I'm off the team?"

BORIS

The team lets me down. It's like they're making this easy for me.

They can't really be *that* stupid can they? I'll be disappointed if that's the case. I like the chase. Like knowing I have a formidable opponent. Facing off against someone who's below you. . . Well, where's the fun in that?

Months of hunting them, backtracking to figure out where they were and where they were going finally paid off that night. And holy cow! If you could've seen the way Hawk put his fist through that other guy's face, you would've paid me big-time for that. Why? Why could that not happen when I had a camera and a tub of popcorn?

Note to self: see if Salim has video footage.

But Hawk's temper did me a big favor. Gave me the opportunity I needed to plant a bug that I could remotely control and attach to one of them. I'm really beginning to think those guys are all brawn and no brains. I mean, it's practically a public service, handing them over to Zmaray and his master.

A few brilliant keystrokes and now. . . "Ladies and gentlemen, we are back in business!" Which means my bank account is filling up, too. Or will be soon. And this time, they're going to pay better. After all, I'm putting *this*—uh, that would be *all* of me—on the block.

I activate the homing beacon then hit a switch. The small vent in the roof cantilevers with a squawk and the small UAV launches out. "Huh. Probably should WD-40 that." I shift my gaze to the screen.

As the UAV rises above me, I set it to lock on to the signal and power up its video feed. Almost instantly a live feed of the bird as it heads toward the base. Within a half hour, the bird is descending.

Comparing the map with its "migration" gives me a surprise. "So, not in the north anymore, are we guys?"

The Little B-1-r-d lands on a wire—not an electrical one. It's programmed to detect those electrical fields and ignore them. As it soars over the barbed wire and sandbagged gate, I take manual control of his flight. The images aren't the best, but they're enough to help me guide the Little B1rd toward the SOCOM building. That's easy to find, with the way the military tends to letter every building with signs. Sure makes it easier for terrorists to find their way around, I suppose.

Little B1rd lands on the eaves.

And I activate my Fly fly. Okay, I can't help but laugh. It's a *fly* fly.

"Hehe. Okay, no wonder you're single, Boris," I mutter as I aim the tiny fly toward the vent. He spirals down and into the building.

Voilà!

Being with the guys again is like coming home for Christmas.

Hm, interesting. Seems we're missing some muscle on the team. Our handy-dandy captain is missing. So is the mouthy guy—Hawk.

"Okay, let's head out." The Italian Stallion is in charge? What. . . why would they do that?

"Wait, wait, wait," I object. "If you head out I can't spy on you. C'mon. Be sports, will ya?"

But they're out the door. Rebellious little thugs.

That's okay. I'm a fly on the wall. A fly on. . .the. . .wall. . . Buzzing above Eagle's head, I am momentarily blinded when one of the guys shoves open the door. But the lens quickly adjusts and we're heading out.

I'm giggling by now. It's so great. Technology totally rawks. These doofuses have no idea I'm following them. I mean—hello? I am *right* there. Can see the dandruff on Eagle's head. "Oh, look! He's thinning already." Cackling, I almost miss him swinging his baseball hat up. He nearly catches my Fly fly.

I whiz the fly out of striking zone but stick with the guys. They head to the motor pool. But hold up. Where's Captain *Uptight* Pants? And my favorite guy? Why aren't they with the team?

Really, I shouldn't be laughing, but being a literal fly on their wall—or in this case, on their Humvee as they head off into the sunset—can it get any sweeter?

Actually, yes it can. The pot can *always* be sweetened. With cash.

Running through my programs, I make the call. Make it impossible for them to trace it back to yours truly.

The line connects. I hold my breath, waiting for someone to speak.

Seconds tick by. "Hello?" I finally say, nerves jangled. "Zmaray?"

"No," a female voice answers. "You will deal with me now."

She sounds pretty. And mean. So not going there. "Not happening. Zmaray was my contact. I don't know you." I reach for the kill switch. "That means I can't trust you."

"You cannot trust the person who deposited 13.2 million dollars in your unnumbered account, *Boris*?"

Okay. Pretty, mean, and entirely too smart for her own good.

For my good.

"You've coded in," she says. "Does that mean you have good news for me?"

"Where is Zmaray?" Yeah, not answering any other questions till I know if they've offed the guy. Because if they offed him, then my neck is already feeling the sting of their blade.

"He is right here. But things have escalated, would you not agree? The Americans killed our Afghan contact. They came entirely too close to uncovering our agent."

Agent? "Do you mean your guy on the base?"

Silence crackled through the line, deafening. Terrifying.

They know too much.

"You are wasting my time, Boris. Do you have information?"

I look to the screen. To the dusting of snow covering the terrain as the Green Berets make their way—I check the compass—south. "I do." Gotta let them know I have value. "But I want to know Zmaray is alive."

"Sorry, that is above your pay grade."

I'll let her snotty attitude slide. Because I *am* getting paid.

CHAPTER 8

Kandahar Province, Afghanistan
28 December—0820 Hours

Wearing her hijab and flight suit, Fekiria made her way to the training rooms. First day of advanced training and one step closer to advanced certification. Surrounded by other pilots, soldiers, airmen, and sailors, she almost felt crowded. Yet an insane amount of loneliness tugged at her soul.

She'd walked out of the apartment six days ago while Zahrah was at the school working with the children. Though Fekiria left a note explaining that she was okay, she had not been entirely honest in her description of her destination and reasons.

Sitting in the classroom as the initial first-day buzz thrummed through the air, she wondered at her reasons. Why was she here? Her gaze skidded around. Men wearing uniforms. Most were Americans, though she spotted one ANA soldier sitting down front. Silent. Isolated. A chill emanated from his direction and mirrored the one wrapped around her.

An involuntary shudder trickled across her shoulders—and with it a gust of wind.

"You ready for this?"

Fekiria jumped at the firm voice of Captain Ripley as he eased into a desk next to her in his flight uniform and a big smile. "Ready?" Was her small laugh enough to cover her nerves? Would he question her about abandoning him at the hookah bar? What about his mysterious "we all have secrets" comment? "It would be vain to say I am, but. . ."

"But you want to be up there more than anything?"

She met his gaze evenly. Their love of flying provided common ground for a friendship. But Ripley wanted more.

She didn't.

Or do I?

A colonel strode into the room and briskly moved to the lectern. The students punched to their feet and stood at attention. Fekiria with them.

Captain Ripley started toward the front, where he smiled and greeted the colonel. Then with a hand on the podium, he faced the class. "Good morning. This is the first day of the rest of your lives—at least, your flying lives. Here, you'll learn the advanced-flying techniques that will ready you for more sophisticated combat aircraft."

He'd said nothing of Sergeant Brian using her real last name, or of the fight, or of her departure. Only that impervious smile and the look that said he was interested in her in a romantic way.

Madar always said she'd wanted a man to look at her with *that* look. Baba's baba had arranged their marriage. And though Fekiria had railed against those "business deals," as she had called them, they were starting to make sense. Men did stupid things when they got romantic ideas in their heads.

The day of lectures, physical fitness, and simulators wore on her. By the time they were done and she stood in line for dinner, Fekiria was exhausted. And sad. The thoughts of her parents and cousin tugged at her conscience.

As she stared at the food in the metal serving trays, she grimaced. What she wouldn't do for some naan and Tandoori chicken. With a sigh, she scooped some slop on the plate and shuffled to a table in the corner. The first bite was blah. The second worse. Finally, she set down her fork and closed her eyes.

It felt wrong. All of it. The food. The people. Being here. Leaving her family.

Why had she been so anxious to—?

"Let's talk."

Fekiria jumped. "You keep doing that to me!"

Captain Ripley smiled. "Sorry. You are very distracted. And depressed. What's going on?"

"How would you know I am distracted and depressed?" Anxiety squeezed her chest. "You do not know me."

"Not as well as I'd like, but yes—I do know you."

Heart tripping over each beat, she held his gaze. Refused to back down.

"Okay." He gave a quick glance around then zeroed in on her again.

"Your name is not Rhmani. It's Fekiria Haidary. You're the daughter of Jahandar Haidary, the biochemist. Cousin to Zahrah Zarrick, daughter of General 'Z-Day' Zarrick."

Had she not already lost her appetite, she would've now. She stared at the mounds of food and her stomach churned. "What are you going to do?"

"Talk."

She met his eyes. Did he mean, he wanted *her* to talk? Or he was going to talk to his superiors? "Is that a threat?"

He shook his head. "If you don't know by now how I feel about you and that I'd *never* entrap you or put you in a bad situation, then we haven't come as far as I thought."

"Captain Ripley—"

"Sandor."

Fekiria stilled. "I. . .I am not. . .cannot—" She heaved a sigh, frustration a noose around her neck, forbidding a decent breath. "Clearly, I am a liar." She couldn't bear to look at him. "Why would you want to do anything except write me up and dismiss me from the program?"

"Dismiss one of our best pilots?" He laughed. "Not even close." Forearms on the table, he leaned toward her. "But I want the truth." He pointed to the table. "Right here, right now."

No sense in arguing, because he wouldn't relent. She wet her lips. "Being female has been my curse since birth. I served no purpose to my baba. Even though I was—am—smarter than my oldest brother, I was a waste. Baba even lamented that he had to pay to get rid of me."

"Fekiria. . ." Captain Ripley touched her hand. "I'm sorry."

"My parents had already tried to marry me off twice, but I made the first man so angry, he rejected me." Staring at her hands did not help the acute feeling of unworthiness. "The second man ran off with my best friend." She gave a halfhearted smile. "Last summer, they were working to marry me to a sixty-something-year-old man who had grandchildren. After the second man, I joined the army. My parents did not know. When they found out, they forced me to quit. They said I brought shame on them."

"But. . .your papers said you've been in since you were eighteen."

A thrill of excitement ran through her. "I. . .I let them believe I quit."

"You stayed in."

With a shrug, she gave him a small smile. "It was not so hard to get away with it. They were not worried about me as long as I was out of their sight. And working part-time with my cousin. She did not know it was part-time. She thought I was there at the school all day."

"So, you've been lying to everyone."

Shame smothered her. But more so, the disappointment in his words. "I know it is awful of me, but I had to make my own life, my own future. If I let them, then I would be married with three children and who knows what number wife!"

Captain Ripley held up his hand. "Easy." He leaned back and crossed his legs. "All this *must* go in your file"—again, he snapped a hand at her when she started to object—"but no one here needs to know this."

"I cannot risk my family finding me."

"They won't. I'll have it documented in your file here, but it won't be uploaded or added to your digital file." He held her gaze. "Not yet anyway."

Fekiria looked away, fighting the mountain of panic surging through her.

"You realize that you are an adult. A woman who knows how to shoot a weapon and fly a helicopter." He had a charming smile. "Fekiria, if I *don't* put this in your file and someone finds out, then it's over. You won't be in the Army and you won't have your certification. You'll never finish advanced training."

Tears burned her eyes.

"I'm just trying to protect you."

—✴︎—

Dulles International Airport, Virginia
28 December—1515 Hours

Duffel slung over his shoulder, Brian made his way up the aisle of the plane and deboarded. As he strode the umbilical toward the terminal, he couldn't stave off the bad mood. Hated this part. Hated seeing people greet their loved ones once they got past security. Or as they stood around the belt at baggage claim.

As always, he'd have nobody there. On his own. Alone.

And now, busted down a rank. No hero's homecoming for him. He didn't even get to hop a flight with a returning unit. Brian ducked into the first restroom and changed into his civilian duds. Jeans, T-shirt, and a leather jacket. He headed out past the security area, where he'd catch a cab.

"Brian!"

Surprised to hear his name, he hesitated then kept going. He was alone. That warm welcome belonged to some other lucky Brian. Not him. He didn't have family. Not any that would greet him. His sister had her family to keep her busy. His mom's parents were still alive, he was pretty sure. As he rode the tram to the main terminal, he realized he'd missed Christmas. Nothing too surprising.

"Brian!"

A few yards from the escalator up to ground transportation, he cast a look to the side. *Not you. Keep going.*

"Brian Bledsoe!"

He gave a quick survey of the area. Pivoted and glanced around. No way he imagined that. But who—? He struck the gaze of a familiar pair of green eyes beneath a thick white mop. His pulse spiked.

"Granddad!" Even as he uttered the name in a disbelieving breath, Brian was caught up into a strong—yet frail—hug that smelled of Old Spice and. . .*home.*

"Thought I'd have to put my running shoes on to catch you, boy."

Released from the hug, Brian stepped back. Held the shoulders he'd once been carried on. Choked back the squall of emotion. "What are you doing here?" His gaze then met the sparkling brown eyes of his grandmother. He bent and embraced her. "I'm. . ." Blown away. Stunned. Shocked. "How. . .?"

Nana smiled and patted his shoulder. "Todd Archer told us you were coming home. Course, your grandfather couldn't let it go. He had to know when and where." She'd always had the warmest smile.

"I know you probably didn't want a welcome, but I said nonsense." Granddad slapped his shoulder. "You were doing good work over there, and I wasn't going to let you return without the welcome owed to you!"

An arm in a puffy winter jacket wrapped around his shoulders. He'd gotten his height and most of his looks from his father's side. Especially from Granddad Jack. "C'mon. Let's grab a steak and you can tell me about your latest exploits."

An acidic pool of dread roiled in Brian's gut. How was he supposed to tell the man who'd received numerous commendations for his heroic acts during World War II that his grandson was on the verge of being dishonorably discharged? That Brian, despite his every effort, had failed the Bledsoe legacy? Just like his father.

In the Cadillac—Granddad always said his Kitty had to have the best—they headed west on 7 toward Dulles Town Center where Granddad pulled into the parking lot at Red Lobster. "Hope you brought your hollow leg."

Brian climbed out, watching as the once-nimble man hoisted himself from behind the driver's seat by holding on to the door frame and side of the car. Upright, he grinned at him. "Ain't as spry as I used to be, but I'm not stopping till they put me in the ground."

"All right," Nana said. "Stop showing off, Jack. Let's get the poor boy out of the cold before you start in on the marathon."

Hands shoved in the sleeves of his leather jacket, Brian looked at his grandfather. "Marathon?"

Granddad winked. "Inside," he whispered conspiratorially. "If I tell you out here, she's liable to beat me with that purse of hers and I'll never see the New Year."

Small talk covered them as they waited and during appetizers. But with each passing minute, Brian could feel his granddad's radar-like instincts homing in on the gaping wound in Brian's pride and career. The meaningful looks. Phrases that felt too perfect to be coincidental.

The waitress returned with a basket of garlic-cheese biscuits and set them on the table. Hands folded in front of her, she smiled at them. "Ready to order?"

"Yes." Granddad jabbed a crooked, arthritic finger at Brian. "He'll have the sirloin and lobster." Bushy eyebrows wagged at Brian then back to the waitress. "He's my grandson. Just returned from Afghanistan. He's a Green Beret, a hero. So nothing but the best for my boy."

Oh man. Just puncture the guilt tank and let it leak all over the table. Brian couldn't even appreciate the way the waitress smiled at him. It just made the hole bigger.

Nana leaned in. "Yesterday, Emory came over with little Benny."

"Benedict!" Granddad spat. "Who on earth names their kid Benedict?"

"Quiet," Nana said with a rueful smile. "He's still your great-grandson."

With a warning look, Granddad pointed to him again. "When you have kids, give them good strong names. Benedict," he said with a curled lip. "Might as well name the poor kid Sherlock."

Brian couldn't resist laughing.

"I never should've told him about that actor," Nana said. "Now, Brian—tell us you've found a girl."

"Of course he has, Kitty. He's a soldier. A right fine one, too." Granddad chuckled. "Where'd you think he gets his good looks from? And I got the best nurse the Army could provide, didn't I?" He leaned over and planted a noisy kiss on her cheek.

"Go on, you old goat," she said with a blushing laugh. The light-hearted banter continued, and Brian couldn't thank God enough for taking the pressure off. Last thing he wanted was to admit he'd failed to this man.

Their entrees came and they quietly prayed then settled into the meal. Brian's guilt and annoyance at eating such a fine meal when he should be relegated to a crust of bread and cup of water made the steak taste bland.

Shaky hands sawed into chicken smothered in a creamy sauce and topped with cheese and shrimp. "When do you report back?"

"First thing a week from Monday." Brian slid a chunk of sirloin into his mouth. The flavor popped and the meat melted in his mouth. . .yet soured in his stomach. *I'm no freakin' hero.* How could he tell Granddad?

"You'll come stay with us at the lake house till then."

Brian set his fork down and leaned back. All day, 24/7 with those expectant, proud eyes watching him? "Oh, I couldn't—"

"Yes." Granddad's gray-green eyes Brian had inherited sparked with firmness. "Yes, you will. You need it."

Nana placed a hand on Granddad's arm. "Now, Jack—"

"I need to go over a few things with you," Granddad said. "I'm not going to live forever, you know."

Brian would rather walk into an IED-laden alley than his grand-father's home. Filled with once-happy memories, the home was also a veritable shrine to the Bledsoe legacy. The very one he'd failed. But it wasn't just the shrine-of-a-home. It was the man, the force behind it. The man sitting across the candlelit table had this terrifying ability of dismantling Brian's defenses, flying in under the radar and digging out every secret.

CHAPTER 9

Kandahar, Afghanistan
10 January—1515 Hours

*R*ed is the color of the blood that flowed. . ."

Fekiria ran her finger over the beads threaded together in a bracelet. Glittering and beautiful, the piece made her spirits pop. She jerked toward the young woman tending the stand. "This bracelet— Who made it?"

Wide, almond-shaped eyes lowered. "I made that one."

Disappointment flowed through Fekiria's veins as she eyed the pieces on the cart. The threads in the scarves bore the same multicolored pattern. *Mitra.* It had to be. Especially the one with gold threads.

"*For the streets of gold we will one day walk down,*" Mitra had told the gathering of children.

Beautiful, sincere Mitra, who had loved Fekiria more wholly, less judgmentally than any other person she had ever met. More than any other *Christian* she had known. Their friendship had been fast and deep, growing up together. They'd been inseparable.

Until Mitra met and married Jacob, who tore her away from Mazar-e and Fekiria.

Soft and smooth, the scarf seemed so much like one Mitra had made her years ago. It didn't bear these colors, but it was similar. *Where are you, Mitra?* Oh, to have a friend like that to confide in. To laugh with.

Laughter had been missing too long in her life.

"I see you still like bright colors."

Sucking in a sudden breath, Fekiria spun. Met the bright brown eyes of her dearest friend and threw herself at her. "I knew it was you!"

Long, thin arms wrapped tightly around Fekiria as Mitra's laughter filled the crowded market row. "You beautiful angel!" Mitra's voice was light and sweet, as always. "What are you doing so far south?" She stepped back and lifted Fekiria's hand, glancing down. "I thought perhaps you had finally married."

Fekiria's laugh turned caustic. "Not yet. Baba tried to marry me to a sixty-year-old man, but I refused."

"Again." Mitra folded her arms and arched an eyebrow.

With a shrug, Fekiria could only stare at her long-lost friend. In a demure blue hijab and modest clothing, she had not aged much at all in the years since she'd left. A few more lines around her eyes—probably from too much laughter—but no other signs of aging. "He was old."

"You said that about all of them."

Fekiria wrinkled her nose and lifted a scarf. "Haven't given up on spreading the *God News*, huh?"

Mitra tugged the scarf out of her hands. "*Good* News." She hung it back up on the rack then drew Fekiria out into the busy market. "And no, I will not give up. Ever." Linking arms as they walked, Mitra gave a very long sigh. "It is so good to see you, angel."

The endearment warmed Fekiria's heart. "I miss that name." Missed having someone who thought highly of her, someone who believed in her.

"So, tell me," Mitra said, bumping shoulders with her. "How are you so far south, so far away from your father's grasp?"

"You would not believe me."

"Of course I would." Mitra turned a corner, delivering them out of the jostling foot traffic and onto a street with a half-dozen or so cars. "I might tease you or roll my eyes, but I will believe you."

Where were they going?

"So, my angel—speak! Why are you down here?"

"I'm a pilot."

Mitra jerked her head toward her then moved in front of her. "A pilot?" Disbelief seemed to widen her eyes. "How is this possible?"

"I never left the ANA."

"But you told your father you had—I was there!"

"I told my father what he wanted to hear, what I needed him to believe so he would not torment or beat me," Fekiria admitted, her heart heavy.

"He was always so hard on you." They scurried across traffic and turned left. The path they took seemed intentional.

"Where are you taking me?"

Her friend smiled, her eyes bright with mischief.

Ah! There is the friend I loved. Fekiria could not help but laugh. "What trouble are you causing?"

Mitra giggled. "Trouble? Oh no, my friend—you are the one with trouble nipping at your heels. I am the one wisdom follows, remember?"

"I seem to remember his name was *Wasim*, not Wisdom."

Another burst of laughter erupted from her friend, who turned a corner then slowed. Head down, Mitra seemed to be lost in thought as she leaned against a large double-hinged door to a building. "I remember Wasim." The way she said it made the name and memory sound as if they were a thousand years old. Wistful, thoughtful, she rolled her shoulder and eased back against the dark wood. "He was so jealous when Jacob came and stole my heart."

Jealousy had not claimed only Wasim's heart. It had been difficult for Fekiria to watch her friend stolen away by a man who shared the religious beliefs of the Christians. A man who was Israeli. "Where is Jacob?"

Eyes glittering, Mitra leaned toward her. "I have a secret to share with you, my angel."

Something about the way she said that worried Fekiria.

"Can I trust you still?"

"Of course."

"But if I do—this must stay a secret." Mitra's eyes resonated with meaning.

"I would never betray you!"

"Even to the ANA?"

"*Especially* to them!" Heart thumping, Fekiria felt as if her character had been questioned or challenged.

Mitra's face brightened, her oval eyes alive once more. She turned, produced a key from her pocket as she gave a cursory glance to the street they stood on. Deftly, she slid the key into the heavy door's lock and pushed it open. "Please," she said as she herded Fekiria inside.

She stood in a courtyard, simple but pretty. A bricked path led toward a center fountain that wasn't running. The path wrapped around the fountain then broke, leading to three buildings. The first, a very small one that could house no more than a single family. The middle structure was large and had two levels. A balcony on the upper level also had a staircase that led to a rooftop terrace, no doubt. The third building looked more like a storehouse of some kind. Plain with two levels as well. Nothing elaborate, but well taken care of.

"This way." Mitra hurried across the open space to the storehouse.

"What is this?" Fekiria tugged her jacket a little closer, feeling a skitter of danger that pulled her gaze to the alleys and shadows of this compound.

But Mitra said nothing as she let them into the two-level home with another key. Inside, where she expected to find some heat and perhaps a woman's touch to the furnishings, Fekiria was let down.

Darkness and chills scampered down the lonely hall void of hangings or tapestries.

"This way," Mitra said as she scurried into the shadows.

Fekiria gulped the dread crowding her. "What is this?" she asked, her voice barely a whisper, a whisper that chased her friend.

Her heart stuttered as silence dropped on her. Black darkness. "*Mitra,*" she hissed.

A flash of light at the other end startled her. There, she could see Mitra hold back a heavy curtain that served as a barrier. Light from the interior room splashed on her friend's face, which was vibrant. "Come see."

Ready to be rid of the chill and fears, Fekiria rushed toward her. "Where are we, Mitra? You're scaring me."

But Mitra only nodded into the room.

Fekiria turned and peered past the thick embroidered curtain. Divided into two parts, the room was not a room. With beds, carpets, pillows, bunks, and a table. "It's a school."

—⁂—

Northern Virginia
12 January—1005 Hours

"Sweet!" Brian set his bottled water on the shop table and stepped back, eyeing the sleek, tough lines of the white 1965 Mustang GT 350 with black racing stripes. "Thought you got rid of this years ago."

Granddad waved at him. "Couldn't do it. Kitty wasn't happy with me, but I couldn't give up the beauty I'd paid for in cash." He opened the door and motioned Brian inside. "Go on. Start 'er up."

In the driver's seat, Brian ran a hand over the steering wheel. The dash—obviously old but in pristine condition. His hand landed on the gearshift. "I can't believe this. It's show quality."

"Sure it is. Used to take it around."

"I remember."

"Had some pretty impressive offers, but"—he again waved—"can't buy something whose price sticker is the heart." He shuffled to the other side and climbed in. Green eyes sparkled with more mischief than Brian had seen from his grandfather in a long time. He held up the key with its pony icon chain.

Disbelief chugged through Brian's veins. Nah. No way Granddad meant for him to take it for a spin.

"One last time?" Granddad finally said, shaking the key.

"Last time?"

Granddad didn't answer, just shook the key.

"Seriously?" Brian tentatively reached for it.

"What, you don't want to?"

Brian snatched it. "Don't put words in my mouth."

Granddad chuckled and tugged the door closed.

The throaty purr of the engine roared through the garage. Brian took a moment to familiarize himself with the instrumentation, eyed the rearview mirror and the view of the driveway.

"Remember—she's a lady. Treat her like one."

Now you're talking my language. "Yes, sir."

Brian eased out and pulled onto the road. They clung to the back roads, taking 15 north toward Point of Rocks, Maryland. The Mustang roared as he crossed the Potomac and took the first right past the MARC station and through the rolling fields of corn and grain.

As they headed back, the engine started rattling.

"There," Granddad said, pointing to a park sign. "Pull in there. Let's have a look at her."

Brian guided the Mustang under a copse of scraggly, naked oaks. Though snow hadn't made its mark yet this winter, the Potomac had icy beams stretching from the bank out a couple of feet.

"Pop the hood," Granddad said as he climbed out.

Brian tugged the release lever then pushed open his door. As he did, his gaze hit the skyline. Gray. Forbidding. "Looks like that storm might hit early."

"Always does. Especially when I take her out." Granddad chuckled. Already bent over the engine, he adjusted this cap. Checked another. "Oil's good. Needs a bit more water, but nothing serious." He scratched the balding patch at the crown of his head.

Flakes drifted down. Hunched into his jacket against the cold, Brian looked up again. Snowing. Broken-down car. Was he cursed?

"I'll give Terrance a call."

"Great." Terrance Crawley had never forgiven Brian for ditching his granddaughter in college. "He won't give you that frequent flyer discount when he sees me."

"Reckon not." Granddad returned to the car and shut the door. "But I never did like that girl. She was too loose."

Shamefully, that was exactly why Brian had dated her. And also why he'd ditched her—when he found out she'd slept with his best friend the first week he'd been at Basic.

Brian watched the windows fog up as they waited for their tow-truck rescue. A thump against his leg startled him.

"Spill your guts, son."

He glanced at his grandfather, feeling an all-too-familiar twist in his gut. Tightening his jaw, he pushed his gaze back to the windows.

"You haven't been the same since we picked you up at the airport fifteen days ago."

Leg bouncing, Brian groped in the void that held his massive failure for the right place to start. How to tell your World War II–hero grandfather that you were on the cusp of being thrown out of the Army?

"I won't yank your chain." Dead-serious eyes embedded in a wizened face, lined with years of military and intelligence work, pierced him. "I know."

Brian snapped his gaze toward his granddad. "You know?"

"He was worried about you."

Pride ricocheting off the betrayal, Brian shifted. "Who?" Who had the gall to go behind his back and rat him out? The dude would pay.

"Let's not worry about that. Let's get the cards on the table," Granddad said as he swiped a hand over a pretend flat surface. "What's happened?"

Ticked that he'd been sold out, Brian had a hard time working past that to admit the truth. "I'm facing disciplinary action." Man, that hurt. The failure, the defeat, the hopelessness came crashing down.

"Why?"

"Fighting."

Granddad chuckled. "Got that heated Bledsoe temper, eh?"

"Look," Brian said, his pulse hammering, "I just want you to know that I'm not like Dad. This wasn't my fault—well, not directly."

"Did you *directly* punch someone?"

Brian gave a soft snort. "I meant that I didn't start it."

"But you also didn't stop it."

"Oh, I stopped it." Brian didn't feel better for saying it. In fact, he felt worse.

"*I* meant, you didn't stop it before it went too far."

"I. . ." Brian clamped his jaw tight.

"It's okay if you don't want to tell me."

"No, it's not okay." He met his grandfather's gaze. "You're my hero. You're the one I want to make proud. And this—this is screwed up." *Just spit it out.* "I made a promise to someone. . ."

"A promise connected to what happened. And you can't break that."

"No, sir."

"But I'm not connected to this." His grandfather seemed to consider him and the situation. "Seems to me you need to let off some steam, so what's it going to hurt to tell me?"

"Considering someone sold me out to you, I can't trust that this won't get back."

"So, you think I'll rat you out now?"

Brian looked down. "I think you'll look out for my best interest, even if you think it might tick me off."

Another hearty laugh. A hand clapped on the back of Brian's neck. "You *are* a Bledsoe, through and through." Granddad tugged Brian toward him. "Son, I said I knew. But I didn't say *what* I knew."

Hesitant and cautious, Brian met his granddad's steely gaze. "Son of a—you faked me."

"I gave you what you needed to talk." Swiping his hand around the interior of the fogged-up Mustang, Granddad smiled. "This conversation stays here." He tapped the spot over his heart. "And here."

Man, he needed to get this off his chest—bad. To spill his guts. Defend himself. So, he did just that. Talked. Ranted.

"I'm proud of you, son."

Brian twitched. "A friend. . .someone was hitting on her, getting out of line. I put him back in line." Then grunted. "Now, I'm about to go down in a blaze of glory, just like Dad."

"No." Vehemence thickened Granddad's response. "What you are doing, that's defending someone. Keeping a promise. What he did. . ." Face pale, he shook his head. Red brightened eyes that seemed ready to cry. He swallowed then coughed. "Brian, you do have to get hold of that combustion that is inherent in our veins, but you were operating out of integrity."

"That time, but"—now Brian swallowed—"but it's in me, Granddad. That demon ready to devour anything to get what it wants. For Dad, it was money, power. For me, it's. . ." He wasn't even sure what it was he wanted.

"Validation."

A raw ache spread through Brian's chest. "Yeah," he said, slow and painfully. He studied his grandfather's face. How did Granddad always *get* him?

"You're not the only one trying to get out from under someone else's legacy."

"But your dad was a great war hero. He was pivotal—"

Granddad held up an age-spotted hand. "See what I mean? Everyone knew what my daddy did. And he never let us forget it. I felt like I never measured up. Had to prove to everyone that I was my own person, that I wasn't like him." He chuckled. "But I wanted nothing more than to be *just* like him."

Brian could relate. He wanted to be *just* like his granddad. A hero. Someone others looked up to. "I don't know how to be that man."

"It'd be easier if there was some magical potion we could drink or some formula we could complete. Go here. Do this. Get that."

With a snort and nod, Brian muttered, "Hooah."

"You've messed up—fighting gets you a quick kick in the backside out of the military, but you also seem to have some strong men behind you."

"Again, how do you know that?"

"Because you're still in."

Brian gave yet another snort. Point taken. The captain hadn't kicked him out. Hadn't handed him his butt on a silver platter. "I don't know how to be what I want to be."

"Son, just *be*. God created you as *you*. Not as me. Or your great-grandfather. Or your father. He created you with all your idiosyncrasies and that fire in your belly for a reason."

"I'd sure like to know what that is."

"It's so that when you're old, you can sit and freeze your assets off on a January night in a broken-down Mustang to encourage someone—maybe even your own grandson—someday."

Laughing, Brian said, "I'll never be as old as you."

Granddad popped him on the head.

CHAPTER 10

Bagram AFB, Afghanistan
12 January—0815 Hours

Leaving the team again meant he couldn't control the situation.

Dean snorted. Hadn't he learned about his severe lack of control when it came to Zahrah? But he had to do what he could within reason to guarantee the safety of Raptor. Being the officer on the team meant more liaising than fieldwork, but it annoyed him not to be completely active with them right now. Cold, brittle wind tugged at the collar of his jacket as he stood at the barrel he'd retrofitted to hold a crackling fire.

Leaving also meant Sal would be in charge. He trusted his friend completely, but something was simmering at the back of Falcon's life that seemed to bleed into his soldiering.

But Sal could handle it. He'd have to.

A mere two hundred yards and a road separated him from the staging area. Dean watched, itching to be there. To coordinate. To make sure Raptor had what they needed and—

"Little late to be roasting marshmallows," General Burnett said as he joined Dean, standing on the other side of the steel barrel, huddled beneath his long wool winter jacket.

"Always did like s'mores," Dean said with a smile. His gaze flicked past the general's ear, watching as Eagle hustled toward the waiting vehicle. In hand, he had his sniper rifle. The eighty-five-pound rucksack didn't slow the old guy down a second.

Burnett eyed him. "How you holdin' up?"

"Fine, sir." He needed to reassure the general. Give him something to distract his mind from following any bread-crumb trail Dean might inadvertently leave that would lead to the team's under-the-radar mission. "Having Zahrah to talk to helps."

Laugh lines crinkled in the older man's eyes. "I bet it does. How is she?"

"As good as can be expected." Over Burnett's shoulder, Dean registered—but didn't let his gaze linger on—the hulking form of Titanis ambling toward the warehouse and disappearing inside. "Still has nightmares, but she promises they're fading."

"And you?"

"I'll never forget." What happened to her, how she'd been used against him, to force his hand, to force hers against her own country.

"Will you forgive?"

Dean let one side of his mouth lift in a sardonic smile. "We'll have to see when we catch up with this guy."

Burnett chuckled. "I guess we will." His smile faded, and for several long seconds he held Dean hostage with a penetrating gaze that probed the sudden gaping silence in their conversation.

If Dean looked away, Burnett would know something was up. But if he continued the silent standoff— "Everything okay, sir?"

"Why don't you tell me, Captain?"

"Tell you what, sir?"

"Start with Bledsoe."

Relief, sweet and swift, surged through Dean's veins. Thank God the general hadn't caught on to the black ops mission. "He's home but will be on the next flight out at 1500"—he did the mental calculation—"tomorrow, I believe."

"And when he gets here?"

Feigning contemplation of Hawk's fate, Dean lowered his gaze. Then glanced up, his heart jackhammering as the general moved to Dean's right instead of opposite him. With the general's quick reflexes and skill, he'd spot the team.

"Hawk will have extra duties. He's going to feel the pain of what he's done. I need him to understand—maybe for the first time—the honor it is to be on this team. To be a Special Forces soldier."

"Extra duties?"

Dean unzipped his jacket and angled away from the fire, forcing Burnett to turn his back on the team assembling at the warehouse. "A month of patrol. Colonel Whitson has a team heading south. They need skilled escorts."

"Patrol."

Dean nodded again, cringing this time as a red glow of lights brightened the evening sky.

He hadn't seen Harrier join the team, but Sal wouldn't pull out without the full working team.

"Trying to teach him a lesson?"

"Keeping him so busy he doesn't have the time or energy to fight."

At the roar of the engine, Burnett glanced over his shoulder. A flicker of concern waggled through his brow, but then he turned back to Dean. Considered him. Then bobbed his head. "Just make sure his head's in the game. Only thing that should be slamming into anyone are bullets into terrorists." He shot Dean a stern look. "Am I clear, Captain?"

"As crystal, sir."

Pursing his lips, Burnett looked down as he nodded. Slowly, his gaze followed the Humvee heading toward the rear gate. He watched as it disappeared around the corner.

If Burnett figured out what he and Sal had planned...

" 'When near, appear far.' "

He knows! Dean's pulse roared with the engine. "Sun Tzu. . .?" He hadn't gotten to the rank he was by giving himself away at the first hint of trouble.

Burnett cocked his head to the side and peered up at Dean with a squinty gaze. "You're one sneaky you-know-what, Captain Watters."

"I don't understand, sir."

"Good." Clapping a hand on Dean's shoulder, Burnett laughed. "Knew I picked you for a reason." He took a step back toward the living units. "See you at 0600."

"Yessir." As he watched the general saunter back to the officers' quarters, Dean let out a heavy, slow breath. *Too close.*

Sun Tzu in *The Art of War* had said those very words, about using the enemy's perception against them. Whoever their coms terrorist was, he no doubt believed SOCOM had pulled out 80 percent of their teams from the field. Only the elite, long-embedded teams would remain hidden in plain sight among the locals. Well, only the elite. And Raptor.

Godspeed, brothers.

—⁕—

Kandahar, Afghanistan
14 January—0925 Hours

"I did not earn my flying credential so I could be a glorified taxi driver!" Indignation coursed through Fekiria, hot and virulent.

Colonel Mahmoud scowled. "You are an ANA soldier and will do as you are commanded."

Fekiria opened her mouth to lob another rejection, heaped with insult, but Captain Ripley smiled and touched her arm. "Colonel, if you don't mind, I need to speak with my flight candidate. Last-minute instructions." He bunched his shoulders. "Won't take but a minute."

With a sharp nod, the colonel stared down Fekiria.

"Lieutenant?" Captain Ripley motioned her to the side, a clipboard in hand.

Moving her legs took every ounce of her will. As she turned, she hissed, "You will not change my mind," to the captain.

"In this morning's lecture. . ." he began, casting glances back. Apparently to put as much distance between them and the colonel before continuing. Near the door to an office, he angled his shoulder toward her. "I realize you are insulted by the assignment."

"You and I both know the only reason I was chosen is because he wants to put me in my place—serving men."

Captain Ripley's eyes crinkled in a small smile. "Actually, the reason you were chosen is because I suggested you."

She drew in a sharp breath. "Why would you do this to me? Do you, too, see me as nothing but—"

"I see you as a capable pilot who is making Afghan military history." His gaze went tender, needling her razor's-edge words. "You will be flying a dignitary, Fekiria. That means, you—a woman—will be in view of a male official. What better way to show them that women are making gains? And if you do a great job and the flight is smooth, he will be more inclined to pay attention."

Disbelief swirled through her. She visually traced the lines of his face, the clean-shaven jaw, so contrary to most men in her country. The stiffness of a soldier who walked and talked with control demanded respect from those who met him. Dark brown hair cut close with a sprinkling of gray. *Gray?* How old was he? The realization that she didn't know startled her.

"Besides, as a candidate in the advanced program, you need to continue flying. And every flight logs hours, and you need those regardless of who is in your aircraft."

How could she have been so wrong? So quick to think they thought less of her? Then again, she'd fought those prejudices her entire life. "It is true," she began slowly, still not believing him, "that you did this? You are not covering for him?"

"Do you really think I'd let them snatch one of my favorite flight candidates out from under me in the middle of training?" He smiled. "Trust me, Fekiria. This is a good thing. It shows you are more than capable."

"But if something goes wrong—"

"Nothing is going to go wrong, because you are going to fly like the ace that you are."

After letting out a leveling breath, one in which she pulled together the fragments of her courage and pride, she gave a slow nod. "Thank you." She met his eyes. In those gray irises, she saw friendship, belief, confidence…and a lot more.

It would not be so bad, would it, to accept his advances? He showed interest. He was a good man. They had a common bond—flying—and …*He's American.*

Perhaps. But he wasn't like most Americans she met. He wasn't like Sergeant Brian.

Why could she not empty her mind of that soldier? His gray-green eyes. His laugh.

"When you get back, maybe we can grab a bite to eat."

A weight dropped into her stomach. Made her hesitate. But enough of this resistance. He was a good man. "Yes, perhaps."

His smile could rival the sun. With her answer, she'd given him hope that something could happen between them. "C'mon. I'll walk your preflight with you."

They headed out to the tarmac where the Mi-17 waited. Captain Ripley handed her the clipboard and took a step back. Observing as she checked the exterior of her craft then climbing in after her for the instrumentation check, he let her set the pace. Gave her the room to do what he had trained her to do. Though he didn't crowd her, it took everything in Fekiria not to feel suffocated by his hovering.

It's in your mind. She had given him an open door to her heart. So why did she suddenly want to slam it shut?

"You are double minded!" Zahrah's words, though more than seven months old, were as sharp and clear as the day she'd spoken them. Then, the context had been about Zahrah and Captain Dean. Today…Fekiria and Captain Ripley.

The irony was not lost on her.

Was she afraid of relationships? Love? *More like afraid of Americans.* And *afraid* might be the wrong term. Perhaps *resistant.*

"Looks like your VIPs are here." Captain Ripley climbed out of the chopper. "See you when you get back."

Fekiria nodded, her heart thumping a little harder than she'd expected when the sleek black limo slid into view. Flags with crests snapped in the cold wind as the doors opened. Fekiria started the rotors. Three men in suits stepped into the gray, wintry day, bundled against the weather and rotor wash.

Colonel Mahmoud rushed toward them and motioned to the chopper. The four of them made their way into the belly of the chopper as the engines roared. A final man emerged from the limo. Tall, broad-shouldered, he seemed oblivious to the elements and engine noise. He glanced to his right and left—then straight into the cockpit.

Fekiria's stomach heaved. She had never been so grateful for the bulky helmet and sunglasses she wore. It was her only protection against the man stalking toward the aircraft. Adeeb, her brother.

—∞—

Bagram Airfield, Afghanistan
15 January—0930 Hours

Sergeant.

Brian stared at the rank on his new orders, a sickening concoction of anger mixing with humiliation and guilt. With a dash of annoyance. *You did this to yourself.* Hard work flushed down the drain of a bad temper. It wasn't that he had a bad temper. He just. . .

No "just."

As he trekked across Bagram to hook up with the mech team heading south, he reminded himself that if he couldn't keep it together, he would never get to prove to himself that he had the good Bledsoe genes as well as the bad. Enough screwing up.

But it was true that evil succeeded when good men did nothing. So, what was he to do when presented with a scenario like what happened at the bar?

Okay, true. If it hadn't been that cocky SEAL, Brian wouldn't have thrown that punch. If it'd been a civilian, he might've restrained himself.

There it was. Pride.

He stepped into the Command building and lingered at the front, taking in the setting. The personnel. The thrum of activity. The fact he didn't belong or know anyone.

"C'I help you?"

Brian jerked toward the voice and found a specialist who stood a full head shorter than himself. Blond hair, blue eyes, she had little makeup and didn't need any more. Hot came to mind. But things had to be different this time. No screwups.

All business. Ruck slung over his shoulder, he shifted his gaze to the other grunts in the room. "Where can I find Captain Mason?"

Her gaze traveled over him, from his tight crop to his tactical shirt with his Raptor patch and his tac pants.

"Sorry," he said, irritated that this hot chick who'd been checking him out had to be ignored. Wanted to ignore it. Would ignore it. "Didn't realize this was an inspection, or I'd have donned my Class As."

Her cheeks reddened, and she dipped her head.

Brian aimed toward the rest of the room and called out, "Looking for Captain Mason."

A head popped up from a desk. "Down the hall, second door on the right."

With a wave of thanks, Brian headed toward the office. He rapped on the half-glass door.

"Enter!"

Entering, he promised to make his time in purgatory short. Do the crime, do the time—then he'd be back where he belonged. With Raptor. "Captain Mason?"

An officer sitting in a metal folding chair looked over his shoulder at Brian. The oak leaf on his shoulder made Brian stiffen. The major frowned, his gaze doing a quick once-over of Brian's uniform and finally settling on his sleeve patch. "Special Forces." He grunted as he looked at the person behind the desk.

On the other side sat a very short, somewhat older woman with auburn hair tucked into a bun. No wedding ring, but an indention there warned him she'd been married. Or forgotten her band. Though, most women wore it like a trophy. "He's mine, Garret," came the amused voice of the officer who wore the silver bars on her shoulders. She folded her hands and met Brian's gaze evenly. "Have a seat. Bledsoe, isn't it?"

"Yes, ma'am." Get his assignment and get out of here. Less scrutinization meant less chance to find something wrong with him and send him home packing. "I don't mean to interrupt. If you'll just give me my orders, I'll—"

"Have a seat, Sergeant," Captain Mason said. "Major Slusarski and I were just talking about this mission."

"Mission?" Something pulled at Brian's nerves as he lowered himself to the chair. "I came here with the understanding this was a routine patrol."

"It is." Captain Mason smiled after sharing a knowing glance with the major. "And it isn't."

Brian set his ruck between his booted feet and rubbed his hands. Swallowed. "Um, no disrespect, ma'am, but I am here temporarily—"

"You're here for disciplinary action worked out through additional duties." Her tone wasn't ugly, but it also warned him she wouldn't brook argument or opposition.

Was this her way of saying she didn't like or trust him? That she had his number and was ready to yank and tank him?

"Make no mistake, Sergeant Bledsoe." She leaned back in her creaky wooden chair. "I want you here. Men like you have instincts and experience I can't buy. My troops are getting shot up and terrorized because they don't have the training you have. With your assistance, we can get done what needs to be done."

Gritting his teeth, Brian bit back his retort. This sounded too much like babysitting. Guard duty. Going out with his team, knowing each of the men whose six he covered also had his—that was one thing. But being dunked in a boiling pot of hostility with specialists and privates who barely knew the business end of their M4s, who didn't know how to recognize and decipher threats from approaching locals. . .

He allowed himself only one question. "What's that, ma'am?"

She narrowed her eyes slightly. Not a threat. Just intense interest. Maybe even a challenge. "We are delivering supplies to orphanages and schools."

"Supplies."

"Don't get overconfident, Sergeant," Major Slusarski warned. "The region has a rash of attacks against supply caravans."

"Besides me, how many will be on the run?"

"Three vehicles," Captain Mason said. "Security in front, the supplies vehicle, then another security."

"Why don't you just paint a target on the side of the trucks?" Snap. There went his sarcasm, and by the wide-eyed look on the captain's face, his humor wasn't appreciated. "You're telegraphing to the enemy that whatever is in the truck is worth being protected."

"So, what?" The captain's voice pitched. "Just leave them unprotected."

Frustration coiled around Brian's head, squeezing. "Yes, ma'am."

She scoffed. The major hadn't taken his penetrating gaze off Brian.

"More accurately, make them look normal. Don't draw attention to them. Instead of three vehicles with one large truck, take four and split up the cargo between all four."

"Some of the supplies won't fit."

"Make them."

"I don't think you understand, Sergeant Bledsoe—we're supplying an orphanage and a school. The crates are too big."

"Break them down." Brian took in a heavy breath, remembering the last school he'd dealt with in Mazar-e. The one that introduced Raptor to the lethal talons of some psycho who'd nearly beat his team captain into oblivion. And the hostility of the Taliban against women being educated was more prevalent here in the south.

Not only did they want him to be a babysitter, they expected him to be a sitting duck while doing it.

Things could be worse—he could be cleaning latrines.

"Ma'am," he said to Captain Mason, shoveling as much contrite attitude into his voice and expression as he could muster. "You wanted me here to help make your supply run a success."

"Yes, and I meant with brute force."

"The strongest force is our brains. If we use them, strong-arming won't be necessary." No wonder things were so messed up in the military. He then shrugged, recognizing he was irritating them. And irritating the captain holding your temporary orders could be a problem. "Just a suggestion, ma'am."

Tensions tightened her lips and eyes. "You'll report to the motor pool at 0800."

Major Slusarski stood. "I'll walk you out."

Duly blown off, Brian pushed to his feet, pulling the ruck up as he did. "Thank you, ma'am," he managed to say without sounding ticked. Which he was. Shouldering the ruck, he trailed the major down the short hall back to the main area.

Slusarski motioned Brian to follow him. "Things work a little differently around here, Sergeant."

Here it comes.

"As a member of SOCOM, you get used to having a voice in mission planning. Briefings are two-way streams of communication." Slusarski pushed open the door and stepped into the bitter afternoon. "Around here, orders are given by officers and taken by enlisted."

"Understood, sir." In other words, shut up and stand down.

"You're a bulldog."

"Sheepdog, sir."

Slusarski chuckled. "Hooah. But you'll need to tone that down if you want Mason to write *plays well with others* on your file."

Was the guy friend or foe? "Understood, sir."

"Keep saying that. You might actually survive this sorry assignment."

Brian shot the guy an uncertain glance.

Slusarski entered a tent where two dozen or so bunks lined up along the length. He pointed to the last bunk. "Home sweet home."

Brian nodded. "Thank you, sir."

"For the record, I didn't want you here."

Foe it is. "Makes two of us, sir."

"Guess God's punishing us both. Don't screw this up, Bledsoe."

Was the guy actually threatened by Brian? "Understood, sir."

BLOODIED BACKS

Shanghai, China
15 January—1130 Hours

They stood in the foyer, sons of former business partners. An alliance started more than thirty years ago on the beaten and bloodied backs of two men who found a strange friendship in the midst of heartache, pain, and war. They had much in common—a son at home, a country in turmoil, and an enemy who had destroyed everything they worked for. America.

Now, the man who controlled the decisions of the company Daniel's own father had cofounded bent his red turbaned head toward Kiew, holding her hand, and placed a kiss on her cheek. "It is a pleasure to see you again, Miss Tang."

Kiew's pale complexion filled with color. "It is an honor, Mr. Takkar."

Heat swarmed Daniel's gut as he watched the exchange. The impudent, disrespectful Sikh he could tolerate. But the humble and subtle actions of the man who bore the name of the company Daniel would own outright one day—he would rather push him off the balcony of his Shanghai penthouse. It was a shame they were the same man. Either way, let the turban unravel and strangle him as he plummeted to his death.

Takkar shifted toward Daniel. "As always, my friend." He nodded. Never finished that sentence.

The teakwood-paneled elevator doors slid open. A guard barely acknowledged the two men as they stepped into the box. Fury had Daniel wishing he could hack the cables and let them drop to their deaths. Anything to rid him of the arrogance that smothered him from reaching the success he sought. Finishing what his father had begun.

Daniel moved to Kiew's side as the doors closed. He grabbed her hands and yanked them up.

Kiew fell against him, clumsily, with a yelp.

"What did he give you? Open your hands!"

Wide eyes told of her guilt. If he did not need to teach her so much, he would end her life. Rid himself of her weakness. But no, she must learn. She must grow stronger.

"Show me!"

"Nothing." She shook her head. "He gave me nothing." With that, she opened her hands, which he held at eye level. Small palms were sweaty but empty. He thrust her backward.

He was not wrong. Sajjan had never kissed her good-bye. He eyed her sleeves. Lunged forward and grabbed her wrists again. He tested his theory, still finding nothing.

"See?" she hissed at him. "When will you trust me?"

"Never! You are *weak*."

"My loyalty is to you, and you alone." Her fire burned, the same one that had drawn him to her three years ago. She stood straight before him. Head up.

Daniel lifted his hand to strike.

"We've had a breakthrough," Kiew said, her voice soft, eyes hopeful.

The words were enough to stem his fury. Still trembling from the anger that had infected his veins, Daniel dared her to have lied to him. "Why did you not tell me sooner?"

"Your guests."

In this she had been wise. They would never give Takkar any more than what the man stole daily. Anger barely abated, he gritted his teeth. "Show me."

Kiew lowered her head.

Accepting her deference, he started for the lower level, stepping beyond the door to his meditation room and entering a code on a hidden panel. They descended a half-dozen steps, and he punched in his master code. "This had better be worth my time."

Steel gave way, sliding into the wall as a series of beams swung out of the way, affording entrance. Down six more steps and he coded in. Then she did. Both or the sensors would attack the unknown intruder. No security was too much with so much at stake. Even Sajjan and his fool Waris had left DNA samples that Daniel had encoded into his system.

Semidarkness gave way to bright lights, hued in pale blue and behind sterile security measures. Several rows of technicians worked intently, heads down, minds engaged. Each assigned a different task. A different way to dismantle the enemy. Spurred by a sense of imminent victory, he allowed the anger to seep from his pores. Rid his body of toxins and focus on the positive forces.

Kiew entered the secure area and walked to the far end, to her station. She was the exception: she had both beauty and brains. It was the only reason he tolerated her weakness. But his instruction had improved her in this area. He would continue the path of discipline and self-control to make her better.

She sat on the stool and logged in. "We have penetrated another layer of defense." Her gloved fingers flew over the keyboard.

"A layer?" Daniel let out a huff. "Seven months and this is all we have?"

"But it is a vital layer," Kiew said, her gaze bouncing to his. "We have been able to get into their communications, disrupt them, confuse them."

"So, no high-security passwords or weapons plans."

"No, that's still outside our reach, but we are close. We're making progress."

Progress? She called this *progress*? Daniel tightened his jaw. "What is taking so long? Why have we not yet dismantled everything? Why are they still operating?"

"We are having trouble. Our commands go and some make it through, but"—she shook her head, eyes pinched in frustration—"it is like they are diluted. Not all succeed."

"How is that possible?"

"They are blocking us," a tech geek said from the side.

Daniel ignored the intrusion in his conversation with Kiew.

"No matter what we do, they thwart our efforts." The man had no sense. No honor. No courage.

"It would seem," Daniel said slowly, "that you think they are winning. That they are stronger than us."

"Yes"—the tech's gaze hit Kiew's and immediately the man reversed his direction—"*no*. It's just that—"

"I think you need a new perspective." Daniel waited as his guards, never more than a half-dozen feet behind him, came forward. "Outside," he ordered, realizing they intended to deliver the perspective in the sanitized room.

The man wrestled against them. "No! No, I only meant—"

Daniel turned his full attention back to the only woman capable of being at his side. Brilliant, beautiful. . .she had so much potential. A little more training and she would be *perfect*. "They are blocking us."

"Not directly." Kiew kept her voice level and smooth. No fear. Only confidence. As he had trained her. It was why she was in charge. Why he trusted her with the delivery of his masterpiece. "The patterns are random. Like a shot in the dark—one or two are blocked, but not all. We have the advantage in that they do not know who or what they are fighting. Our programmers have implemented ghosts. The time they take chasing them affords us time and room we need to maneuver."

How many times must he say it? "I want complete control of their systems."

Kiew looked down at her keyboard. "Then we must return to Afghanistan."

The danger of exposure, of failing, increased on enemy ground. But the challenge, the delicious victory of upending the Americans in their borrowed backyard. . . "Upstairs." He pivoted and left the suffocating sanitized room. Felt the tendrils of peace unraveling. As he passed the meditation room, he sensed it calling him.

Behind, he heard the second *hiss* and *whoosh* as the secure chamber accepted then released Kiew. Her footsteps were almost silent on the marble floor as she trailed him up into the living area. "Why must we return?"

"The greater the distance between our servers and theirs, the more time is lost. We can do a faster capture. And if we can insert someone onto their bases—"

"We have someone."

"He is locked in the north. We must have an asset in the south, closer to—"

"You think I am a fool? If they are discovered, the entire effort collapses."

"Those you have hired are completely loyal to you. They would rather kill themselves than lose this. If we succeed—"

"*If?*"

She cocked her head and looked down, a microshake of her head. "*When* we succeed, not only will you be in the position you want and deserve, but China can topple the Americans. We will no longer be second."

"You are making me impatient, Kiew." He did not care about China. He cared about resetting the thrust of power from the West to his hands. "I must get in. We are running out of time. The longer we are in their system, the more chances they have to trace us—and if we plant too many people on their bases, the chance of capture is great, too."

"Meng-Li," came a raspy voice.

Daniel turned, his heart catching. "Mother. What are you doing out of bed?" He hurried to her side and wrapped an arm around her bony shoulders. Shoulders that had carried so much weight. That had literally transported water and food across a mountain to ensure he got an education, that ensured he could take his place at Takkar as his father had vowed. "Come back to bed. You must rest."

He led her into the room that spanned the entire west wall of the tower. Exquisite fabrics wrapped her in elegance. Tapestries, curtains, rice-paper dividers that gave her a sitting area, a dressing area, a bathroom and shower.

"There." She pointed a gnarled finger toward the chaise by the window. Her favorite spot.

With care, he eased her onto the gold brocade cushion and smiled at her, taking in her aged appearance. But instead of age, instead of wrinkles, he saw wisdom. Grace. Strength. Beauty. All wrapped in a small package with white-gray hair.

"You worry too much." She smiled.

He needed her to hang on a little longer to see his grand victory. To see her husband—his father—honored in the highest possible way. "Soon, Mama, we will honor Father. His name will be above all others. The world will know Meng-Li Gang."

She patted his face as she leaned back on the long cushion. "You are such a good son." She let out a sigh. "Your father would be so proud."

Infused with her praise and the promise of words he would never hear his father whisper, Daniel was reminded of what must be done. What he *must* finish.

"Be nice to her," his mom said as her eyes fluttered closed.

It took a moment for Daniel to catch up with her subject change. Kiew. His mom had introduced them. Designed their upcoming marriage.

"I want grandchildren."

As he drew a blanket over her frail form, Daniel tried not to scoff. "Rest, Mother." He did not want children. Not now. Did not have time for them. Not until he succeeded. Not until he cut the breath from the lungs of his enemy as they had done to his father. Not until America died a brutal death.

CHAPTER 11

Undisclosed Location, Afghanistan
15 January—1010 Hours

Let's get some eyes up." Salvatore Russo secured the doors and nailed light-blocking material against the windows. The building had two entrances and sat in the center of a bustling shopping area, making it easier to come and go. Camping out in the middle of the enemy's territory heightened the risks as well as the possibility of finding those responsible for the attacks.

"Almost there," Sergeant Grant Knight said from the bank of laptops and monitors. At his feet lay panting the MWD as renowned for his skill in taking down predators as he was for licking peanut butter. "It'd already be done if your coms specialist was here. I don't know this stuff the way he does."

"Nobody does." Eagle draped himself in camo netting. He lifted his sniper rifle and gear. "Heading topside."

"Roger that." Sal checked his watch. "Anyone heard from Titanis?" he asked as his secure sat phone rang. "Go ahead."

"Set up?" Dean's voice came through the line firm but quiet.

"Eighty percent."

"I'll be there when I can."

"Understood." Sal studied the most recent map of the city tacked to the wall that had chunks of plaster missing. "You're sure Riordan isn't floating us a fast one? All the way out here, in the middle of a crazy-busy city. Lot of eyes to see what nobody wants seen."

"We're not sure about anything right now."

"Copy that."

"But the intel is reasonable—best place to get lost or go unnoticed is in the open," Dean said. "Talked with Hastings this morning. They finally pinned down the coordinates of the call that led us to that ghost village. Couldn't get an exact location but pinned it down to within five klicks of your location."

"Hooah," Sal grunted. "Just made our job a little easier." While they might not be closer in terms of solving this insanity, at least they were *physically* closer to whoever or whatever was hunting them.

"Keep me posted."

"Roger that," Sal muttered as images sprang to life on the bank of monitors.

"Hooah," Knight said. "We are live and recording."

Dean laughed. "Wish I was there."

"We'll save you some fun," Sal said. The call ended and he focused on the feeds. He taped labels to the different monitors, indicating what angle they provided. The enemy might be messing with SOCOM's communications, off-grid, off normal channels, Raptor had a hair's breadth of a chance to nail these punks.

"Movement at the watchmaker," Knight hissed out, his words fast and precise.

After a glance at the feed that showed the front of the shop, Sal swung his M4A1 to the front as he hustled up to the side of the trapdoor. Whoever came through that door without authorization would find permanent authorization embedded in his forehead.

Thump. Thump. Thump-thump-thump.

Inhaling a breath, he eased his weapon down and slipped back.

The panel slid open and the hulk of an Aussie SAS soldier folded himself through. "Door's a little big," Titanis said with a grin. "Think you could find a smaller one?"

"Then we couldn't fit your ego through," Knight said with a chuckle, the camaraderie he'd established with the team on the mission six months ago still evident.

"What's this," Titanis said in his deep, gruff Oz accent. "Little Bird has found a sense of humor?"

Harrier looked up, his face a mask of sincerity. "Who was humoring?"

"Raptor Actual made contact. Said our target is within five klicks of this location."

Titanis tossed his eighty-pound ruck into a corner as if lobbing a tennis ball. "Good. We can start scouting."

"What's this target going to look like?"

"After we're done, he'll look dead," Titanis said.

"Easier to barbecue that way," Knight added. "But before we grill 'em, how do we find them?"

Jokes about killing annoyed Sal. And their sarcasm grated along his raw nerves. "This is going to take time. We're Green Berets. It's what we do—recon, develop relationships."

"In other words, we'll be here awhile." Knight set out a collapsible bowl for MWD Ddrake and filled it with water.

"Unless you know how to find this son of a gun faster. Unless you're holding back on intel that could solve this for everyone so we can go home to our families."

Titanis's gaze hit Sal, alerting him to his tone and his aggravation.

"Long and short of it is—Zmaray wants us hiding behind our bunkers back at Mazar-e. We're going to let the Lion think we're doing that, all while we're sniffing right up under his big schnozz."

"Then cram a grenade up it and send him back to his maker," Harrier said.

Sal resisted the urge to bark at the guy about his bloodlust. Truth was, Sal was tired. Tired of the killing. Tired of people dying. Tired of *his* people dying.

—⁂—

Two Hours Outside Kandahar, Afghanistan
15 January—1030 Hours

Fekiria stayed in the cockpit. The flight out to the private estate was smooth. Even with the winter winds, there'd been no accumulation of ice. The skids touched down without a hitch, and the men were hustling into the sprawling home without a backward glance.

Including Adeeb.

Fekiria let a long breath out between her lips as she watched him disappear into the house. *What* was he doing here? With these men? Connected to the ANA? Since when had Adeeb been in the Army? Her stomach clenched as the realization hit her—if he was ANA and connected to those high enough up, he could find out. . .everything.

Captain Ripley had noted her real name in her file. That would get digitized, no doubt, and then it would be far too simple for him to discover her secret.

She closed her eyes, images of being dragged into the street and being stabbed. Shot. Whatever means they wanted to use to kill her. In the name of the family honor, of course.

In the name of idiocy! Anger flared through her.

"November Romeo Three One Two, what is your status?"

Relaxing against the seat, Fekiria breathed a little easier at the sound of Captain Ripley's voice. She keyed her mic. "This is November Romeo. Arrived on time and delivered VIPs."

"Roger that, November Romeo. Well done."

She smiled. Those two words were a balm to her soul. "Thank you." She bit her tongue. The instructors made it clear that the coms weren't for informal chatter. "Expected departure is at 1500."

"Roger that."

Fekiria signed off and sat in the cockpit. She'd have to walk the chopper again, but doing so risked her brother seeing her. What if he was near that large window overlooking the beautiful terrace?

A security guard approached from the house.

Fekiria busied herself, running through her after-flight checklist. Making notes. Feigning distraction.

A soft thump against the Plexiglas window startled her.

The security guard waved her outside.

She held up her clipboard, since shouting would only draw more attention, and she wasn't sure he could hear her anyway. Certain he'd go away after a few minutes of being ignored, she kept her head down. But when she looked up again, she knew it was no good.

Outside, she continued ignoring him, focused on her board.

"You must come inside," he said, his tone a bit. . .off.

"I must do my after-flight walk of the chopper."

"No good. It is too dangerous. If someone targets the chopper. . ."

Fekiria stared at him. Then at the house. She refused to look into the sky. What on earth would someone be targeting and why?

Like anyone needed a legitimate excuse here. If one faction was angry with another, then they blew up the house. Burned down businesses. Slaughtered families.

"Come," the guard insisted. "Inside."

"I—"

"You can stay in the back kitchen with the staff."

She swallowed her objection. That should be safe enough. She'd keep to herself. Remain hidden. Finally, she gave a slight nod and followed the guard around the side of the house and along a rear garden path. He banked down a flight of stairs to a small door.

Something in her stomach curdled. Standing at the top made the door appear smaller than it was. That psychological impact left her feeling threatened.

"Come," the guard said.

Being in the ANA, she had basic self-defense training. But could she unarm and subdue this man? What if there were more on the other side of that door?

He must have understood her fear because he nudged open the door and motioned inward. "Look."

Tilting her head, she peered in. Red tiles spilled inward. She barely saw the corner of a counter, the side lined with shelves of baskets of what looked like roots and vegetables.

Fekiria released her hesitancy and trailed him inside. The cooling room spread to her left for at least twenty or thirty feet. Straight on only ten feet. The guard crossed the tile and climbed a flight of four whitewashed steps that creaked beneath Fekiria's feet. Almost as soon as her foot hit the slate floor, a blanket of warmth cocooned her shoulders and neck.

The large stove and oven provided the heat that warded off the winter chill.

A large woman, bent over a pot on the stove, slid a glance in Fekiria's direction. Sprigs of unruly gray and black hair coiled out from beneath the tan hijab. Sweat mottled the woman's complexion. "Sit," the cook ordered then turned to a teen girl. "Get her some naan and water."

Fekiria held up a hand. "Thank you, but I am—"

The cook shouted to someone else to check the bread in the massive stone oven that reminded Fekiria of ovens of old that were hewn in the walls of the home from rock.

Unwilling to argue with the cook and draw more attention to herself, Fekiria tucked herself into the corner table and did everything she could to be invisible. Within a few minutes, bread and cup were planted before her by a young girl, who hurried down into the cooling room then returned a minute later with a basket of chickpeas.

Quietly sipping the drink, Fekiria ignored the naan. It was too sweet and heavy for her stomach—especially knowing she sat beneath the same roof with Adeeb. Of all the people. . .why must it be him? As fierce and traditional as their father, Adeeb had no reservations about honor killings. Or putting a woman in her place.

This woman he'd put six feet under without hesitating.

The hard wood chair dug into her bones as the hours passed. Growing fidgety two and a half hours later, she stood and debated about whether she should say something to the cook, who was now well into making pastries and baklava—Oh, mercy! Fekiria's sweet tooth ached for the parchment pastry—but then decided the cook would not care if she was here or not.

She caught the young girl who'd served the bread. "Excuse me, I must speak with one of the guards."

The girl, eyes larger that pomegranates, shook her head.

"I must. My boss will be angry. We were supposed to leave thirty minutes ago."

"I will get the guard. Leave the girl alone," said an older man who appeared in the kitchen. He then shuffled out.

Waiting, she tried to keep to the shadows. What if he brought Adeeb instead of a guard? Maybe she should just go to the chopper—

"What is it?" the guard demanded, a scowl darkening his beady eyes.

"I am an ANA soldier, who was on orders to fly the gentlemen out there, but we were supposed to be back at the base by now. I could get in very serious trouble."

His scowl grew. "What do you want me to do, stupid woman?"

"I must either radio in that we—"

"No! You cannot go out there."

Fekiria drew back at the venom in his words. "I must. If I do not report in, the Army will come looking for their aircraft and me."

"Let them look."

"You cannot stop me from going out there."

He snapped his weapon at her in a not-so-subtle challenge. "They said no one out there. That means you, too."

Anger pushed her boldness to the front, beyond her fear of reprisal. "Then go tell them I must radio in, or I'm going out there."

"And I will kill you."

"Then you will have to explain to your masters why they have no pilot to get them back to the base."

He snapped his mouth closed.

Aha. She had him. Triumph sent her thundering heart into an irregular beat. Trembling coursed through her hands, but she refused to show weakness to this man who found power only in threatening a woman.

He made to strike her, and she stepped back. Embarrassed, he hurried from the kitchen amid the laughter of the cook and the girl. Fekiria stumbled back, but her legs went rubbery. She steadied herself at the table, giving herself time to regain her courage.

Stomping feet preceded the guard who stalked into the kitchen, his face all rage. Behind him strode a man in a suit.

Fekiria drew herself up, silently thanking Allah that it was not Adeeb.

"What is the problem?" the suited man demanded.

"My name is Lieutenant Rhmani, and my orders were to deliver four men to this estate three hours ago, and to return two hours later."

"They are not finished." He dared her to argue, and the smug grin of the guard behind him only frustrated Fekiria.

"I understand," she said. "I only ask that I may go to my aircraft and radio."

"That would be unwise."

The threat in his words could not be clearer, but she would use the "stupid woman" belief to her advantage. "What would be unwise, sir, is if I do not report in."

"You dare counter my words?"

"What is happening here?" a voice demanded from the kitchen entrance.

Fekiria's stomach vaulted into her throat. She stood, frozen, as she met Adeeb's fierce gaze. Her heart felt as if it exploded with each beat.

"What is the matter?" Adeeb barked, looking from the others then to her. Recognition flickered through his face.

"Ad—"

"I asked what is happening here," Adeeb shouted at the men.

"Sir, this woman insists on radioing to the U.S. base."

"I must," Fekiria said. Why had he not named her? Shouted at her? Hit her?

"You are the pilot." His voice betrayed nothing but irritation.

Confusion circled her brain like vultures over a dead, rotting carcass. Why had he not acknowledged her? His question felt as one he'd ask a stranger. *Perhaps that is what I am to him now.* Besides, she still wore the flight suit, so refuting it would be foolish. "I am. If I do not report in, then not only will more ANA soldiers come, but the American military will come looking for their property."

His gaze raked her soul. But he said nothing. It felt like minutes, but it had been only seconds. "You will radio in and let them know we will not be leaving tonight."

Fekiria started. "Not—what?"

"You will return tomorrow morning."

"The flight orders said we would return an hour ago!"

Voice and expression impassive, he said, "Plans change." Understanding spread across his face. "Escort her out there and back." His gaze never left her face. "Then lock her up in a room. Make sure she does not leave again."

The guard and the suited man escorted her out to the helicopter. With her headset on, she radioed the base. "November Romeo to Sierra Alpha Bravo Two."

"Sierra Alpha Bravo here. What is your status, November Romeo?"

"Delayed," she said, exasperated and yet relieved to hear Captain Ripley's voice again. Had he been sitting there at the controls the whole time? Why did it have to be him? "The VIPs have had a change of plans, sir."

"Come again?"

"They have said we will not be leaving until tomorrow morning."

"Negative, November Romeo. You are ordered to RTB immediately."

"They will not allow me to leave."

"November Romeo, is this a threat level red?"

Threat level red meant hostile. Meant Captain Ripley and who knew how many other American soldiers would come rushing—assaulting—to her aid. What would happen to Adeeb then? She stared out at the guard, who happily kept his weapon trained on her.

He had been the devil himself. Did she care what happened to him?

Perhaps not. But she wanted to know why Adeeb was here. "No, sir. Just. . ."

"Just them holding us over a barrel."

"Sir?" His American phrases did not always make sense to her.

"He's got our hands tied. He has you, the aircraft, and if there's no threat, Colonel Mahmoud knows we won't do anything." Captain Ripley sighed. "Am I right?"

"Yes, sir."

"I don't like this."

"Neither do I." She glanced against the muzzle of the M16.

"I'll be waiting for your preflight check-in."

"Yes, sir."

"If I haven't heard from you by 0800, I'm bringing the cavalry."

BORIS

Have you found them?"

She didn't need to get all snippy about it. Boris pulled back his frustration and indignation. "I want to know about Zmaray."

"Do not toy with us, Boris."

I smirk. They really have no idea who they're messing with. "This isn't toying with you, Highness. This is ensuring my safety."

"If you keep Osiris happy, then you are ensuring your safety."

"Osiris." The name is an anesthetic to my brain. I can't think. Can't process. I know that name. I do. Somewhere. . .at some time. Shaking out of my stupor is the only way I guarantee staying alive. "Zmaray. I want to know about him."

With more of that unnerving silence she is so good at dishing out, I wait. And wait.

"Check the e-mail."

Warily, I reach for the screen. Touch the icon for my e-mail. It opens. And explodes with a gruesome image of a man—a *dead* man—sporting an extra hole in his head.

"For the love of—" I race to close the browser. My stomach is climbing up into my throat. With a flick of one hand, I open one of the cantilever windows. With another, I reach for my sport drink. "Was *that* necessary?" My voice is shrill and my fear rancid. I gulp the drink. Grateful for the cold sensation of the liquid dumping down my system.

"I don't know, Boris. *Was* it?"

"I don't work well under death threats, Miss. . ." How is it I don't even know her name? Honestly how did I know anyone I met or worked with was who they said they were? It came with the trade. All sleight of hand. Smoke and mirrors.

It's bull crap. No need to get ugly and hateful.

I can pull the plug. I can get nasty with my viruses and programs that snake into a system. Lay dormant for decades if I want. . .and then unleash the demon within when I want. Do they realize what I can do? *Do they?*

I'm so mad, my hands are shaking. How dare they threaten me!

"Please, Boris. I would not threaten you." Her voice seems to purr, making me angrier. "This was not a threat. I tried to distract you from the question about Zmaray. But you persisted. Even *threatened* me."

"I didn't threaten." There is a fine line with these types. You threaten, then you push them over the ledge. Which pushes you over a *real* ledge. Your body is found weeks, months later, eaten by crows and wild animals. Not enough left to identify except through dental records.

"You were willing to withhold your cooperation if I did not tell you."

In the movies, a guy in my place would wet his pants about now. "It was insurance."

"And are you *insured* now?"

I shove my hand through my hair, noticing the sweat. The tremble in my fingers. This chick—I don't like her. She's worse than Zmaray. And my mind is in denial. Maybe that image wasn't the guy I'd dealt with. The one who showed up here and had his thugs throw their weight around. "I just—you have to admit that a person in my situation has to be careful. Just as you have to be careful."

"Are we past the handshakes yet? Can we get on with business?" She was a cool cucumber.

Why people used that expression, I don't know. Because I hate cucumbers. They give me gas. Give me a chilled apple. Better yet—a chilled Cayman Jack. *That* would settle my nerves. Well, right now, it might take an entire case. . . Maybe I need to visit Salim's.

"Okay." I wipe my hands over my face, warding off the chill—it is January after all—and sweat that coated my body after the standoff with the queen of Sheba. "Okay, look. I don't know their exact location. They've gone south. I've narrowed it down to Kandahar or a nearby province."

"Find them. We must know their location."

CHAPTER 12

Bagram Airfield, Afghanistan
16 January—0910 Hours

Okay, listen up!" Sergeant Brennan, a wiry guy with a deep voice and a wicked sunburned nose, waited as his members of the 10th Mountain, 1st Sustainment Brigade gathered.

With his HK416, Brian sauntered into the staging area where a dozen or so grunts were gathered around—

Hold up. What was this?

Brian couldn't help but grin as he took in the four, not three, vehicles. So someone was listening after all. Even if they didn't want him here—and heck-fire, he was all in with that sentiment—they knew he had something to contribute.

The echoes of boots thudding across the tarmac made Brian's hackles rise. He pivoted and brought around his HK416, easing his finger toward the trigger well as he sighted the boots. Friendly. He relaxed his grip and stance as they hustled toward the group.

"Davis, Parker—you're late!"

"Sorry, sir." Specialist Parker circled up with Davis. And only when Davis looked in Brian's direction did he make the connection. Blond bombshell who'd gone red when he blew off her flirtatious glance.

I am cursed.

"Today," Brennan continued, "we have the experienced brain and brawn of Sergeant Bledsoe."

Brian touched the rim of the baseball cap he wore in a mock salute.

"Trust his lead, his instructions. If he says pull back, then do it."

Surprised at the command authority he was being given, Brian had this crazy, crawl-out-of-his-skin agitation. What was it? What bugged him?

Only when the private next to him skated Brian a glance did he figure it out. They're kids. *They're freakin' kids.* The punk to his right didn't even have enough peach fuzz to need a razor. What was this? Kindergarten roundup?

Be nice, be nice. He'd been there once, green and wet behind the ears. Eager to serve. Wetting his pants when his convoy hit the first IED.

"Okay, let's load up," Brennan said as he took a step toward Brian and extended his hand. "Adam Brennan."

"Call me Hawk."

"Good to have you on board." As they moved toward the MRAPs, Brennan asked, "Special Forces?"

Brian nodded.

"Rumor's going around that SOCOM's calling in all the teams."

He said nothing.

"You'll ride with me in the lead." Brennan climbed in the rear, navigating around boxes stacked on one side. Supplies. Counting and verifying what they had as he moved forward.

Trailing him, Brian noticed the man stumble over the small obstacle course–like space. One of the grunts looked pale, his knees bouncing as he sat on the bench lining the other side of the vehicle.

Brian slapped his shoulder, trying to give him a boost of courage. Instead, the kid jolted.

"Need some air?" Brian asked, taunting him.

Face red, the kid licked his lips. "I'm good, sir."

Brian snorted and kept moving. His gaze hit Davis. "You ready for this?"

"Not my first rodeo, sir."

"Good to know." He then hoisted himself into the right, front seat.

The convoy made radio contact with each other then lumbered off the base. Taking a normal route, they raced toward their destination. Wisps of green stuck up defiantly against the winter weather that stripped most bushes and trees of their leaves. But mostly, more of the same—brown, gray drab, and rock—smeared across his mind with the minutes.

Brennan's grip on the wheel kept rolling, his gaze shooting back and forth.

The team's tension was tighter than a det cord. They needed something to lighten up the mood. "And on this side, we have a glorious field of rocks," Brian spoke over his shoulder. "On your left, if you'll take a moment to gaze out the blast shields, you'll find another stunning field of rocky barrenness."

"I think I buried my pet rock there."

Brian laughed and glanced back—surprised that Davis had the wherewithal to be lighthearted. But she was the only one. Nobody else laughed. Or even looked out the windows. "Got a tough audience, Davis."

"Yes, sir."

Eyes front, Brian stiffened. Before them, a village of huts and plaster-walled structures stood like a ravenous animal in the middle of the road. A starving animal who saw its first meal of the day—the convoy.

Scanning. Assessing. Processing. Brian had eyes out, probing the shadows. Not more than twenty or thirty sardine-packed structures, but plenty for the enemy to hide in. A blur of striped fabric warned him of someone hustling out of view. A man in tan pants and a long tunic raced across the main road and dove down an alley.

Not good.

The MRAP slowed.

Brian snapped a hand to the left. "Don't slow down. You're tipping them that you're nervous. Barrel in." This wasn't just a small road. It was the main road that led to their supply target. Houses and small shanties had shot up around the paved road that had more windows than the structures.

The sergeant hesitated for only a second.

"Do it," Brian barked, his adrenaline spiraling. The truck lurched forward, pulling them faster. *Relax. No need to nuke what little courage these grunts had.* "When was the last time you were outside the wire?"

Brennan shot him a nervous glance. "I just got back over here."

"How long have you been sergeant?"

Head down in a defeated posture, Brennan muttered, "Two months."

Brian rolled his shoulders, trying to shake the frustration. "Well, Sergeant, you have to man up. These terrorists don't care what rank you are. You're a target. They don't stop and check rank first. They shoot to kill. Period. There's no playing nice, no PC crap out here. The rules of the playground here are very different than they are at home."

"Figured that out last time."

Brian jerked toward the sergeant. Beneath the brain bowl, all of a sudden he looked maybe fifteen. Beads of sweat dotted his forehead and upper lip. The guy was scared spitless. "You got family, Brennan?" A startled smile distracted him from his nerves. Blue irises sparked with memory. "Yeah. Got married last Christmas. Jennie."

"She's a beauty," Davis added from the rear.

Brian again noted Davis, who had it more together than her first sergeant.

"Not sure how I rated to get her," Brennan said, his tone sheepish, "but I'm no dummy. Married her before she could change her mind." His sweat had turned to joy.

"You kidding me?" Brian slapped the guy on the shoulder. "She married a real American hero. I think she's the one who knew to marry you before you could get away."

A goofy laugh competed for volume with the MRAP's engine, but Brennan's smile couldn't be missed.

Something the guy had said poked at Brian's awareness. Gaze raking the terrain, he searched for snipers. For heads popping up on the patio rooftops with shoulder-mounted RPG tubes. "Hey, what did you mean about the last time?"

"What?" Brennan was all confusion again.

"You said you figured that out last time." Brian wasn't sure he wanted to know the answer to this, but being ignorant got people killed. And he so wasn't dying during babysitting duty. "What last time?"

"Oh." Brennan swallowed. "Four days ago. They tried to make the supply run but got ambushed."

"They?"

He nodded. "How do you think I ended up as team leader? My sergeant was killed in the blast."

"Son of a biscuit," Brian whispered. So that's why they wanted him on this mission. They didn't need one Special Forces operator. They needed a whole team.

But that wouldn't happen with SOCOM pulling teams to safety.

He adjusted his helmet and his position in the vehicle. "All right, listen up," he said into his coms that went into every headset. "Every driver—listen up. We are not stopping. I do not care what is in the road—cows, chicken, children—we do *not* stop. Am I absolutely clear?"

"Clear," Brennan said, his voice squeaking.

"Blue clear."

"Red clear."

"Clear on Green."

Nerves drumming over the daunting predicament, Brian ground his teeth as he eyed the windows, blanket-covered doors, and the alleys that seemed to play host to demons. "How long's this been going on?"

Brennan swerved around a pothole large enough to swallow a small car.

"Months." Davis leaned forward. "The closer we get to turning over things to the ANA, the more blue-on-green attacks and the greater the hostility. Especially here in the south."

Brian nodded. He knew that. Knew the Taliban had retaken southern Afghanistan. But they weren't technically in southern Afghanistan.

As the buildings loomed on either side, Brian shifted into warrior mode. His gaze traced the rooftops and windows. The corners. Shadows. "You're doing great," he said to Brennan. "Remember, no stopping."

"Right."

More than halfway through the small village. But his adrenaline surged. Reminded him of the mission that took half of Candyman's leg.

Ghost town. Deserted. "Notice anything. . .?"

"No people," Davis said.

Instincts blazing, he anticipated it.

The car that leapt into the intersection.

Brennan slamming on the brakes.

"No! Don't stop, don't stop, don't stop!"

But Brennan's brain had shut down. Survival instincts controlled him.

A man stepped from a shop, a long tube on his shoulder.

CHAPTER 13

Forty Klicks Outside Bagram, Afghanistan
16 January—1618 Hours

Brian lunged over the foot-wide instrumentation and yanked the wheel hard right.

BooOOOoom!

Brian braced against the concussion, which pitched the MRAP to the right. Tossed it into a building. The impact thudded through Brian's neck and brain. Dropping back down, the vehicle rocked. Cement and plaster dribbled onto the hood of the vehicle. The front end created a triangle-like impression. They were stuck.

"Back up! Back up!" Brian shouted.

But Brennan was dumbstruck.

Brian slapped his arm. "Move!"

Finally, Brennan responded. Rammed it into Reverse. Gunned it. The MRAP cleared the structure. Brennan threw it into gear and barreled down the alley. They jounced and bumped, the hull ripping chunks of plaster off the buildings.

"Red, Blue, Green, report!" Brian glanced over his shoulder to Davis. "Get us a route out of here."

The enemy wouldn't stop. In fact, because Brian had managed to extract and save the team, the terrorists would race them to the next intersection and try to take them out.

"Blue is here—took some fire, but we're good."

"Green here. All clear."

Who hadn't reported? "Red, report!"

"Here. We're . . . They're . . ."

Brian pounded the door at the sound of the simpering voice.

"Left, go left," Davis shouted.

Brennan flung the MRAP around the corner.

But they still hadn't heard from the last vehicle in the convoy. "Red, what is your status?"

"Sir, we've taken a direct hit."

"Can you move?"

"Uh. . .yes. Yes, we're clear. Moving again."

Relief whooshed through Brian's chest. "Good. Keep going. Take a left at the shop with the blue awning."

"Copy that, sir. We see the tail of Green."

"Good. Green, keep them in your sight."

"Roger that."

—⁓—

Mazar-e Sharif, Afghanistan
16 January—1640 Hours

General Lance Burnett stormed down the hall to his office. "Tell me this isn't happening." He flung a paper back to Captain Watters. "You seeing this?"

"Seeing," Watters said, "but not believing, sir."

"You and me both." He threw open the door to his temporary quarters. In the middle of the sitting area, he stopped. Considered the lamps. The floral arrangement. The fruit. The pictures.

"I'm thinking the same thing, sir."

Lance turned and walked back out then locked the door. Teeth grinding, he made his way to the Cup of Joe For A Joe portable building. The barista took their orders for vanilla lattes, then Lance and Watters sat in a corner.

"I haven't been this ticked in years." Lance reached for the bottle of glycerin tablets in his coat pocket. "How in Sam Hill did they find out the 1st Sustainment would be there?"

"Either they've managed to bug our command centers or we've got another mole."

"Or both." Lance tossed the pills in his mouth and slurped his latte. Then cursed when the liquid singed his tongue.

Every mission. Every protocol. Every directive. Every *thing*.

With an arm on the table, Watters angled his shoulder as if to protect not just his flank but their dialogue. "Sir, they got in, didn't they?"

"Official word is no."

Watters grunted.

"No, I'm serious. We can't find a way in or a hack trail." Lance heaved a breath and roughed a hand over his semi-balding scalp. "We're just operating as if nothing's secure. Mother of God, help us."

Glancing at the thick paper cup, Watters snorted. "I think you'd be better off talking to her Son right now."

"Don't give me your tongue right now. In my mood, I'm liable to cut it out."

Watters gave an amused nod.

Lance could barely swallow around the thought lodged in his brain. He'd looked the other way when Raptor went dark and into enemy territory. What if they didn't make it back?

"If I'm reading your face right, General," Watters said then took a slow sip of his drink. "Don't worry about them. They're checking in every hour. Falcon knows the danger. They all do. We already walked into one ambush. Won't do that again if we can help it."

"Forget the dang ambush. If this piece of crap knows everything we're doing—then he knows Raptor's location."

"He doesn't."

The captain's confidence unseated Lance. "Get cocky and you'll never see the bullet that hits your gray matter."

The man smiled. Actually smiled. "This isn't cockiness. It's cautious confidence. We have a level of vigilance most do not have because we have been in the sights of this lunatic already. We were almost put six feet under because of this guy, so my men know what's out there. That every situation, every person, can be a trap. They know they're being hunted. We have protocols in place that nobody else knows."

"Watters, so help me God—do *not* trust that. What do you think we were operating under when you went out to that ghost village?"

"Understood, sir." Unflappable courage was what made Dean Watters one of the best operators out there. He had a long career ahead of him. Assuming he could outlast their hunter. "But that protocol was directly from SOCOM. We—"

"No." Lance stabbed a hand up between them. "I don't want to know any more. I trust you. Just. . .recognize what we're up against."

"A ghost."

Two Hours Outside Kandahar, Afghanistan
16 January—1700 Hours

I will die tonight.

Her brother had locked Fekiria in an upper room. One with carpet. Carpet. So. . .there would be no messy killing. She might live after all.

Poison? Was that how he'd do it—force her to drink her own death? To cleanse the family name. Redeem their honor. Or simply to punish her for not doing what they wanted her to do? She wasn't sure, and right now it was really hard to think. Rubbing her temples, she closed her eyes. Her family was a good one. They had connections, notoriety, and her madar worked hard to make sure they were fed, clothed, and felt loved.

But Baba ruled. What he said even *overruled* whatever Madar said or wanted.

A glance at the clock explained her headache. Dehydrated and stressed, she struggled to think beyond the building pressure. Four hours, she'd been locked here. "Why must you torment me and make me wait, Adeeb?"

Maybe it was good he hadn't come. Death would be on his heels.

She stomped to her feet and immediately regretted the action at the eruption of pain and lightheadedness that pushed her back onto the thick, soft mattress.

Ludicrous! That a woman's desire to work, to be validated as useful beyond a bedmate for a man and a vessel to bear his children, was considered evil. Wicked. Western.

Western or not, there was more to her than beauty.

Perhaps Zahrah had something right.

Rubbing her temple, she gave a soft snort. Her cousin had a lot of things right, though Fekiria probably would never admit that to Zahrah's face. But the one thing that had always irritated her was Zahrah's proselytizing. She believed in *Isa* as the Messiah. Not a messiah as Muslims believed.

Yet for all her zeal, all her passion about Isa, Zahrah had accepted Fekiria without reservation. Yes, she'd shared openly about her Christian beliefs—perhaps too openly, for Fekiria's taste. Then again, she had been just as insistent that her cousin never speak of the Christian Bible. She didn't want to die, after all. Still, Zahrah had embraced her as a sister. Loved her. Mitra had done the same.

She shows more love than my own brothers.

Why was that?

Did Sergeant Brian believe the same way? Were all Americans Christians? A silly thought, of course. There were Muslims in America who were doing all they could as Mohammed—peace be upon him—had instructed. They were not killing as her people did here. Adeeb had said it was because their faith, their love of Allah, was not as pure.

Fekiria ambled across the thick Persian rug to the windows. Rich gold drapes with an intricate brocade pattern and silk trim framed the double doors to the balcony. She nudged aside the sheer panel and peered at the darkening sky. By nightfall, it'd be an endless canopy of black sprinkled with twinkling lights. Something in her craved that freedom again, to be up there, with mile upon mile of openness... She loved flying. Loved being among the stars and heavens. Closer to Allah.

But was that all she was meant to do—fly? Be a blight on her family's name? What was so wrong with having dreams and goals? With being *free*?

Flickering movement on the lawn drew her attention to where she'd landed the helicopter earlier. But even as she caught a glimpse of the rotors, they vanished.

What was this? A trick?

She squinted, demanded her eyes focus. What were the men doing? Cupping her hands on the glass, she peered through it to avoid the glare. Why were the men messing with her chopper? Whatever it was, she wasn't about to let them mess something up. It was her name, her career, her certification that would be stripped away if they damaged it.

She flipped the latch and swung open the door. Moving onto the upper balcony, wrapped in an icy blanket of cold air, she stared out to where men hoisted six poles and secured a camouflage netting, effectively concealing the helicopter. Not just from the air but from her. If there truly was a threat from attack, it made sense to cover it. Shield it from view.

So...why were the guards not leaving now that they'd put up the cover? Voices carried through the bitter cold, tugging at Fekiria's hijab, but she ignored it. It was her duty to protect her helicopter. Her entire career! Her freedom.

"What are you doing?" She gripped the stone balustrade and leaned over. "Leave that aircraft alone!"

Several faces swung toward her. Shouts went up, and the dots that had faced her now bounced against the dark canvas. Two guards bolted toward the house. Boots thumped against the lower terrace as two others pointed and shouted.

"Smart. Just draw Adeeb's attention and sword." She had never cowered before her brother. Even when he struck her. She in fact swung back. And he laughed. Shoved her backward, as if she were an ant, and walked away. Which infuriated her more.

But getting *hit* and getting *killed* were two different things. And here, Adeeb had more than his bad temper to motivate him. Fekiria slipped inside and closed the door. Perhaps they would not know which room—foolish idea. Of course they knew. She was a prisoner here.

Doors slamming and boots thudding—or was that her heart?—sounded in the hall. Coming closer. . .closer. Fekiria hurried back outside. Studied the balustrade. Could she escape? Climb down?

This was no fairy tale. There was no Aladdin with a magic carpet to carry her off.

Fekiria turned in time to find two fat guards rushing her. Dark faces hemmed in black hair and beards, they grabbed her arms. "Release me!" She swung her arms up and rammed down over theirs, breaking the hold. Another guard caught her as she twisted away.

She reared. Punched him in the face.

The guard stumbled back, hands covering his now-bloody nose.

Lifted off her feet from behind, Fekiria screamed. Did as she was taught and let herself go limp. Slid from the man's hold. She wrested free then jumped to her feet.

"Stop!" She held her ground. "Listen to me!"

The stunned guards did stop. For a second. Then the fatter one came toward her, the smell of liquor on him as thick as his body odor.

"I want to see Adeeb." Her demand went unheeded. She connected gazes with the guard from earlier, the one who'd helped her in the kitchen. "The man who told you to take me to the chopper—I want to speak to him!"

The men laughed, then one said, "He is not someone who can be summoned by the whims of a harlot."

"I am no harlot, I am—"

His hand flew hard and true against her face.

Her head snapped back. Stinging pain radiated across her cheek.

Two guards grabbed Fekiria, wrangling her off her feet. Lifted like a sack of vegetables, she snaked her body, trying to liberate herself. Thoughts of death—and worse—coursed through her mind. She knew what men had done to her cousin. To many women. Surely Adeeb would not let that happen to her.

Then again, he hadn't come to her. Did he not recognize her? How could he not? Perhaps he'd disowned her, and for that reason, he refused to acknowledge Fekiria.

They dragged her into the house, cursing her. Threatening violence. But she gave them some of her own violence. She focused on fighting. Not on being a weak girl. She had self-defense skills. Captain Ripley and Captain Rashidi, a female American officer from Saudi, had taught them well. Fekiria would use it. Make them proud. Use the tactics she'd seen Sergeant Brian use against the other soldier. Anything to keep herself from being harmed. Or killed.

Her efforts paid off.

Her foot slipped free. She swung it upward, nailing the shorter guard in the head. He tumbled backward and hit his head against a table. The other started for his friend then realized his mistake when Fekiria used it to gain her balance. With a hard elbow jab to his nose—followed by a loud *crack!*—she freed herself from the fat one.

Standing, she turned ready for the fight and found the butt of a weapon flying at her.

Pain exploded through her temple. Her world vanished.

CHAPTER 14

Forty Klicks Outside Bagram, Afghanistan
16 January—1640 Hours

*O*bjects in mirror are closer than they appear.

"Go, go, go!" Brian pounded the side of the door again.

Brennan punched the pedal, but gunning it in an MRAP was different than Granddad's '65 Mustang. "We're too close."

Brian bit back the retort as the massive mine-resistant vehicle lurched forward. But not anywhere near fast enough. What Brian wouldn't do for Raptor, for his boys who had the instincts of wolves and reflexes like cobras. Guys who knew what to do without anyone having to shout at them once, let alone a half-dozen times. Frustration cinched around his throat.

We are dead meat.

Another man on the roof joined the RPG launcher. Two? Two trying to kill them? The newcomer waved at the man with the launcher then motioned for him to put it down.

"What the. . .?"

When he didn't immediately comply, the second man rushed forward and yanked down the tube. The dude complied.

What the fluff?

Brian glanced over his shoulder, searching for a clear view to confirm what he'd seen. Because he wasn't trusting his eyes. This wasn't right. Brennan swerved to stay on the road. Brian double-checked the mirror, disbelieving as the two villagers stood there on the roof. Just stood there. Like this was a parade.

Why were they calling off the attack? They had time and distance on their side. Manpower. Brian's MRAP was first in the convoy. Even if they couldn't hit Brian's, they had the opportunity to take out the last one.

Whoops and hollers went up as the convoy gained speed, racing away from the ambush. The newbs were ecstatic to survive their first ambush and come out with all parts intact.

But. . . Brian couldn't take his gaze off the sideview mirror. Didn't make sense. Why'd they stop? *They had us.*

Out of ammo?

Then why would the villager aim at them? Why would the other guy try to stop him?

Okay, so it was loaded.

"Don't look so mad that we made it," Brennan said, his voice squeaky and tired with a trace of laughter—relief. "Give us more credit."

Brian eyed the guy. The sweat on his brow and upper lip. In forty-degree weather? Even geared up he shouldn't be sweating like that. "We're alive. But we're not there yet. Let's break out the bubbly after we get there."

In fact, they had two more villages they'd encounter before hitting the city where they'd have to navigate busy streets to get to the orphanage. That didn't bother Brian. Ironic that he felt less threatened in a city with thousands more people than in a remote village with a few dozen. But he knew the ropes. Knew the Taliban soaked up remote locations so they could evade authorities and attention. And it was so much easier to lay a trap for soldiers traveling through and far from help.

"You okay?" Davis asked, her voice just over his left shoulder.

"No." *Right, make them panic, genius.* "Yeah. We'll be fine."

Brennan white-knuckled the steering wheel and burrowed into the drive.

"Just. . ." Brian didn't have anything solid. Just a gut instinct that this wasn't right.

But that same instinct had gotten him into the Green Berets.

"Just stay alert." The next twenty minutes felt like a wound-up jack-in-the-box. Any second, any turn, an explosion, another guy with an RPG, and then they'd be either dead or wishing they were dead.

"You got a girl back home, Hawk?"

Irritation scraped down Brian's spine at the question. *That* was the guy's idea of small talk? "Got a lot of them." Wasn't true. He *had* dated a lot. But bored easily.

Brennan's laugh was caustic. "Should've known."

This time, Brian glanced at him. But bit down on being baited into a conversation like this. His personal affairs—*nice choice of words*—were his *personal* affairs. He didn't even talk about that stuff with Raptor. Somehow, dating made him feel. . .wide open for trouble. What it did to Captain Watters—the guy had gone all nutso over Double Z and then ended up a POW, tortured and left for dead outside a base.

"You can't tell me some girl hasn't caught your eye," Davis said, her voice way too soft and silky.

Didn't chicks know what that did to a guy?

And why in this freezing, dusty world did Fekiria Haidary's face blast into his mind just then? He'd been too quick with a promise, knocked senseless by a pair of ultra-green eyes and those full lips.

Aw crap. She was in his head. He didn't need that. Besides, she had that butter-bar, slicked-up officer who seemed to negate her "No American Soldiers" mantra.

"What's her name?"

Brian skidded a glance to his left shoulder, where he found Davis's knowing smile and pretty blue eyes. "Sam. First name, Uncle."

Laughing again, Brennan shifted in the seat. "Give it up, Davis. Guys like Hawk don't date girls. They're married to the Army. They're machines."

The words burned like acid in Brian's veins. Dialogue like this ended in bad places, ones that usually forced him to set records straight. But he was going to keep it together because there was something bigger than his pride, than his ego, than demanding the respect he'd earned, happening here.

"Nah, guys like Hawk have girls flocking to him," someone called from the back. "He's a freakin' Green Beret. Right, Davis—you got the hots for our own personal hero?"

Brian snapped his gaze to the back of the MRAP where the half-dozen other grunts sat. The way the grunt had spoken reeked of disrespect, jealousy, and way too much attitude. He nailed the source of the words with a heated glare. "She's your battle buddy. Treat her with respect. She may be the one who has to save your sorry carcass."

Twenty minutes of tension and laughter over Brian's unwillingness to engage in the middle school conversation about girlfriends had to be endured before they reached the next village.

"Speed up." Brian keyed his mic and ordered the other vehicles to do the same.

"We're only stopping if we're dead or at our destination," he spoke over the coms.

The situation drenched the interior of the MRAP with anxiety. Palpable, palm-sweating anxiety. Next to him, Brennan radioed in an update of their location and progress. Barreling along, Brian gauged the time and distance to the final destination. Another hour. Maybe ninety minutes if they hit some messed-up traffic in the city. Or a snafu here.

Wind swirled dirt over the road like a demon dancing in the sand. Demon. Why'd he have to go there?

"How long are you out here with us?" Brennan asked.

"Till the job's done." Brian's gaze tracked over the buildings. "Eyes out. Watch for unfriendlies."

Another gust of wind whipped dirt across their path twenty yards ahead. The wind was strong. Much stronger than—

Every muscle in Brian tightened. He saw it. Saw the trap. "Hard right!"

Brennan complied. Curses and yelps erupted from the back.

"What'd you see?" Brennan demanded.

"Convoy, road trap!" Brian shouted into his coms. "Veer right."

"Too late!" someone from the back shouted. "Red ate it."

—◊◊◊—

Forty Klicks Outside Bagram, Afghanistan
16 January—1700 Hours

Checking his sideview, Brian glanced at the mirror again. Sure enough, the third vehicle had caught the edge of the trap. The front wheel hung down at least four feet, the vehicle tipped at nearly a forty-five-degree angle, its underbelly exposed.

"Go back! Go back!"

Brennan turned the MRAP around. Gunned it back to the other vehicle.

"We'll need to get them to safety, protect the vehicle."

"Davis," Brennan said, "radio in for a recovery vehicle."

"Roger that."

"Eyes out," Brian said.

Brennan put the gear in NEUTRAL then pulled the yellow button. A loud pop and hiss signaled the setting of the air brake.

"Be ready." Securing the chin strap of his brain bowl, Brian eyed

Brennan. "They trapped us here. That means they're not done. Get your people to safety. I'll cover, but I need three on me."

Davis—no surprise there—volunteered first then SmartMouth and Parker.

"Everyone else with Brennan. Get the team in Red to safety." Brian rolled out of the vehicle. He dropped to the ground, his weapon up as he traced the three one-story structures right that formed a south wall to the incident.

Behind him, he heard the scritch of tactical pants and the crunch of boots following him. With two fingers, he pointed to the buildings. "Eyes out. Davis, twelve o'clock. Parker, monitor our nine." He glanced at the other guy's name strip, figuring he'd probably set off the grunt calling him SmartMouth. "Redding, stay here. I'll take our six. You see anything, let us know."

The three spread out, a loose perimeter around the capsized MRAP. Brian slid up to where Brennan and his soldiers were already ushering the team from the vehicle.

On a knee at the side of the second MRAP, Brian focused on the two-story plaster building directly opposite. Especially on the drab sheet that hung in a long window. It riffled on the wind.

But there's no wind.

If he were with Raptor, he'd radio in the possible threat. But this team wouldn't understand. Frustration mounted.

"How we doing, Brennan?" Brian asked through his coms.

"Two left inside—one unconscious, and the other broke a leg."

"We have spectators," he muttered, trying to hint that they had unwanted eyes on this situation.

"Can't believe they get off on watching us," someone replied.

"Perimeter team, report." Peering through the scope, Brian eased his weapon to his right, scanning and assessing.

"Redding here. All clear."

"This is Parker. Normal with a few stragglers and kids kicking around a ball in the alley."

Just another day in the neighborhood while Mom and Pop kill some Americans.

"Davis here." Her voice sounded tight. "I— There's two women in a shop."

"Sounds like a mighty big 'but' coming, Davis." Brian brought the scope back to the upper window. Nothing changed. He went higher, to the roof.

"They seem. . .preoccupied with something or someone. They're huddled in a corner."

"Stay on them," Brian said as he returned to that window.

His heart jammed up into his throat as a long tube pushed the dingy sheet outward. Even as he took aim, he heard a shout through his coms.

"RPG! RPG! Take cover."

His mind ricocheted over Davis's words. Did she see the same one he was sighting? Or. . . He steadied his breathing. Aimed, approximating where the shoulder. . .chest. . .placed in connection to the shoulder-mounted RPG launcher. He fired twice.

The tube flipped up. Vanished behind the makeshift curtain.

Fire breathed down Brian's neck a split second before a strong concussive fist punched him forward. The ground rushed up at him. Brian dropped his shoulder and rolled through it. He came up and perched on a knee, sighting through the chaos, through the burning hulk of the MRAP that now lay in its own personal grave dug by terrorists, to the far side where Da—

"Davis! Report." Brian scooted back up to their MRAP for protective cover. In a hunch-run, he scurried up toward her position. "Davis!"

"I'm—I'm here. A little shell-shocked, but here."

"Where'd that RPG come from?" Almost at Blue's MRAP, Brian slowed, the hairs on the back of his neck prickling. *Something's not right.*

"The rooftop, sir. Above the two women."

Brian nodded as he pressed his back against the steel hull and glanced back to the window where he'd shot whoever tried to hit them with another RPG. "All right, team, we have multiple targets. Eyes. Let's get everyone—"

Tink! Thunk! Thunk-thunk!

As the sound of bullets pinging off the side of the vehicle, Brian dove to the side, rolling beneath the MRAP. "Taking fire! Taking fire!" Prostrate, Brian peered out at the wreckage of the other mine-resistant vehicle spewing black smoke and flames into the sky—well, as much as he could see. He scanned for hostiles, shutting down the fear. Homing in on the warrior within him. The one who made sure everyone came home. The one who did what it took. The one most people didn't understand.

There, across from a small well-like structure, he barely saw two forms. One held a rifle, the other wrangled a launcher. "Eyes on target," Brian spoke into his coms, his tone deathly even.

"Spartan platoon, you are ordered to stand down."

Brian frowned. *What the. . .?* "Eyes on hostiles."

"Sergeant Brennan, get your team to safety and get out of there."

"Sir," Brian said. "Sta—Sergeant Bledsoe here, sir. I have eyes on target and can neutralize the threat."

"Negative, Bledsoe. Pack it up and RTB."

Angry, Brian hesitated. "Sir—we are taking direct fire. Getting in the vehicles puts the team in direct danger, sir."

"You're not listening to me—get out of there!"

Ticked, Brian decided to ignore the booming voice ordering them back to base under a deadly situation. He pressed his cheek to the stock of his weapon and once again sighted the enemy.

"One more mess up, and you're gone, Hawk."

His palms went slick as Captain Watters's words pierced his mind. He swallowed. Tried to shake it off.

But he'd lose everything.

Biting back a curse, he balled his fists. Glanced down the sight just in time to see the enemy take aim at Davis and Parker, who were rushing to the MRAP.

"Nooo!" Brian shouted. "Davis, Parker—"

The drilling sound of automatic weapons drowned his voice. Davis and Parker went down, face-first, into the dirt.

Like a vacuum, Brian sucked back his grief. Gulped it down. Replaced it with fury. He resolved right then to kill the terrorists who had ambushed the supply convoy. Whether he had authorization or not. Fury ripping through his muscles, Brian lined up his sights.

—◊◊◊—

Two Hours Outside Kandahar Airfield, Afghanistan
17 January—0710 Hours

Through a haze of blurry memories and vision, Fekiria woke. With a groan, she pushed herself off the mattress, the material warm and soft beneath her hand. Rolling her shoulders did nothing to dispel the ache in her neck. She rubbed the spot and squinted around the room. Sunlight peeked between curtains on the far window.

Disorientation faded as the surroundings settled into her mind.

She remembered the rifle butt flying at her. Instinctively, her fingers went to her temple. A prick of pain darted through her head, shoulders, and neck at the touch. She cringed and groaned.

A noise—a jangle that felt entirely too loud and annoying—pulled her gaze to the left. To the dark wood door that swung open.

Colonel Mahmoud stood just over the threshold. "How long will you keep us waiting?"

Fekiria shoved to her feet, yelping at the spike of pain that felt like a steel rod shoved through her skull. Heel of her hand to her forehead, she crossed the room. "Where. . .where are we going?"

"Where do you think we're going?" Snarl in his voice, he pivoted and stalked out of the room.

Feebly, Fekiria followed him. Outside the room, two guards straightened at her presence. They fell into step with her as she made her way to the sweeping staircase and descended. With the loyal guard dogs on her heels.

Ahead of her, the front door swung open and light burst in.

Pain radiated through her corneas, stabbing the back of her eyeballs. Fekiria ducked but kept moving. Outside. To the chopper. Back to the base. Just had to get out of here. Get back to. . .what? Captain Ripley, the one man who wanted her but she did not want?

Why was she even alive? What purpose did she serve?

"Wait."

The strong voice was unmistakable. Fekiria tensed, the move making the headache pound. Stiffly, she turned.

Adeeb strode toward her. With a flick of his wrist, he sent the guard dogs scurrying back to the shadows. *Who is my brother that they obey him so completely?* He stepped into her personal space. Glanced out the door. Indecision glimmered in his dark brown eyes. He pressed his lips together then met her gaze. "If you speak of anything you have seen here, I will have you killed."

Disgust squirmed through her.

"It would take just one word from me to tell Baba what you are doing"—his gaze slid down her body, taking note of her flight suit—"for Baba to have you hunted down and killed like the worthless—"

"I may be worthless in your eyes, but I am an excellent pilot." Fekiria lifted her chin ever so slightly—not enough to arouse his anger but enough to show him she did not fear him as he wanted her to. "I delivered your terrorists to your door—"

He grabbed her hair bundled beneath the hijab at the back of her neck then slammed her face into the door. A sweet but metallic taste filled her mouth. "Release me," she hissed.

Again, he slammed her head against the door. "Do not think that because we have the same blood I would not hesitate to make an example of you."

She yanked free, readjusting her hijab and catching the warmth sliding down her chin. She narrowed her eyes at him.

"Go. Do not keep them waiting. They cannot be late." With that, he thrust her out the door.

Fekiria stumbled, surprised and angered at her brother's animosity. "And you say I am the dog." She spat at his feet then stalked toward the helicopter, the back of her hand pressed against her mouth where he'd split her lip.

She walked the helicopter for her preflight check, disconcerted about what the men had been doing last night. But she found nothing out of place. In the cockpit, she tucked on her headset and adjusted the microphone.

"Let's go. Why are you so slow?"

The words didn't speed her up. They did make her go a little slower, however. After powering up the bird, she made radio contact with Kandahar. "November Romeo to Sierra Alpha Bravo Two."

"This is Sierra Alpha Bravo," came the voice that was distinctly *not* Captain Ripley. "What is your status, November Romeo?"

"Powering up to RTB."

"Copy that," came the reply, filled with relief and yet some apprehension. "What is your ETA?"

"Forty minutes."

"Copy forty minutes. Safe flying, November Romeo. We'll see you when you get here."

"Copy. November Romeo out."

CHAPTER 15

What have you found?" Dean strolled over to the bank of laptops and devices, glad to be back with his team. He sidestepped to avoid cables strewn across the floor and zigzagged into one of two power strips.

Sal straightened in his chair. "A whole lot of nothing." He pointed to the map of the city—some parts redrawn by a Sharpie and others, a lot in fact, marked off with large *X*s—and shook his head. "We've ruled out a lot but haven't gotten any closer."

Dean lifted one of the chatter transcripts. "Ruling them out *is* closer." He shuffled the papers, skimming as he searched for keywords. *Zmaray.* Lion. Though they'd had a massive confrontation with the guy who'd tried to take his victory out of Dean's back, they hadn't found the source.

The papers revealed exactly what Sal said—nothing. Dean flicked the pages onto the table and looked around. Bunks lined one wall. A curtained-off area probably concealed the bathroom or shower. They had to make do with whatever was left of the run-down shop.

"Where are the others? Titanis?"

"Titanis is out checking a hookah bar. Said he's seen some regulars so he wanted to hang around, see what he could pick up."

Dean nodded. "Good, good."

"Harrier is Stateside for a while." Sal stood and moved to a small cabinet. He extracted a bottled water. "Thought the general didn't want to know where we are or what we're doing."

"He doesn't." Dean studied the map. "And things are picking up. Radio chatter is constant—and wrong. Got word that Hawk's supply run in a southeastern province went south. He's fine, but not everyone was."

"Imagine he'll be kicking and screaming to get back here."

Dean rubbed the fuzz covering his jaw. "Yeah. Probably."

"You letting him back in?"

"In?" Dean glanced at the team daddy. "He was never out. Just needed to get some things straight."

"Like his head."

"For one." Dean smirked then noticed the way Sal was staring at him. Expression tight. "What's wrong—you disagree with him coming back?"

"He's a loose cannon."

Dean folded his arms over his chest and lowered his chin, listening as the newly minted warrant officer spoke.

"He can't obey orders. He gets mad at the drop of a hat." Sal held out his hands in exasperation. "Don't tell me you can't see that."

"I can." Dean gave a nod then met the man's steely gaze. "But if I had to yank and tank just based on things like that, this team wouldn't exist. *I* wouldn't be here—not after what happened with Zahrah."

"That was different."

"You didn't think so seven months ago. In fact, you went to Burnett about me."

Sal took a step back, his head lowering. "Just looking out for the team."

"I want you to look out for yourself."

Sal scowled. "This is a team, it's not—"

"Whatever's eating at you, Sal, fix it. If you need my help, I'm here."

"*Me?*" The guy's thick, black eyebrows drew together. "You're putting this on me?"

Dean held out his hands in a placating manner. "The only thing I'm putting anywhere is the truth. Something's going on. It's not affecting your decisions, but it's affecting your relationships with the team. I won't push as long as your performance remains at the high level it's always been at. But Sal." Dean sighed heavily. "I see it. They see it."

Sal's jaw muscle flexed and popped.

"So." Dean turned back to the map. "Looks like the northeast sector needs some eyes. I'll suit up and head that way."

"No," Sal said, his word still tight and tense.

Dean considered him, wondering if he'd have to pull rank.

"You're too white. Besides," Sal said, running his hand over his thick beard, "my beard's better." A bit of the old sparkle returned to his brown eyes. "It's better that you're here, processing the data, directing the team, staying in touch with Command. Maybe even figuring out how to get Hawk back here so he can work his geek magic on that equipment and laptops."

"Copy that."

"I can go with Ddrake," Knight offered.

"We'll both head out."

—ɷ—

Kandahar Airfield, Afghanistan
17 January—1115 Hours

"Lieutenant Rhmani?"

Fekiria rubbed her forehead. "I told you, there was nothing I could do. They took me at gunpoint and locked me away. I had no weapon. No way to return to my aircraft."

"It's a little hard to believe, considering the facts."

She frowned at the flight commander, Major Stuckey. "What facts?"

After several long moments where he simply looked at her, he plucked a file from the bottom of his stack of documents, glanced at it, then slid it across the table to her.

Wary of what this file contained, Fekiria considered the commander. American. Intense. Confrontational.

Like another American soldier she knew. But maybe not so mean.

Well yes, that too, she supposed.

As her fingers separated the pages and opened the file, she kept her attention on the commander. She couldn't help but wonder where Colonel Mahmoud was, what he thought of the Americans interrogating her. Then again, she was being trained by the Americans and with one of their training choppers.

Finally, she looked down. The heat drained from her face in a nauseating wave of fear and dread. Her picture, stapled to the middle of the file folder, had the name Haidary, Fekiria boldly stamped below it. "What about your brother, Lieutenant?" Stuckey asked, plenty of insinuation in his voice. "Are you close to him?"

"Which one? I have more than—"

"Adeeb Haidary. Are you close to him?"

"He is my brother." She folded her hands over the file and stared at the gray table.

"Rumor has it you are not on good terms with him."

She narrowed her eyes at the interrogating officer. He almost seemed to know Adeeb was at the compound, but how would he know? And she certainly would not confirm it, not with her brother's warning hanging at the back of her mind. "In America, you might accept women in your armies, in your government, but here, it is still something many men do not want or accept. My brother is one of them." She touched the scabbing knot on her cheek. "This is what happens when a woman speaks her mind in my family."

He made a noncommittal sound. It was almost as if he *wanted* her to be guilty of stealing the chopper and making all this up. And in a stomach-churning moment, she realized that was exactly what the commander thought.

"Your family doesn't know you're in the ANA—is that why you've concealed your true identity, which I might add, is a crime?"

"Yes. I hid my identity because if my family found out, they would have killed me. My baba—father—is not a progressive. He misses the old ways, the times before the Taliban and wars. So he demands his wife and daughters adhere to the old ways—it is the only thing he can control."

"So, you can be controlled."

She lowered her head. "He thinks he can control me. Baba has tried to marry me off many times." This would be endless. And she was very tired of telling the story and just plain exhausted. "Commander, I assure you, my loyalty is to this program."

"But not to the military."

"To the ANA, yes. One hundred percent."

"And the U.S. Army who's training you?"

"For that, I am grateful."

His head bobbed, but he said nothing. His expression didn't change.

"Please—I am tired and hungry."

"Okay. For now, that's all I have." He slid a document toward her. "I'll need your signature on this."

Fekiria didn't care what it was, she just wanted out of here. Wanted to eat something, grab a shower, and sleep till the sun rose tomorrow. Not necessarily in that order. Released, she headed out of the building. Across the air base to her bunk. Forgot the food. And even the shower. Dropping into her bunk and escaping was all—

"Lieutenant Rhmani!"

Curse the man! If she kept going, maybe he wouldn't—

"Hey, hold up," Captain Ripley said as he sidled up alongside her.

Fekiria mustered internal fortitude not to show her annoyance. "Oh. Hi." She sounded fake, but she did not care. "Sorry—I'm just tired."

"Yeah, I figured as much." A frown tugged his eyebrows together as he spotted the swelling on her cheek. Captain Ripley ran his thumb over the spot.

Fekiria stepped out of his reach and tucked her chin.

"Sorry. I keep forgetting. . . I just wanted to make sure you were okay."

"I am fine. Thank you for your kindness."

"Kindness."

Guilt choked her. "I. . ." She shook her head. "Please, forgive me. I am tired, it's been a scary night, and I just want to forget it happened." Fekiria pointed to her bunk. "Sleep will help me be nice again."

Captain Ripley's slow nod warned her she'd lost points.

But when had she been trying to win them? Especially with him?

"Listen, a panel will naturally need to review everything. They'll be the ones to reinstate your flight status."

"So, I'm grounded."

"It's SOP—and temporary. As your flight advisor, we'll need to go over the incident."

Fekiria flared her nostrils, and she lifted her shoulders in defense.

Captain Ripley held up a hand. "But we'll start tomorrow."

Fight deflating, she relaxed a little.

"Get some rest. I'll see you at 0800, in my office. Okay?"

At his smile and recognition of her state of mind and exhaustion, she relented. Though she would have preferred not to repeat the story a millionth time, she owed it to him. And should be grateful for the break he afforded her. "Thank you. Tomorrow then."

But she had withheld information that could very well cost her everything—the part about the men secretly working around or on the helicopter. She'd made it back to the base without incident so perhaps they were just looking for secrets about it.

Perhaps. But then, why could she not shake the thick streak of dread plaguing her?

BORIS

Never hurts to have two hands in play. With the way these Chinese are rolling the die, I need the backup. And I gotta admit, it's fun screwing with guys who run all over the world playing hero. Guys who think they're *all that and a bag of chips.*

The only chips they have are the ones on their shoulders.

It's like in high school when the jocks are brought down by a science geek's flubbed experiment. Doesn't matter that the experiment fails. If it ruins the jock's day, the job is done.

So probably by now, people would guess I had a rough time in school.

Nope. Wasn't me.

But keep trying. You know how I like games.

My phone tweetles, giving me a split-second heart attack. But one check of the screen and I'm feeling pretty good. "Your highness," I say after answering.

"Have you gotten back in?"

"I'm a skip and a jump away." I'm hammering at the keyboard as we talk, knowing that minutes equal millions to these people. Well, to me, too, if I can reestablish their connection. Not having eyes on the team and the military Command puts a serious kink in the fabric of our little insurrection.

"We need you to get us in."

"Working on it, baby."

"No. I mean *in.*"

My fingers form their own private revolt. My brain shuts down. I can't think straight. She seriously did not say that. "I. . .I don't think you realize what you're saying."

"If you cannot do it, we can find another freelancer."

"Nice try, but you and I both know if you wanted some warehouse hacker, you'd have hired him. But I'm not that guy. And if you want me—"

"Do you see your monitor, *Boris*?"

When they start a threat that way, it's never good. I'm already sweating by the time my eyeballs lock on to her meaning. There on the right-hand side an icon has appeared. I mean—just appeared. "No. That can't— You can't. . ."

I recognize the skull with the anime-face overlay. It's mine. They are freakin' using my own hack against me. How in the name of—?

"Do not try to run your interface, Mr. Kolceki."

Oh that is not good. *She knows my name!*

I can't breathe. Can't move. This is *not* happening.

"I need you to listen very carefully. Then you will carry out the instructions and wait for my next call."

When the connection dies, a little piece of me does, too. Wait for her next call? I don't think so. They crossed the biggest line in the sand. Invaded my personal and private space. That's not going to work. If they know who I am, I will never be safe.

It is time to vacate the premises.

As I shift around and make my way to the door, I hesitate. *This is what they want.* I move, I leave now, they are probably sitting there waiting. Or maybe they don't know where I am, but they're waiting for me to make that move that gives myself away.

Stunned by the thoughts, I straighten. Look around my cyber nest. No, they know. They had to get that hack on my system. Though I have a million reroutes and dead leads, they're on to me. Whether tonight or tomorrow, they'll know where I am.

Tonight. I'll leave under the cover of darkness. With a quick glance at my watch, I calculate it's three hours till dark. Thank God it's winter and darkness comes sooner rather than later.

But still—waiting? Three hours?

What if they're tracking. . . ?

Lunging toward the main console, I tap my code into the system. Send my data to a remote server and shut down. Kill the power. Then climb into the front seat, thinking. And sit in the darkness.

CHAPTER 16

Bagram Airfield, Afghanistan
17 January—1345 Hours

Flexing and unflexing his fists, Brian couldn't get the lifeless body of Specialist Davis out of his mind. Anger roiled through his system like a toxin. Did what they said to do. *Obeyed* the order. Stood down.

And freakin' watched a subordinate die in front of my eyes.

Gunned down.

By the very person Brian had his sights on.

How did that make sense? Obey the order.

Molars grinding, Brian remembered her face. Attractive. Blue eyes behind those closed lids. Spatters of blood kissed the right side of her jaw and neck. As if kissing her good-bye.

Davis had what it took to make a difference in the Army. Gave it her all. Chin up, attitude out, she'd faced every bit of his indifference and the tough act he threw at her. Every challenge they encountered, she was right there. Thinking. Strategizing.

She trusted me. Trusted me to watch her six.

And they freakin' tied my hands.

A slap on his shoulder snapped him up, his fists coming up ready for a fight. He drew down the instinct and looked up at Sergeant Brennan.

"You did the right thing," Brennan said.

"Yeah, and it's sunny in the Caribbean."

Brennan gave him a deer-in-the-headlights look.

Only as her coffin slid into the belly of a plane did Brian connect with the fact they'd landed. "Doing the right thing didn't do her"—he stabbed a gloved finger at Davis—"much good, did it?" He stomped across the tarmac toward his temporary bunk.

This was seriously muffed up. *God, Granddad believes in You like I believe in my team.* Brian shook his head, his mind still tethered to the image of Davis, dead on that stretcher. He gritted his teeth. *But please get me back to Raptor.*

"Sergeant Bledsoe?"

He'd never had been put in a situation like that with Raptor.

But he'd lost the right to serve with his brothers because he didn't obey orders. Didn't keep the Code.

So he did. . .he actually kept the code, played nice the way they told him to, and—BAM! A young, beautiful specialist—

"Bledsoe!"

Brian snapped his gaze to the left.

Major Slusarski stood at the Command building, arms folded over his chest, a scowl gouged into his face. With a nod to the side, Slusarski headed inside.

Obeying orders hadn't done him much good today. He seriously considered just heading into his bunk and pretending he hadn't understood the silent signal. He sure didn't feel like getting chewed out. The greater fear for Brian was that he'd unload on the major. Give him a piece of his mind. Or his fist.

Nah, he'd better not go to the major. He still had too much pent-up anger. At his bunk, Brian dropped his gear. Shed the Kevlar vest. Rubbed his forehead as guilt nagged him. Doing the wrong thing here wasn't justified because someone made a royal screwup on the call.

He pivoted. Stalked through the dusk and bitter wind to the Command building. Inside, he stood on the small mat to wipe boots and waited for the door to close. And his temper to settle.

Right. Good luck with that.

"Bledsoe." Slusarski eased over the threshold of Captain Mason's office.

Head down, Brian drew up his courage. And gave himself a mental flogging not to mess this up. He entered the office and gave a nod to his superiors.

Mason, poised in her chair as if she sat on a throne, met his gaze with reinforced steel behind her eyes. "How are you, Sergeant?"

"Good, ma'am." *So not in the mood for this.* "Ready to get out there and kill some bad guys." In other words, let's get it done.

Her lips flattened, his unspoken message had apparently come through loud and clear. "I'd say quite a mess hit the fan out there yesterday."

Brian said nothing. It wasn't a question. She didn't ask for information. He kept his peace. Slusarski sat at the end of the captain's desk in a folding chair. Elbows on his knees, he had his head down. Impossible to read the major.

Mason sat forward and slid on silver-rimmed reading glasses as she lifted her chin to peer down at the paper she held. "You were given an order to stand down."

This was it. They'd hand him his orders and ship him back home. And ya know what? He didn't care anymore as long as his DD214 read "honorable." But with his track record, that was a long shot.

She tugged the glasses off so fast, sprigs of her dyed-auburn hair came loose from its bun. The glasses landed and clattered against a nondescript white coffee mug. "You disagreed with the order."

Brian held her gaze, unbending. He would *not* open his trap and get in trouble. He might be direct and unafraid of sharing the truth, but he wasn't stupid. No way he would fill out the discharge papers for them.

"Is that right?"

Not answering a direct question would get him slapped with insubordination. "Yes, ma'am."

"In fact"—she plucked the glasses from her desk again but didn't put them on—instead she read through the glass—"you even argued with the officer in charge."

"No, ma'am. I did not argue."

In her nasally voice, Captain Mason read from the transcript:

> OIC: *Sergeant Brennan, get your team to safety and get out of there.*
> Bledsoe: *Sir. Sta—Sergeant Bledsoe here, sir. I have eyes on target and can neutralize the threat.*

She brought her dull brown eyes to him again. "I'd call that arguing."

Brian resisted the urge to correct her. He wasn't arguing but offering a solution that had not yet been considered.

After an intense but brief glare, she continued. "And then you go on and give a situation report to OIC, as if he had no idea what was happening."

Armchair generals were always the worst. Couldn't see what's happening and yet they felt they had better insight into whatever the boots on ground were seeing and doing. Did it matter to them that nobody could see what he saw? That he had a bead on the guy, could've stopped this madness? That if he'd taken that shot, this conversation wouldn't be happening?

The squawk of Mason's chair snagged his silent aside as the captain sat back. "Well, Sergeant? What do you have to say for yourself?"

Dare he come clean, call it like he saw it? What would happen? This wasn't like Raptor where his opinion mattered. Or was even considered. He'd been stuffed here to fill a "warm body" slot for a supply run.

But he'd never been the kind to go down without a fight. "Permission to speak freely, ma'am?"

She considered him, no doubt aware of the way he wielded his tongue. "Go on." She held up a finger like an old schoolmarm. "But tread lightly, Sergeant. I warn you that you are on thin ice here."

Thin ice. Brian wanted to curse. "Ma'am, I meant no disrespect to anyone on oversight with the supply run, but I had eyes on ground that Command did not have. Considering my unusual insertion with your team and previous experience with my Special Forces team, I felt it prudent to be sure the officer in charge knew I was capable of neutralizing the threat posed against the soldiers. That I could"—*easy, easy*, Brian warned himself as his pulse amped up—"that I could prevent any loss of life."

"You think you're that good?" Slusarski's head came up only after he asked the question.

"I know I am, sir."

"Mighty arrogant, aren't you?" On his feet, Slusarski's lip curled. "After a lower-ranked soldier dies?"

"She died, sir, because my hands were tied. I had eyes on the terrorist. I saw him take aim at her and Parker. That's why I stepped into the conversation about withdrawing."

"Conversation?" Mason scoffed. "That was an order, Sergeant."

"I understand, ma'am. But—"

"No. No more buts."

Brian's heart kick-started. "You're blaming me for this?"

Mason and Slusarski glanced at each other, faces full of meaning. Intent.

Son of a biscuit! Brian worked to constrain the swell of rage.

"No," Slusarski finally said. He slid his hands onto his belt. "It's worse than that."

Un-freakin'-believable! I obey the order, breaking my own moral code— but I do it because I was told to, then two soldiers die, and now they blame me!

"Major—"

"He should know," Slusarski said quietly as he faced Brian. "The order to stand down never came from us."

CHAPTER 17

The days were dark and only growing darker. A bleak thought, but Brian couldn't shake it. Skies laden with thick clouds and the cruel wind digging its icy fingers through the tents and portable buildings left him with a chill deep in his bones. Something was off. Something was brewing.

Or maybe he just wanted to get back with the team.

That much was true without the weather or sense of doom plaguing him. But he felt it, the nudge that said. . .

He wasn't sure what. Just felt it. The way some athletes feel an approaching storm in their joints. For some, the indication was painful, for others it showed up in the form of an annoying ache that created little more than a "hurry up and pass" wish. That's where Brian was right now. Whatever it was, whatever was coming, he just wanted it to be over. Life was dishing him a whole lot of junk right now. He was so over it. So ready to get on with his life. Get back to normal.

A chuckle rattled the air to his left. Though Brian didn't look, he could tell one of the Airmen had a device of some kind. By the sound of it, the guy was streaming back home because that voice was a woman's voice. And it wasn't a friendly or sisterly voice. That was an "I want you home" voice.

The woman's voice and the baby's giggle whispered through the void in Brian's life, stirring an ache in his chest he hadn't known was there. Dad was too entrenched in his work at the university to help at home, and Mom liked her pity parties too much to indulge in a bigger family.

Worked better for Brian. At least another kid didn't have to endure what he did. Imagine the fun when Dad's scandal blew wide open.

The baby's belly-gut laugh burst through the connection.

Brian dropped his gaze and reached for his HK416. He removed the bolt carrier group, which consisted of the firing pin inside the bolt carrier and the charging handle, and laid them on the wool blanket.

A girl and a baby back home. What would that be like?

Awesome.

No. Awful. Nobody would hang around six, twelve, or eighteen months while he secured freedom in some other country. Even if he was home.

He snorted. No chick was stupid enough to put up with his crap. She wouldn't stick around. That's why he flirted but kept his distance. He didn't need more humiliation in his life.

"You're worthless! What's wrong with you? Use that brain of yours!"

The problem was, he *had* used his head. Not good enough for Dad. Sucked to be a borderline genius when your father was a Mensa.

A really *stupid* Mensa at that.

Got hung up on that brain of his. Thought he was above everyone, even the law. Especially Mom. The scorn, scandal, and shame of his father's idiocy underscored to Brian that it didn't pay to have head-smarts. While his father served his life prison sentence, Brian played the dumb jock and bought himself a pass out of geekdom. He cleaned the cam and pin with a small patch, a brush, and lightweight oil.

Getting into the Army and discovering he could be physical and mental at the same time settled any question about what he'd do with his life. He'd found his niche. Being in the Army took care of his body, and being a communications specialist kept his mind engaged. And being Special Forces did all of that in one blink. And his skills served the team.

Well it would have served the team. If he'd been authorized to take the shot.

Or. . .if the terrorist hadn't interrupted communications.

It would've taken *one shot*. And Davis would still be alive. He'd sit here without her blood on his conscience. He was sick of this. Sick of the bad guy having a leg up on them. Baiting them. Ambushing them. *Killing us.*

The jerk had thought he was so much smarter.

Just like Dad.

What was the terrorist's point? What did he want? If he had a point, he needed to make it. Because if they encountered him, Brian wouldn't wait for kill authorization. He'd do it.

With each piece carefully cleaned and replaced, he reassembled the weapon. Racked the slide. Now that he'd taken care of his weapon, time to take care of his body. He went outside, a brittle wind nipping at his ears as he ran a couple of circuits, beating off the boredom and sense of isolation. As he jogged toward the gate, the swirl of snowflakes caught his attention.

Great. Freeze his assets off while they played hide-and-seek with a terrorist who had more *seek* capabilities than should be plausible. Maybe it was time for Brian to reverse the poles, swing some favor in their direction. Put the brains his father belittled to some use.

And just like then, it was time for him to do something. His boots crunched on the dirt and gravel as he headed to the Command building. At this time of night, most personnel would be either at dinner or bedding down for the night. Perfect time for Brian's nimble fingers and brain.

Bathed in a swath of dimness, the building sat like an ominous challenge to his goal. A few cubicles cradled grunts, battened down. Some groaned when the wintry mix swarmed in with Brian before the door clattered against the frame. He took a moment to orient himself. Which monitor. . .? One in a dark corner. But where he could keep an eye on anyone coming. Not near a camera.

A familiar face peeked up from a monitor. *Crap.*

Slusarski's eyes widened. "Hawk."

Play it cool. Brian moved that way. "Hey." He shrugged off his jacket and met the guy halfway across the room.

"You lost?"

More than anyone could ever know. "Is there a terminal I can use?"

Confusion skittered across the major's face. "They have terminals at the—"

"No." Brian leaned in and lowered his voice. "My specialty is communications." He hadn't admitted to this in a decade. "I thought I could dig around, maybe find a trail. Maybe back-trace."

Lifting his chin a little, Slusarski seemed like he was about to turn Brian away. "This about Davis? The village?"

Brian said nothing. It was about Davis, but it wasn't. The scope on this terrorist's head had widened. Brian had yet to figure out if the guy was targeting him—it was starting to feel a little personal—or if he was just screwing with the entire military coms system. That was the more logical, less-paranoid answer.

"You know they have guys working round the clock to find—"

"Nobody will know I was here."

"*I'll* know."

"Didn't mean that. Just meant I wouldn't screw things up."

Slusarski sighed and looked around the communications room. "You really think you can find something nobody else has?"

"After having my hands tied and watching a soldier die when I could've stopped it, I'd like to think I have a little more invested in making this stop than some grunt out there who's been staring at code and traces for the last week or month."

After another heavy sigh, the major started out of the room. "Come with me."

Kandahar Airfield, Afghanistan
17 January—1930 Hours

Reviewing her manual to stay fresh while the panel reviewed the event, Fekiria sat at a table poring over the flight instructions. The intricacies of advanced flying skills. Sitting here for three hours hadn't made the information seep into her brain, which was locked on the team who had gone over the aircraft then the flight recordings. All to determine if she had done something wrong. Or should have done something different.

Like never climbed in the cockpit.

Chin resting on the heel of her hand, she let the questions overtake her again. What was her brother doing there? He'd always had a particularly sharp tongue, little patience, and even less tolerance for her antics. But this? Outright wickedness? Waving guns around? Holding his own sister hostage?

She almost laughed. Keeping her hostage would've been something he'd have taken pleasure in as an older brother. Not because of any malice but because he was her brother. But now. . .

Was there a darkness in Adeeb? Something wicked that drove him to wield a gun at her. Command men who answered to a terrorist? A darker, graver thought worried her—did this make Adeeb a terrorist? What would Baba think?

Oh! Fekiria pressed a fist to her breast. Madar would be shattered, knowing her son went down the same path that had brought so much war and death to their country.

They were traditional in their values, committed to Islam.

Am I?

The question, the very doubt that lingered in the back of her mind like a. . .a stain on her soul, bothered her. *Of course I believe in Islam!* What craziness!

There had been too much stress. Too many incidents that left her afraid and. . .uncertain. What *did* she know? What *did* she believe—about life, about love, about everything?

The thoughts, gaining strength and vigor, rushed her like a gale trying to toss down an aircraft that didn't belong in its domain. Fekiria cupped her hands against her forehead and closed her eyes. She was independent and successful. A self-made woman.

"Yet more confused than ever," she whispered over a throat raw with thick emotion.

Warm pressure came to her back as a voice said, "Are you okay?"

At Captain Ripley's question, Fekiria straightened and purposefully tucked aside her doubts and tears. "Yes. Just. . .tired." Her gaze fell on the open manual, and she hoped it was enough to convince him she wasn't lying. She pressed her spine into the chair as he sat beside her.

"You look more than tired." His brows knotted as he considered her. Then he reached up and brushed the side of her cheek. "That's a tear. . ." He said it as if he didn't believe what he saw.

And neither did Fekiria, who glanced at his fingertip, surprised at the shiny drop. She wiped her eye to make sure there weren't any more. "I. . .I guess it was from yawning too hard." The nervous laugh didn't cover her lie, and she hated lying to Captain Ripley. He was a nice man. "Anyway, why are you here?" It was not like he was just dropping by with the way she had sought an out-of-the-way spot to study and think.

No, that wasn't true. She had wanted to be alone. Away from her classmate who kept telling her she should date Captain Ripley. Away from the safety officers assessing her every move, looking for a reason she might try to steal or sabotage their aircraft. And away from the man sitting here with her now. Mostly because she wasn't sure what direction to go with him. Was she being unreasonable?

"I got word from CID that their decision is coming close. An inside source"—at this he winked—"told me that things looked pretty positive. He doubts they are going to levy any punishment, let alone ground you permanently."

She drew in a breath and let it out slowly. "That is very good news. I am relieved." Her stomach turned and twisted, knowing that wasn't the only reason he'd come here. Maybe she should leave before—

"Fekiria?"

Warm dread poured down her. She hated that he used her real name. It felt wrong. Invasive, somehow. She slid a wary gaze in his direction.

"I care about you, and I'm concerned."

Her pulse skipped a beat. Where was this going?

"You haven't been the same since you returned." Captain Ripley leaned forward. "Are you okay? Did something...something happen...?"

Crazy the way a simple shake of his head seemed to speak so much. "No. I told you everything." Except about Adeeb. That wouldn't— couldn't—come out. The panel would ground her for sure. "Why? What do you think happened?"

"I don't know. You've been withdrawn. When you see me coming, you look like you want to hide. The openness and free spirit I'd always admired is gone."

Fekiria chewed her lip, nervous. What he described had little to do with the event a few days ago and everything to do with wrong impressions. "It is true, I am stressed. Scared, even. They could take my wings away." She pushed her most fearful expression toward him.

Captain Ripley, facing her, placed a hand on the back of her chair. And it seemed to jam her breath in her throat. "I won't let that happen. You're a great pilot—you have strong instincts up there. If they come back with a negative decision, I will fight it." He was close. Too close. "I won't lose you."

She blinked. *Won't lose me?*

Before she could react, he leaned in.

For a kiss!

Fekiria jerked her face to the side. Shame raced through her. And anger. She grabbed her book and shoved to her feet. "I'm sorry. I should get some rest." Though she didn't look directly at him, she could see his downward gaze, his disappointment. "Thank you for trying to cheer me up." Right. With a kiss?

She turned and headed out of the small classroom, manual clutched to her chest. Heat washed down her spine. She was furious. Scared. Not because she had almost been kissed by Captain Ripley. But because she had worked too hard and too long to gain her flight status, and if the panel even saw a hint of romance between her and Captain Ripley, it would all be gone.

As she pushed open the door, her heart thumped hard. One of the majors from the panel stood in a library office, phone in hand, staring out at her. The message he telegraphed made her fears seem realized.

The possibility of losing everything seemed more real than ever before.

NECESSARY RISKS

"Meeting here is dangerous."

Hands in his pockets, Daniel stared at the man who'd sold out his country, sold his soul, for money. Disgust swirled through him as he watched the uniformed man look around the open desert road they stood on. "Do you not feel safe?"

Blue eyes caught his. "With the stunts your people are pulling? *No*, I don't feel safe." He hunched his shoulders, apparently against the bitter wind.

"You mean with the stunts *you* are helping us pull off." Daniel watched the man squirm. For the right price, the soldier had compromised his own people but could not accept the blame that sat so squarely on his shoulders.

"Look, I'm here." He scowled and looked around again. "What do you want?"

Though the freezing temperatures tugged at his coat, Daniel refused to let it affect him. Refused to let this weak, impudent American destroy so many months of hard work. He slid his gaze over the landscape. The mountains bordered his homeland and felt familiar. Freeing. "We need 'eyes in' again."

"No." The man seemed to have found his manhood. "Not again. They know they're being watched. They're sweeping randomly, and if I'm caught—"

"You *will* be caught." Daniel felt his own heart thud, giving away a piece of his plan. But he watched the man grow uneasy. "*If* you are careless. Risk is a game we must all play to succeed. It is inherent in every decision we make. Some risks are higher than others, but they exist."

"Look," the soldier said, his hair mussed by the strong fingers of winter. "This isn't me. I don't betray my country. I just need the money—got a sick kid back home. After the furlough, we couldn't afford his treatment."

"Now you can." Keeping the curl from his lip, Daniel focused on the weakness he must exploit. "It is clear your son means a lot to you, and the opportunity to afford his treatment is one you would not ignore. You are a dedicated father, and it's obvious you would do anything for him."

The man looked perturbed. "What good does it do if I die?"

"Now, you are being dramatic. I thought your son was what mattered to you."

The soldier cursed, and Daniel knew he had him. "I need access to a system. One of my people will show up at this location." He handed him a slip of paper. "You need to make sure they get in. And out."

"I'm telling you—it won't work. They are only letting specific personnel enter those facilities now." He stuffed his hands in his Army-issued heavy jacket.

"But you will make it happen." Daniel straightened and turned toward the waiting car. "I know you could never forgive yourself if your son died because you were too weak to take the necessary risks to ensure his well-being." How did men like that get so high up the ranks in the Western military? The man would have been handed a gun and left to take care of his own failings in China.

"Are you threatening him?"

Daniel closed the door, the tint-darkened view giving him no pleasure. "It is a promise."

CHAPTER 18

Bagram Airfield, Afghanistan
17 January—2205 Hours

Nothing frustrated Brian more than knowing there was a lead somewhere in a mess of a code and not being able to find it.

He took that back. One thing frustrated him more—even angered him. Knowing someone was toying with him. Being made a fool of. That's what his efforts here tonight felt like. Every turn, every pathway he ventured down seemed to turn back on him. Like some twisted time loop that had him bumping into himself over and over.

But yeah—this guy was in here somewhere. Staring right back at him, if Brian guessed right. He'd find him. Eventually. Because it was impossible to remove every trace of a hacker's identity. Humans were humans. They made mistakes. Which meant the dog meat messing with his friends was out there, had left a signature, a fingerprint, a piece of DNA, so to speak.

And the only trick was knowing where to look.

But that was like trying to find one maggot in a bag of rice.

Shoulders knotted with tension, he roughed his hands over his face, trying to brush away the burning in his eyes. Exhaustion plied a yawn out of him. He stretched, a fist over his mouth, as another yawn took hold.

But he wasn't giving up. Not with the way this guy nearly killed Raptor. Brian clicked around, read some code, wondered what Captain Watters would do—or what he was doing. *Probably sleeping, like a sane person.*

Or visiting his girlfriend. Didn't guys do that? Lose track of time when they're hanging with a chick they're into?

Sad to say, he'd spent too many nights crashing at a girl's house. That was in high school. Time and deployment didn't afford him that now. Of course, the older he got, the more the one-night flings didn't satisfy.

Granddad would have a long talk prepared for that type of behavior. Brian sat back, the chair tilting as he did, and thought of Granddad. Wondered how that Mustang was doing.

How had Granddad known the lines to read between Brian's streaming code of silence? He'd nailed the problem. *He knows me.* A weird thought. Nobody knew him.

Nobody *wanted* to know him.

Brian had worked hard and long to keep it that way. Keep people at a safe distance so they couldn't know what Brian Bledsoe was really like. And as long as they kept a safe perimeter, nobody would know.

She would know.

Brian stilled, the thought out of the blue startling him. A pair of green eyes and pink full lips swam before his mind's eye. It still annoyed the crud out of him that Fekiria had thrown him to the wolves because of his nationality, but she was all over that officer.

Apparently, Brian wasn't good enough.

That's what you get, numbskull, for playing it safe.

Playing it safe kept him alive. Kept him from getting his head bashed as a teen. Building bulk and benching brains—that is, pretending he didn't have them—moved him into the cool crowd. Made him the "poor kid" whose father went to prison for life. Got him a scholarship to a university for hockey.

But he'd abandoned that after his mom's death. Just had to get away from it all—the people, the pity, the pressure. The accusations. The truth.

But justice demanded action. He'd done the right thing.

Yeah, and if you hadn't, Mom would still be alive.

No. There was no way to know that. Brian shook his head. Shook off the thoughts and shoved out of his chair. Too many hours staring at a screen was dumbing down his brain. He went for the coffeepot down the hall.

A cup of joe to get his mind buzzing again, back into the coding and ciphering. He wasn't giving up. This guy had hit the team hard time and again. Hand on the coffeepot, Brian stilled.

Hit the team.

Hit me.

Had he hit anyone else? Anyone outside Special Forces—outside of Raptor?

Right. Because it's personal.

He yanked the coffeepot, chiding himself for staying up too late and letting paranoia dig its fingers into his skull. The pot practically flung upward, it was so light. He finally looked at the carafe. Empty. He slammed it back down. Checked the clock. Three in the morning. No way would he make more.

Maybe it was his cue to grab some rack time.

Scratching the back of his head and stifling another yawn, Brian headed back to the office Major Slusarski had tucked him in. He backed out of the programs and cleared the history. He deleted markers that left *his* virtual fingerprints and powered off.

Halfway down the hall, he heard something. Voices.

Correction: one voice.

Brian slowed, easing up to the juncture where the hall intersected the main area. He passed at the corner, concealed, as he attuned his ears to whoever was talking.

A man. Talking on the phone if the one-way conversation gave a clue.

Brian craned his neck forward for a quick look-see. Hit eyes on the target then snapped back so he wasn't seen. A guy in a heavy jacket stood in a darkened corner of the office area, talking on the phone.

At three in the morning?

I don't think so.

Brian slid his Glock 22 from his side holster and held it low as he slid around the corner, sticking to the shadows. The guy shifted, angling away from Brian, who almost smirked. *Just make it easy for me, dirtbag.* Nobody was here, making calls in the dead of night and under the cover of darkness.

This guy probably was the leak. Maybe even the one who'd given the terrorist access to the system. Which could mean this guy was responsible for the deaths of Parker and Davis.

And nearly taking out Raptor. *Me.*

"Hands!" Brian shouted. "Show me your hands!"

The guy jerked around. Whites of his eyes bulging, he cursed. Slammed down the phone.

Brian moved in swiftly. "*Hands!* Or I put a bullet in your brain!"

Hands up, the guy wagged them at Brian. "Easy. I work here."

"Move away from the desk," Brian ordered, still closing the distance. When the guy shifted to the left, he started to lower his arms.

"Hands!"

Fingers stabbed upward. "Easy, I'm telling you—"

"Name and rank."

"Sanderson, Mike. Specialist."

"On your knees, Specialist Sanderson." If that *was* the guy's name. Brian wasn't taking chances.

"Are you kidding—?"

Brian stared down the barrel of his Glock and let that be his answer. Sanderson huffed but complied.

A shadow to Brian's right flickered. He eyed the spot and found Slusarski emerging from an office.

"What's going on, Sergeant?" Slusarski glanced down at the kneeling specialist.

"Came out to get coffee and heard this guy on the phone." Brian let some of the tension ease up, but not enough that he couldn't get a shot off if necessary. "He says he's a specialist—find that mighty suspicious that he'd be here at this time of night making a phone call."

"He is." Slusarski hadn't stopped considering the specialist. "He's one of mine." The tall, thin major stalked around the room and came in front of the specialist. "What're you doing here, Sanderson?"

His shoulders slumped a little. "It's my kid's birthday. I wanted to call him before he headed out to school. I set my alarm, but when I woke up my phone was dead. Rec center's closed up tight. Same with the USO's."

Slusarski gave an exasperated sigh as he eased onto a folding chair in front of the specialist. "You realize making personal calls is against regs?"

Sanderson gave a defeated nod.

Brian holstered his weapon, teeth grinding. What if the guy was making it up, about his kid?

"Go on," Slusarski said with a wave. "Back to your bunk. Zero six hundred comes early when you don't sleep."

After a furtive glance to Brian, Sanderson came to his feet. "Yes, sir. Thank you," he said to his CO. The guy left quickly, a swirl of wind and snow dashing in before the door thumped closed.

Once the door shut, Brian turned to Slusarksi. "You believe him?"

Slusarski rose and went to a cubicle. He lifted a framed photo and handed it to Brian. "His wife left him. Sent him a Dear John letter."

There was a name for chicks like her, and it rhymed with *witch*. "If his wife left him, he could have motive."

"To what?" Slusarksi pinched the bridge of his nose. "I know where you're going. And you're right." He looked as tired as Brian felt. "I'll have the number he called verified. We'll keep an eye on him."

The guy could walk out and find another phone. Notify his contact. If he had one. But there wasn't much Brian could do about it. This wasn't his base. Wasn't his team. Wasn't his CO. Wasn't his problem.

Unless it was *him*.

"With all that's happening, I felt we couldn't take chances." Brian gave him a nod. "Good night, sir." He really hated calling this guy sir, but with the chain of command. . .

"Thanks for watching out for us."

Brian gave another nod then headed for the door. He punched the level and was met by an angry squall of icy snow and wind. An instant reminder he'd forgotten his jacket. He pivoted and caught the door before it shut. He hustled down the hall, into the office, then snatched the coat off the back of the chair.

When he did, he saw something on the monitor. *Wait. I turned that off.*

"I thought you left," Slusarski said as he stepped into the cramped space.

Lifting his jacket, Brian smiled.

Slusarksi laughed. Clapped Brian on the shoulder. "Be thankful we aren't in the mountains. I hear a monster storm is brewing. Should hit in about a week."

"That's why I'm staying right here. Night." As he moved behind the major, he caught a line of code streaming across the screen. A series of numbers: 051|215.

Slusarksi grunted. "What the devil?" He shook his head. "The system has been messed up the last few weeks."

"Yeah, I wouldn't trust anything." Including the man standing in front of Brian.

—⁓—

Kandahar, Afghanistan
26 January—0745 Hours

"Did you rest well?"

Fekiria stretched out the aches in her back as she glanced around the dim room empty of elaborate or luxurious furnishings. In fact, it had very little. Last night, she had reported in and informed Captain Ripley she would be staying with family in the area for the weekend. Though she was not blood related to Mitra, she was more deeply connected to her than anyone. Except Zahrah.

Though it'd been more than a week since her abduction at Adeeb's hand, the weight and opression of that night hung over her. She wanted a break. And helping Mitra with the children was her best option. Her only option for an escape.

She moved to the small table where three children sat with bowls of something that looked like watery flour. "What are they eating?"

With a forced smile, Mitra said, "What the Lord has provided"— and her voice dropped to a whisper—"during desperate times."

"You need a new lord if that's all you have."

Pain snapped through Mitra's expression, but she refocused on the girls. There were six in all, including Mitra's four-year-old daughter, Hadassah, a girl with bright eyes and a ready smile.

"Finish your meal then on to chores."

A collective groan flittered through the girls at Mitra's instruction. Once their bowls were emptied, they carried them to a bucket and set them inside before heading out a rear curtained-off area. Each time the fabric flapped back, it gave Fekiria a view of the dark juncture where walls had missing chunks and plaster had cracked and broken off.

Could anything good be back there? The thought felt ridiculous considering the poor shelter even *this* room offered. "What is back there?"

"A bathroom," Mitra said as little Hadassah clung to her mom's legs.

Fekiria suppressed a shudder at the thought of what that bathroom must look like and turned her focus to the little one. Ebony hair hung down her back, the clothes a bit too thin for the winter weather and too short at the ankles and wrist. Her shoes were simple flats that probably did little to keep the cold from her toes. Fekiria glanced over to the sleeping area then wandered over there. Feather mattresses were covered with thin, often torn sheets. Atop them, dingy gray blankets. Wool, but so thin they might as well be paper.

"Mi—" Fekiria stopped as she turned to find herself in an empty room.

Where was Mitra's husband? Why did they not have food, warm

clothes, and bedding? She started for the rear room but her friend reappeared. "Mitra, what is going on here?"

The little girl trailed her mother, holding on to the hem of her long tunic. Mitra bent toward her daughter and whispered something, which sent her scampering out of the room.

"Where is Jacob?" Fekiria asked, stalking across the room. What kind of man would make his wife and child live like this?

"It was not long after Dassah was born, I visited my mother in Mazar-e. While I was there, men set upon Jacob. Ordered him to renounce Isa or leave Afghanistan—alone." She tidied the room then lifted a stack of books from a shelf. The move reminded Fekiria of Zahrah. "They vowed to kill me and Dassah if he did not."

Fekiria stared at the table with five plastic chairs gathered around it. She did not want to vocalize the horrible truth lodged in her brain. But the question freed itself. "And he did not."

Mitra gave an almost-imperceptible nod.

Which meant her husband was dead? By the grief evident in her friend's face, she could only guess this to be true. Though she'd heard of stories like this, and Baba had said his sister had been threatened, it had never happened to someone so close to Fekiria. Except Zahrah— but that wasn't connected to faith or jihad. It was knowledge that had gotten her cousin into trouble. "Why did Jacob not tell them what they wanted to hear?"

"If he would deny what he believed just to save his life, then he did not believe it."

"But is it not better to tell a lie and save your life? How could he not think of you and his daughter?"

"He did think of us." Fire sparked in her friend's eyes. "What life would he have if he had to live with guilt for the rest of his years knowing he bowed his knee at a threat?" Mitra shook her head. "Even I would not want Jacob to do that."

"But they killed him! Now you don't have him."

"I have his strength, and more than ever, I believe in Jesus. He has provided for us—"

"Provided for you?" Fekiria heard her own voice bounce off the roof. "Look at this place, Mitra! You have no heat, no decent food, and the clothes—"

"We have a roof over our heads and enough to keep us sustained!"

Mitra blew a breath through puffed cheeks. "Forgive me for speaking so harshly. I know you do not understand. But. . .try." Her friend's expressive eyes pleaded with her. "Please."

"But Hadassah will not know her father."

Kindness never left Mitra's face. Unshakable. "And what would she know of him if he lived by denying Isa? That he was not strong enough to defend his faith? That at the hint of challenge and danger, he would walk away from those beliefs?"

"No, that he loved his family enough to do whatever it took to live for them!"

Stretching across the gap between them, Mitra touched her arm. "Denying what one believes just for temporary comfort is the sign of a weakhearted man. A shallow belief. If we cannot stand for our beliefs, we will fall for everything."

Fekiria placed a hand over her forehead, her mind spinning. It made no sense to die for something so. . .intangible. "And how is that different from those who jihad?"

"Because Jacob did not die to kill someone who would not believe as he did. He died for Someone who gave everything for him, in the hopes that those watching would know that his belief is resolute."

"You and Zahrah—I never understood you."

Mitra sighed. "I know. And it is okay. I still love you, angel."

"And now, you are here teaching these girls. Do you not realize what will happen if the Taliban find out? They've been killing girls in the area, Mitra!"

"You are a pilot, yes?"

Fekiria drew back. "What does that matter?"

"I remember standing in the room when you told your father you left the ANA. But you didn't. And now you are a pilot!" Mitra's smile was infectious. "What bravery you have shown to do what you believed in!"

But I lied to do it! And now she was running and hiding and lying more. Fekiria gave a low laugh. "I see what you are doing."

"Even you believe in teaching the girls," Mitra said then turned and gave the girls instructions. "As someone who has her freedom, surely you would not take away their chance just because of danger."

Almost as if on cue, the half-dozen girls quietly returned, taking places at the table where Mitra had set out the books and papers.

"Girls." Mitra placed her hands on the shoulders of a girl who looked about ten years old. The faded yellow hijab and blue tunic gave a striking contrast. "This is Miss Haidary. She is a pilot."

Awe and gasps infected the young faces.

"You fly planes?" the oldest girl, who stood just a little shorter than Mitra's five-six height, asked. A horrid scar marked a line down her jaw and neck.

Fekiria gave a stiff nod. "Sometimes. I prefer helicopters."

Another cluster of *ohhs* and *ahhs* went around, followed quickly by a dozen questions. Her friend had been clever in ambushing her with this dialogue. With tempting the girls to unleash their questions on her.

"See where learning to read and do your math can take you?" Mitra pointed to the table with a winning smile. "Now, let's work quietly."

Defeat and frustration clung to Fekiria as the morning wore on, but she could not walk out of here, abandon her friend and these girls. She used her day off to clean and bake naan, which she had bought the ingredients for at the market. They had so little. Innocence stayed here. They did not deserve the scared little men with their big guns and mouths who tried to rob them of the right to learn and grow.

The greatest irony was the lie Fekiria had believed about her friend. Mitra was supposed to have the perfect life—a husband, child, and a future. Fekiria had so envied her when she left Mazar-e Sharif with a bright, prosperous future ahead of her.

Not . . . *this*. Poverty. Fear. Widowhood.

"Are you well?"

Fekiria looked at her friend. "How can you do this? Be alone, take care of these girls? Where. . . Why. . .?"

"I am not alone."

Rolling her eyes would only upset her friend, but Fekiria couldn't stand it. "You mean Isa."

Mitra laughed. "Well, yes, but I meant Baktash and Belourine, the couple who live in the smaller house and help as they can."

"Oh." Corrected, Fekiria felt chastised. "You have help then?"

With a kiss on the cheek, Mitra gave her a hug. "You love me, so you are angry to see me in need."

She understood? "Yes!"

"Then come help us."

Fekiria's heart dropped. She'd walked away from her part-time work at the school in Mazar-e because of what happened to Zahrah.

"I could use the help, and the girls—especially Sheevah—would love to have you around. It is not so bad after you have gotten used to it."

"Sheevah?"

Mitra glanced toward the eldest girl, whose red-tipped ears were giving away the fact she'd been listening to the conversation. Her curiosity and admiration had been obvious when she asked questions earlier of Fekiria.

Expectation and danger came hand in hand here. What happened in Mazar-e, what she witnessed, and what her cousin endured could repeat itself.

"Do these girls not deserve a chance to learn?"

"Of course they do." Hearing her own conviction seemed to give it more weight. These girls did deserve that chance, and so much more. Perhaps she could find a way to get them supplies so the girls weren't on the verge of starvation or freezing to death. Fekiria straightened her shoulders. "How can I help?"

―◆―

Mazar-e Sharif, Afghanistan
26 January—0815 Hours

Dean jogged across the compound, heading toward the showers when the staticky rendition of reveille echoed through the winter morning. He stopped in his tracks, turned toward the raising flag, and saluted. Things might be out-of-control crazy. A sadistic terrorist might be targeting the military. But there was Old Glory.

Inspiring. A symbol of courage. Of thousands of soldiers, sailors, airmen, Marines, Coasties who had served before him. Lives sacrificed. And the untold number who would serve after him under the banner of the Stars and Stripes.

When the song ended, Dean continued toward the showers.

"Captain Watters?"

Dean pivoted, surprised to find a major heading his way. "Yes?"

"Colonel Coffino sent me over with this." The officer handed him a sealed envelope.

Apprehension weighted Dean's muscles as he turned the envelope over. "What is this?" The addressee was one SFC Mitchell Black.

"Don't know, sir. We tried to locate Sergeant Black—"

"He's in the field."

"Yes, sir. This is unusual, but could you be sure to deliver it to him?"

Why did this feel like he would be handing Mitch a death sentence? Then again, Dean would rather bad news—nobody sends good news like this—get delivered by a friend than a stranger. "Of course. Thank you." He saluted the major, who headed back to the Jeep he'd abandoned.

He tucked the envelope with his things and resumed course for the showers. His secure sat phone rang. Maybe he should give up on the idea of a shower. "Watters."

"We may have a problem."

Dean almost laughed at General Burnett's comment. "When do we not?"

"Meet me at Command in ten."

"Yes, sir." Dean grabbed a three-minute shower and changed then hustled over to the Command building. Gathered in the office were the general and his administrative officer, Lieutenant Brie Hastings.

"Got a call from Bledsoe," Burnett said.

Dean hesitated. "Hawk?" Frowning, he looked between the two. He knew better than to ask if everything was okay. It rarely was when it came to Hawk. "What's going on? I thought he was down in—"

"He is." Burnett lifted his Dr Pepper and slurped. "Seems some strange things are happening."

"Strange is the new normal."

"He has a theory," Burnett said.

The general's sense of humor had vanished. That he didn't laugh or acknowledge Dean's comment unseated what little confidence Dean had left. "I'm listening."

"He thinks this is personal."

Dean snorted. "Everything is personal to Hawk if it involves him. It's why his fists land in other people's faces."

"I think he might have something."

Again, Dean was surprised. "Okay."

"Communications between the base and Bledsoe were disrupted, and he was given an order to stand down—an order that cost the lives of two soldiers."

Dean lowered himself to the empty chair. "I'm sorry to hear that."

"You and me both, especially since the base didn't send that message." Burnett stabbed a finger at Hastings, who laid out a series of papers on the desk. "These are all the disrupted communications—or at least the ones we know about."

Shifting to the edge of his seat, Dean looked at the incident summaries. Not full reports but one-page synopses. Included was the ambush in the ghost village. An incident by a river that nearly had them taking an icy swim.

"Notice anything?"

Yes. Dean saw the common thread. And the dread pushed his shoulders down. No...this couldn't be... "There has to be an explanation."

"There is." Burnett's chest puffed out, his eyes sparking with meaning.

And Dean knew the implied explanation. "It *is* personal. They're going after Raptor."

ACRID WEAKNESS

Shanghai, China
27 January—0815 Hours

Weakness had a smell. It was acrid and pungeant, dipping deep into the soul of a person. Few were able to rise above the inherent stench, to learn and grow. To become better. Worthy of those who must endure their failings. Most people were not willing to make the sacrifices. Willing to brave the pain of growing beyond their shortcomings. Most lingered in it, steeping like a bad tea or rotten fish. Their rank scent infiltrated those around them, diminishing them. Lessening them.

Hands stuffed in the pockets of his slacks, Daniel waited. Watching as she stepped out of the car. Which would she be? The rotten fish stinking up his company, his name? Or was she as the tiny irritant of sand in the clam's shell that became a beautiful pearl?

Pearls. He should buy her pearls. They would rival her complexion.

Kiew now stood before him, her skin as porcelain. Her lips glossed and as enticing as the bloom of a flower. The roses of her cheek so perfect.

Daniel brushed her cheek with the back of his hand. When she lowered her head and eyes, pleasure erupted through him. *Good.* "You are learning, my pearl." She would not understand the endearment. The way she raised her eyes—yet never met his gaze as she should not since she was not yet equal to him—proved right. He kissed her, savoring her. She responded, as she had since their first introduction three years ago. Her curves pressed against him.

Good.

She must want him.

Daniel stepped back, his hunger warring with the knowledge he must still teach her discipline. Even to the detriment of his own desires.

But she would not refuse him, were he to taste of her virtue again. She never had. "What did you find out? Why are they silent?"

She swallowed, her gaze down. "They do not trust the communications, so they are not using them."

Rubbing his jaw, Daniel turned away from her. That was not good, the Americans abandoning communications. It had been his direct link to crippling them. If they abandoned that, then his efforts would succeed but would not inflict the intense personal damage he sought.

"Our contact. . ." Kiew rarely left a sentence unfinished. Doing that indicated weakness. Uncertainty. He tolerated neither.

Hand on the hard lines of a crystal decanter, he waited for her to finish that thought. He did not want to have to punish her for the lapse. Or perhaps this hesitation was her way of protecting someone. She had a soft, kind heart. One that did not belong in someone who held the position she did. He'd told her that. Trained her to discard that shortcoming.

Her lingering resistance told him what he needed to know. "You protect him though he fails us, though he defies us." In his periphery, he saw Kiew tuck her head. He must push her to know and do what she knew in her heart rather than surrender to her proclivity toward compassion. "Kill him."

Now, her head came up.

The stench of the pearl singed his nostrils. "You would defend him?"

"No." At least she had the common sense not to raise her voice, though she argued with him. "I believe we still need what he can do. Changing the operation, finding someone else suitable—"

"*Everyone* is replaceable."

"Yes, but not everyone is invisible and able to stay that way to the Americans. If we bring in someone else, they could be the weak link to break our chain."

She had thought it through. Daniel lifted his chin and considered the beautiful woman. Had he underestimated her? "Have you begun to squeeze him?"

Her eyebrow arched ever so slightly and she tilted her head. Almost smiled. "I have."

He breathed in deep, pleased. "Good." The perfume of her confidence distilled the room of the putrid scent.

CHAPTER 19

Kandahar, Afghanistan
2 February—1920 Hours

For a week she had given her evenings to the girls' home and school—with Captain Ripley's approval. Fekiria had vowed no more lies. At least, ones she could avoid. He'd wanted to come. To volunteer as well, but she saw it for what it was: he wanted to push into her life.

Why can't you give yourself to him?

He was a good man.

American.

Even she must admit they couldn't *all* be bad. Not if she wanted and demanded the same respect from the Americans regarding her own people, who were just as affected by the Taliban and terrorists scarring her country.

He was charming.

Yes, perhaps too charming.

And his green eyes.

Fekiria stilled. No, Captain Ripley had gray eyes. Who. . .who had green—? Her heart jolted as she made the match between the green eyes and their owner: Sergeant Brian.

"What is his name?"

Fekiria blinked as she looked up from the table where she had been looking over Sheevah's writing. "What?"

"You've been sitting there staring at the page, but you haven't been reading it." Mitra sat across from Fekiria. Mitra's hooked nose added an exotic flare to her features. "So, I am left to imagine there is a man who has captured your attention." Elbows on the table, she leaned in with a mischievous grin. "Yes?"

"You know Zahrah always said you were a bad influence because you had more mischief in your eyes than I did."

Laughing hard, Mitra threw her head back. "I do not think it is possible to outdo you!" She patted her arm. "Now, no success diverting me. What is his name?"

Fekiria knew she could not mention Sergeant Brian. It was foolish that she had even thought of him when she'd never see him again anyway.

Unless Zahrah married Captain Dean. Then Sergeant Brian might come to their wedding. Still, she'd stick with the less scandalous story. "His name is Captain Ripley, but it's not what you think. He's my flight advisor, and he likes me."

"Is he handsome?"

"He is. . .easy to look at, yes."

"And is he smart? Rich?"

"Smart, yes. Rich—he's an American soldier."

Mitra's mouth fell open. "No. That is not possible."

"Exactly. It's not possible."

Wide brown eyes stretched in disbelief, then Mitra drew back, apparently weighing the conversation. "Does he like you—I mean, like that?"

"He does. Maybe too much. He is not quiet about his feelings."

"But you don't like him?"

After setting aside the papers, Fekiria moved from the table and started organizing the books on the shelves. "I don't *not* like him."

"Then what is the problem? Is he old?"

"No. Well, not like Habib. Captain Ripley is only in his thirties, I think."

"So, what *is* the problem?"

And again—her mind betrayed her. She saw him. The *other* American soldier who had a fast smile and an intensity that drew her like gravity to earth. Which was ridiculous because they had not seen each other since he went to prison for her. Since she made him angry and he ordered her out of the prison and his life. He would not speak to her again, let alone make good on the innuendos in his words and actions.

"There is another man?"

The words came from right behind her, startling Fekiria. She realized she stood staring at the bookcase. "No." Because there wasn't. Sergeant Brian would not want her. Would not speak to her. They wouldn't see each other again. "It's just that Captain Brian is too perfect."

Mitra blinked and shook her head.

"You know?"

"I think so, but—"

"What?"

"Is that some kind of nickname? Captain Brian?"

Her heart tripped. "I didn't say that."

"You did." Mitra lifted a basket of dirty clothes. "You said, 'Captain Brian is too perfect.'"

She did? This time, Fekiria blinked. "You must have heard me wrong." Had she mixed Captain Ripley's rank with Sergeant Brian's name? She must be more careful. "I...I should go."

Mitra came closer, a hand on hers. "I am sorry if I pushed." With a slight head tilt she smiled. "You are as my sister, and that is why I am nosy about your love life."

Fekiria's laugh came out hollow. "Love life? I have none!"

"But—"

Shouts in the courtyard startled them both.

Mitra spun, her expression slamming down from fun and light to deathly serious. She raced to the hall, only to collide with an older woman. "Belourine!"

"They are coming. Baktash saw their car. He's slowing them."

With a strangled yelp, Mitra darted to the rear door. "Fekiria, come quickly!"

A moment's hesitation and worried look to the older woman churned Fekiria's stomach into a thick knot of dread. Belourine moved faster than a woman her age and size should be able to. At the shelf with the schoolbooks, she released a tassel at the side. A thick tapestry whooshed from the sides, covering the shelves and board.

"Go!" Belourine said, noticing her standing there. "Help her at once!"

Fekiria shoved herself forward, her pulse sputtering. In the dark rear hall that led to the bathroom, she hurried after her friend. "What is happening?"

"Hurry, girls." Mitra herded the girls down a dark hall. She slipped into the bathroom, and then one by one the girls entered.

They would not fit in there! "Mitra," Fekiria said as she stepped toward the bathroom.

To her shock, a corner of the bathroom floor had lifted, the tiles vertical to her. Mitra held the trapdoor, helping the little ones into the space. Sheevah seemed to vanish right into the floor.

"Come." Mitra waved Fekiria closer. "They will take any girl found here."

"Who?"

"The Taliban!"

Fekiria's heart pounded. "I told you this was dangerous! You put—"

"Shut up! In! Now!" Fire sparked in Mitra's eyes as she gripped Fekiria's shoulder and guided her down the wood steps.

Sand or dirt crunched beneath her feet. She had to squat to fit into the cramped space. Whimpers and yelps sounded as she stumbled over one girl after another to find a space. "Here," Sheevah's soft, steady voice came as cold fingers wrapped around Fekiria's and drew her to the left. No sooner had she touched the dampness of a stone wall than darkness clapped them in tight.

At first, Fekiria strained to make out shapes, forms. Desperate to make eye contact with her friend, to find reassurance. *I'm an ANA soldier! A pilot—surely they won't harm me.*

But she knew the truth. Knew the Taliban would take great pleasure in making an example of a woman who dared take a man's role. And these girls. . .she could not imagine what horrible things men like that would do to such beautiful, innocent children.

Beside her, she noticed the trembling of Sheevah. Though the girl had been a strength when Fekiria had fumbled, now she, too, sat fully aware of the horrors that could swallow them up. In a move to comfort the girl and offer reassurance that she would do everything she could to protect them, Fekiria put her arm around her.

Sheevah shoved her face against Fekiria's shoulder and shuddered.

The minutes fell like anvils against her thudding heart. Each creak, each thud, each distant voice snatched her breath. Reminded her of the tenuous line they walked as women in a country where some men sought power and domination.

Above them came the unmistakable sound of voices. The clopping of feet. What if they walked over the trapdoor? Would they notice a variation in the sounds on the floor? If she and the girls were discovered, they could throw in a grenade or IED and there would be nothing to bury. Nothing to hold against them.

Her heart ricocheted off her panicked thoughts.

Sheevah pressed harder against her, as if trying to escape the fear through Fekiria's embrace. Fekiria tightened her hold on the girl. She should give her reassurance. Tell her everything would be okay. But that was rarely the truth.

Dirt dribbled down on their heads.

She ducked, burrowing her face against Sheevah's hijab. What surprised her was that where she had expected to smell a homeless girl, she smelled lavender soap. Fekiria closed her eyes, thinking of all Mitra had done for these girls.

And what good will it do if these girls die here?

—⁂—

Bagram Airfield, Afghanistan
3 February—1320 Hours

"The world is some kind of messed up, Granddad."

Wizened, creased eyes smiled back through the grainy iPad stream. "Only if you let it be, Brian."

Leaning forward with his elbows on his knees, he glanced at the dirt floor. "I'm not sure how to change it. I've never felt so powerless."

"I think you have," Granddad said. "You just don't want to remember—because that feeling is a terrifying one."

Brian grunted. "Right between the eyes again." He hated to admit how right his granddad was, but truth was—he'd take a wide mile around those memories. Why was he even here anymore? What good was he when he couldn't save his own team members?

"Listen, I'll be praying for you. I reckon there are things you can't tell me, but God knows them. I'll have fireside chats with Him every morning and ask Him to show you, to protect you, to give you wisdom."

Brian nodded. "I'm not. . .not exactly religious, Granddad."

"Good. Neither am I."

Looking up through his brow, he frowned. How was that? Granddad was one of the most religious guys Brian knew. His mom had been the same until Dad went to prison. Then her life crumbled. And so did she, right into the grave.

"God isn't about religion and performance. He's about relationship. Talk to Him. He's waiting for you to do that. I thought that would've gotten in your thick skull back when we took ya to Sunday school."

"Slow learner, I guess," Brian said with a smirk. Nana and Granddad had taken him to Sunday school every week he lived with them after his mom's death, but there was so much he'd had to work through that church, which was always too quiet, left his thoughts and guilt screaming. And what did God have to do with some terrorist hack dismantling the U.S. military's super-secure computers? Compromising communications?

Forcing me to watch one of my team members die when I could've stopped it.
He'd obeyed the command.

The one that wasn't legit.

The one that cost Davis and Parker their lives.

Brian closed his eyes. Pinched the bridge of his nose. When he'd first hit the base, he thought getting back to Raptor would solve everything. Then he found out he wouldn't be reuniting with them. He missed those guys. Missed the connection. But he wasn't sure about that anymore. To be fair, he wasn't sure about anything. He was just fed up.

"I'm sending you some verses," Granddad said. "Promise me you'll read them each night. Can you do that?"

Religion. A fake Band-Aid on wounds that didn't heal.

"If I can promise to get up early and talk to God on your behalf, the least you can do is promise to read a few words each morning, too. Can you do that?"

"Of course he can, Jack," Nana's sweet voice called from somewhere in the background and brightened Brian's mood.

"Okay," he said, knowing Granddad would not let up.

"Need you to hurry home, son. This Mustang is hurting for a good drive again."

Brian smiled. "Hooah." And felt the smile warm him. Maybe it was time to go home. Weird—when was the last time he thought of anywhere as home? But yeah. He was ready for something different. Was it worth it? Was any of it?

His phone chirruped.

"That's the verses."

"Don't waste time, do you?" Brian snickered as he glanced at the screen. Sure enough, his granddad had sent two verses. He scanned them, his heart thumping on the second one:

"Though youths grow weary and tired, and vigorous young men stumble badly, yet those who wait for the Lord will gain new strength; they will mount up with wings like eagles, they will run and not get tired, they will

walk and not become weary."

Wouldn't that be nice? To not become weary?

Too late.

"Bledsoe!"

At the shout of his name, Brian sat straight on his cot and looked over his shoulder.

A specialist stood at the tent opening and thumbed over his shoulder. "Command wants you."

With a two-fingered salute, Brian shifted his attention back to the iPad. "I have to go."

"Okay, son. Take care. I'm praying for you, and know this—God's with you every step you take. He gives His angels charge over you!"

"Yessir." He wasn't sure he believed all that, but it sure made him smile to hear his granddad say it. "Thank you, sir. Bye." After stowing his iPad, Brian grabbed his gear and weapon. Weapon slung over his shoulder, he tried to shake the depression that had clung to him.

The mess with the terrorist, watching Davis die, and whatever was happening with the system/communications. . .

"You sure move slow for a Special Forces operator."

Brian pivoted, stunned to find himself staring at— "Captain," he breathed. "What. . .?" No way he was here for Brian. Had to be a coincidence. "Everything okay?"

"No, actually, it's not." Hands on his tac belt, Captain Watters shook his head. "I need my communications specialist back."

Brian's heart kick-started. "Seriously?"

With a one-shouldered shrug, the captain said, "Unless you want to recommend a replacement."

Hesitation killed. But things were so messed up. Brian just wasn't sure what he wanted and didn't want anymore. What mattered. "No, sir."

"You don't sound sure."

"I'm not sure what it's going to take to bring this freak down. Or if I have what it takes."

"Only one way to find out."

Brian nodded.

"I heard about the supply run ambush and those two soldiers who died."

"Davis and Parker."

"Right."

"I could've saved them."

"No doubt."

"But they're dead."

"Which is how I'd like to make our enemy."

"Hooah." Brian looked around the base. "How do we know. . .? How do we make sure our coms are secure so this piece of crap doesn't screw with us again while we hunt him down like the dog he is?"

Watters grinned. "We've been working some tricks, but I hoped you could come show us."

Dare he hope? "I can come back?"

"I thought that's what I said. Do you want to?"

Be with his brothers? Be with the men who thought and warred the way he did? Men who acted as a single unit with power and precision? Those who were actively working to bring down the psycho having entirely too much fun beating the snot out of them?

"Hooah."

BORIS

Son of tortoises! They completely turned the tables on me. Trapped me. Forced me into doing what they wanted. Even now I can feel their Chinese breath blowing hotly down the back of my neck. I didn't leave, though I sat in the dark for hours, debating. Arguing with myself.

Some might say I'm a big fat chicken.

They would have two of those right. But I'm no chicken. It's more a duel of wits with these power-hungry types. Or maybe it's more about revenge, because I am smelling a whole lot of personal stink with this whole endeavor to sabotage the American military.

The thing of it is—I'm the expert hacker. Sure, whoever the cash-lord is—he's got some serious geeks behind this. Like the chick. Clearly she has some serious skills to be able to track me down, so running would be a moot effort.

"Have you found them?"

"No!" I have no patience for her anymore. And there's no need to show the deference I once did. Not with the way they pulled down my pants in front of God and everyone. *Figuratively, of course.* "No, I have not found them. You ticked them off. Now they're off grid. This isn't like running passports at Customs, okay?"

"No, it is not okay. You find them. Or we will—"

"I said I would, and I will."

"Osiris wants them found."

"Look, one thing you might need to learn about Americans is if you attack them, if you ambush them, they're going to be pissed. And if they're pissed, it's going to come back to bite you in the a—"

"You are wasting time, Mr. Kolceki."

"I'm sorry. Who started this conversation that has gotten us nowhere?" Raising my eyebrows can't be seen, but the motion puts more emotion in my voice. Like it needs more. "Are we through here?

Because you're interrupting my progress."

The line went dead, and though I feel a squirt of fear at upsetting them—because clearly I had; Asians aren't one to take disrespect lightly . . .they have that in common with Muslims—I am just glad to have her off my back.

"Now I know what a nagging mom is like," I mutter as my fingers continue over the keyboard.

The systems behind me are running facial recognition against the video feeds I've intercepted from the various bases. Surely, one of these guys has to report in or something. I mean, I know Hawk is sitting pretty—well, pretty ticked—after the stunt Kung Fu Madame pulled on him. It was pretty surreal, watching as he just lay there and did nothing. Never thought I'd see a soldier like that lie down and play dead.

Yeah, yeah—I know he was obeying orders. But seriously? What kind of guy just sits there and does nothing? That is some serious kind of messed up.

Beeping draws my attention to the far-right system and I turn around. There on the screen is an enhanced image of Hawk. "Oh, for cryin' out—" Wait. I scoot my chair toward that monitor. It's Hawk, but he's not alone. Right next to him is his boss man, Captain Watters.

Heart in my throat, I double-check the time. Ten minutes ago. Holy cow! My fingers are flying as my heart ramps up to a speed that makes me wonder if I'm going to end up at the hospital. If I'm quick enough, those two will still be on the base. If that's true, then I can get Fly fly to hitch a ride. I giggle, which is sad, really. A guy my size should not giggle, but it's too much to endure.

Scanning. . .scanning. . .scanning. "C'mon, c'mon, c'mon," I mutter as Fly fly scours the base for— "Bingo!"

Hawk is jogging toward a building, and his captain steps out into the snow-laden mess.

It's cold and wet. Fly fly might object so I double-check his systems. Confident my mechanical fly will survive the elements, I have him over the unsuspecting idiots. Right to the nondescript vehicle they climb into.

"And away we go." I salute the two soldiers and thank them for making my job oh-so-easy, then I lift my phone. Punch in the phone number for Kung Fu Madame.

"What?"

"I've got them."

CHAPTER 20

Kandahar, Afghanistan
10 February—1820 Hours

You have to move away from here."

Mouth slightly open, Mitra stared at her.

"It's the wise thing to do. You aren't safe here." Fekiria motioned to the children working on their math. "Neither are the girls!"

Mitra's glance slid behind Fekiria to the the long hall that led to the front. "How could you bring him here? You have endangered everyone!"

"He's a friend, Mitra. An ally!"

With a caustic laugh she turned and fled to the small kitchen area. "You, calling an American a friend and ally." She shook her head, her yellow hijab dull against her beautiful complexion.

"He is a good man."

"But not good enough for you to consider for marriage, and yet you want to throw my life and the girls' lives into his hands?" Narrowed, angry eyes held hers. "If word of our location gets out to the American soldiers, it will make it to the ears of the ANA." Her nostrils flared. "It will only be a matter of time before the Taliban raze this building!"

"What of last weekend, Mitra? They were so close, and you cannot live like that!"

"What do you know of our plight?"

"I was here! I know how close they came to discovering us."

"You make too much of it. Do you know how many times they have come and searched?"

Fekiria drew back. Considered her friend. "They've been here before?"

"Often." The fight seemed to leach out of her friend. She whirled around and dropped against one of the small shelves as she touched her temple. "But they have never come so quickly, nor have they searched the bathroom as they did when you were here." She shook her head.

Fekiria went to her knees and took her friend's hands. "Let us take you out of here. Captain Ripley can get help from the Americans. We can move you and the girls safely to another location."

"Then it will just start over."

"But it *is* a start. A chance to be free."

"I. . .I will pray about it. But I must tell you, it does not feel right."

Pray. Fekiria wanted to roll her eyes. "Every day you are here is a day they could find you."

"If we leave, we have nowhere to hide. No friends who will shelter us." She sighed and lowered her gaze. "We fight for what we have, but we do have it. This is our home. We have no money to start over."

"But—"

"If it was only me, I would go. No doubt. And I would thank you. But there are six of us. Five children. They cannot flit from place to place."

"You could get killed!"

Softness and what looked like sympathy crowded Mitra's face. "We could get killed anywhere. It is safest for us here."

"If I can find a place in another town, will you go?"

"I will pray about it. That is all I can promise right now."

Pray. When lives were in danger. Fekiria wanted to scream. Instead, she gave a nod as she considered the girls—and stilled. Captain Ripley squatted next to the table, smiling at Aadela, the six-year-old with dark, expressive eyes that could captivate anyone. And she apparently had captivated the captain.

The little one asked if he was Fekiria's husband. Then she went on to explain that he must be because he was here with her alone.

The prevalent male-dominated world was much more prominent in the south, where the Taliban had taken hold again.

Captain Ripley looked up at Fekiria, and she saw his hopes as clear as she could see the snow-capped mountains that stood in the distance, beyond the window, abutting the city. He pushed to his feet then joined her, touching her arm lightly. "Are you okay?"

"She will not leave."

"I agree with her."

Fekiria frowned. "They are in danger!"

"They will be in danger anywhere in the country, especially if they are being educated. That doesn't change."

"It is safer in the north."

His gray eyes probed her response, and she knew he was thinking of Zahrah. Of what happened at their school. "It was different with my cousin."

"How?"

"She drew their attention because she has a degree in quantum cryptology." Fekiria folded her arms. "I do not know what to do."

"You help her," Captain Ripley said, his voice gentle but firm. "We can probably get some people at the base to donate items. We'll do it quietly so we don't draw attention. Little by little, we can get them supplied."

Fekiria stared at him, surprised and impressed at his consideration. His willingness to help them. "Why would you do this?"

He smiled at her, his touch once again warm against her elbow. "Because it means a lot to you."

Tugging her elbow free only fueled her irritation. "Do not do this to get me. Do this because it is right!" With that, she crossed the room and said her good-byes to Mitra. They must return to the base. "I'll come tomorrow and help."

Mitra hugged her. "Please do not be angry with me."

"I just want you to be safe."

"Thank you. God will protect as He sees fit. I trust Him."

"Even when your husband is dead?"

"Jacob is not here. God is. He has never left me. Never made me go without. And now, He has sent you." Mitra's smile was full and almost ethereal. "I am blessed!"

They hugged again. Fekiria could not help the laugh that bubbled up. "For once, I understand how frustrated my parents and cousin were when I refused to do what they wanted."

"And would you change anything?"

Fekiria shook her head. "That is not fair. I was a rebel."

"You were a young woman who knew what she wanted."

More firmly, Fekiria said, "I was a rebel. . .who knew what she wanted."

—⁊⁊—

Kabul, Afghanistan
11 February—1140Hours

The truck idled noisily after a supply run as they waited at an intersection for traffic to loosen up, gazes swinging to rooftops, doors, alcoves, alleys. . .constantly assessing for possible threats.

"Hawk," Dean said quietly. Firmly. "I need to know."

Clogged traffic was the perfect ambush opportunity. Brian's nerves thrummed, and he stayed eyes out. "Know what?"

The captain eased the truck forward and cleared the intersection as Brian took in the buildings, the people. Tried to talk himself out of the adrenaline rush crowding his brain. This wasn't Bagram Airfield.

Taillights lit up in front.

The captain nailed the brake.

Brian reached for his Glock.

"Easy," the captain said, a hand held low as he navigated around the sudden jam. Once they were moving freely again along a wide multi-lane road, his CO cleared his throat. "When you were in holding, I saw the logbook of visitors. Last entry was Zahrah."

Brian frowned. "Double Z never visited me." He looked at his captain. "Is that what you think? Me and Double Z—?"

With a laugh, the captain shook his head. "No. I know how she feels about me."

"Then what is this about?"

"Why was Fekiria visiting you at the jail?"

Brian shoved his attention to the dilapidated buildings they cruised past. Then the hospital that loomed on the right. The grocer right next to it. He'd been back with the team almost a week and the questions hadn't come. The others had respected his privacy, but Brian knew eventually the captain would call him on it. He'd wanted answers. The time had come. "I can't answer that."

"Why?"

"It's not mine to tell."

"But she was there?"

Brian said nothing.

"I don't understand."

"You and me both." And it still stung that she hadn't come out of concern for him, but to save her own hide. A woman with that type of self-absorbed interest wasn't worth his time.

"The SEAL you fought with said it was over a woman."

The insinuation hung icily in the truck despite the buildup of almost warm air.

"Hawk, I need to know I can trust you."

"You already know that. If you didn't, no way would you have picked me up at the base. No way would you let me back on the team." He didn't mean to come across so strong, but he wouldn't break his word. Even though she stiffed him. "You also know I'd tell you if I could. But I can't—I gave my word. But it's nothing that would jeopardize the team. I wouldn't do that."

Walls closed in on them as they wove through a series of alleys. The captain cut the wheel tight. Drove through a wide opening covered with a heavy tarp. The material thumped softly against the vehicle. No sooner had their vision blanketed than it cleared. A double door swung open wide, and they careened into the open area.

The captain revved the engine and raced into a narrow area that didn't look like it had enough room. But he never hesitated. Brian felt himself sucking in his breath and trying to thin his shoulders as they raced down another alley then veered left. Into a warehouse.

Light blinked out before the rip of the brake.

"Home sweet home." The vehicle creaked as the captain climbed out.

Computers, monitors, and printers dominated the bulk of the room from the far left all the way to a small curtained-off area that must be shielding bunks. Cables snaked in and around everything, making it look like a spaghetti factory exploded in the room. A fridge and what looked like a door that led to a bathroom sat off to the right.

Headphones on, Falcon looked up. Gave Brian a curt nod.

Feeling's mutual. The WO1 never had much love for Brian, their personalities like oil and water. And Brian had to admit, it bugged him. Falcon was so much like his father, and no matter what Brian did, it was never good enough. But his mistakes were always the end of the world. Hard to have respect for a man who held others' mistakes over their heads.

Which. . .is exactly what you're doing.

"Drop your gear over there," the captain said as he went to the command center. "We have a lot to get done. There's a massive storm coming in. Should be here in a couple of days. Best if we're cleared out by then."

Brian tossed his sack and let it slide across the dirt and cement floor. "Two days?"

Eagle shrugged. "Give or take, but it's a beast. Could knock out power."

With a sigh, Brian headed to the computers. Eyed the systems. Eased into a cold metal chair and started scrolling through feeds and data. A couple of hours later, he looked up. Met the captain's eyes. "This all we got?"

"For the most part." He flicked a finger toward the team daddy. "Falcon's got a lead on an Asian chick."

"She's been very busy but also very repetitive," Falcon said. "Took me awhile to lock on to her."

"Repetitive? How?"

"She has friends in high and low places—ISAF and ANA officers, dignitaries, and a secondhand shop. She visits him every other day. Vanishes inside and is there for an hour. We can't figure out what she's doing."

"She's rich, and she has an entourage," Titanis added. "I've tried tailing them, but they're experienced."

"*Too* experienced," Eagle said. "We lose them every time."

"What about the bogus orders? We figured out anything else about them?"

"No," the captain said. "Burnett has a team working on it."

"Speaking of," Falcon said. "They pinged us, verified our location."

Captain Watters's eyes seemed to spark with hope. "Think they found something?"

"Or he just wants to make sure we're actually working," Falcon said. Though it sounded funny, it wasn't. Not by the look on Falcon's face.

"I'll do some digging around," Brian said. "Oh—and it might be nothing, but I caught sight of a hacker name at Bagram."

"Nothing can become something fast," the captain said.

"Osiris. I think our terrorist is Osiris, or maybe that's the name of the operation." Man, it was good to be back. To get active again. Quit sitting on his thumbs. "I'll dig around in chat rooms and the like to see if anyone's heard anything. With what he's accomplished, it's got to be there."

"Work fast," Falcon said. "You've got forty-eight hours."

—∿—

Kandahar Airfield, Afghanistan
13 February—0950 Hours

Preflights. Walk-arounds. Run-ups. Instrument sweeps. Fuel checks. Old hat. Yet it never got old.

Fekiria sat in her cockpit, helmet on, feeling the *thwump* of the rotors. The vibration rattling through her entire body. The whine of the engines as they screamed to life. One hand on the cyclic and one hand on the collective, she eased it forward and the bird dipped forward slightly as the tail lifted. As the helicopter rose, it leveled off and pulled her up into the clouds. They settled into a steady pattern as she practiced maneuvers over the city surrounding the base.

"Doing good," Captain Ripley observed from his seat. "Nice and smooth, Lieutenant Rhmani."

It was weird hearing that name. Hearing it from him when he knew the truth. Did it bother him to call her that?

"Storm's rolling in thick," Captain Ripley said as they streaked through some heavy cloud cover, precipitation caressing the hull.

The condensed water vapor created a wall-like feel, blocking her vision. The air felt heavier, colder. It wasn't just claustrophobia.

"They say it's going to be a bad storm." She voiced her thoughts as they broke cloud cover. After a glance at her instrumentation and fuel gauge, she calculated they had been out about twenty minutes.

"Let's take it up some. Head northeast."

Fekiria judged the instruction. Looked in that direction through her tinted visor. One end of the Hindu Kush stood mighty and proud before them. "The mountains?" Her heartbeat spiked a little. "Really?"

"A quick pass should be fine," he said, his voice deep and a bit staticky over the mic.

She adjusted course before he could change his mind. The chopper veered upward, skimming the mountainside with enough room to protect them against unexpected wind gusts. Or unfriendly fire.

The bird rattled a bit, making her palms sweat.

"Nice and easy," Captain Ripley said, his words reassuring and warm.

Fekiria breathed a little easier as they crested the top. She traced one of the spines, smiling down at the incredible view. "It's so much more beautiful than the view from the city."

Snow had already covered the higher peaks and was dusting the lower ones now. A thick coat painted such a beautiful, monochromatic tapestry with trees shooting up out of the white defiantly.

Her gaze hit a path of snow rutted by wheels of a vehicle. Or maybe several vehicles. "Cannot imagine living up here. Too cold. I think the altitude would get to me, too."

"But you'd have one spectacular view of Afghanistan."

"This is true," Fekiria said with a smile. She looked to the south and spotted several long stretches of paved lines. "Is that an airport?"

"I've heard a local prince or something owns it."

As she circled back, Fekiria leaned the bird a little. A decent-sized structure jutted up out of the snow and rugged landscape. Not a shanty, one probably used by Bedouins or sheep/goat farmers. The tracks she'd noted earlier dead-ended at the building. In fact— "What is that?" She spied a half-dozen trucks parked around the building. Not old, broken-down pieces of junk. But newer, all-terrain vehicles. "You seeing that?" She captured the images on her chopper's underbelly camera.

"Pretty interesting, considering the storm coming."

Fekiria noted her fuel gauge and made the obvious call. "Guess fun time is over." She smiled, invigorated by the incredible view of the Hindu Kush.

"Command is predicting all aircraft will be grounded."

She shivered, even with the flight suit and her thermals. Something ominous hung in the clouds, and she was very glad she'd be holed up on the base during the storm. Or she might try to purchase some supplies and take them to Mitra and the girls.

She took care and precision in landing the chopper back on the tarmac. As they ran through their checks and logged the flight, Fekiria couldn't stop thinking about her friend. How would the girls do if the storm knocked out power?

"You heading to dinner now?" Captain Ripley asked as they went inside.

"Actually, I think I'm going to visit Mitra and the girls. I'm worried about them with that storm coming. I think I'll grab some blankets and food for them then head over there."

"Can I help?" Expectation once again hung in his gray eyes. The color of the olive flight suit amplified the hue.

"I. . ." Even as she hesitated, she saw his shoulders drop a little. She had no legitimate reason to refuse him. "Sure. Meet back here after showers?"

He smiled and nodded. "Done."

At least he hadn't said, "It's a date." Fekiria headed to her locker. She worked the combination lock and opened it then snatched out her toiletries. After a quick shower, she returned to her locker. She pulled out her clean uniform.

A manila envelope slapped the floor.

Where had that come from? She retrieved it. No markings on the front or back. She undid the clasp and opened it. Two pieces of paper slid into her hand. Her heart vaulted into her throat. In Arabic script one read:

It seems you have forgotten you are a Muslim first and foremost. An opportunity for forgiveness is coming.

With trembling fingers she separated the letter from the printed-off image of Captain Ripley. Not just any picture, but of him. Today. On the tarmac—with her. Her head spun as she read the words scrawled across the bottom: *Obey or he dies!*

MITCH

Mitch sat on the edge of his cot with a military-grade iPad in hand. He pulled up the latest e-mail Sienna sent a few days ago. He'd watched the attached video a half-dozen times since. But heading back into the field after a medical recertification course, he wanted to burn these images, their voices into his head.

"*Hey, Mitch. It's me.*" Sienna tucked her chin and smiled. She looked like she might actually be blushing. "*The kids have a special thing they've put together for you. We hope it makes you smile—a lot. But. . .uh. . .be nice.*"

Even though he'd watched it many times, her voice and warning to be nice to his own kids made him smile.

Sienna glanced over her shoulder, blocking his view of whatever she was looking at. Her long neck was tanned and bore a plain silver chain. "*Ella, you ready?*"

"*Yes yes yes! Get ready, Daddy,*" Ella shouted from somewhere off screen.

"*Okay.*" Sienna whirled away from the iPad.

Mitch leaned forward, confused at first with what he saw. He finally realized a sheet had been hung along the back wall. Styrofoam piled up made a snowman. There were paper snowflakes dangling from the ceiling.

Music played in the background.

Tears came to Mitch's eyes as his daughter and son once again acted out and sang a scene from the movie *Frozen*. His little girl was quite the actress. He'd called her a drama queen from the beginning. Thought of her tiny hand clutching his fingers when she was a toddler. She knew how to work him over the same way her mother had.

Mitch opened another video Sienna had sent shortly after their aborted Six Flags trip. In it, Ella read a picture book—word for word. It was her favorite book about how much she loved him. He loved watching this video because it was normal. In the midst of his insane life and fighting terrorists, it was good and comforting to know his kids were home safe, living a normal, quiet life. That's what he worked for. That's what he fought for.

After that one, he surfed over to the one of Noah at baseball practice. The kid had a good swing but tended to close his eyes and miss the ball. They'd work on that when Mitch got back home soon.

His iPad cut the video off, indicating a Skype call from Sienna. His pulse kicked up a notch as he answered the call. "Hey."

"Hi." Bright brown eyes met his through the feed.

"I was just watching the video. I can't believe you got them to do that."

She smiled. "Ella had more fun. I think Noah hated being Kristoff, but it was that or Anna's sister, Elsa."

Mitch laughed. "I bet!" Man, he appreciated her. "Thanks for being so good to them. I hate not being there."

"No worries. I love them, so. . ." She shrugged then looked away, her throat processing a swallow. A nervous swallow. And then he saw it. Saw her hesitation.

"You okay?"

"I. . .I just—"

"Harrier!"

At the sharp bark of his name by Captain Watters, Mitch sat straight. Glanced at the iPad. "I'll call you back."

"O—okay."

He hit End and looked up as Watters's long stride carried him into the tent. "What's up, Captain?"

He thrust his chin toward the device. "On a call?"

"Just ended. I'll call her back later."

Watters's left eyebrow winged up, but then he held out an envelope. "Came in from the CO. You weren't on base, so they asked me to deliver it."

A sickening dread filled Mitch's gut. He tossed aside the iPad and stood, taking the envelope. "What is it?"

"I'd wager it's not good news." Watters stood with his hands on his tac belt, watching.

So. No privacy. With a breath for courage, Mitch slid his finger under the envelope flap, tearing it open. "It's from JAG." The only words that would register in his mind were the most ominous:

Leitner Vs Black

His heart plummeted as he read what he'd anticipated. "My in-laws are suing for custody of the kids." He lowered the notice. "My kids. *My kids*, and they want to take them away from me!"

"Nothing like getting stabbed in the back while you're fighting a war."

"They never liked that I was in the Army, but this. . ." He waved the letter. "Couldn't have dreamed they'd do this. Ella and Noah already lost one parent. I might not be there all the time, but when I'm there, I'm *there*."

"What're you going to do?"

"Fight it," Mitch said, working hard to restrain the pitch from his voice.

"Leave during this mess?"

"How can I not?" This time, his voice rose. "If I stay here and ignore this, they'll move forward without me. I'll lose Noah and Ella!"

CHAPTER 21

Kabul, Afghanistan
16 February—1905 Hours

Hawk, anything?"

Brian roughed his hands over his face as he dropped back against the rickety chair and glanced at Falcon. "I got a whole lotta nothin'." With a shake of his head, he tucked his hands up under his armpits and stared at the monitor. "And that's telling."

"Telling you what?" the captain asked as he spun a chair and straddled it backward.

"I have no idea." Brian shifted and straightened in the seat. "Normally, there'd be some type of chatter, probably not anything that would be really helpful, but noise. Street talk about something happening. It's crazy quiet about what's happening here, and a mess like this with our communications would have the cyber underworld lit up like New Year's."

"Command's probably keeping a tight lid on this."

Brian snorted. "You can't keep a lid on something like this." When he saw the narrowing of Falcon's gaze, he leaned on the table. "Geeks talk. And we know how to talk so most of you normals don't know."

"Wait." The captain cast him a strange look. " 'We'? " He slapped his knee with the back of his hand. "You including yourself in the geekdom?"

There it was. The ribbing he'd worked to avoid all his life. The taunting he'd seen his friends dish out to his father and brainiacs in school. "I'm just saying I know where to look and what to look for." He wouldn't hand them a get-out-of-jail-free card to harass him. "And that's what you want me to do, right?"

"Absolutely," Falcon snapped. "But you're not doing it."

Brian balled a fist. Did he just want him to produce it out of thin air? "If I had workable, usable information, I could get it done."

"Easy," the captain said, his voice laden with warning for both Falcon and him.

Brian met his steady gaze. Again, this was going to be all on him if things went wrong. Never mind the unrealistic pressure. *Ungodly* was more like it. Because what they were facing, the sick jerk taking too much pleasure out of taunting and ambushing them, had no trails. No hint of existence to be found other than he was screwing up their missions and endangering their lives.

But the anger? It wasn't worth it. *Is any of it worth it?* In his mind's eye, he once again saw Davis collapse with a sick thud against the ground. Dead. Davis was dead. He could've stopped it. But instead, Terrorist Number One—TN1—forced him to stand down and watch the bloody tragedy.

Brian shrugged. He pushed up out of his chair and stepping back, he swung his leg over the spine of the chair. "I'm going to get some air." Right now, he wanted to breathe the air of another country. Maybe even another planet.

He batted aside the thick tarp that served as the first barrier to his escape. He strode across the small room and flung open the steel-wood door. Wind slapped his face as he stepped into its bitter embrace. Good. The cold felt good. A wake-up call, of sorts. Getting all hot and bothered in the safe house, they'd lost sight of how little they could control.

Walking a few laps around the inner courtyard where they'd parked the vehicles left Brian drained and his skin tingling. Hands under his armpits, he crouched in a corner that shielded him from the driving wind. An eight-foot cement wall protected them from prying eyes. Shoulders hunched and head back against the freezing plaster, Brian let out a long, slow breath, which puffed around his face. Snow danced on the hazy light of a street lamp positioned outside the compound.

He pushed his gaze upward. Instead of a sprinkling of stars and blinking lights from aircraft, he could only see a wall of clouds. What lay beyond the storm?

It could be a theological question. *God. . . You up there?*

Or a metaphorical question. *Would he survive what was coming?* If they didn't find this TN1, would any of them survive?

Did it matter?

Brian wasn't sure anymore. *Why am I here?*

He once believed in this, in war.

But that. . .that was about making a name for himself. And he'd done that. Became a Green Beret. A quiet professional. A soldier who didn't have to tell anyone what he did because he was that confident in his abilities.

But that hadn't been good enough. For too long he'd had to make his point, his mark loud and clear. Fists and all, if necessary.

Which was stupid. Being a tough mudder didn't save Davis.

The side door squeaked open. A shadowy, hazy form drifted into view. The tall build of the team commander warned Brian a lecture would accompany his arrival.

"That was a first."

Here it comes.

"Good call, walking away like that." Captain Watters stood beside him, propped against the wall. "I thought I was going to have to peel you off him."

The words pricked Brian's conscience. He didn't know what to say.

"What's going on with you, Brian?"

Jaw clamped, he watched the snow again. The frenetic, unruly path the flakes took under the violent fingers of the wind reminded him of his life. Crazy. Unpredictable. "Just. . .thinking."

The captain slid down and sat, forearms on his long legs. "I have that problem, too."

Brian smirked.

"Watching someone under your command get hit is hard." The captain nodded, his gaze out. "It's hard when a friend goes down, but when you're responsible for them—"

"She wasn't under my command."

"But she looked to you, right? And if I know you, I'd bet you felt responsible for every grunt and newb they sent out on that supply run. Right?"

Brian gritted his teeth, trying to push away Davis's face. The thump her body made when she fell. "She was a *good* soldier. She was ready, she followed orders. Had a good mind for strategy." And TN1 blew it out of her skull. "I think she had the makings of an officer."

Taunting whispers of doubt carried on the wind as silence fell between them. The same accusatory, icy whispers that told him he should've followed his gut, not the order. That Davis and Parker would be alive. "I'd been working so hard to be good, to do what was expected of me, to"—he swallowed hard—"earn back your respect. And that son of a biscuit tied my hands and made me watch her die."

The burn started at the base of his throat, forcing another hard swallow. He hated this. Hated feeling weak. Hated giving anyone an opportunity to mock him. Put him down. Compare him to his father. "You know—my dad screwed up his life and, in doing so, screwed up my life and my mom's. I've never forgiven him for that, and now I realize I bear the same shame as him."

"For what?"

"Davis and Parker."

"You're kidding me, right?" The captain shifted, an arm slung over his knee. "Dude, that's out of your control. You did everything you could've—"

"No." He cut his eyes to his captain. "I could've taken that shot."

—⁂—

With a breathy grunt, Dean shook his head. "Man, don't do this to yourself. There was no way for you to know that call wasn't legit."

When he'd signed off on the disciplinary action against Hawk, he had no idea the man that would come back would have this on his shoulders. This wasn't the frame of mind the guy needed. Or one the team needed.

"Are you with us?" Dean had to ask. Didn't want to question one of his brothers, but there could be no doubts here.

Hawk stared out at the snow. "Yeah. . ."

"Can you say it maybe like you mean it?" With the snow and darkness, he wasn't sure, but he chose to believe Hawk smirked. "Listen, I need to let you know"—Dean's heart cinched—"you never lost my respect. I might've been disappointed in your choices, but I know you, man. Like I said back then, you're a top-notch soldier. I wouldn't have you on this team if I thought otherwise. I wouldn't trust you with my back."

Hawk eyed him. "When they put my dad away, I had to fight every day for the respect I ended up with."

"That's the difference here, Brian." Dean waited to make sure he was looking him in the eye. That he really heard him, because Dean had a feeling this was vital for the fierce fighter not only to hear but believe.

"You don't have to fight for it here. You've got it."

Hawk looked down then away.

"What's happening here? What is the denial written all over your face?"

"Nothing."

That *nothing* was a big *something.* "I need you to be straight with me. We have our lives on the line."

"It's just. . ." Hawk ran a hand over the back of his neck. "Nothing. It's nothing. Okay?" He came to his feet.

"No." Dean wasn't going to accept that and stood to face him. "Something's—"

"Hold up!" Hawk craned his neck forward, looking over Dean's shoulder.

"Hey, don't—"

"Cap'. Look." Hawk hurried forward to the old Hummer they'd driven back from the base. As Hawk moved, he freed his Glock, took aim, and fired—into the air.

"What're—?"

Clank. Thunk. Tink.

Dean looked to his right, stunned.

Something crackled and popped—electrical!

As if running for his life, Hawk raced toward the thing, picked it up, and messed with it. Though Dean had no idea what the communications expert was doing, he was *doing* it—fast.

"What is it?" Anticipation and fear tightened frigid fingers around Dean's throat.

Hawk plucked something free. Shot a glare at him. "Someone knows where we are."

Axles popped loudly as tires crunched over the snow. Slivers of light attacked the wood gate that served as the only barrier between them and whatever vehicle approached. And there shouldn't be anyone approaching at this hour. Even someone lost would have to take a lot of wrong turns to end up back here.

As swiftly as Hawk pulled his sidearm, so had Dean. He sent Hawk to the left and he sprinted right just as the wood gate groaned open. They waited until the vehicle pulled in and stopped. On Dean's signal they scurried forward, weapons aimed at the driver and the passenger. He could take out the front two. Hawk would have no problem nailing anyone in the back. They had it covered.

Hands aching from the cold, Dean was warm from head to toe from the surge of adrenaline as he barreled down on the car. "Hands, hands!"

From the other side, Hawk shouted, "Give me a reason not to kill you!"

CHAPTER 22

Kabul, Afghanistan
16 February—1940 Hours

Out of the car, slow and easy," Dean shouted over the engine noise and wind. His heart hadn't slowed since the car entered, even though he felt confident they had it contained. He hoped Sal and the others saw this on the feed and were on their way.

"Hands up or I shoot," came Hawk's yell from the passenger side of the vehicle.

"Out," Dean ordered.

The driver-side door creaked, the hinge no doubt stiff from the cold temps, and gently opened. Two hands appeared over the window frame. Then a heavily graying head.

Dean sucked in a breath and let it out. "General Burnett. Sir. You weren't expected."

"That was the point, Captain." General Lance Burnett pulled his wool coat tight and clutched the lapels beneath his chin as he shot a look at the other soldier. "Am I enough reason not to kill me, Bledsoe?"

Holstering his weapon, Hawk gave a curt nod. "Yes, sir."

Burnett laughed. "Good. I like living."

Thud!

Dean pivoted, his weapon still in his hand, instincts buzzing. Falcon, Titanis, Harrier, and Eagle burst out of the building, guns bared. "Stand down," Dean said.

As the creak of another door drew everyone's attention, Sal started forward. "General."

Hawk reached for the door and drew it open fully as a tall, beautiful blond emerged, and from the rear came two more—Lieutenant Brie Hastings and a male officer, Lieutenant Smith.

A curse froze the chilly air.

Dean glanced at Sal, who had already turned and headed back inside. He stopped hard at the door, glanced at the blond then at the general. "I'm not doing this. No way." And he went inside.

Dean looked to Burnett and the blond. Waited for an explanation, but the way the woman lowered her gaze somberly told him enough. He shifted and angled toward Burnett. "What's going on?"

"A long story. Let's get in out of the cold." Burnett wagged his fingers at the woman.

Dean waited, watching as she joined the general, the other two officers trailing behind as the threesome followed the well-built general into the building. The blond had a thick satchel in hand. Wore Army dress blues.

Class A's? Out here?

"Cap?" Hawk asked.

"Let's find out."

—ɯ—

Lance shook the snow off his wool trench coat as they crossed the room. He'd already told Lieutenant Walker to let him do the talking, initially. And he was glad to see she understood his order. Bringing her in was a risk, but she had intelligence and could help.

"Sir, we didn't have word that you were coming."

"Exactly." Lance turned to Watters as he and the rest of the team came in and shut out the cold. "With coms compromised, we felt it best."

"My men and I could've shot you."

"Could've." Lance grinned. "But you didn't. And good thing." He motioned to Walker. "We might have some good news."

Watters and the others exchanged nervous but hopeful glances.

Rubbing his hands tighter for warmth and effect, he said, "In fact, we have two pieces of good news." The men looked a bit haggard. Better not give them too much excitement. "At least, we're hoping you can verify that." He motioned toward the lieutenant. "This is Cassandra Walker with the DIA's National Military Intelligence Center."

Lance didn't miss that Salvatore Russo had abandoned propriety and shoved his nose into a computer.

The captain stepped forward. Offered his hand. "Dean Watters." With a motion she could follow, he introduced the men. "The one on your right is Hawk. Next to him, the big guy is Titanis, for obvious reasons. Eagle is there with Falcon."

Walker's gaze hit then fled Russo's. No small amount of frustration and tension balled up between Lance's shoulders. He turned to Hastings and Smith. "Why don't you two show them what you found." With that, he took Walker by the arm and led her to the side. "You said this wouldn't be a problem."

"It's not." But again, her wide eyes betrayed her as they bounced to Russo.

"I need you here, Cassie." He made sure she heard him, left a pause for emphasis. "I need eyes on the data, on what they're seeing so you can figure out—"

"I'm fine." Her naturally soft voice hardened. But only a fraction. She knew she needed to offer an explanation or apology. "I just didn't expect his reaction to be so. . .violent."

"I warned you—"

"You did. And I'm a professional soldier. I'll do my job." She met Lance's gaze with unwavering resolution, fiery determination in blue eyes that could melt the strongest soldier. Except Sal Russo. "To the mission, sir."

Lance nodded, feeling the pressure in his chest ease a bit. "Good. Because I need your eyes, Cassie."

"You have them, sir."

"Don't let his attitude mess with you. Put the past out of your head. You're here on my orders, and he'll deal with it like the Special Forces soldier he is."

"Of course, sir."

Lance wanted to say more, to reassure her—and himself—that this would work out. But they didn't have the time. With a bob of his head toward the rest of the crew, he rejoined the others.

"Now, I can get something done," Bledsoe announced as he dropped into a chair.

"The audio isn't the best," Hastings said.

"Doesn't have to be." Leaning toward the monitor, Bledsoe went to work.

"Now you see why I risked getting shot to bring you this?"

Watters gave a lopsided smile, but then he looked at Walker. "What's in the satchel?"

She blinked as if she'd forgotten. "Files, footage, metadata from the situations Raptor has been involved in to date."

"But most important. . ." Lance said as he held out a hand to her.

Opening the satchel, Walker darted a glance to the side—to Russo—as she dug into the leather portfolio. She lifted it out and held it out to him.

"Go on," Lance prompted. She needed to bolster her confidence. Walker had a unique specialty. An uncanny one, really. She could read a situation unlike anyone he'd ever seen. But that wasn't why she was here.

"This is Meng-Li Jin. He adopted the name Daniel Jin a few years ago." Walker passed the photo off to Watters, who studied it then handed it to Straider.

"He looks pretty chuffed with himself," Straider said, his thick accent seemingly thicker with the southern drawl Walker unloaded on the room.

"He is. Rich, powerful, bachelor." Walker crossed her arms. "He's part owner of Takkar Corp."

"Hold up." Bledsoe looked up from the picture, trying to hand it off to Russo. "Takkar?" He turned to Watters. "Isn't that—?"

"Yes," Lance interdicted in the conversation. This information had to be controlled. "Sajjan Takkar's partner."

"Hold the fluff up." Bledsoe folded his arms over his thick chest. "Are you saying Takkar is targeting us now?"

"No, we're not."

Bledsoe shook his head. "Do we know which way is up yet?"

"What we know," Lance slid his hands in his pockets, "is often not verifiable, but I have it on the best authority that Sajjan Takkar is not involved in any actions against us."

"Okay, so why do we care?" Bledsoe asked.

"Because"—Walker lifted her chin, cast a nervous glance to Lance, who gave her an affirming nod—"I believe Meng-Li is your problem."

"*Our* problem?" Watters cocked his head. "How?"

"To be more accurate," Lieutenant Hastings said as she circled the room and stood between Lance and Straider, "he's the entire U.S. military's problem, and for any American."

"What have we done to him?" Todd Archer asked.

"Decades ago, Daniel's father went into business with Dilraj Takkar, Sajjan's father. They had a start-up poised to take off. Then Operation Desert Storm happened. The American government promised all kinds of monetary and military backup if the people would rebel."

"Yeah, we've heard this story before," Archer said. "Didn't end well."

"No, it didn't." Lance hated what happened more than anyone in this room because he'd been part of the command structure during ODS.

"In fact, it ended in tragedy for Meng-Li Gang." Lieutenant Walker went on. "After the Americans pulled out, he was brutally murdered, as were many Iraqi locals who participated in the uprising. Their voices were smothered. Their lives snuffed out. Daniel and his mother lived with one relative after another, until he was old enough to take over his father's position."

"Hold up—how long ago was that?"

"Twelve years."

"So, Takkar let him just waltz back in?" Bledsoe asked.

"It was better than that," Lance said, the bitter taste of irony on his tongue. "Sajjan—whose own father died five years ago—invited Daniel Jin to take his father's place. It was a demonstration of honor and respect."

"So why aren't we calling into question the man who's been helping us?" Bledsoe scratched the side of his face. "Because that's who Takkar is, right? The guy at the A Breed Apart gala? I'm not understanding why he's not suspect in this. Is he friendly or—?"

"*Or.*" Lance let the nonqualifier stand. "Our situation here is Meng-Li—Daniel Jin."

"If he's in bed with Takkar, shouldn't we—?"

"Bledsoe. Listen up, all of you." Lance tried to stow his own frustration. "Takkar will not be discussed. Clear?"

They didn't like it. Neither did he. But they couldn't lose focus, and he couldn't answer questions about Sajjan Takkar. Not here. Not now. Not ever. The fact that he couldn't discuss the foreign operative should be enough to silence the team. They would read between the lines.

"So, why do we need Walker?" Bledsoe's tone wasn't belligerent. "Just curious."

"Because I'm fluent in Mandarin, and"—her very expressive eyes drifted to Russo, who, by the tilt of his head and the set of his jaw, was listening—"I interned with Takkar Corp.–Shanghai for a year."

Sliding his hands in his pockets, Lance leaned on the table. "Walker worked as the assistant to Meng-Li's admin. She has some knowledge on his inner workings. She was the one who came forward with the leads on this case."

Metal scraping against metal announced Russo's move. He stood, fingers resting on the table. "That alone is enough to question everything she says. I vote she leaves."

"Fortunately for me and this mission," Lance said, "this is not a democracy. You have no vote here. If you don't like it, suck it up. She's staying. Get your focus back on the target—find Meng-Li's claws in our system and chop them off!"

CHAPTER 23

Shanghai, China
18 February—0930 Hours

His pearl lay on the satin sheets, her beauty rivaling the opulence of the room, the incongruent beauty of the pearl. He set the symbolic pearl ring on her pillow and stood back, appraising the two. So similar. She had been an irritant, but he recognized that with refinement, with endurance, she would become a gem.

Showered, dressed, he left the room. Sailed through the penthouse and met his assistant, who inclined his head as he gave an upper-torso bow. How he missed the days of kneeling bows. As his people had long done before their emperors. Respect in physical form.

In the elevator, he turned and, before the doors slid closed, saw Kiew emerge from his bedroom. Long black hair tumbled over her ivory shoulder as she stood wrapped in the sheet, the pearl between her fingers as she watched him. Questions danced in her eyes, but he would not answer them. Not with words, not with a smile. Give her too much encouragement and her weakness would return. She would stop trying.

Several hours in the air aboard his private jet gave Daniel time to meditate. Empty his body of the stress toxins and clear his mind so when he arrived he could move forward confidently. He noticed an obvious decline in his stress levels as the Lear descended into Kabul International Airport.

Singular focus must be maintained to guarantee the success of his mission. Coat buttoned, he hustled down the steps of the jet and into the waiting black SUV, where he loosened the coat. The driver pulled away as soon as Daniel slumped into the rich, ebony leather seats. Congestion through Kabul city caused numerous delays, but they were to be expected—and avoided. The driver detoured time and again onto freer streets, affording Daniel even more contentment when they pulled up in front of the large, multistoried building precisely on time.

Never early. Never late.

The door popped open, and Daniel climbed out. He stood, securing the buttons once again as his gaze rose skyward. To the top of the steel-and-glass structure that bore not the name of his father and his partner. But of only the partner. Takkar Corp. glittered despite the thick clouds and snow billowing off the mountains. A northerly wind tossed the flap of his coat against his cheek. A slap, as it were, from the spirit of his father, who did not appreciate being forgotten. Being excluded.

It would be remedied.

Teeth grinding, he stalked up the ten steps to the front door, where Waris Singh met him with an acknowledging nod then escorted him to a private elevator, accessed only by a special key Waris inserted after sliding away a metal plate on the wall. What looked like a tiled wall split in half and opened onto an elaborate elevator adorned with granite, mirrors, and gilded trim. Much more luxurious than his own private elevator in Shanghai.

Waris said nothing, and Daniel repaid the courtesy. *Or discourtesy?* He would not speak to this underling, and he knew the man held no little disgust for him.

After ascending, the doors slid back silently. No *whoosh*. No *ding*. Nothing. Just opened and secreted them onto a floor that provided two paths. To the left where an Exit sign offered a perilously exhausting journey to the roof and basement. And to the right a set of scanners and panels guaranteed a more profitable venture.

Daniel started walking. It was not the first time he'd been here. And there would come a time when he would wait on the other side of the door for the guests. It must be remedied that he held no office here. That his father's name did not gleam above the city as Takkar's did.

Again, the paneled wall recessed and a door appeared. Waris accessed it and stepped back for Daniel to enter.

He crossed the threshold, and what met his eyes stopped him cold.

A portrait, at least four-by-five feet, reigned over the large foyer. His belly afire, as if a dragon had been unleashed, he stared at the likeness of Dilraj Takkar.

"It is an incredible likeness, is it not?"

Daniel forced himself to turn toward the voice. To douse the fire within and portray an unaffected facade. "I would have the name of the artist to commission one of my father."

Sajjan Takkar, distinguished in his expensive suit and bloodred turban, stood at the end of the long hallway. "Indeed! Come, friend. Have a seat." Beyond him spread a massive view of the ancient city of Kabul, crumbling like a forgotten, unimportant statue of a prince no longer valued.

Daniel moved toward the man. Though Sajjan was in his fifties, he looked no more than Daniel's own forty years. When he entered the open area, he found lavish sofas huddled around an open fire. All gleaming over the city in which Takkar reigned. And there, reclining on one of the burgundy sofas, was a woman.

American.

"Have you met my wife?" Sajjan turned with an outraised hand. "Nina, meet the son of a friend of my father's."

The woman rose and glided to Sajjan. Something was familiar about her. Something. . .dangerous.

"Meng-Li Jin, meet my wife, Nina Laurens Takkar."

He did not have time for this, for pleasantries. This trip had been made for business, not to leisurely recline on sofas and meet American whores who sought money over morals. Though he gave an acknowledging nod, Daniel turned to Sajjan. "I would speak with you"—it hurt to say the next word, but for the sake of civility and pretense, he did—"friend."

"Daniel, I asked Waris to bring you here so we could have privacy and openness."

He slid his gaze to the woman.

"Mom, you ready?" Another woman emerged from the side, this one dressed in black military pants, hiking boots, and a jacket. "Tony? Ready?" Behind her trotted a massive dog that seemed to control the entire room. And trailing the beast of a dog—

Daniel took an involuntary step backward. *Stop! No weakness.* But that man—*he* was familiar, not personally, but that he was a soldier. He had the bearing that shifted Daniel's confidence. That knocked his reassurance out of alignment.

"Baby, I was born ready!" Though the man's words were casual, lighthearted, there was nothing light or casual about the way his gaze raked Daniel.

"That's my cue." Nina turned to Sajjan, kissed his cheek then whispered something before she spun and smiled at him. "It was nice to meet you, Mr. Jin."

That was why he did not like Americans. Why he used their stupid American name—because they did not understand Chinese name structure. That his name was not *Mr. Jin.* It was Mr. Meng-Li. His first name was Jin. Irritation clawed its way up his spine, digging into each vertebra with razor-sharp talons.

Silence draped the luxurious room, making the cozy setting feel empty. Icy. In his own, temporary isolation, he warned himself not to let this upset the meditation that had secured peace of mind. Sajjan Takkar would not devastate his plans, neither for peace of mind, nor destruction of the American military.

"Daniel, are you well, friend?" Sajjan's voice broke through his thoughts.

He turned to face the Sikh. "I would ask for your help, Sajjan."

The man turned his head, considering. Weighing. As if he might find something lacking about Daniel—absurd! "I'm listening."

Listening. Had he not earned more than a platitude of "listening"? Where was the commitment their fathers had sealed in blood decades ago? Had he been wrong to think this man would work with him to tear down their common enemy, the one Muslims termed the Great Satan?

"You know what I like about you, Daniel?"

The words drew him away from the window. When he turned, he found Sajjan sitting on the massive sofa that dwarfed the rest of the living area. Waris had taken a seat on a bar stool, one leg propped on the foot support rung near the bottom.

"Your dedication is unshakable." Sajjan straightened, forearms resting on his knees as he scooted to the edge of the dark cushion. "While you had so little, you fought and created an empire."

"With no thanks from"—*careful*, he warned himself—"those capable of assisting."

Sajjan stood, slid a hand in a pocket, the other coming to rest on Daniel's shoulder. "But your strength, Daniel, is that you did not need their help. The fire within you burned hot and you forged your own way."

"And now," Daniel said, his anger dulled by the generous words. "I come to ask for your help. Does that make me weak?"

Laughing, Sajjan stroked his beard. "I would like to think that makes you wise." He waved a hand to Waris. "We all have those whose counsel we seek."

"It is not counsel I seek." Did the man think him so beneath him that he needed others to tell him which way to walk? How to run? "It is cooperation."

"You have it, old friend."

Daniel's heart pulsed hard. "You have not heard what I need help with."

"But our fathers made a pact years ago that you and I both agreed to maintain."

Lifting his chin, Daniel could not help but stare speculatively. "Perhaps you should know the facts before you agree."

"Then you should think twice before you lay it on the table."

"Where does your loyalty lie? With the Americans? With the Afghans?"

"My loyalty," he said, lifting a cigar from a tray before facing Daniel, "is where I lay it." He sliced the end of the cigar, lit the end, then puffed on it.

"Are you saying you can be bought?"

The man's expression went dark. "You are a friend so I will forgive your indiscretion in questioning my character."

"No insult, I only meant—"

"Have you a favor to ask?" Hazy circles puffed around his head as Takkar stared with those dark eyes, pinning Daniel. "Or a demand to make?"

Indignation coursed through him, hot and virulent. How dare this man! He had taken full control of the company, made it his own, lived fat and rich in a skyscraper when— "The Americans need to be dealt with."

"And how would you propose we do that?"

"Takkar Corp."

"Explain."

"You have one of the best security and technology divisions in the country. I want help disrupting their communications."

"To what end?"

Here was where he'd need to get creative. "With one hand they have played their cards well, pretending to leave the country as agreed."

Sajjan leaned against the sofa, arms crossed, the cigar smoking in his left hand. "And with their other?"

"They have planted rogue teams to remain in country."

"This is old news, Daniel." Sajjan straightened and walked around the room, hovering at the window for a few minutes. "Do not play your own cards here at my risk." He leveled a decisive glare at him. "Takkar Corp. will help you, but only with absolute openness so I can prepare for and contend with the fallout."

Daniel stood stunned.

Sajjan puffed on his cigar. "What do you need?"

CHAPTER 24

Kabul, Afghanistan
19 February—1915 Hours

All truths are easy to understand once they are discovered; the point is to discover them.'" Brian stood before the wall dribbling plaster with years of use. They tacked up their map, the trail, the clues.

"Wise words," Lieutenant Hastings said as she joined him at the wall. "Who said it?"

"Galileo." Brian couldn't make sense of the information they'd gathered. It felt as if he was crawling out of his skin with the lack of progress.

"You know, your personnel file shows you could probably become a Mensa."

Disgust spiked through Brian. He shot her a glare. He wouldn't get caught up in dwelling on his dad. He had to solve this. They had to stop this guy.

"You've sat there at the computer for days working on stuff I've seen some of the brightest minds do back at Langley and the DIA." Hastings folded her arms and studied him. "Yet every test you've taken with the Army, you've passed. Nothing spectacular but just above average."

He gritted his teeth.

"In light of what happened with your father, I can't help but wonder—"

"Don't." Brian pivoted and returned to the bank of monitors where Falcon sat, tracking troop movement, radio coms. "We need something to work with here." Anything to get Hastings off his back.

"Bledsoe." Hastings remained at the wall but faced him. "I believe you can solve this. Why haven't you?"

His jaw dropped. It actually dropped—just a fraction—but he couldn't believe the woman's audacity. He slowly straightened at the insinuation lingering in her words. "What are you saying?"

"Nothing complicated." She went on even as Titanis moved in behind her. Was the Aussie defending her or stepping in to stop her—which really would be protecting her as well? "Just that you've always avoided being labeled anything close to your father, but there's an intelligence in that head of yours I'd bet is off the charts."

"That right?"

"Yes." She wasn't wavering. "What do you need to figure this out, Bledsoe? This doesn't take fists or guns. This is technology, and that's LEGOs to a guy like you."

"LEGOs." *A guy like me.*

"Yeah."

Heat flared across Brian's shoulders but then dumped out just as quick. She was trying to bait him. Egg him on. But it didn't matter. "We're up against a monstrosity of technological engineering." And they didn't have a prayer. Fighting the unfightable. Searching for the invisible.

Elbows on the table, Brian held up his hands, letting them express his point as much as his words. "It's like you—sitting in your comfy ergonomic chair in your snazzy dress blues and thinking you *actually* know how the heck a tactical operation should go, how the men on that team should solve the terrorist attack of the decade just because *you* decide"—his voice pitched at the same time a hand came to rest on his shoulder—"a guy with a brain should've already solved this crap."

Beside him, Captain Watters gave a gentle squeeze of his shoulder muscle. A nonverbal cue to be both careful and calm down. "I think we're all doing our best, and I'm certain Lieutenant Hastings is not implying anything."

Her eyes widened. "That wasn't even close to what I meant."

Brian gave her a mock grin. "I guess I'm not as smart as you thought."

Her eyes narrowed.

He returned his focus to the notes he'd taken, the chicken scratch from hours of scanning the IP trail that ricocheted across the globe. He had the IP hits sorted by location, repeats, unique hits, length of time—anything that might possibly become something.

And yet, it was nothing.

"You okay?" the captain asked.

"Fine." Brian lifted his IP trail and hammered in the coordinates. *Just need a* Titanic-*sized break in this iceberg.*

And of all the stupid, asinine things—to accuse him of *not* trying. The woman didn't know how close to the mark she'd hit with that comment had this been ten years ago.

Or even six months ago.

But he would do anything to chop TN1 into a thousand pieces.

"I'm rarely wrong," Hastings countered.

The woman just didn't give up. "Tell you what, baby," Brian said, feeling the thump of his pulse against his temple. "Give me something to work with, not this rat bait you've suffocated our time with, and I can solve this. But *this* is like a microscopic needle in a haystack. If you had something useful—an e-mail, a voice mail, a recording of—"

"We have a recording," Hastings said.

Brian stilled. "What?"

"We have a recording," she repeated, verifying with a quick look to where Burnett emerged from the other room with Walker.

"What recording?" the captain asked.

Hastings gave Brian a sympathetic look. "It's from Bledsoe's ambush with the supply team."

I'm going to be sick. God had a cruel sense of humor. Though his gut roiled at the thought of having to break that down—

"We've had teams going over it." Burnett sounded like he was justifying.

"Give it to me." Keeping a civil tone wasn't important right then. Figuring this mess out was.

"Our experts have gone over it—"

"Why are you still talking?" Brian knew he was out of line now. "Sorry—but your experts haven't had their butts handed to them. They don't have a vested interest in finding this warped puppy and shutting him down the way I do, the way the men in this room do."

"He's right," Burnett said. "Let's see what he can do with it."

Relief jettisoned the futility Brian experienced sitting in this room, staring at the same figures, numbers, locations over and over. Within minutes, she'd forwarded the file. Slipping on the headphones, he braced himself.

Nothing made him feel disembodied more than hearing himself all but beg for STK authority. He pinched the bridge of his nose as the shots exploded against his eardrums. Cruel images paraded across his mind's eye. Davis. Parker.

He saw her fall. Again.

Again.

Again.

Simultaneously, her saw her smile. Heard her laughter. Her soft but firm voice. Heard her fall again. Saw her fall. Saw her blood-spattered face and gear.

"Hawk?"

As if he'd been immersed in a vat of thick goo, he extracted himself but felt the past, the defeat clinging to him, hot, sticky, and heavy.

"Hawk?"

He opened his eyes. *When did I close them?* "I'm good." He sniffed. "I'm good." Maybe if he repeated it, they'd believe him. Compartmentalization was the only way he'd survive this. He had to shut down the Brian who took a liking to a smart, aggressive soldier. Put her in a box on a shelf at the back of his mind.

Shift over a few aisles to the "locate and destroy" section. Find something useful. Find it, locate this guy, and stop him. "Permanently," he muttered as he went to work. Broke down the noises, the frequencies. Layers of noise. Honed in on the incoming commands. The muezzins. Cars. Anything distinct.

Hours became cloaked in stealth. Though the plunging temperatures permeated the building, Brian felt the fire of a possible lead simmering within. He'd figure this out. Somehow. *For Davis.*

He replayed the recording, over and over. "Whoa." He slid the progress bar a fraction. Released it. "Muezzin," Brian said to himself, listening. "It's close." Whoever made the call for him to stand down sat in a location close to a mosque or tower.

No. The projected voice wasn't dulled the way a voice amplified over a great distance was. No echo. It was there. "In fact, it was very close." But something else was there. . .something—the static crackled. A quick, sudden interruption. Something loud. Something. . .strong. "A bomb. Or an explosion."

His gaze rose as he processed the information, stunned to find the team huddled around the tables watching him. Right. "Wherever this is—there's a mosque close by. And an explosion happened while they hijacked the coms."

"Bombs aren't exactly uncommon here," Walker said.

Falcon straightened. "But in a city where there's a mosque putting out a call to prayer—that should be easier to track down."

"Get on it!" Burnett ordered.

Already ahead of the general, Brian was cross-checking and running possibilities. An expectant hush, filled with research and tapping fingers on keyboards, fell over the structure.

How long had Burnett sat on this? That explosion had been two weeks ago! As Brian's anger crested, his brain registered the address on his computer. His pulse hiccupped. "You gotta be kidding me," he muttered. Double-checked the coordinates: 34°32'06"N 69°0'11"E.

Made sure that's what he'd keyed in.

Yep.

"Holy crap." He snatched a stack of papers, the ones that had the ping-ponging IP. Adrenaline shot into the back of his throat. He sucked in a hard breath as his head snapped up. "Kabul—was there an explosion or ambush there?" Brian glanced at the cities with a mosque that had a report of an explosion nearby.

Hastings looked up from a computer she stood over. "Kabul Polytechnic had an explosion in their science lab exactly two weeks ago." She straightened, hands on her small waist. "There's a mosque within a block of the university."

Brian was on his feet. "Hooah! Getting out of this stink hole."

BORIS

They're in Kabul." I feel like a middle school tattletale as I report in. But this chick is one person I'm not willing to mess with.

"Address."

Biting my tongue, I resist the urge to make her say please. Instead I rattle off the location and hope this staves off her desire to turn me into dog chow. Even as I finish the information, I get a tweetle on my personal monitor. Another monetary donation to the Save Boris Foundation. *Cha-ching!*

The line is dead before I can bother her anymore. And really, it's just better that way. Because with them out of *my* hair, I can get back to work on my exit strategy. One more payment and I'm outta here.

It's hard not to curse myself. This wasn't exactly rocket science, this gig. And it doesn't take a genius to figure out I'm working with some seriously messed-up people. Normally, taking advantage of someone so eager to do wrong to another person is easy. And lucrative. Even before they come off the adrenaline high of their victory, I'm half a country away. This time, I'll be on the other side of the world. As far from their slimy, deathlike grip as possible.

Seriously. These people are a major wake-up call. I'm getting careless. No way should they have been able to find me.

But to be clear—they haven't really found me.

Not the *real* me.

They found the newest me.

But not the born-from-my-mother me.

And they won't. He doesn't exist anymore. Can't exist. If he exists, I die. And I mean *me*. Flesh-and-blood me.

Now that I've got some money and milked them for what they're worth, maybe it's time for some payback. Just. . .need to figure out how. On my tiny Fly-fly screen, I watch the team. They're in this new place.

207

Big improvement on the last place, which was deeply hidden—well, not from me, of course—but a rat-infested, falling-apart ghetto.

This. . .at least the windows actually have glass. There are curtains. Thick rugs run the length of the room and cushions provide these hardened soldiers a place to lay their heads. Real shower and bathroom. A working kitchen. None of that makeshift crud for them here.

Say it with me now, "Aww."

Gag!

Let's keep it real—they're as good as dead.

But what if they're not?

The rebellious thought is thick and sweet on my tongue. "Now, wouldn't that be the ultimate payback? The Rich and Famous want these men dead."

Eyeballing the monitor, I watch as they lean over a table and some maps. Geared up, tough-looking, the men are ready to brave the oncoming storm. That would, of course, be quite literal since a total whiteout is predicted for the area in the next twenty-four to thirty hours.

"What if the prey goes to ground? What if they don't die?"

Assassin Chick will be on my butt again, but I'm good with that. I can handle her. At least—I can lie really convincingly. How would they know who helped them? I've helped them once before. Idiots didn't even know.

Don't get me wrong. I'm not taking sides. Unless it's *my* side.

Yeah, I need to let this annoying assassin chick know that they don't rule the world. But this will have to be done in a way they can't figure out it was me.

They asked for the location.

Which means they plan to hit the team.

What's the fastest way to hit them?

Dispatch a local team.

Right. Sending toy soldiers against professional mercenaries. Men trained to detect trouble.

So I'm guessing they'd send something a bit more high-powered. Something less able to be detected or escaped from.

A bomb?

Hm, maybe. But a little overkill.

Unless it's an aircraft with a strategic hit.

"Ohhh." To do that, they'd have to launch from somewhere close.

Because with this storm, they don't have long-range time. As my fingers hit the keys, I'm suddenly hearing Commander Data from *Star Trek* singing that song—the one about "tiny little life forms."

CHAPTER 25

Ease off the stick."

Fekiria obeyed, though her instincts warred with the decision. "It feels...wrong." Chastising herself for such a weak response, she searched for a more technical term.

"Remember," Captain Ripley said, sitting in as her wingman, "weather affects the birds, even the steel, multimillion-dollar ones."

His words were instructional. She knew that. But it was hard not to feel patronized. She did not have the experience or number of hours he had, but she knew when her aircraft felt...wrong. *Bah!* Why could she not figure out what was wrong?

That was it—nothing was *wrong*. Just...off.

With a quick glance at her navigation controls—*wait!* She snapped her attention back to... *What?* What had she seen?

I am going crazy!

"Okay, let's RTB."

Frustration choked her. She sighed. "Roger that. RTB." After notifying the flight tower, she aimed them back in that direction. Wind buffeted the aircraft, but she managed the controls just fine.

"Whoa, Rhmani. We're heading south, southeast."

"Negative," Fekiria spoke to Captain Ripley, staring at the indicators, her navigation control, and maps. She scanned the skyline, mostly hidden by the swirling storm that had overtaken most of Northern Kabul. "I am—" Fekiria snapped her mouth closed. Felt a cold rush down her spine. The readouts—*what on earth?* Her mind raced.

"Correct our course, Lieutenant," Captain Ripley said, his voice calm, void of alarm.

But that alarm spiraled through her. She had not entered this course. How— Why? *What is happening?* She brought the aircraft around and headed back north toward Kandahar Airfield.

Her heart thudded still as she set down the bird, uncertain what had happened. After their postflight walk-around, Fekiria still felt shaken. And she did not want to talk to Captain Ripley about it. Hopefully he would just think it was a rookie mistake.

But it wasn't! I am a skilled pilot.

"Hey," Captain Ripley called as he came toward her. "Are you okay?" With a furtive nod she tried to wave off his concern.

"Your voice sounded strained."

"I—" She could not lie. "I do not know what happened. Things just. . ." Could she trust him? Would he believe her?

"Obey or he dies!"

The threat silenced her. "Yes, I guess I'm too tired." She started toward the hangar, ready to put it all behind her.

"Weather really mucks up the navigation. All the same, you did a great job out there."

"You are very kind—and a bad liar."

Captain Ripley laughed. "Guilty as charged." He opened the door for her and waited as she entered. "Are you headed out to see the girls tonight?"

"No, I will go tomorrow. Stay the weekend with them, help as I can."

"I enjoyed last weekend."

"Mitra was very grateful. She has told me several times how much they appreciate the extra supplies you gathered."

"We've got a truck with supplies coming in tomorrow morning. A friend up at Mazar-e sent down some kids' clothes and shoes for them," he said as they entered the narrow corridor that, at the end, split off to the locker rooms. "I'm hoping they can use some of it."

"You asked them to send the clothes?" Surprise wiggled through her.

He held her gaze for several long seconds. Then, in the space of a heartbeat, his fingers caught hers. "They needed them. Besides, our troops aren't here just for combat and scenery." His smile widened. "We want to see the people taken care of and treated well. Besides, I think Aadela might be my new girlfriend."

"She is quite taken with you."

Captain Ripley inched closer. "She doesn't have anything on you though."

He was so different. Not at all like Sergeant Brian. Arrogant. Angry.

Attractive. Captain Ripley was attractive. But not in the same way. Or more correctly, his appearance did not affect her the way Sergeant Brian's did.

"I should go." And yet, she didn't move. She let herself stay there. Gave herself permission to see what would happen next.

The softness in his gaze remained as he slowly craned his head forward.

He's going to kiss me.

Her stomach knotted, his cologne, crisp and strong, tickling her nose.

"It seems you have forgotten you are a Muslim, first and foremost."

The note—it was a threat against Captain Ripley.

Which meant she must protect him. Protect them both. She took a step back. "I'm sorry." And she was. Curiosity had her by the throat. She wanted to know—would a kiss change everything between them?

It would. It absolutely would.

Because they would kill him.

Fekiria knew in that moment that her brother was somehow connected to the note. To the threat. All her life, he had been as adamant as Baba about her obeying their customs. Restrictions. As the eldest son and because of the power Baba allowed, Adeeb acted as an authority figure to her and her siblings.

"See you in class Monday morning," Captain Ripley said, disappointment thick in his words.

"Good-bye." Fekiria headed toward the locker room. Bathed in darkness, the room had a chill to it. A shudder rippled through her as she reached for the light switch. The lights flickered on the fluorescents popping to the left.

Cold steel pressed against her temple. "Time for forgiveness."

MITCH

Mitch removed his ruck from the overhead bin and shuffled down the aisle of the plane with the rest of the passengers. He made his way out of Dulles International and headed to his truck. Nothing like being home. Driving his own truck. But even if he was out of the combat zone, they couldn't take the fight out of him—not even driving down the highway, assessing situations. Instead of seeing a shrub on the side of the road, he saw a potential hiding spot for an ambush. A soda can tumbling down a sidewalk triggered IED memories. He'd gotten used to the hypervigilance and learned to manage it. Forty minutes later, he pulled onto his street and noticed the white Toyota Avalon parked in front of his townhome.

Sienna.

His heart did this crazy jig, comprised of excitement and apprehension. He liked her a lot more than he probably should. And in ways that left him troubled and yet anxious to hear her voice and see her smile. But her dad... Had Will tainted Sienna's view of him?

Only one way to find out.

Mitch grabbed his ruck from the seat, climbed out of the truck, and headed up the steps. He let himself into the house. The warm, sweet scent of tomato and—he lifted his chin to inhale the spices... sausage?—hit his nostrils. Laughter reverberated from upstairs—Ella was giggling over something.

Smiling, Mitch dropped his gear and headed toward the kitchen... which sat empty. But on the counter was a baking sheet with steaming french bread. A bowl of salad. The oven light was on, giving away the apple pie baking. His taste buds squirted across his tongue. On a cooling rack, he spied the culprit of the spices and tanginess he'd detected when he first came in—lasagna. His mouth watered.

Lasagna. Salad. French bread.

He turned and stopped short.

Wearing a pale blue blouse and jeans, Sienna leaned against the pantry smiling. Her hair hung loose and curled around her long neck. "Trying to steal some before dinner?" She looked amazing, like. . .*home.*

Mitch hauled his brain back into line and held up his hands. "No, ma'am."

Her expression sobered as she stepped toward him. "It's good to have you back, but I'm sorry. . .sorry it's under these circumstances."

This close, he could smell her perfume. "It's not your fault."

She tucked her chin, worrying the edges of a pot holder she'd picked up. "I feel like it is. I think, 'if only I'd shown them more of the father you are,' or if I'd—"

Mitch touched his finger to her lips. The visceral reaction to that startled him. He felt his gut clench. Noticed her eyes widen. All in a split second. "It's not your fault, Sie." He brushed the hair from the sides of her face, telling himself he was crossing a line but unable to stop.

Sienna shifted, just marginally, but enough for him to notice the hitch in her breathing.

"Daddy!" Ella's sweet voice burst into the moment.

Mitch turned and caught his six-year-old daughter in a bear hug, forcing himself to act like nothing happened. "How's my angel-bear?"

"Hungry!" she said.

"Me, too. When are we eating?" Noah trudged into the kitchen with a gaming device clutched between both hands.

"In fifteen minutes." Sienna handed a stack of plates to Noah. "Set the table, please?"

"I'm going to shower up real quick. I feel like the sandman." It took him less than ten minutes to shower, change into some clean duds—which he'd put a little more effort in choosing than normal—and appeared as the food was set out.

Dinner went quickly—too quickly. He wanted these minutes, what felt like "last minutes" with his kids. Not that he thought he'd lose. What judge in their right mind would take away kids from a soldier? There were legal measures in place to protect soldiers from stuff like this.

After their meals, Mitch herded Noah and Ella into baths and then into bed. It felt good, right, to be with them. Aches wormed through him that the Leitners could rip this all from his hands. The thought weighted him, depressed him.

Thankfully, Ella was oblivious to the storm hanging over them. She wrapped her small arms around his neck and hugged him, planting a noisy kiss on his cheek. She snuggled in with her Tweety toy and said good night. Heart aching, he made his way to Noah's room.

On his bed, Noah had a book propped on his legs. The bed lamp cast a cool glow across the bed and his son.

"What are you reading?" Mitch asked as he lowered himself onto the mattress.

Noah slapped the book closed. "Why is Pawpaw trying to take us away?"

Mitch deflated. "How do you know about that?" He sighed. "Ya know what? It doesn't matter. He can try, but it's not going to happen. I'm your father, and I'll fight for you with my dying breath."

Noah looked up at him. "I know you will, but sometimes, life isn't fair."

Folding his son into his arms, Mitch wished an eight-year-old hadn't learned that lesson so soon in life. "I know, son." Losing his mom had taken a big toll on Noah. He kissed the top of his head. "Get some rest. Long day tomorrow."

Noah hugged him tight. "Love you, Dad."

Throat constricting, Mitch squeezed his son closer. "Love you, too, champ." Again, he kissed his head. "Proud of you." He might just cry. "Now, get some sleep."

Eyes burning, Mitch turned off the light and headed into the hall. The possibility was real and cruel. He'd heard of it happening, heard of soldiers losing their kids in unreal scenarios, but he never imagined he'd have to fight this fight.

He made his way into the kitchen, where Sienna loaded the dishwasher. "You don't have to do that."

"Almost done."

Mitch watched her place the last few pieces into the trays. "I appreciate the dinner and—all you've done for the kids." He steadied his voice. "For me."

Sienna lifted her head at that and met his gaze. "Of course. I love you guys." She closed the dishwasher and then wiped down the counter.

"Sure wish we could clean up this mess as easily as you're doing here."

Folding the hand towel in half, then again, she set it on the counter. Smoothed it out. She seemed to be avoiding something.

"Sie?"

She shifted toward him, her hip resting against the cabinets. "I. . . You know I'd do anything for the kids, for you."

His heart beat a little harder. "You've done a lot already. You're like a mother to them, almost more than Ellery ever was. So yeah, I know you would."

Sienna came nearer. "Mitch. . ."

With his gaze, he traced her oval face. Brown sparkling eyes. Pink lips. Auburn hair that hung just below her shoulder. He brushed her hair away from her face again. He just couldn't seem to stop doing that.

When her fingers touched his abs, they tightened.

Mitch slipped his hand around the back of her neck and tugged her closer, telling himself he shouldn't do this. Things were too messed up. The hearing. . . He eased off, resisting the temptation.

Sienna pushed up and kissed him.

Surprised, he stiffened.

Then dove into the passion. Slipped a hand around her waist and pulled her into his arms. She tasted of cinnamon and apples. Sweet. Mitch relaxed into and savored the kiss, savored her in his arms. Wished for more time in the days ahead to explore this. But fighting for his children might put a wedge between them.

CHAPTER 26

Kabul Polytechnic, Afghanistan
23 February—1507 Hours

Book bag slung over his shoulder, Brian sauntered down the main street that led through the university. In traditional Pashtun garb, he wore a fake beard and huddled beneath the warmth of a thick, heavy jacket. "This sucks," he muttered into his coms as he continued, his shoes crunching on the buildup of snow.

"Quit whining," the captain's voice came through taunting.

Brian eyed the obscenely modern cafeteria. "At least they take their eating seriously." The circular building stood in stark contrast to the decades-older structures—student housing, staff office, and the two primary educational buildings—which were in serious need of upgrade. In fact, one of the buildings had been updated, but it still bore the unique marks of the 1970s and '80s. Nothing yet that reeked of high-tech and necesssary to wreak havoc on the U.S. military. But someone from here had somehow hijacked their systems. He'd find them. And destroy whatever they used to do it.

He headed up the pseudo-sidewalk to the first of the two educational buildings. "Entering now," he said low and quiet.

"Copy that," Captain Watters said. "We have you on visual."

Thanks to Brian, they'd hijacked a helmet cam and hotwired it to transmit to a laptop.

"I'd feel better with Eagle looking over my shoulder."

"Breathing down your neck," came the sniper's almost whisper.

"Creepy." Brian stood a little straighter. Felt his ears burn and his hackles rise, but also felt more confident as he walked down the hall, trying doors. Most of the students were gone because of the storm. "Blue one clear." He went to the left. Opened the door, peered in. Rows of tables and chairs. Not the high-end stuff you found in American classrooms, but simple, practical furniture. "Blue two clear." To the right.

"Blue three clear." And so on. All the way down the hall.

"Getting bored," Falcon yawned around his words.

"Join the club," Brian mumbled. He pivoted and started back the route he'd come then banked left. "Crossing."

"Reacquired," Eagle said.

"Entering alpha now."

Another half hour of room clearing and checking. He hit the stairs. "Entering lower level."

"Copy that," the captain responded. "Making good time. Keep it casual."

"Roger." Brian cleared the first two doors without a problem. As he went for the third, the hall ahead darkened. "Contact."

—m—

Kandahar Airfield, Afghanistan
23 February—1540 Hours

"Go." The man ordered her to a helicopter.

On the tarmac sat the Mi-17 she'd been training on. Armed. They wanted her to kill. Fekiria balled her fists. "No. I will not do this thing," she said through gritted teeth. "I am loyal to my people, but there is no need to kill innocent people."

"They are not innocent!"

"Lieutenant Rhmani?" Captain Ripley's voice echoed through the building. "Everything okay?"

"Of course." She tried to smile. "J—just showing *Hanzeer Bacha* around."

The weapon thrust against her spine.

She swallowed the yelp. Calling her captor "son of a pig" was as bad as calling him any other of a dozen curses but without actually cursing.

"If you're sure." Captain Ripley eyed the man as he joined them.

"Captain Ripley," someone called from the side—Colonel Mahmoud. Fekiria's hope leapt. Maybe if he saw. . .

"I must speak with you about the closures." He waved the captain over. "Please. It is important."

"Okay." Captain Ripley turned back to her, but like lightning, his fist shot forward. Right into her captor's face.

The weapon flicked from his hand. Skittered across the cement floor.

A shot fired.

Fekiria frowned at the weapon. Had it gone off?

Another shot.

Captain Ripley grunted and stumbled.

Fekiria saw red bloom across his shoulder. She lunged forward, glancing back and finding Mahmoud with his own weapon raised. "Captain Ripley!" That's when she saw the pool of blood around his throat. He'd been hit twice.

Gray eyes struck hers. Then he collapsed like a table with a broken leg. He just went down. Right out of her hands. "No!" Fekiria tried to catch him.

Hands clamped on to her. Jerked her backward.

"Help!"

The weapon swung in front of her face. "Shut up!"

"Kill me," she screamed at the man. "Then you won't have anyone to help you."

"And what of your friend?"

Tears stinging, Fekiria looked down at Captain Ripley. So still. So bloody. Right there. At her feet. "You've already killed him!"

"And the girls? Mitra?"

She sucked in a deep, painful breath. How did they know about them?

"In the chopper or our first target will be your friend and those girls." The man's beady eyes seemed wild. Cruel. "Now, or I will make a call. They'll die. One by one."

"Stop! You don't have to do this." Hot tears raced down her cheeks.

"Good." He waved the gun toward the bird. "Let's go."

Somehow, she stumbled to the chopper, glancing back more than once. Captain Ripley tried to save her. Protect her. And they'd killed him for it.

Numb, terrified, grief-stricken, she tried to remember what to do. Walk-around.

"No preflights."

"*Dalaal.*" Strong words, calling him an idiot, but he was just being stupid now. "If we don't do them, then—"

"They've been done." His eyes narrowed as he wagged the gun toward the cockpit. "In."

Robotically, she climbed up into the cockpit. She settled into her seat, lifting her helmet as she did. Glanced to the right. To the hangar where Captain Ripley still lay. Her chin trembled. *I am so sorry.*

"No radio contact," the man ordered as he dropped into the secondary seat.

"You can't leave without radio contact."

"It's been taken care of," he said.

Again, her gaze hit Colonel Mahmoud, who stood just inside the hangar. By Allah, if she lived, she would make sure he died. For what he did to Captain Ripley. For whatever he was helping orchestrate now.

"Head to Kabul City," he ordered.

Fekiria powered up the bird, and within minutes they were lifting off. *Dear God—whichever one is out there and real, help me!*

The chopper droned as they made their way out to the city, though the weather made the controls feel sticky and uncooperative. But even as she made her way into the city, somehow the navigation must've mucked up again.

Panic started threatening as buildings grew familiar. This was close—*too close*—to Mitra's home. The girls. She tried to adjust course. Scowled at the controls. "What. . .?"

"Is it clear to you now, who is in control?"

"What are you doing?" Even with the driving snow, her mind filled in the blocked visual cues. A weapons-lock light exploded on the instrumentation. "No!" Her nerves vibrated with panic now. "What are you doing? You promised—"

"Remember what I did to your American boyfriend?"

Arguing that he wasn't her boyfriend wouldn't matter. "Yes, and I did what you asked."

They were within a couple of miles now. She could see the compound with its crumbling roof on the upper level of the main house. "Please! Do not do this. *Please!*"

How were they controlling the instrumentation? How had they taken over her aircraft?

They zipped over the compound.

More tears trekked down her face and trembling overtook her limbs. Breathing hard, she tried to gather herself.

"You must learn a lesson."

The weapon launched.

"Noooo!!!!"

CHAPTER 27

Kabul Polytechnic, Afghanistan
23 February—1600 Hours

Detouring, Brian entered the bathroom.

He pressed his spine against the wall and turned his head toward the door, toward the sound of the approaching man. "Hello?" the man called in Pashto. "The school is closed. You should not be here."

Neither should you.

No need for a body count on a recon mission. Not if they could help it. And he could. Brian slid closer to the door, waiting. His pulse climbed a little, but not too much. Taking down one man—child's play.

The door swung inward, covering Brian.

"Hello?" The man stepped in, holding the door.

Brian slid along the wood. As the Pashtun moved forward, so did Brian. He slipped his right arm around the man's throat and hooked his forearm upward, cutting off air to the man's windpipe.

Thrashing, the man tried to free himself.

With a slight push forward against the back of the man's head, Brian anticipated the sudden shift to dead weight. "Target down," he muttered. He eased the man to the ground, patted him down, located and extracted his wallet. "Moving out."

"Eyes wide, Hawk. The mission just escalated."

"Roger." In the hall, he rifled through the man's wallet and plucked out Afghani banknotes. He checked the next two doors and called them, folding the money into his tunic. This wasn't about stealing. This was about protecting appearances. That man would report being mugged. Having his money stolen would deter suspicion.

But with the man unconscious, a dozen other problems could present themselves. What if he wasn't alone? What if someone was waiting on him? What if he woke up?

Brian's skin crawled. He sped things up but not enough to draw attention. Just four doors left. "Red seven clear." His hand coiled around the next knob. He turned it.

Click.

He looked at the door. "Red eight locked." The narrow vertical window was barricaded with what looked like cardboard. Primitive but effective. "No view."

"Hawk, you've got company coming."

"Clear out. RTB," came Captain Watters's quick command. "We'll make another hit tomorrow."

"Copy. Clearing out," Brian said as he strode to the end of the hall, dumped the wallet in a bin, then pushed his way through the door. Again, the wind smacked and tugged at him. The frigid temps bit at his cheeks.

"Hawk, might want to speed things up," Eagle said. "Two unfriendlies coming into that building from the south. If they find your bathroom friend. . ."

"Understood."

Brian angled right. Through the student housing and quickened his pace.

Sirens wailed in the distance.

Brian's pulse thumped.

"Running might be good," Eagle said in a calm tone that belied the necessary urgency.

Brian broke into a sprint. Targeted a five-foot wall and launched himself over it. He landed in a narrow alley. Jogging, he kept a steady, even pace. Enough to put distance but not enough to make him look like a criminal being chased.

"Two blocks," he whispered as he rounded a corner and tucked himself into another tight alley where he could move moderately undetected. "In view."

A green police truck spun around the corner, sirens screaming.

"Company." Brian threw himself back against an old jalopy, hand on the rusted metal, as he slid around the back side, gauging his surroundings, his options. He watched the truck race past.

Brian peeked out again. Checked the safe house. And broke into a sprint.

The door opened.

Brian dived through. He dropped to the floor, breathing hard. Laughing. "Nothing like a brisk walk in the snow."

"Get up, gear up," the captain said, extending a hand. "Eagle's watching our location. If we're compromised, we clear out, rendezvous with him."

Hopping onto his feet, Brian shook the adrenaline tremoring through his fingers. "Only one room locked—I'm thinking that's the jackpot."

"We can't verify that right now."

"Roger, but I want to hit it tonight."

The commander turned, scowled.

"If we wait—they'll have it cleared out by morning. They knew something was happening. Somehow, they got tipped off."

"Location is too hot," Eagle's calm, steady voice whispered through the room.

The captain's shoulders rose. "Fall back." A beeping pervaded their safe house. "Rendezvous at the market. We'll retrieve you there."

"Copy that."

Freezing out there, and Eagle had to hoof it to the Najeeb Zarab Market a couple of miles away. They'd originally chosen the Pul-e bazaar, but that took him right past police headquarters.

"Okay, gear up. We're"—Captain Watters looked around, scowling—"moving. . ." He turned a circle.

Helmet and boots on, Brian shouldered his way into his ruck as he shuffled toward one of the laptops.

A steady vibration wormed through his boots. "What's that noise?" His gaze rose to the sky.

"Choppers?" Falcon stood. "In this weather? The rotors would ice!"

Brian felt sick. Something was very wrong. Why did he feel like he had a neon target painted on his chest? He glanced at the monitor.

His breath hiked into the back of his throat. A message with a single word. "*Osiris*," he whispered. Then saw a blinking red dot approaching— "Get out!"

—⚔—

The weapon launched. A missile streaked out from the belly of the bird, snatching with it Fekiria's breath. She watched as it tore northward. "I will kill you," she shouted. "I will kill you a thousand times and leave nothing of you for those virgins!"

She flicked the protective cover of the fire switch and tried to shoot down the missile.

Laughter filled her headset, the son of a pig mocking her.

Anger swooped in.

The missile changed course. Darted east then veered.

Fekiria brought the bird around, watching the trajectory of the bomb. "Where. . .?"

"You have done a good thing for Islam, for Afghanistan today."

She trailed the path of the weapon barreling over the city and tracked it as it angled downward. Streaked into a building.

Boom!

A fireball shot into the sky.

Fekiria aimed away from the natural concussion of the explosion but wanted to see what had been so important that the Taliban would kill a captain, kidnap her, and force her to blow up something. "What is it?"

"An American safe house."

—∭—

Can't outrun death.

The concussion lifted Brian off his feet. Tossed him violently, like a giant had grabbed him by the ankles and flung him to the side.

Silence cracked like two beefy fists against his ears.

White-hot light exploded.

Blinded and deafened, Brian knew he couldn't afford to lay there. He peeled himself out of the wall he'd been thrown into, shards of pain knifing through his resolve.

Boom!

Another explosion punched him in the chest. Shoved him backward.

He looked up, feeling a tickle of something along his shoulder. He batted at it, and his fingers came away slick. Must've blown his eardrums. Bent in half, he worked to regain his balance. His orientation.

Peering up through a knotted brow, head throbbing, he saw Captain Watters. Mouth wide open, arm waving. *He's shouting.* But only a warbling noise, like something out of a Charlie Brown movie, reached Brian. How did this keep happening to them?

As his wits returned, he saw something in the sky. Behind the captain.

The chopper! "It's coming back," he shouted. He raced toward the old Humvee. Flung open the rear. Grabbed a rocket-launcher tube. The captain was there, retrieving the rocket. Brian knelt, his knees stinging from the cold water.

Water?

Snow. Snow melted from the fire. He shook his head, ignoring the blazes behind them, and took aim. The captain loaded the rocket, slapped his shoulder, and Brian focused on shooting down that hunk of metal that tried to wipe them out.

"Come to Papa," he muttered, leaning his cheek against the tube. Targeting.

"Hawk," came a warning from Falcon, as if the team daddy thought he'd miss. Or miss the opportunity.

But he wasn't going to rush. He'd do this right and take down this terrorist.

"Hawwwwk," Falcon whined.

"Easy," the captain said. "Take your time. Nail him."

And in three. . .

Hawk cleared his mind.

Two.

His finger rested in the trigger well. His eyes focused clearly on the reticle.

And he eased back the trigger.

Fire streaked out of the tube with a high-pitched whistle. Tore into the sky. Antiaircraft fire barrage tried to dispel the rocket. But too late.

The rocket tore a hole in the hull of the chopper—right where the copilot sat. A fireball erupted. *Whirp-whir* of the dying rotors put the bird in a spin.

A blast of smoke poofed over the bird. Dark and fleeing, an ejected seat shot into the sky.

"Pilot!" Brian shouted.

"Load up!" The captain ran to the front of the Humvee, which had taken on some charming new dents from the explosion, but the old beast worked fine.

Titanis, Falcon, and Brian climbed in. Doors still swinging shut, the Humvee pealed away from the no-longer-safe safe house.

"See him?" the captain asked.

Brian crawled up into the gun turret and searched the sky for the telltale parachute that would safely deliver the pilot to terra firma.

"Cloud cover's too thick," he called.

"Nocs," Titanis said as something thumped against Brian's thigh.

He grabbed the binoculars the Aussie handed off and scanned the sky. Nothing. Nothing but blurry white snow and— "There." He lowered the nocs. "Due east, east. . .northeast."

The Humvee veered that way.

Brian scanned the terrain below as they rose over a bridge. He was able to get a good line of sight on where that pilot was being deposited. Thank goodness they still had daylight. But not much.

"Near the Pul-e Kheshti Mosque. He's going down south of the mosque."

"The market," Captain Watters said. "Is that where he's headed?"

"Can't tell," Brian muttered, watching as the parachute glided down, tossed often by the strong winds of the storm blowing in. "Weather's not making this a perfect guess."

"There's enough of us. We can find him," the captain said. "Sal, get on the horn with Burnett. See if they can get us some sat backup on this."

"Roger." Falcon lifted his secure sat phone from his tac pants.

"Titanis, make radio contact with Eagle. Tell him to get high near the mosque. We need high eyes."

"On it."

"Keep your eye on that terrorist, Hawk."

"Hooah." Brian braced himself as they spun around hairpin turns, raced roundabouts, and took hard rights. All the while he kept the nocs on that pilot. "Still heading to the mosque—wait. No. He adjusted course."

Interesting. All this time and he hadn't navigated. Had the pilot been knocked out when he ejected?

Within minutes, they were on Nadir Pashton Road and headed toward the mosque.

"Hawk, Titanis, Falcon—on foot. Find the pilot," Captain Watters said. "I'll patrol the roads and keep moving."

"Left, turn left," Hawk shouted as he watched the pilot disappear among a tangle of buildings. "Market!"

The captain turned into an alley and slowed.

Brian deployed. Boots on ground, weapon cradled in his arms, he jogged toward the market. Behind him, he heard the thump of more boots.

"All right, Eagle has eyes on the pilot. Went down by the bird market."

Bird market. Right. Only in Afghanistan. Brian headed that way, angling southwest of his current position. But even as he moved, he knew—*knew*—the pilot would head to the market. "Cap', if this guy makes it to the market, we'll never find him."

"Then don't let him make it there," the captain said. "I'll head there in the Humvee."

Even as he toed up toward the main street of the market, Brian raised his weapon. Slowed his breathing. Slowed his racing mind. Being out here, in tac gear, wouldn't be embraced openly. But at this point, he didn't care. They'd get this guy and get out.

Sliding from the crowded street into the smothering market, Brian lifted his chin. *Stay calm.* A lot of people. A lot of things could go wrong. A lot of ambushes could happen here.

His mind warred with the variety of vendors. From the hanging animal carcasses on one side to the narrow stall packed with *shalwar kameez.* A dozen paces down—kites. Fruits.

People. So many people.

"How the heck are we supposed to find this guy?"

"Flight suit will probably give him away? That, and he'll probably run when he sees us," Titanis said, his humor flat in light of the mission.

Despite the cold weather, snow, and pending storm, the people were out in force. Probably stocking up. Something buzzed at the back of his mind. Brian slowed to a stop, scanned through his sights, and paused on an old vender with an opaque eye. The guy's single brown eye shifted to something behind Brian.

Nerves sparking, Brian pivoted, weapon trained.

White flapped as if waving at him. Taunting. Brian hurried forward, grabbed the nylon material wadded in a corner. It hadn't been cut but released. "Got the chute. Pilot's here." Lifting the thick nylon material, Brian walked over to the half-blind vendor. Held out the material. "You take," he said, then said in Pashto, "Where did he go?"

It was a phrase they'd used before in other manhunts.

"I see no man," the vendor said in broken English to match his broken, yellow teeth.

Brian tossed it at him. Scanned the open area. . .and then. . . *What?* He walked to a dried-fruit vendor and toed a slick spot. *Blood.* Into his coms he said, "Pilot's injured."

CHAPTER 28

Kabul Market, Afghanistan
23 February—1615 Hours

Follow the blood!"

Great. Now I'm a bloodhound. "Copy," Brian said as he searched for the next stain.

I prefer sheepdog.

The scattered trail led him down the main market path.

"Raptor, group up around Hawk's location," Captain Watters said. "Pilot is nearby and injured. Let's close the trap."

Brian navigated the congested market. Finding blood would be challenging with the heavy foot traffic and variety of vendors.

"Just passed slaughtered lambs," Falcon said. "Tell me again how we know the blood Hawk found is human?"

"It was next to the chute." Brian searched the packed, cracked path, his eyes bouncing faster than a Ping-Pong ball. His gaze struck a shalwar-kameez vendor stall.

Why were the people just standing around, watching him? And not just watching, but...*anticipating* him. His gaze traveled the clothes that packed the wall of the stall. In particular, he noticed one thing. Closing in, he edged around a couple of men who refused to move. Brian eyed a hanger with a missing floral tunic and hijab. The wide-leg pants... He leaned in closer. Tilted his head. A smear across the hanger and a corner of the pants.

Brian turned out of the stall and moved to the middle, turning a slow circle. "I think our pilot's dressed as a woman."

"Come again?" the captain asked.

"White silk tunic with purple flowers. Same hijab." He smirked. "Probably still has his flight suit and tac boots on."

What a picture that made! He moved along the path, noting the difference of those who stood, staring openly at him. Defying him. He used their nonverbal cues as his clue to the pilot's path.

"Guys, Kabul police coming your way," Eagle said.

"Copy. Storm's kickin' up some wind. Let's get this guy found fast," the captain said. "Report."

Brian eyeballed a mother and daughter who looked at him, guilt scrawled all over their faces, then ducked quickly. "Still tracking." Two yards past them, blood—a big smear. He hurried onward. "Located more blood."

"Coming up on a parallel path," Titanis said.

"Copy," Brian said as he came to a juncture. He scanned the location, the path, the stands. The people. He turned a circle. Crap.

He pivoted. Backtracked a half-dozen paces. Then continued past the cross point seven or eight feet. Had he lost the pilot?

"Hawk, we need to find this guy."

"Roger." Which would be fine if there weren't fifteen thousand people in this market right now. Brian tugged his thermals from his pack and scanned. Nothing. He grunted. Turned.

A blur of a face smeared across his mind.

Brian froze, his mind assembling the information. His heart thundered, telling him it was impossible. His mind was playing tricks on him. But that hijab was white and purple. *That was our guy.*

He pivoted. "Got him." Rushed forward, cheek against his weapon. Toward the spot he'd seen the person disappear. When he reached the apex, he paused. Wanted to curse. A long dark alley led out of the market. A half-dozen doors on either side. At the end, a fence with a hole across the street.

But no target.

"I lost him," Hawk muttered. "Alley off the market."

"Converge on Hawk," Captain Watters ordered.

After a round of "rogers" rang out, Brian let his shoulders slump. He could go in there, try to find this piece of dirt. But he could also end up slaughtered.

White popped out of an alcove.

"Stop!" he shouted, his voice reverberating off the walls. "Stop right there!"

And, of course, the target ran.

Brian sprinted down the narrow alley, weapon in his arms.

The pilot slipped through the fence. Shimmied around a broken board in a fence.

Brian was right on his tail. "Stop!" For an injured target, the guy moved pretty fast. And. . .odd.

Around a corner. Into a compound. The gate closed even as he raced up to it. But that didn't stop Brian. He flung his weapon on its strap over his shoulder. Launched at the wall. Threw himself upward. Caught the lip of the upper section. Felt a snag but pulled harder. Scrabbling, he toed the wall and hauled himself on top of it. He spotted the target limping toward a three-story structure. Believing he was safe.

Brian landed with a soft thud. Took a knee and whipped his weapon around in front, aiming. He moved along the perimeter, his back to the wall, M4 at the ready. With each step, he prayed he hadn't lost the team.

An eruption of lights and shrieks exploded just outside the compound. Brian stilled, clinging to the shadows. Listening behind him, over the wall, to the chaos unfolding there but never taking his eyes off the door his target had gone into.

"Cap'—you there?" Brian whispered.

Nothing. No response.

Brian frowned. "Captain? Falcon?" He checked his mic and nearly cursed at the severed coms cord. *What now?*

Acquire the target. No way he was walking away from this.

Brian slid along the shadows. As he approached the door, he heard voices. Somebody lived here? The place looked abandoned or deserted. No lights. No toys or things left at the door. He scooted into the alcove of the door.

Whispers came from the other side.

Brian took a step back. Lifted his tac boot and slammed it, heel first, through the wood door. It gave easily, weakened from years of disuse.

Weapon up, he clicked on his shoulder lamp. Saw the white material fluttering away from him. "Stop!" But stopping would be too easy, wouldn't it?

Brian lunged after the guy. Two large strides caught him up with the pilot. He rammed into the guy. Drove him into the wall. A yelp.

Brian moved with purpose. Grabbed the guy's shoulder. Jerked him around and drew back his fist, ready to drive it right into—

Green eyes!

Brian froze, fist poised. Heart ricocheting. *"Fekiria?"*

A subtle *whoosh* from the side was the only warning he had before his world went black and he heard a strangled scream.

—m—

Kabul Market, Afghanistan
23 February—1700 Hours

"What did you do?" Fekiria dropped to her knees, hovering over Sergeant Brian. Blood flowed from the side of his head. She pressed a finger to his thick neck, checking for a pulse. It was steady and strong.

"He injured you!"

"No, that is not true." It was a very difficult, confusing story. His team shot down the helicopter, but if Adeeb's men hadn't taken her. . . "Get something for his head. We need to get him out of there, into the room with the fire."

"How do we move him?"

Fekiria considered him. Broad shoulders. Thick chest—the vest made him look bigger! "I. . .I have no idea. But we can't leave him here." Only then did she see his communications device. Fekiria unplugged it and removed it. "Here. Throw it in the fire."

She positioned herself behind him, and after some finagling she managed to remove his large rucksack. Then she did her best to lift his shoulders and slip her hands beneath them. . .then under his arms. But she was too small. She couldn't encircle his chest.

He groaned.

Fekiria eased him down and swung around to his left side, looking down on him. "Sergeant Brian?"

"You know him?"

She shot a look to Mitra but then focused on the American soldier. "Sergeant Brian." She touched the side of his face. Felt a spark in the pit of her stomach.

Another groan.

Fekiria withdrew her hand and rested it on his shoulder. "Sergeant Brian, can you hear me?"

Ash and dirt covered his face, and now blood mingled with it.

His eyes fluttered. With a long, loud groan, he came to. "Holy. . ." He pulled himself off the floor and swung a hand out for balance. Then held his head, eyes squeezed tight.

Fekiria caught his arm, as much to stop him from accidentally hitting her as to help.

"What happened?" he said with a grunt.

"Sorry." Mitra hovered above them, arms wrapped tightly around her small waist. "I thought you. . .she said you were. . ."

"Mistaken identity." Fekiria dabbed the edge of the silk hijab against his bleeding temple. "I thought you were a soldier trying to kill me."

His gray-green eyes fixed on her. "You. . .*you* were the pilot?" A storm worse than the one swinging down from the mountains moved in across his handsome face. "You bombed my team. Tried to kill us!"

"No." Fekiria's heart climbed into her throat. She could not let him believe that. "No, that's not what happened."

"Bullspit!" Anger churned in his eyes. "I was there! The explosion threw me through a wall. My team—" He looked at the door. Back to her. "My team. How long have I been out?" Faster than she thought possible, he was on his feet. Moving toward the door. "How long was I out?"

"No!" She threw herself between him and the exit. "You can't go out there!"

Fury lit through his expression. His brow knotted. With flared nostrils and colored determination, he clamped his hands on her shoulders. Lifted. Turned and planted her.

"Please, no. They'llkillyou!" Her words tumbled out on top of each other as he stepped into the snowy afternoon. Desperate to protect Mitra, the girls, and even him, she lunged forward—

Sergeant Brian collided with her, throwing her back against the wall. Hands on either side of her head, he grunted hard.

The door slammed shut. Apparently he'd kicked it.

His eyes bored into hers. "I just got shot at!"

Fekiria stared at him, stunned. He terrified her with the ferocity of a mountain lion, and yet, she knew enough of him to know he wouldn't hurt her. Would he? "Come inside."

"Answers. *Now*," he growled, his forehead almost touching hers. "Who's out there? How'd you know—?"

"In there. All the answers you want." Why was it hard to breathe? Why did she just stand here, compelled under his power not to fight the way she'd done with every other man? "Please."

He hesitated, a shift in his expression so slight but so significant. And somehow, his hesitation hurt more than anything her father had said to her in a lifetime.

"Please," Fekiria repeated, the ache raw that he did not believe her. Trust her. "I promise."

A flicker of a frown creased his brow, but he relented. Sergeant Brian pushed back. Stumbled. She hurried to him and put a hand on his back and one on his bicep that dwarfed her hand span to steady him. When she leaned in to help him again, he pulled away. Held out his palm. A definite "I'm fine" response.

He moved into the room, sluggish, heel of his hand pressed to his temple.

The girls huddled on the bunk made some noise.

Sergeant Brian snapped alive. Went for the handgun holstered at his thigh.

"Children," Fekiria said as she stepped in front of him, touching his tac vest as she steadied him. "Just children."

He took in the cluster of girls, his jaw muscle popping as he made his way to the rickety table and lowered himself into one of the chairs. "Get them away from the exterior walls. If a stray bullet makes it past the plaster. . ." The rest didn't need to be said. He lifted a large phone from his leg pocket. Punched in numbers.

Fekiria covered the phone. "Please, don't."

His jaw muscle popped again. The way he looked at her bespoke the anger he clung to, and he stepped out of her reach. Put the phone to his ear.

She was so tired. So rattled from the last two hours. "Sergeant Brian, for the children I beg you." But her words fell on deaf ears.

"Hawk here. . .I'm good. In a"—he looked to the side, to where the girls huddled beneath the blankets and peered at him as they hugged each other—"situation." Hand on his tac belt, he walked the length of the room. "No, pinned down. Can't leave."

Fekiria glanced at Mitra, whose face had gone white.

"Yes. A half-dozen others." He nodded as someone on the other end talked, and then he glanced back at her. "I got the pilot."

Fekiria felt as if a window had opened with the icy blast he sent her way.

"I'll lay low then make the rendezvous after dark. . .roger. Hawk out." Sergeant Brian lowered the phone. Let out a long sigh. Roughed his hand over his face—and hit the slick spot of blood.

She motioned to the rickety table. "Come. I will clean your injury."

"No." He came toward her with a menacing expression. "I want answers. You bombed our location. Tried to kill us." He practically snarled at her.

"Sit at the table. I will dress your injury and tell you whatever you want to know."

Again, he resisted her.

"You are angry with me. I understand."

"No, I don't think you understand the first thing about what I'm feeling right now." He angled a shoulder in toward her. "Do you realize how many men you nearly killed firing off that rocket? Men who are my brothers? Men I took an oath to protect? And you want me to sit at a freakin' table and act like that didn't happen? And *where* is my coms piece?"

Fekiria shot him a fierce expression to match his. Then moved her gaze purposefully to the children. "*Please.* Come sit." She tugged his arm.

The brooding man was like a reluctant bull being led by the ring in his nose. "Sit? You want me to sit when men are out there shooting at us?"

"I want this to stop. I want you to listen to me." Her anger flared across her chest, heating her.

"Why were you flying that bird?"

With her own nostrils flared, she moved to the table. Folded her arms. Waited.

Mitra came forward with a bowl and a hand towel.

Sergeant Brian stood unmoving, but she could see the turmoil playing out behind those green eyes. "No time for that. We need to get somewhere safe."

Mitra set down the bowl. "This is it. With the storm, there is nowhere to go. The children will not last in the snow and wind. We have no friends beyond those in this compound."

He stalked toward the rear hallway. "What's back here?"

"Bathroom, empty rooms," Mitra said.

Fekiria closed the distance between them. "You are scaring the girls."

"They need to be scared. This is—"

BooOOOooom!

CHAPTER 29

Kabul Market, Afghanistan
23 February—1800 Hours

*D*own!" Brian wrapped his arms around Fekiria and dove to the ground. Plaster and dirt peppered his head and back.

On his knees, he hauled Fekiria from the dirt and propelled her toward the far wall where the girls were huddled. He scrabbled up behind her and looked to the other woman. "Exit—we need a safe exit!"

"The back, but"—the woman shot Fekiria a worried look—"the children. They're not dressed. They need shoes, jackets—"

"Do it. Hurry." Brian shifted to Fekiria as another mortar round shook the building. "Help her." He shuffle-ran to his rucksack on the floor. After shouldering into it, he knelt. Lifted the sat phone from his pocket as he eyed the women and children. He wanted to curse. How he ended up in a situation like this. . .

Phone to his ear, he waited for the call to connect.

"Watters."

"We're being hit." Brian watched an older girl help the smallest into a jacket and shoes. "I have six innocents. Children."

"We can't move, Hawk."

His gut cinched. "They need help. This place is going to come down. We have to get out of here or they won't make it."

"Hands are tied. Nothing's moving, and I can't get there. It's too hot. Command won't budge. Stay there. I'll—"

"They're *pummeling* us with mortars." Brian gritted his teeth. "This building's going down. We have to move."

"Then get out. Find shelter."

Brian screwed his mouth tight. "Roger." He pocketed the phone and shifted his attention to the woman bundling up a small girl. "Do you have a vehicle?"

She glanced at him as she stuffed the girl's arm into the sleeve jacket. "It was stolen last week."

Irritation clawed up Brian's spine. This night had gone from awful to nightmarish. It was a wonder he was still alive, that he hadn't killed anyone. Yet. He was still ticked with Fekiria. She had some serious secrets. His mind warred with the divergent images of her. Piloting that chopper and blowing up their building. And now the petite woman, head no longer wrapped in that silk number, bent over a little girl and buttoned her jacket.

Girls. Five of them. They couldn't be any older than ten. And the youngest—thank God they weren't toddlers. It was inevitable that a toddler would scream and give them away.

How did this happen? How did he end up a babysitter? To a bunch of kids. Unbelievable.

On a knee beside Fekiria—he wasn't letting her far from his sight, not after what she'd perpetrated against him and his team—Brian checked his weapon and extra magazines. As geared up as he could get considering the situation, he looked at the others. "Ready?" Though he barked it, there was something unsettling about the half-dozen pair of wide eyes that watched him.

Were they afraid of him? Or expecting him to be the hero and save the day?

Neither made him happy. He didn't want to be here. Didn't want to face the questions about Fekiria that had exploded since he found himself face-to-face with her.

"Mitra?" Fekiria eyed her friend then spoke in her native tongue.

Brian hated being the odd man out. He had no idea what they were saying.

Or planning.

No, don't borrow trouble. These women needed to get to safety as much as he did. And they were smart enough, he hoped, to realize he was their way out.

Mitra rattled something in Pashto and seemed to go even paler. She rose and started across the room.

Brian shoved to his feet. "Whoa. No." He caught her arm. Looked down at Fekiria. "Where's she going?"

Joining them, Fekiria explained, "There is an older man and woman who live here, too. She wanted to see if they are okay."

"Not outside. She's not going out there." Was the woman crazy?

Fekiria gave his response to the woman, whose face twisted up in grief.

He handed his secure phone to her.

She shook her head. "No phone."

Over the howl of the wind outside, Brian heard a distinctive, more ominous howl. "Down!" He grabbed Fekiria and pulled her close as he went down, covering both women.

Crack! Thud!

Brian's gaze shot to where the girls had stood. His heart spasmed—between him and them, a pile of debris opened the ceiling. Snow and sleet pelted the mound. Crying, the girls grouped up with the eldest holding them close to the wall. *Smart girl.*

Fekiria shifted beneath him. Brian met her large green eyes. What he saw—a mixture of fear, expectation, and uncertainty—made him feel like a chunk of an iceberg had broken off his heart. "You okay?"

She gave a furtive nod as she pulled herself off the ground.

Brian offered his hand, and she hesitated for a fraction of a second, her gaze bouncing to his then to his hand as he placed hers in his. He tugged her upward, catching her back as she found her balance. Mitra was already over to the girls, and by her tone, she was reassuring them.

"Let's move," Brian said.

Fekiria spoke to the others. "Sheevah, help Aadela."

But the little six-year-old shook her head violently. Shoved herself back against the wall, rigid with fright.

Sheevah started toward the girl, who just kicked and screamed.

He'd seen this before. It wasn't unusual for a child to react so violently to a situation like this. "She's in shock. Tell her to go easy on her."

Fekiria translated, but the little one still wasn't having it.

Brian stepped over to the two, touched the older girl on the shoulder, and nudged her toward the little one sitting on the cot, waiting. He slid his weapon around behind him, out of her sight. Anything to reduce the threat-stress levels she was experiencing right now.

Reaching into a side pocket of his ruck, he squatted before the little one. Winked at her. Drew out a candy bar. He'd learned from his former teammate, Tony "Candyman" VanAllen, to always have a bar or two ready to win local favor. And right now they needed her favor because if he had to haul her out kicking and screaming, they might as well have a homing beacon on them.

He held it in his hand but didn't extend it. She had to come to him. *And quick.*

"Aadela," came the soft whisper of Fekiria's voice in his ear.

He nodded but said nothing.

Aadela. Bright-eyed, short-cropped black hair. Hands and knees held close to her chest, she watched him. Warily. As if gauging whether she could trust him. The seconds felt like hours, with the threat of another hit any moment, as he waited for her to decide he would be safe.

"Tell her I need a friend," Brian said to the side, to Fekiria who hovered behind.

The words came sweetly in Pashto.

Aadela looked to Fekiria then back to Brian.

He turned his hand so his palm faced up, exposing the chocolate bar. An offer. But not an extension.

Aadela shook her head.

Okay, maybe he needed to take the forceful route.

She pointed to his shoulder. Brian glanced at his shoulder lamp. Unhooked it and held it in front of him. Aadela scooted forward. Took it.

Brian lifted her into his arms and rose at the same time. "Go now!"

—◦◦—

Kabul Market, Afghanistan
23 February—1815 Hours

"What do we know about his location?"

Grim-faced and exhausted, Sal scratched his beard as they sat under a bridge in the Humvee, avoiding detection. Avoiding exposure. "It's hot. I don't know what lit that area up, but there's no way we'd get in without being seen." He turned to the small radio he held and grinned. "Bumped into a cop."

And apparently bummed the guy's radio. "What're you hearing?"

"Craziness. They're talking so fast, it's hard to catch—" He craned his neck, listening. Shook his head. Though none of them were fluent in Dari or Pashto, they all had a passing knowledge, able to pick up bits and pieces. Sal had the best grip on the language though. "They're looking for a woman. I can't tell what reason they're giving."

"So, what? They've hit the wrong house?"

Sal lifted a shoulder then went back to listening.

"Can we get them out though?" Talking out loud helped Dean think through the situation, but it also gave the opportunity for one of the others to offer up a solution.

"Unlikely," Sal said. "They've got police, and I've heard some ANA chatter."

"That's a lot of activity for Hawk," Titanis put in.

"So, what? Hawk's in the wrong place at the wrong time?" Dean wasn't buying it.

"Wouldn't be the first time," Sal said with a grunt-laugh.

"But not this time." It felt different. Too quick. "They were on that house before we even got there." Like it was planned.

"Guys," Sal said, his voice strained. "This. . .this isn't military chatter. Or police. It's. . ." His dark brown eyes hit Dean's. "This sounds"—he tilted his head, thinking or listening—"this sounds like normal Taliban chatter."

"You're telling me the Taliban are after him?"

"Or after that woman. Didn't Hawk say he had two women with him?"

Dean nodded. "And the pilot. He's got nearly a dozen innocents on his hands."

Radio in hand, Sal shifted in his seat, the Humvee rocking beneath them. "If we could get back to the base, we could coordinate—"

"It's more than an hour north," Dean said.

"There are kids there—Hawk has children," Eagle said, his tone conveying his frustration. "This goes global if kids die. We'll be put on a spit and roasted."

It was true. Kill as many adults as you wanted, but kill a kid and you ended up on the front page of the news, labeled a murderer. Kids. *How did that happen?* He didn't get the whole story from Hawk and knew he couldn't over the coms. Though their phones were secure, they were all too aware that nothing was "secure" anymore.

"Look, I'm willing to face whatever risk to go in there and help him," Eagle offered, his words thick with concern. "This whole just-sitting-here-talking isn't working."

"But going in could put them in more danger than not going in," Titanis countered.

"So, we just leave them?" Eagle's voice pitched. "In this storm—

it's about to dump a truckload of snow, and the wind coming with it could chew through granite. Hawk has limited weapons and supplies. Children and women depending on him, and we just walk away?"

"Easy," Dean warned. "No decision has been made. We're talking."

"We need to quit *talking* and get moving."

Eagle was right. They couldn't leave Hawk with women and children who were being targeted. "Okay, let's do it."

"Command won't like that," Sal said.

"They rarely do." Dean pointed to the wheel. "Get us over there."

23 February—1825 Hours

Crouched in a darkened alley, Fekiria held Wajmah close as they rested against the damp, cold wall. They'd escaped through a hidden door at the back that led into this narrow enclosure. Wind and snow snaked through the tight space, threatening. Chilling. Mitra slumped beside them, her daughter in her arms. Trailing them, Sheevah and Jamilah hugged each other. Hawk crouch-ran a few paces past them with a monkey-like Aadela clasped around him.

Slowly, he lowered Aadela, motioned for her to stay, then raised his weapon. Head back against the wall. Bracing himself. Preparing himself. With a finger, he nudged aside a board. Peered through. Then to the other side.

He turned his head, and his gaze struck Fekiria's. With a nod, he motioned them forward. A buzzing seemed to rend the air, though the wind howled and in the distance sirens still screamed their presence.

Sergeant Brian grabbed at his leg pocket, digging out his sat phone. He had no pale blue light to give away his location. He pressed the phone to his ear. His words were tight, controlled, low.

Fekiria moved closer, careful not to be noisy. Cautious that she did not upset Wajmah, who shivered in her arms.

Sergeant Brian looked at her as he listened. "Roger. Good." He nodded. "Okay. Ten mikes." He put the phone away and waved at the others. "We have a rendezvous."

Relief spiraled through her. Wait—had he said ten mikes? Was that minutes? That meant. . . "Where?"

"Two klicks northeast."

"Two kilometers?" She tried to keep her voice as controlled as his. "They are children!"

"If they want to live, they move." He handed her his gun. "You know how to use that, right?"

She nodded, mute.

"We go three at a time." He placed a hand on her shoulder. "Cross the street. Take shelter in the next alley up. Bound and cover. No straight lines. You know the drill, right?"

Fekiria's heart pounded. She looked through the wood slot to the spot he'd mentioned. To get there, they'd be out in the open for a solid minute or two. Plenty of time to get gunned down. She would be responsible for making sure the girls were covered. "Are you sure?"

His expression seemed to soften. "You'll do fine. Just keep moving. Do not stop. No matter what."

"You trust me?"

"Yes," he said then smirked. "But if you don't keep moving, they shoot you."

"Right."

"I'll cover you and bring up the rear."

"So you have nothing to lose by sending me first." *He's American. Of course he doesn't care about us.*

Surprise and hurt crowded his expression. He frowned. Then scowled. "You think I'm trying to get you killed?"

Fekiria stared up at him. He stood at least a foot taller. Shoulders broad. Neck thick. He seemed to dwarf her. A measure of guilt coursed through her, but she would not take back the words. She had been betrayed by too many men.

"Baby, if I wanted to kill you, I'd walk the other way. I can hide and never be seen for months. With seven of you, I'm a sitting duck." He leaned into her. "There are easier ways to kill someone. Now, you done holding us up?"

He might as well have smacked her. In truth, his words had. And it hurt. A lot more than she thought they would. "Sheevah," Fekiria said, not breaking his eye contact.

The fourteen-year-old came to her side.

"Take Wajmah." Fekiria turned away from Sergeant Brian. Away from his accusation. But she deserved it. The man infuriated her! "Let's go." She nodded to the opening.

Wide eyed, Sheevah sucked in a breath. Shook her head.

"Across the street, to the alley," Fekiria said. "I'll be right behind you. Do not stop. Run, and run hard."

Shouts and shooting far away startled everyone, gasps and yelps echoing through the dark alley. "See?" Fekiria said. "They are not near us. We must hurry." And with that, she turned and angled herself through the wood slats Sergeant Brian held open.

She scanned the ever-darkening neighborhood. The wind and snow tugged at her collar and hijab as she waited for Sheevah to emerge with Wajmah. A second later the two burst through and took off running.

Running behind them, her back to the pair, scanning and aiming at the same time, Fekiria could only hope they made it. It felt surreal to be on the ground in her own country fleeing for her life. Down past two walled homes and another compound, then they banked right. Slammed up against the plaster wall of the final compound.

Panting hard, she worked to steady her nerves. They'd made it. No one had shot at them. No danger presented itself. Maybe they would be okay. She reached over and squeezed Sheevah's hand. "Stay here. Don't move."

"Where are you going?" the teen asked.

"I must cover for Mitra now." Fekiria inched along the wall to the corner. There, she knelt and waved at Sergeant Brian. The distance was not a great one but enough that she could not tell if he was still there.

What was taking them so long? Her pulse hiccupped. What if he *had* left? Abandoned them? Her stomach squirmed at the thought. Even as she was pushing onto her feet, a shape emerged. Then another.

They ran toward her.

Her fears allayed, she resumed her watch, ready to protect Mitra, her daughter, and Jamilah as they hurried toward her. But the thought plagued her: Had Sergeant Brian left?

Why would he?

Because he's American.

But he had helped. He would not do that. . .would he?

Crack!

Fekiria blinked. Jolted. *What was that!?* In that second, the wind seemed to stop. The earth and its elements yielded to the violence of the moment. Because she saw more than she wanted in that single blink of her eye. Jamilah pitched backward, right into Mitra, who fell. Little Dassah tumbled from her mother's arms. Jamilah's shriek filled the dark alley.

CHAPTER 30

The explosion of wood registered as Sergeant Brian barreled out of his hiding spot. Took a knee. Sparks flew, and she knew in that instant he was shooting.

Did he accidentally shoot Jamilah?

No. No, she realized he was shooting at someone beyond them. Back in action, he fired at someone behind and to Mitra's right. Moving decisively, he kept shooting.

Fekiria snapped out of the stupor. Spun. Tried to find the shooter. *Where are they? Who. . .?* Muzzle flash gave away the enemy. She aimed. Fired.

The *rat-tat-tat* of Sergeant Brian's controlled bursts told her he wasn't giving up. She ducked as plaster exploded around her. *They're shooting at me!* Fekiria threw herself back, out of view. Inspired, she rushed to the other side of the wall, ordering the girls to follow her. From this vantage she could see Sergeant Brian—he'd made it to Jamilah and was helping her up.

Unlike Hollywood, Fekiria didn't have an unlimited supply of ammunition. On her belly on the thin layer of snow that had fallen, she peered around the corner. Saw the shooter. Fired.

She heard the thud of boots from the other direction and knew Sergeant Brian was closing in on the safe spot. Fekiria needed to keep the shooter's head down so they could make it.

Another wave of shots peppered them.

Fekiria flattened herself as dirt and snow spattered her face. Covering her head, she hoped they continued missing. Again came the familiar *rat-tat-tat* of Sergeant Brian's weapon.

She resumed her position. Started firing so he could get to cover.

Back and forth. It took awhile, but he finally hustled into the alley. "Keep moving," came the breathy grunt from him.

On her feet, Fekiria turned—then froze at the sight of all the blood. She then followed the others, marveling at the way Sergeant Brian carried Jamilah over his shoulder as if he'd just been carrying a heavy sack. Mitra and Sheevah both carried one of the smaller girls, and she lifted Aadela, who had been running as fast as her little feet would go, a hand hooked onto a strap on Sergeant Brian's leg.

The eight of them hurried down the street, turned left onto another street, then went right. A dizzying pattern designed to confuse their pursuers. A few minutes later, Sergeant Brian slipped into the partially open gate of a compound and motioned them all inside. He gently laid Jamilah down and went to a knee. His chest heaved against the exertion of having transported the teen through the city streets.

Jamilah's face had gone pale. The accumulation of snow beneath her quickly grew red. "Fekiria," she whispered.

"Shh," Fekiria said. "You'll be okay."

Jamilah nodded, her face slick with a sheen of sweat.

Breathing hard, Sergeant Brian pulled out his phone again. "Hey"—deep gulp of breath—"Yeah. Got hit." He breathed hard, peering out into the street, then tucked the phone between his shoulder and jaw as he dumped his pack on the ground. Dug into it and pulled out a smaller bag. "One seriously injured." He huffed, his nostrils flaring as he worked to control his breathing. "Can't make it."

Medical kit.

He dug out bandages and pressed them against Jamilah's side. The girl cried out, but Sergeant Brian kept working. He glanced at Fekiria, taking on a third task. His gaze locked with hers. "I need a street name."

Nervously, she nodded, but Mitra whispered, "Haseb Sayee."

Sergeant Brian paused as he considered Mitra then looked at Fekiria. "Was that the street?"

She nodded, still rattled. Still out of her element. She was a pilot and soldier! She should be stronger. Like him.

"Haseb Sayee," he repeated into the phone then flung it aside.

"Are they coming?" Fekiria couldn't help but ask.

"On the way," he said as he sprayed something against the open wound. Jamilah whimpered but bit through it.

But he was still working to tend the wound. "Keep watch for my team. Black Humvee. Old."

"I'm not leaving her!"

"If you want her to live, you'll do what I say." Finally, he looked up. Then to the gate. "Now."

"I—"

"If you miss them, then she dies."

Furious, she pushed away. Onto her feet and stumbling to the gate, dazed. Angry—at the men who shot Jamilah. At Sergeant Brian for being so unfeeling. So insensitive. Cruel.

He saved your life!

Had he not followed her. . .had he not ordered them into the streets during a storm. . .

If her friend died—if any of them died, she would not forgive him. She sagged against the gate, clutching the wood, shivering. Clinging to it as if her life depended on it. And perhaps it did. This whole thing was crazy. Who was behind all this? Who would do such a thing?

The rattle of a car engine stabbed the wintry night. She eased the gate to give a little more, not wanting to betray her location if the car was the enemy.

The Humvee rolled into sight, slow. No headlights.

"That sounds like them," came Sergeant Brian's voice, followed almost immediately by the sound of his steps. She felt his presence before he even cupped his hand over hers on the gate.

He pressed close, his presence warm. He looked over her head. "Yeah." He nudged the gate just wide enough to reach through. Stepped around her and exposed himself. With a single wave, he signaled the vehicle.

The engine revved, and the Humvee swung toward them. Sergeant Brian opened the gate enough to allow the vehicle to roll inside, the engine dying as tires crunched over the pebbled path and the snow.

Men spilled out of the vehicle. Armed American soldiers—and from the passenger seat came Captain Dean Watters. Zahrah's boyfriend. Though it was foolish to think she could still keep her secret, Fekiria drew into the shadows as he jogged closer.

"We can't take everyone, but we'll take the injured and youngest," Captain Dean said.

"Why?" Fekiria's demanding question revealed her presence, but it was the least of her concerns.

"Not enough room," another soldier answered.

Hadassah clung to her mother, refusing to release her hand. A soldier with a kind face and a bit of years on him lifted Dassah into the Humvee.

"Okay," said another with a dark beard and eyes. "Two more. The rest have to walk."

"I'll stay with Hawk," said the one who'd put Dassah in the vehicle. Sergeant Brian nodded then motioned to Fekiria. "She goes with the little ones. The teens can walk with me."

"No." Fekiria placed Wajmah inside the vehicle, surprised at how crowded it was in there. But even as she stepped back, Wajmah let out a shriek.

Mitra rushed forward and comforted her.

"Go." Fekiria nudged the twelve-year-old inside. "Stay with them. You will be safe."

The men started back to the vehicle.

"You okay?" Captain Dean asked Sergeant Brian, handing him another weapon and ammo.

"Fine." He thumbed toward Fekiria. "She's ISAF trained. Give her a weapon."

The captain hesitated. Glanced at her, and the frown erupted across his face. "Fekiria?"

"It's a long story," Sergeant Brian said. "One I haven't even fully heard, but you can interrogate her later. And I'll help, but right now time is short."

"Roger," Captain Dean said without breaking eye contact. "Does Zahrah know?"

"No."

A man built a little bigger than Sergeant Brian handed her a fully automatic weapon and two extra magazines. "I'll need those back."

His accent—European? Wasn't British. "Thank you. I'll return them."

Crying and an ardent "no!" turned them all toward the vehicle.

Sergeant Brian looked like he was trying to wrestle a monkey with the way Aadela avoided being drawn off his back. "C'mon," he growled. She crawled around his back and shoulders. He groped, missed, tried again.

Aadela railed, screaming. Arms and legs thrashing, she arched her back hard when he finally pulled her free.

"Hey." Sergeant Brian wrapped her in his arms, and almost immediately she settled. "Easy, chiefette."

Two of them went to Jamilah, lifted her, and transported her to the vehicle.

Captain Dean gave a terse nod then shifted his attention back to Sergeant Brian. "Already contacted the general. He's mustering backup, but—"

A bright explosion of light lit the night.

Fekiria felt herself flying backward.

Rammed into something solid.

The world blinked out.

CHAPTER 31

Kabul, Afghanistan
23 February—1845 Hours

Fire rained down. The wall to the left of the Humvee erupted, spewing cement and plaster into the sky. "Go, go, go!" Brian shouted.

The captain, Falcon, and Titanis dove into the vehicle. Brian grabbed Fekiria's hand, the bundle of screaming terror still clinging to the front of his vest. Eagle rounded up the other two and they rushed to safety.

Brian was freakin' fed up with this terrorist who seemed to have a tracking device on their location. Could they not get a break? His arms ached and his legs felt like putty.

The fleeing Humvee had drawn the enemy so they had a free run for the first mile. They hurried down through a warehouse district, putting as much distance between them and the location as possible.

"Hey, hey," Eagle huffed, slowing. He nodded backward and started in that direction.

Backtracking, the little one clinging to him like a frightened monkey, Brian saw the vehicle. A sedan sitting alone next to a building where a lone light shone on the second floor. "Someone missed the storm warning," he muttered then jutted his jaw toward the car. It wasn't old and junked out, but it also wasn't so new that hotwiring wouldn't work.

Eagle made quick work of jimmying the lock.

"In, in." Brian ushered the three women and little girl into the backseat. He climbed into the passenger seat as the older Raptor member hotwired the car.

Pealing out of the parking lot would make a cool exit. But they needed stealth. Eagle knew that and eased the car out of the parking lot with as little noise as possible. Once they hit the main road blanketed in snow, he gunned it. The tail wiggled a little, but the tires caught purchase. "Which way?"

"Away," Brian said. "Just drive for an hour, Eagle. We can sort it later. Just need distance between us and them."

"Who is 'them' anyway?" Eagle asked.

"No idea." Brian peered over his shoulder to the women and little girl. He never would've said Fekiria was afraid, until today. With those wide eyes and the pale sheen on her face. . . But that wasn't enough to stay his anger. She had a lot to explain. "Now might be a good time for those answers."

—⁂—

Kabul, Afghanistan
23 February—1925 Hours

His attitude irritated her.

Maybe she did owe him, but did he have to act like that? The only good thing was that Mitra, Aadela, and Sheevah didn't understand English enough to know what she was about to confess. "It was an accident."

"Right. An accident. Bombing a building is an accident?"

Fekiria's anger simmered. "I did not—" She clamped down hard on her tongue and cringed, drawing a concerned look from Aadela. "Somehow, the navigational guidance of the weapon. . .didn't work right."

Sergeant Brian shifted, looking her right in the eye. "Seriously? That's your story? My team nearly got burned to death and you're going to blame a screwy navigational system?"

Fekiria looked away, hurt and angry by his unwillingness to listen and believe her.

The other soldier driving gave Sergeant Brian a pat. "Hey. Fits with everything else, right?"

"What?" Sergeant Brian frowned. "You believe her?"

"Not surprising that someone would have her bombs target us, right?"

"But she—she hates Americans."

"Come on," the other man said.

"No. Serious. Dead serious—she told me to my face."

"If you hate olives," Fekiria said, "smash them all with a hammer?"

"If they're green and salty, heck yeah." Sergeant Brian wasn't giving her a chance.

"Hey," the other soldier said. "Give a listen. Hear her out." He pointed out the windshield. "It's going to be tough and quiet. I could use a distraction."

Sergeant Brian dropped against the seat, saying no more.

"Thank you." Fekiria met the pale blue eyes of the man driving. "It is a long story, but I believe my helicopter was tampered with. I was taken at gunpoint into my chopper and forced to fly into the city. They killed my flight advisor—an *American* Air Force captain whom I admired and respected."

Sergeant Brian flung around. "Wait. That's the guy you were with at the hookah bar?"

The heat drained from her face. "He is dead. Please respect his memory."

He jerked toward her, held her gaze, then yanked forward.

Though she wasn't sure what that was about, she felt his disapproval keenly. His rejection. His anger. And why it scalded her heart, she didn't know. She hated him, so arrogant, so. . .*direct*.

She drove her gaze back to the *nice* soldier. "They threatened me by making me think they were going to bomb the school with the girls." Fekiria hugged Aadela a little tighter, the thought of the little one nearly dying. "I was so relieved when we veered off but then terrified when I saw the bomb hit that building. I swear I did not know what it hit. Next thing I know, I'm taking fire. The rotors were taken out, and I ejected."

"So, you were the one we were trailing through the market?" he asked.

Fekiria nodded. "I knew if I could get to the school, Mitra would protect me." She considered her friend, whose shoulders pressed against hers. Wanting to hide her tears and shame, she buried her face in Aadela's soft hair, damp from the snow.

"She's asleep," Mitra whispered, nodding to the six-year-old.

"So, who hit the school?" Sergeant Brian asked without turning around.

"I'm not sure," Fekiria answered. "Mitra was hiding from the Taliban, who wanted to kill her and the children."

"For what?"

Fekiria snorted. "For existing. For wanting to learn."

Sergeant Brian looked at his friend. "Taliban and Chinese terrorists. Working together?"

"It's a stretch," the man mumbled. "But pretty much everything we've faced recently is a stretch."

"Yeah, but we're talking Plastic-Man stretch here, Eagle." Sergeant Brian shook his head and looked out the window.

Barreling down the highway in driving snow made it almost impossible to see. But Eagle drove fearlessly. She couldn't pretend to understand why whoever it was forced her to bomb their building. Was it a coincidence? What were the odds that she'd end up in the car fleeing Kabul with the man who'd worked detail with her cousin's boyfriend?

Eagle glanced in the rearview mirror. "You're Double Z's cousin, right?"

"What does that mean?"

"Sorry." He gave a one-shouldered shrug as they barreled along the highway. "I mean, Zahrah—she's your cousin?"

Fekiria nodded.

Eagle glanced at Sergeant Brian. "I don't know, Hawk. There are some pretty wild coincidences here. Maybe too wild."

"Right? See what I'm saying?"

"No—you're implying it's me, that I did this," Fekiria snapped.

"Hey, you had motive and you had opportunity."

"I would never do that. Unlike you, I haven't been in jail."

"Hey!" Brian again jerked toward her. "You—" He screwed up his mouth tight. "You got no class, throwing that at me." Turned back around, muttering.

Guilt and shame slipped a noose around her neck. He was biting his tongue because he'd made a promise, one that had landed him in jail after defending her honor. At least, that's what he thought it was. Maybe. She hadn't let herself think about it much. All that mattered was that he'd promised to keep her secret—a secret that no longer seemed important. But he'd kept her secret, hadn't he? That was why he would not say anything just then, though he seemed ready to yell at her the way her father and brother always had.

And yet, he hadn't.

The dull lights of the panel cast a strange glow, accenting the shape of his head and shoulders. He was a thick mass of contradictions and . . . *strength*.

A weight pressed against her hand, and she looked over to find Mitra and Sheevah asleep. A few more minutes and the teen was snoring softly.

"What is the plan?" Fekiria whispered.

"The plan?" Sergeant Brian glanced back at her, a little calmer now. "To stay alive."

"Can you not give me a straight answer?"

He shook his head and snorted. "You gotta be kidding me! Seriously. The plan is to stay alive."

Eagle gave a sigh and rolled his eyes. "We'll drive for an hour, or until we can't see in front of us," he said, pointing to the flurries rushing into the windshield. "Hit the next village or town and try to find a place to hole up for the night. If we can, we'll reestablish contact with our team."

"Why wouldn't you be able to?"

"Long story," Brian said.

"What is your problem?" Fekiria demanded, tired of his snippy answers and attitude.

"You! *You* are my problem!" He shook his head again. "Every time you're around, I end up fighting for my life."

Eagle swatted his shoulder again.

Sergeant Brian raised his hand sharply. "What? It's true."

"Go easy. It's been a hard night for everyone."

He looked out the window, roughing a hand over his head and neck. He might seem angry. He might be gruff and annoyed with her. But Sergeant Brian would fight to the death to protect them. So would Eagle.

One just might be nicer doing it than the other.

Fekiria rested her head against the back of the seat, watching him. Wondering what made him tick. What type of man he was outside of this war and her country. The monotonous motion of the vehicle and almost whiteout conditions of the storm lulled her to sleep. She felt safe. She was even beginning to warm up.

"Watch out!"

CHAPTER 32

South of Kabul, Afghanistan
23 February—1935 Hours

*P*_{op!}

Crack! Crunch!

Brian's head rammed into the passenger window as the car whipped around. Using the vehicle's support, he braced himself.

But flipping. Tossing. Banging. Crunching.

Pain streaked down his neck. A scream rent the air. He begged God to stop them. Twisting, crunching, flipping. *Are we going to die?*

Glass shattered.

Metal crunched. Whipped to the other side. Upside down.

Thud!

Violently, everything stopped. Silence. Deafening. He got his bearings—they were still upside down. Glass glittered on the fresh-fallen snow. An embankment or something had stopped them cold.

"Get out," Eagle shouted. "It was a trap."

Brian freed himself from the belt. Dropped to the roof of the car. The little girl was there, dangling unconscious from the seat belt. The woman was on the floor cradling the teen, who cried hard.

Where was Fekiria?

Brian's gut clenched. His gaze shot to—*missing door!*

He scrambled out the opening, catching his weapon and ruck before leaving the vehicle. "Fekiria!" He clambered to his feet, using the car for balance against his dizziness. "Feki—"

Sparks flew against the belly of the car. *Shots!* Brian dropped to a crouch. Looked out over the snow-blanketed landscape. He waited for more, but none came. Maybe he was being paranoid. Maybe the spark was a gas leak or something.

But even that couldn't be verified. As he got his bearings, he realized they'd crossed the road and landed upside down in a ditch. He crawled to the edge and strained to see into the darkening day and through the barrage of snow.

"Fekiria!" A sound carried on the voice of the wind, low and distinct. "Fekiria's out there," he said to Eagle. "Can't tell where."

The other three were crawling out of the overturned vehicle. Brian guided them to a safe spot, away from the upended sedan, and—if there was gunfire—away from stray bullets. He pointed to the ditch, which gave them cover and safety against the storm. "Stay." He made motions with his hands but couldn't tell if they understood. The older girl nodded, so he hoped she did.

"I'll check across the road," Eagle said.

"I'll take the embankment." Crouch-running along the ditch, he repeatedly called her name. She had to be in some serious pain after being thrown from a car like that. What if she hadn't survived?

No, don't go there. Stay positive.

"Fekiria!" he shouted again, listening into the howling wind.

"Here," came a faint reply.

Brian rushed forward and found her pushing up onto all fours. He dropped at her side and nudged her into a sitting position. "Are you hurt?"

Hair disheveled and loose around her face, she shook her head. Then quickly held it with a groan.

"That good, huh?"

She scowled, and he saw a trickle of blood on her face.

"Well enough to still hate me." He chuckled.

"I do not hate you."

Brian hesitated a fraction. Mostly trying to figure out why that made him so happy. "Good to know." Really good. "Come on. Let's get back." He hooked an arm around her waist and helped her up—but not all the way. "Stay low." The tire spikes. He'd seen them but not in time. They'd been placed there by someone. And that someone could be taking a bead on them right now.

It surprised him how small she was, her waist thin and her frame light, considering the size of the fight in the woman. He helped her back to the others, and she dropped down. The little girl threw herself forward—not at Fekiria, but at Brian. He caught her, startled.

"Eagle," Brian shouted as he shifted the small child to his other side. "Found her!"

"Copy," came a pretty distant shout.

The visibility out here in the storm sucked and played tricks with sight and sound. He thought he saw Eagle coming up from the south, but the way the snow swirled and danced, he couldn't be sure it wasn't just a shadow.

"We'll have to walk," he shouted to the girls over the howling wind, "to find shelter once Eagle returns."

With a nod, Fekiria and the teen huddled together.

"Eagle, hurry up, man!" Brian squinted and strained but didn't hear a thing. Or see a thing. In his arms, the little one went rigid. Let out a shriek.

A couple dozen feet down the road, a shadow coalesced into a form. Not just a form. A man. With an RPG tube. "Run!" He pushed around, the child in his arms. The women scrambling in front of him.

Seconds felt like an eternity. The snow some demon working against them. Clutching their feet. Slowing progress. They headed down the ditch, but lights swinging—*flashlights!*—shoved them up the embankment. Fekiria scrambled, grunting as she helped the girl climb.

"Go, go, go!"

Halfway up the incline, Brian heard the *thunk* of the grenade.

The powerful fist of the blast punched him into the snowy rock face. Shoving out his hands provided scant protection for the little girl clinging to him better than Velcro. He grunted but kept moving as white-hot fire behind them lit their path.

Ahead, Fekiria and the teen stared backward, eyes wide. The injured woman kept her head down.

"Move!" he shouted, quickly reaching them. "Take her." He tried to extricate the child—whose arms and legs snapped tight around him again. Once Fekiria pulled the girl free, Brian knelt. Took aim.

He glanced up—saw Fekiria's stricken expression as she stood over him, watching. "Go!" With a shove, he reacquired the targets.

Two men were running toward the ditch. Brian eased back the trigger once, twice. The men crumpled into the snow.

Brian pivoted, swung the weapon behind him—and froze.

Coming down the road, he spied at least a half-dozen sets of headlights.

Eagle. *Where's Eagle?* "Eagle! Pops!" He scanned the road but couldn't see anything. He had to trust the guy knew protocol. Knew to get to safety then rendezvous later. Brian knew the same drill. And he had four innocents whose safety he'd have to ensure as well.

Brian scaled the embankment and nearly cursed when he realized it only afforded a small break—straight across a half-dozen feet and up again, or they'd be exposed once their attackers caught up with them. Go north or south and it was an open plain.

For a second, a crazy, idiotic second, he wondered if the men were still chasing them. That was, until snow poofed up at them. "Keep moving. Up!"

Fekiria frowned but started climbing.

Scaling backward wasn't entirely 100 percent effective, but it provided cover fire. It also told Brian how high they were going. *Not good, not good.*

But away from the enemy *was* good. High ground best. And the hill would provide cover once they could clear the incline. They'd get away and find shelter somewhere. Maybe find another vehicle to get them back to the team.

"Where?" Fekiria gulped air as she waited around a small outcropping. She moved again, stumbling. Caught and righted herself then continued. . .stumbling yet again. With the extra load of the girl, she was tiring quickly.

"Just go. Keep moving." He caught up and lifted the girl from her arms. He tucked her into his jacket, felt her body trembling against his tactical vest. They'd need to find a way to better insulate her against the cold since she wasn't walking, which kept the rest of them warm and their blood circulating. First, they had to get away from trouble and bullets.

As he wrapped his arm around the little girl, he tugged up his sleeve and checked the GPS. But since the whiteout made it impossible for him to verify visually what the GPS said, he'd have to use blind trust. "That way." It wasn't as steep and would keep them from ascending.

"But—"

"No talking. Conserve." He pulled himself along the rocky terrain. With a quick glance to the child in his arms, he verified she was okay still.

"There's a snowstorm," Fekiria shouted, her rebellion once again obvious.

"Really?" He hauled himself up using jagged clefts for leverage. "Hadn't noticed."

"But we're heading into the mountains."

"Want to go down? Explain to the guys shooting at us that we can't climb up because the mountains are up there?" Navigating the rocky terrain with the girl in his arms proved not only tricky, but downright dangerous. His hands weren't free to break his fall.

Brian tugged his sat phone free and glanced at it. Froze for a second. Glanced at his leg pocket, stunned. A hole in the material told of the bullet that had seared its edges. And the cracked screen and curled-inward frame had surrendered the bullet that had bent it, but the damage was done. Still, he pressed the Power button, praying— begging—that this wasn't happening. They had to make contact with Raptor. Had to find a way out.

He mashed the Power button.

Nothing. No faded blue screen. No vibration. No nothing.

He cursed. Slammed the phone against a jagged rock thrusting upward out of the ground. He grabbed the sim card from it but tossed the rest.

"Don't we need that?" Fekiria demanded.

"If it worked, yeah."

Shock riddled her features. She blinked. Her mouth opened but nothing came out.

"Let's go." Brian nudged her onward, but she shook her head.

"How will we get out of here?"

"We fight our way out." He gave her a mean look. "Now, *move!*"

The three older females formed a straight line, huddling close to block out the wind and push through the elements with courage, walking fast, heads down. Each step, each placement of their feet, risked injury. The blanket of snow was deceptively even, with only subtle rises and depressions to indicate a possible wrenched-ankle trap. Or a crevasse that could cause all sorts of chaos in their escape plan.

Behind them, he heard the *pop* of weapon's fire answered by *rat-tat-tats*. He could only pray that Eagle was okay. That somehow Raptor had caught up with him.

Pray. Yeah. That. Brian had grown up with a grandmother who delivered him to church every Sunday morning and Wednesday night. He went because the girls in the junior high and youth groups were cute. Because it gave him a chance to get away from his dad and the eventual disgrace. But then it caught up with them. Kids found out. Taunted him.

But Granddad had been resolute. Told Brian he'd prayed for him every day. That God was never more than a whisper away, that He was waiting for us to call on Him. *"A gentleman never forces his way. . ."*

A strangled cry snapped Brian's attention to the women.

Fekiria was standing over Mitra, arm still hooked. The teen girl waved frantically at him, calling for help. A red stain blossomed on the snow.

Brian swung his weapon around, sighting as he knelt and aimed at the pursuers who'd shot the woman.

23 February—1945 Hours

"Mitra!" Fekiria gasped, clutching her friend.

With a pained expression, Mitra climbed to her feet. "It's okay. Only a scratch." Running for the shelter of a large rock, she held her arm close. Together they dove for the protective cover. Up against the cold, wet rock, Mitra checked her side.

It didn't look bad. But it was bleeding. That could cause a lot of problems for her friend but also for them. A trail for whoever wanted to catch them. Fekiria tugged free her hijab, which was mostly around her neck now, and wrapped it around Mitra's arm. "We'll look at it as soon as we get to a safe place."

Mitra nodded.

Like a giant blur, Sergeant Brian rushed toward them and dropped to his knees. His green-eyed gaze hit them both.

"We're okay." Fekiria nodded to her friend's arm. "A graze."

"Can't stop," he said. "They're down, but I doubt they're alone or the last. And now, we have a trail." Raising his chin, he searched their surroundings.

"What are you thinking?" Fekiria lifted herself off the snow, the cold digging past her winter clothes and outerwear.

"Need to change course. Take a less obvious route."

"That would mean a less accessible route." She nodded at the snow-ridden landscape. "We are nearing the Tera Pass. It's not heavily populated, but there's a reason for that."

His gaze rammed into hers. "Then that's where we need to go."

"Have you lost what little brains you have?"

"Yeah." Terse and unyielding, he shifted in his crouch. "Pretty sure they were tossed out of the vehicle when we flipped."

What did that mean? Was he mocking her since she'd been thrown out of the car?

Again, he was searching their surroundings, looking for options. "Nobody in his right mind would be out here." He met her gaze again. "But then, we weren't given a choice. We can't stop moving. Night is coming. So is the storm."

"I think it's already here." Mitra raised her eyebrows to the swirling snow.

"Don't kid yourself. This is just the beginning. In an hour or two, we won't be able to see two feet in front of us." He pushed off his knees. Motioned between Fekiria and the teen. "Rest time's over."

A little ebony head twisted around, seeming to search for Fekiria.

She hunched next to Sergeant Brian and smiled down into the pouch-like space he'd created for the small girl. "How are you, Aadela?"

"Scared," she whispered.

"You are in the safest place." Fekiria said the words as much to reassure herself as the child.

On their feet, they trudged now in an easterly direction. At least, she thought that's where they were headed. The snow and heavy cloud cover made it too hard to tell. Sergeant Brian was leading. They entrusted him with their lives.

"Do you believe that?" Mitra asked about thirty minutes into their trek.

"Believe what?" Fekiria glanced back to Sheevah, who was slowing.

"That Aadela is safest with him?"

Surprise teased the edges of Fekiria's awareness. "It was a figure of speech." She swallowed hard. "I did not mean in particular with him. Just that he's a soldier. He knows what he's doing."

"But you watch him," Mitra said in their native tongue.

"Of course, I do! It will not help to get lost." She trudged a little faster, each step soaking her pants. Legs leaden and needles of pain pricking her nerves, she tried to put a little more space between Mitra and her. She didn't want to answer questions about something she didn't understand herself. Something that left her confused. Angry. It made no sense. She barely knew him. And he was American.

Like a flash, she recalled their argument in the car before the crash. The way Sergeant Brian had been about to yell at her, but he stopped. Turned back around.

He made a promise. . . never to tell. And even though her secret was out now, he kept his word. In that small gesture, the man with hulking shoulders, a thick neck, and fierce eyes had shown more honor than some Afghan men she knew.

With a hop forward, she closed the gap between them. "Thank you," she said, but the wind ate her words. Fekiria shuffled forward again, though the act of putting one foot in front of the other grew harder with each step.

Sergeant Brian snapped a look in her direction.

"Thank you," she said a little louder.

Scowling, he considered her. "We're not out of this yet." He indicated ahead of them. "Still plenty of terrain to die in."

Time lost meaning and power here in the mountains. And that's exactly where they were headed—higher, deeper—despite their best efforts. Wind and snow dominated. Demanded submission. Held victory over those who dared tempt its hand. Walking hurt. Or didn't hurt. That's what scared her. *Not* being able to feel her feet. In her pockets, she worked her fingers into fists. Straight. Into fists. Kept walking. Flexing. Had to keep the circulation going.

They'd find safe ground and help soon. She was sure of it. Until then, she'd keep her head down and her hopes up.

"Hey!"

Fekiria collided with Sergeant Brian.

He caught her, his gaze sharp and assessing. "You're slowing down."

She blinked. Was she? "I—I was just walking."

"Where's the teenager?"

"Sheevah?" Fekiria turned, glanced behind her to where Mitra had joined them. But. . . Her heart skipped a beat. "Sheevah!" She pushed herself forward just as a shape emerged in the darkening day. "Sheevah," she breathed. "Thank God!"

Sergeant Brian frowned at her for some reason. He shrugged out of his ruck and dug through it. Rope in hand, he moved toward her.

"What are you doing?"

After tying a knot, he used a metal hook and clamped it onto his tactical belt. He then moved toward her. Leaned in. Wrapped his arms around her waist.

Fekiria stood frozen, awareness flooding her as he worked a knot into the rope, effectively anchoring them together. Next, he tied Sheevah then Mitra—but around her hips to avoid the wound in her side.

"Here." He removed Aadela and handed her off.

Fekiria held the girl close, not entirely sure how long she would last holding her, but if he felt it was necessary, if he was tired. . .

He knelt, working the straps on his pack. Sergeant Brian shifted then patted the upper part of his shoulder.

Fekiria wasn't sure at first but then caught on. She placed Aadela on his back and instructed her to hold on. Then she assisted Sergeant Brian with sliding the rucksack over Aadela so she was sandwiched between his vest and gear. Also, being on his back, he would block her from the wind and elements.

He tightened the strap around his chest and waist. Then angled down a little toward Fekiria. "Is she okay?" he shouted.

She brushed a hand over the little one's face, barely visible beneath the part of his ruck that shielded her. "Hold on and keep your head down," Fekiria said, and Aadela nodded. "She's good."

The American soldier held out his hand. Without hesitation, she reached for his grasp. Not sure what he intended but willing to do whatever he wanted. She trusted him. Knew he'd get them out of this.

He placed her hand on a strap on his vest, just above his elbow. "Hold on!"

Fekiria curled her aching, raw fingers around the strap, not entirely able to feel it.

"Have the others group up. Stay close." As he tied a keffiyeh around his neck and face, she gave the orders to the others.

Grouped up, they would not only stay together but block the wind from each other. As they walked, she found she was able to stay up easier. Walk easier. She couldn't feel her toes still, but she could move.

They walked for a while. She had no guess how long. They were at the mercy of the terrain and the weather. It might have been an hour, or two hours, when she once more collided with Sergeant Brian.

He twisted, not breaking their holding pattern, and tugged the keffiyeh down from his nose. "Stay here." He motioned to a slightly curved rock. "Stay close and don't separate. I'm going to find shelter."

She caught his arm as he freed himself from the metal hook. "Wait!"

Though he'd started away, he gave her a reassuring nod.

Fekiria turned to Sheevah and Mitra, waving them in closer. "Come together." She guided them against the rock. They squatted in a tight huddle.

"Where did he go?" Sheevah said, her teeth chattering.

"To find shelter." Fekiria glanced at Mitra's wound. "How are you doing? Does it hurt?"

Her friend smiled. "I can't feel it," she admitted with a shrug.

The wind growled through the space where they waited.

Fekiria stilled, thinking. Waiting. Wishing Sergeant Brian would hurry.

Growling clicked through the rocks, popping.

Another growl.

That isn't the wind!

A pair of hollow, yellow eyes blinked at them.

BORIS

I'm not the violent type. Not really. I mean, that's why I prefer my keyboard and monitors from the safety of my home-away-from-home. It's sterile—in terms of violence—and noncombative.

Okay, if anyone believes that, he's nuts. I have a small island in the middle of Afghanistan I'd like to sell him.

Are they paying attention? I'm waging a serious war here in a *very* combative way. A passive-aggressive way, but does the delivery method matter? No. It's the outcome. The end product. And that's the utter defeat of the men who are so full of themselves they can't see it coming.

Yes, I know what they're thinking—Raptor got my Fly fly.

But that's where their intelligence ends. Do they seriously think I'd only send one Fly fly? Or that those are my only devices in play? Get real. I'm not that stupid.

Speaking of stupid, these Chinese overlords are pushing some serious buttons. They have been digging in my systems, trying to find me again. Trying to control what I do because they know that if I can get them inside the American establishments, there's no reason I can't get in theirs. *Especially* when I'm continuously transmitting data to them.

Now, these guys aren't near as fun as the Americans. Remember—they were going all WWE on us. I've watched for a while now, but I have yet to see any ninjas.

Maybe that's the point. One never knows ninjas are there until it's too late.

And true—they found me once. But if they show up again, I've got a few surprises of my own.

So back to the Americans. They've taken a beating. Hawk is out there not being quite so hawk-like, dragging his sorry carcass through a blizzard. The guy wouldn't freeze to death. He's got too much fire in that gut of his. But I've got to hand it to him. I hear he's dragging two kids and two chicks with him up a mountain in a snowstorm. But I wouldn't want to be him—because those kids will die.

C'mon. I'm not being mean. It's just logistics. It's freezing. It's snowing. They have little shelter. Doesn't take long for hypothermia to set in. Frostbite to chew through fingers and toes.

I can't help but snicker. And he thought watching that female soldier die was bad? Hawk will need serious psychiatric help after this. Of course, that would be necessary only if he survived. Which he won't.

He'd have a chance if the others weren't there. But there's no way in that wintry hell he's going to make it out alive. That makes me tear up.

Not really.

I mean, I am, after all, the one sending the Chinese in after him. It's not real difficult to swing a few satellites around and find the nearest shelter—which, sadly for my counterparts, is their southern safe house, their waypoint. And because I need them to believe I'm still on their side—*let's review that I'm only on the side of the money flowing into my accounts*—I've got to send them the notice because they've got that safe house up there, the one they've been running half the operations out of. If they don't bug out now and he shows up. . .there will be explosions.

And Mr. Special Forces will survive that encounter. It's what they do. Because the dude is a fighter. He wants to live. The snow, however, has a chance because Hawk will believe himself impervious, and each minute out there will numb him and his body parts to the freezing defeat. But Hawk is a little too egocentric, and having to save the damsel in distress will push him. He doesn't want another person to die on his watch—yeah, that mess in the village totally did a head job on the guy.

It was a genius move, sending that bogus stand-down order. The dope totally bought it. Just brilliant, playing his own insecurities and weaknesses against him.

So here, with a few keystrokes, my Chinese dictators will have the best intel to attempt yet again to take this team out.

Has anyone besides me noticed how they're totally like Energizer bunnies, never dying?

Dudes. We need some bodies. The dictators are going to get peeved. They won't believe I'm doing my job. And trust me, I am. Day and night.

If I weren't so committed to seeing this through, I'd declare the pain of killing these guys not worth the effort. Too much work. And each time you punch them down, they snap back up. Like those stupid targets at the county fair.

But the endgame is in play. Their day is coming when they will fall. And stay down.

MITCH

Sergeant Black," Judge Cartwright said, his nasally voice grating across Mitch's nerves, "I'm not seeing proof that you are able to take care of these children."

Heart stalled, Mitch straightened in his chair. "Sir—"

"You're staying in the Army?"

"My time is up in two years."

"Two years? What are those kids supposed to do for two years?"

"Sir, I have an arrangement with—"

"Kids don't need an arrangement. They need a parent! At home, looking out for them." Cartwright huffed as he shuffled papers on the surface in front of him. "Unless you can prove to me that you will be there for these children, I am inclined to rule against you, Sergeant Black. I'm sorry, but I have enough experience to know how these things go when children do not have consistent supervision, love, and support."

"Sir, my love and support for my children has never wavered. It never will."

"Can you leave the Army?"

Mitch blinked. Leave the team? Leave Dean and the others out there. . .? He swallowed. "I. . .I'd have to put in for discharge."

Cartwright grunted. "More red tape, which means more time those kids don't have a parent at home."

At the other table sat the Leitners, who had gloated over the last several hours of testimony and witness-calling. They'd berated him. Chided him. And now, Will Leitner lifted his chin with the smug, knowing look of his impending victory.

"Sir, I do everything I know to do. I'm a soldier. I fight for my country, for the freedoms represented here in this courtroom—"

"I know that, son," Cartwright said, his bushy eyebrows tugging together in a furrow. "But this isn't about you being a hero. This is

265

about you being a dad."

"On the contrary, sir. It's about both. If—"

Cartwright held up a hand. "Enough. Unless you can provide reassurance that you are going to be there, I need to move forward and rule in favor of the Leitners, who can provide a stable, loving home for your son and daughter."

"Sir." Mitch's throat constricted, choking him. "Please."

"The Leitners showed proof that you'll be out of country yet again in less than a week. And you're gone for months."

"Please. *Please* don't do this, Your Honor. There are thousands of troops deployed who cannot predict their schedule, but all the same do not fail to love and provide for their children."

"But this isn't about them. It's about you."

"Sir," Mitch bit out, his eyes burning. "Please—"

"I'm sorry, Sergeant Black, I—"

"May I speak, Judge Cartwright?" A lone clear voice shot through the tension.

Mitch glanced over his shoulder and found Sienna standing behind her parents. He frowned at her, but she wasn't looking at him. She was trained on the judge.

"Miss Leitner, we've already heard your testimony."

"Yes, sir. But I have a question for you, if I may." Her hands trembled and her chest rose and fell unevenly.

What was she doing?

"You want to question me?" Cartwright asked incredulously, tugging off his glasses.

"Not question you, but may I ask—if Sergeant Black were married, would he be permitted to retain custody of his children?"

Cartwright grunted. "What kind of question is that? Of course he would—there would be a wife to take care of the children." He slid on his glasses and looked over at Mitch. "But you don't have a wife hidden somewhere, do you, Sergeant?"

"No, sir." Mitch frowned again, once again stealing a glance at Sienna.

"Not yet, he doesn't," Sienna said firmly. "But he will."

Mitch scowled now. "What—?"

"Where is he going to get this wife, Miss Leitner? Mail order?"

"He's going to marry me, sir."

"What?" Mitch froze. That's what the other night had been about.

"Look here, young lady." Cartwright wagged a thick, hairy hand at her. "You will not make a mockery of this courtroom. Marriages of convenience are wrong. And if you're doing this just to help Mister Black—"

"I'm not, Your Honor. At least, I don't think I am. Not after the way he kissed me the other night."

Mitch dropped his gaze, feeling the heat of embarrassment rushing up his neck. He could feel his in-laws staring. Heard them gasping and reprimanding Sienna.

"Is that right, Mister Black? You have feelings for this young woman?"

Mitch had never been one to air his laundry, dirty or otherwise. But the judge demanded an answer. "I do, your honor. It wasn't intentional. Just. . .happened."

"If we marry, Judge Cartwright, will you allow us to keep the kids?"

"Sienna, please," her father said. "Don't do anything rash."

"It's not rash," she said, a fiery tone to her words. "I've waited two years for him to realize how I felt. He's just a little slow on the uptake."

Mitch swallowed a laugh, and it came out a breathy grunt. He shook his head, admiring Sienna. She'd always been a take-charge woman.

She finally met his gaze, and a crimson tinge shaded her cheeks.

Only then did he realize the courtroom had fallen silent. Mitch looked to the judge, who was staring at him, hard. "Well, Mister Black?"

"Sir?"

"Would you marry Miss Leitner?"

"I. . ." Mitch looked at Sienna. Take her as his wife? He'd had no plans to marry. Put another woman through his deployments and minor PTSD issues. But he'd never dreamed he could win a woman like Sienna. "I probably would, sir." He saw the faintest glimmer of a smile on Sienna's face.

"Then get to it."

Mitch flinched. "Sir? Now?"

CHAPTER 33

Tera Pass, Afghanistan
23 February—2135 Hours

Driving snow and darkness wrapped him in a nightmarish cocoon. Only nine o'clock, but it looked like midnight. Aadela had returned his shoulder lamp, affording Brian illumination as he patted surfaces in his search for indentions that would give them more shelter. Fekiria and the older girls were waiting on him under a small copse. He'd prefer a small cave or an overhang to protect them from the storm. Cold was one thing. Cold and wet an entirely different matter.

He had four girls under his protection. That normally didn't work out so well. Look at Davis. The captain must be pretty ticked about now that he hadn't obeyed orders, that he'd gone after the pilot. . .who was Fekiria.

Fekiria! Of all the women in the world, it had to be her.

Of course it was her. The woman who didn't want anything to do with him because he'd been born in the wrong country. How twisted was that?

And who cared? It wasn't like they were going to date or something. Her father would probably behead him. Besides, he'd deliver her back to safe ground, and she'd be all hate and disgust again. Women like her didn't change.

Heck. Look what it took to affect *him*—a woman's death.

Davis had it all—looks, brains, gumption.

Fekiria had that in spades, too. Took a mighty strong woman to go against her family, learn an entirely new vocation. And not just any career, but a pilot. Dude. That was hot.

No. No no no. He wasn't going there.

His hand slid. Brian pitched forward. What the. . .? He angled his shoulder lamp to the side. Only snow and. . .wait. Brian sucked in his gut—which didn't really help considering he had another body between him and his ruck, which made it impossible to shrink his size to fit through. Around a hairpin juncture. Light probed the black. Darkness bled into deeper, darker darkness.

Poetic. Perfect. In a crouch, he followed the depression. Went back at least eight or ten feet. Got smaller and smaller, but it would work. It'd shield them through the night. He'd given up hours ago on getting down the mountain before nightfall. His only thought had been to keep the women safe.

He reached back toward the little girl. She could stay here, out of the elements. But it'd take him a good fifteen, twenty minutes to get back with the others. That would probably terrify her. After one more once-over to make sure there weren't any leftover bones from a kill, no bats clinging to the top, and no critters, he pivoted in his crouch.

Behind him came a soft murmur.

He glanced over his shoulder to the little girl. "It will be okay," he said in Pashto. It was a phrase they'd been taught assisting locals. Brian slid the keffiyeh back up and navigated his way out of the cave again. He back-traced his steps and had just hit the lip of the small rise he'd climbed when a sound stopped him.

Brian crouched again, listening. Was it a shot? A scream?

No. It seemed more. . .

A moaning sailed through the storm.

Brian froze. "No."

The sound came again. Followed by a piercing scream.

He threw himself down the embankment, rock and snow avalanching beneath his weight, and the little one screaming in his ear. At the bottom, he hit the ground running, pulling his weapon up. He stayed in his original path but was more concerned about moving fast.

That sound— "Okay, God. Here. I'm praying," he huffed as he ran. "Don't let this be what I think it is. Really. Please."

Wide and flat, the land between the women and the overhang had to be twenty yards long, if not more. He'd deliberately gone away from their path, but now he regretted it. *Too far from them. Too far.*

A lull in the wind, thanks to the high peaks that overlooked the tract, afforded him a view of the location. Darkness warred with the glare of the white snow. A surprising peek of the moon between the clouds gave Brian the view he needed.

Snow and rocks seemed to roll and swell.

Crap! He hated being right.

He dropped to a knee. Sighted down his M4 at the big cat. *Really, God? A snow leopard?*

They were rare. Few had seen them beyond the zoos and wildlife preserves. Incredible, amazing cats. Beautiful. Fierce. The cats couldn't roar. They growled—the sound he'd heard on the wind—and chuffed, like tigers.

Despite a healthy respect and admiration for the large cats, Brian had more important assets to protect.

When the big cat crouched, its shoulders rippling as it hunched to pounce, Brian took aim, certain nobody hunkered behind the cat should the bullet go clean through. Steadied his breathing. And just as the cat's muscles ripped for a lunge, he fired.

Fekiria's scream echoed through the small valley.

Brian broke into a run—would've been a sprint if it hadn't been for the monkey-girl attached to his back—straight for them. "Everyone okay?"

On her feet, Fekiria stared down at the cat. Her wide, glossy eyes seemed wider and brighter than he'd ever seen them.

"Fekiria. You okay?" He cut off her view of the now-dead snow leopard and touched her shoulder.

She flinched. Looked at him. Shuddered. And wilted against him.

Surprise exploded through him as he let his arm wrap around her shoulder. This chick had never shown that she was even capable of affection. And especially not fear. *Until she met me.*

Right.

"C'mon." Taking her by the shoulder, he gathered up the other two, whose cheeks were pinked by the cold and hot tears. "Let's move quickly. I found a cave. We need to get them out of the elements."

He tethered up and led them across the open area, keeping eyes out in case the big cat had a mate or sibling bent on revenge. They made it over the clearing and up the rocky, snow-swirled incline as the wind once more raged. Snow came in sheets. Brian tucked his shoulder against the drifts, staying attuned to the others. To Fekiria, especially. Though it was a brutal climb, she didn't falter, whine, or complain. She struggled up the mountain, slipping more than once, but she never quit.

They were tired. Too tired. And frozen. Frostbite was a real concern. He'd check them once inside the cave to make sure they had full use of their digits and toes, though he wasn't sure at this point what he could do if there was frostbite. Out here in the elements, with no help in sight, options were limited at best.

"Here," he said, as he pointed to the hairpin area.

One by one, starting with the teen, they wound their way into the cave. Brian edged in right after Fekiria, the progress slowing as they dropped into the cavernous part. The teen sat against the back wall, completely wrecked. The other woman—Mitra?—held her side as she lowered herself next to the teen.

Brian trailed backward into the cave, swiping away their tracks as he went deeper. It'd be insane for someone to find them up this high, but the freaks chasing them were very determined. That was okay. *I'm more determined.* Nobody was dying. Not this time.

"Here." Fekiria indicated to Brian's pack. With her help, the little girl came free and scooted over to Mitra.

On a knee, he dug the thermal blanket from his ruck and handed it to Fekiria, who draped it over the younger girls, the two miraculously finding something to giggle about.

Shivering violently, Fekiria watched them, smiling.

"Hey," Brian said as he dug out his med kit and nodded to the blanket. "Get warm."

"N–no. I'm–m okay."

"Bull. Get under there with them." Why did she have to be so stubborn?

She gritted her teeth and opened her mouth.

See? He knew her mean side would come back. "No arguing." He gave her *the* look. "*Now.* You can be brave and strong in ten minutes. Right now, I have to tend to your friend. She'll need the blanket when I'm done, and then I won't argue with you. Deal?"

Her lips tightened. What would she do if he kissed those lips? Knock a tooth loose, most likely. Better steer her toward something less *him* oriented. He pointed to the smallest girl. "Quit thinking about yourself for once. Your body heat will help warm up the little one faster."

Eyes flashed at him. "Her name is Aadela."

There. That's what he needed to see: her fight. "Well, *Aadela* needs you to think about her for ten minutes."

Relenting, Fekiria joined Aadela and Sheevah under the blanket as Brian knelt beside the woman. "I need to check your wound."

Fekiria translated, her teeth chattering over the words.

Mitra nodded.

When Brian leaned toward her, the lamp beam hit her. A sheen of sweat coated her face. She wasn't as pretty as Fekiria, but she had a prettiness all her own, and right now, it was coated in a pale gray. He laid out his tarp, which wasn't sterile but would protect her against the wet ground, and motioned her to lie down.

Gingerly, she obeyed.

Being a soldier, he'd been through emergency field training. He knew how to dress a wound, splint a break, and apply a tourniquet. All the jazz necessary to save a life.

There was just one problem: he hated bodily fluids.

They were great. Necessary. *On the inside.* That's where they belonged.

Teeth clamped, he cut away the fabric around her injury, knowing he'd have to bandage her up pretty tight when he was done. The bullet tore through her coat, tunic, and the waistline of her pants. It wasn't good. Not the holes in the clothes nor the one in her side. He wasn't a doctor, but he had a bad feeling about this injury. With no exit wound, it meant the bullet was still in there, digging around, agitating organs and tissue. Infecting. If they were out here too long and she didn't get medical attention, she'd go septic.

So much for Fekiria's promise that it was a graze. He'd have a word with her later. This should've been addressed earlier. Warm blood gushing over his hands gave his brain mixed signals—grateful for the heat, but knowing that heat shouldn't be happening. His stomach roiled as he cleansed the injury, applied the stasis foam to the bleeding, and wrapped her up tight.

"She should keep still for a while," Brian said to Fekiria, meeting her green eyes evenly. "Have them lie next to her with that thermal blanket. I need to check toes and fingers." Fekiria wrapped the blanket over them and tucked in the supplies then brushed back the hair of the little one.

A soft whimpering started from one of the girls as Brian cleaned up the medical supplies, and Fekiria urged Aadela and Sheevah toward the woman. They cuddled next to her, barricading themselves at the back of the cave, but the whimpering only grew worse. They were getting warm, which would mean if they had frostbite, they'd probably feel a prickly sensation if not outright pain in their digits as circulation returned.

Brian squatted beside those huddled beneath the thermal blanket and smiled at them, taking the teen's hands. She snapped her gaze down. He glanced at Fekiria. "Tell her what I'm doing."

As Pashto flew between the two, Brian checked her fingers, the tip of her nose—he'd avoid her ears since she wore a hijab—then her toes. Pinkish but not gray. He pinched her skin and she hissed.

"Good." He moved to the little one and smiled at her as Fekiria moved in behind her, softly explaining what he was doing.

His gut tightened as he held her fingers. A grayish tinge had already crept into them and the tips of her ears. "She's showing signs of frostbite," he said as he lifted her leg. "Talk to her. This might hurt." He tucked her foot beneath his arm.

Wide eyed, Aadela stilled. But then he saw the shift to pain. Her face screwed up. She cried out. Tried to wrench her foot free, but Brian held her firm.

"It'll pass," Brian reassured. She needed more protection against the elements. He'd have to go back and get the pelt from that snow leopard. He didn't relish the thought of skinning it, but he had no idea how long it'd take them to reach civilization. Or if they'd be confronted again by the terrorists.

Fekiria wrapped her arms around Aadela as the girl's cries softened, *shh*ing her and rocking.

"Keep massaging her toes." Brian lifted Fekiria's booted foot and started unlacing it.

—◊—

23 February—2313 Hours

Startled at the intimate touch, Fekiria yanked her foot back and snapped her gaze to Sergeant Brian, her heart thumping.

Hands up, he cocked his head a little. "I need to make sure you don't have frostbite."

"I don't." She swallowed as something in her stirred at the thought of him touching her feet.

He held her foot again. "Pardon me if I don't believe you. Wouldn't be the first time you've lied to me."

"I've *never* lied to you." Her own admission shocked her. It was true. She hadn't deliberately lied to him about anything.

"True," he said, unlacing the boot. "But you've omitted a lot. And I wouldn't put it past you to omit that you can't feel your toes right now." She froze as her boot slid off.

Sergeant Brian cupped the back of her foot with one hand and peeled back her sock. A rush of heat shot through Fekiria. Embarrassment. And shame. Feet were considered dirty by Muslims. But no, that's not what filled her cheeks right now. It was. . .his touch.

His hands were strong and callused as they squeezed and rubbed her foot. "A bit pink for you, but—" When he looked up at her, he stilled, his gaze roaming her face.

She yanked back her foot. Tugged up her sock. "I told you I was not lying."

"So you weren't." He handed her the boot, something unreadable in his expression.

She snatched it and stuffed her foot in. Even as she secured the laces, she could feel him watching her and refused to acknowledge him.

"What about your other foot?"

She flicked a mean glare his way, her heart about to jump out of her chest if he touched her again. "I'm fine."

"Ten toes, but each one counts." He shrugged as he squatted before her. "Not sure you'd forgive me if you lost one because I didn't check it."

"That will not happen." Neither him checking it nor her losing one. Because her toes were fine. *She* was fine. When she finally looked up, she felt a squirt of heat through her stomach. She pulled her gaze back down but couldn't ignore what she felt. What she saw—though she wasn't sure, she thought she saw a hint of a smile.

Still crouched, he wheeled around. Grabbed a couple of items. "I'll be back. Stay here." When he shifted, he handed her the weapon again. "Use it if someone comes without giving you the password."

Fekiria blinked as she took the gun. "What password? Wait—where are you going?"

"Out. Need to take care of that cat before someone sees it."

Oh. Yeah. That made sense. "What's the password?"

"Pink toes."

"You are laughing at me." Stunned, she shoved her attention to the ground, squished the hurt she felt.

"Only a little." He touched her chin and nudged it up. "Hey, it was cute. I didn't mean—"

"Just go." She hated that she'd had such a visceral reaction to his touch.

Her words vanquished Sergeant Brian's lightheartedness. He considered her for a moment then turned and left. Grateful she could once again breathe, Fekiria tugged Aadela a little closer. Almost as if the six-year-old could protect her.

From what? Yourself?

"He is a good man," Mitra whispered.

"He's *American*." Throwing that out there did nothing to lessen the cracks in her resolve or the searing memory of his touch. Of his gentleness even with those large hands. Of his commitment to helping and protecting them—*despite* being American.

He'd held her without comment or retort after he killed the snow leopard. Shock had stripped her of common sense, falling into a man's arms like that. She could even still smell him.

"You are a dear, sweet friend." Mitra pulled in a hard breath and stiffened for a minute. Slowly, she relaxed, her eyes fixing again on Fekiria. "But you are being childish and foolish."

"You said the same thing to me when I would not listen to your proselytizing," Fekiria shot back.

Mitra smiled. "I confess I was zealous then." Her expression grew serious. "You are a smart woman. Don't let rash thoughts and quick judgments smother your future."

"Future?" Fekiria laughed and came around her friend's side, tucking her in a little better beneath the thermal blanket. "I think you are more ill than you realize."

"I hope not," Mitra said with a grimace. "Because I feel terrible and I do not want Hadassah to grow up an orphan."

Sobered by the words, the plight of her friend, Fekiria focused her attention on the situation. On their desperate need to get back down the mountain. Not on Sergeant Brian.

"Where did he go?" Sheevah asked, curled on her side next to Mitra.

"To get the skin from the leopard." Fekiria stared at the opening, half expecting him to be there or to come through it. But it was dark and empty. What if he took off? He'd be quicker and faster without them.

"Did he leave us?" Aadela asked, tears pooling in her eyes.

"No," Fekiria answered quickly. Decisively. "He wouldn't do that."

And somehow, she knew it was true. Knew he was a good man, just as Mitra said. "He takes care of us and will make sure we are safe again before he leaves."

The thought seared her heart. He would leave, wouldn't he? As an American soldier, his loyalty was to his country. Not Afghanistan. Not her.

Stupid. Why was she even thinking like this?

Fekiria pushed to her feet, remembering how he had to duck to walk in the cave, and made her way to the opening. Cold air pulsed against her. Surely it didn't take that long.

A thumbnail between her teeth, she eased into the narrow passage that switched back. She scooted along until she could see out. Threat of danger kept her from stepping into the open. But she couldn't see anything. The way the snow fell in blankets felt as if she were facing an opaque wall.

She shimmied back into the cave, frustrated. Afraid. Rubbing her arms, she tried to ward off the chill seeping into her bones. Into her very soul.

"His binoculars."

Fekiria turned to her friend. "I'm sorry?"

"Use the binoculars. He's been gone. . .too long." Eyelids drooping, Mitra looked toward Sergeant Brian's ruck.

So it wasn't just her. She hurried to his large camo pack and retrieved the binoculars. She returned to the opening and strained—even with the long-range vision—to see anything. After scanning the hills, the open area between this incline and the jutting mountain opposite, she searched for the spot where he'd killed the snow leopard. Where he'd saved her life.

Tightening up the contrast, Fekiria froze at what came into focus.

Two men. Attacking Sergeant Brian.

CHAPTER 34

23 February—2330 Hours

Pain exploded across the back of Brian's skull. His knees buckled. He shoved his hands out to break his fall and landed on all fours. Head dangling, he groaned, his only thought the women in the cave depending on him. Fekiria. She could die if he didn't—

A boot came into view.

Brian swiped it. Caught the back of the slick heel and flipped the guy.

Thud!

Snow puffed up as the man hit the ground. Brian pounced. Slammed his fist into the face. Heard the crack. Felt the spurt of hot liquid. The attacker went still. Brian leapt up, reaching for his weapon. . .that wasn't there.

Scrambling, he came to his feet, hunting for the other two. They'd come out of nowhere when he was knee deep in the leopard blood. He'd been there, shielded against the worst of the wind and snow, when he noticed them come over the rise. He snatched up his modified Glock, but he hadn't been aware of the third Talib—right behind him.

Burning awareness rushed through him. He was badly outnumbered. Women were depending on him. And he didn't have a prayer.

Actually—he did have that. Or could. *God, help me!*

An invisible fist punched him. Knocked him backward. Brian grunted—he'd been shot. Though he could see, he couldn't breathe. Felt like a rocket had slammed into his chest. The ballistic inserts of his tactical vest prevented penetration but didn't prevent the impact. He blinked. *Breathe!* But there was no air. The edges of his vision started ghosting.

No! He couldn't die. Fekiria. The women. He had to get them to safety. If he died and these Taliban found them. . .

Snow crunched to his left.

Another assailant coming closer.

Brian grabbed a tendril of air. Choked. Coughed. Coiled onto his side, his vision returning.

A boot dropped on his face.

Cringing against the pain that spirited down his neck and shoulders, Brian grabbed both ends of the ankle. Twisted. Upended the guy. Brian rolled to the side. Something hard and cold hit his hand. He knew that feeling! His frozen fingers coiled around the rifle. He glanced, identifying it as a Kalashnikov. Brian shoved to his feet, lifting the rifle. Then struggled to stand, bringing the weapon to bear.

Brian aimed it at the attacker. Fired.

Something wrapped round his neck.

Brian grabbed at it. Felt the rope. Focused on the attacker. Dropped his full weight down. Dragging the guy with him. The man fell forward. Brian drove his elbow into his face.

He stumbled back, freeing Brian.

Twisting around, Brian sighted the attacker.

Blood dribbling down his chin, the man sneered, the fight still burning in his heart as much as in Brian's. This duel would be bloody and to the death.

So be it. Brian dove into him. Tackled him. They rolled. And rolled. Brian tried to control the ending so he was atop the attacker. But the man whipped him around.

Pain erupted across the back of Brian's head and neck. He pitched forward. Dropped onto his knees in the cold, biting snow. With a groan, he tried to shake off the spots in his vision. He reached for his Glock. The holster was empty. He'd given it to Fekiria. As the realization hit him, so did another—crunching snow. Coming closer.

Brian looked for a weapon. He saw nothing but a rock. A stock. Dead leopard. The thing was bloody and strewn across the snow five feet away. If he could get to it, he could swing the thing.

A shout in Pashto or Farsi froze him.

To his left, the man loomed over him. So this was it. Fight like a demon to protect the women only to end up in a puddle of leopard blood. Options. He needed options. But he didn't have any. He'd already run through the mental checklist.

If he feigned surrender, could he gain the upper hand? Or at least the man's Kalashnikov? Hands raising and mind racing, Brian slowly came to his feet.

The man aimed.

Brian tensed.

Crack!

He blinked, waiting for the searing pain. For death. In the split second it took him to realize he hadn't been shot, the man tumbled forward.

Thud.

Crumpled to the ground, the man's body was limp. A dark stain spread out from his head.

Brain catching up with the scenario, Brian searched his surroundings. His heart jump-started when he saw a blur racing toward him. First instinct: fight! Grab the guy's weapon.

Two seconds later, a small form plowed into him. His mind registered her—*Fekiria!*—only as he brought his hand up to punch her. Her arms flung around his waist. Snapped tight.

Okay. Okay, he could live with that. Better than a bullet or another fist. And this was twice now she'd thrown herself at him. He didn't care. He held her tight. Grateful she'd been there. Grateful she'd had firearm training. Grateful that propriety and national boundaries vanished in the heat of battle. This girl he liked. This girl, he'd be willing to take home to Granddad.

She shoved him back. "Why did you come out here alone? It's too dangerous! You could've been killed." She shoved him backward again. "Then what would we do?"

She was worried about him. He couldn't help but grin. This hot, kick-butt chick who hated American soldiers was worried about *this* American soldier. A smart-aleck comment danced to his lips, but he stopped it.

"I saw all the blood, saw you sprawled out—" Her words caught in her throat.

Brian's excitement over her reaction crashed and burned in the pain shining in her eyes. She was scared. Really scared. He cupped her face. "I won't leave you." Staring into those green, frightened eyes did something screwy to his chest. Made it hard to breathe. "Not if I can live and move."

She slapped his chest. "That's the problem! They were going to cut you down."

"They didn—"

"Don't you know what country this is? How these men feel about—?"

"Hey—"

"Don't be so stupid and get yourself killed, leaving us—"

Brian caught her mouth with his. Awareness and excitement whipped his good sense right out of him. Her lips were soft, though dry from the elements. Though cold at first, they quickly warmed as she responded. Returned the kiss.

Shouldn't be doing this. With body armor on, he couldn't feel her curves against him, but he had enough imagination to fuel the kiss deeper. It was like an electric bolt right through him. She tasted sweet. And salty. Like. . .*tears.*

Brian broke off. Tears? Was she sweating? Or crying?

Fekiria dropped her gaze fast. Held on to his biceps without moving, her fingers digging into his arms. She stood there in the snow, the heat of their passion the only thing warming them now. And really, it shouldn't be happening. There were a million reasons why.

They'd just been shot at. She was Muslim. He a Christian. She hated Americans. They couldn't let stress and exhaustion whittle away their values and beliefs. Standing out in the open while attackers were out here—

Yeah, why don't you just flip on the neon We're right here sign? Stupid as it gets. Didn't he remember that talk he'd had with himself earlier? The one where he'd said chicks like her didn't change?

Finally, she released him and pushed away. Stomped away, head still down.

"Fekiria." Brian stood there, cursing himself and his foolishness. "Wait. We need to stick together." *Right. Kiss the tar out of her and expect her to just act like a soldier again?* He'd never taken dating seriously before. He'd never thought twice about kissing a girl.

Until now.

His entire universe had shifted. It was insane, and he couldn't explain it, but he didn't want to hurt her. And if there was something Brian Bledsoe excelled at—it was hurting people he cared about. He stood there, feeling as if God had placed a glass rose in his hand.

His big, clumsy hands that were more often in fists than open and welcoming.

But would God put a Muslim girl in his path?

That doesn't even make sense.

—⁓—

"Hey, stay close."

Fekiria stopped, hating herself. Hating him. Hating the world. She wanted to cry—no, she *was* crying! She batted the tears. The way he'd kissed her. . .she'd never felt like that before. The explosion of heat in her breast. The urgent but gentle way he held her, the way his lips caressed hers.

"Give me ten minutes," Sergeant Brian said. "I'm almost done with the pelt."

Huddled against the cold, she kept her back to him. "Why did you have to skin it?"

"Aadela needs more protection against the cold. If she goes hypothermic, we'll lose her."

Fekiria snapped toward him. Stopped, her mind racing at the thought of the little one dying. But she couldn't look at him, not without thinking about the kiss.

Turning away from him, she sat on a rock, looking out over the small plain. They couldn't do that again. That's why she hated herself— she *wanted* it again. Wanted the strength that poured out of him when he was close. Wanted the way he looked at her. Touched her. But she couldn't give herself to anyone when she didn't know who she was. He's American. She was supposed to hate Americans. Had been raised to believe that way. To hate that way.

And God. Or Allah. Some said they were the same. Zahrah and Mitra disagreed. Most converted Muslims preached they were not the same. Though her mother was a good Muslim woman and she knew many, many good Muslims, Fekiria could not deny the tug she'd felt for years to find the truth. Yet instead of searching for the truth, she had run. From anyone and anything that had to do with religion.

Fekiria lowered her head and rubbed her temple. *I don't know what I believe.* She never had. It had always been so twisted and convoluted. How many times had her people declared they were a religion of peace yet sent women and children with suicide vests to bomb in the name of jihad? Centuries ago, Christians had done the same with the Crusades. Many religions had waged war in the name of peace and their gods. It was one thing to fight for what you believed in. Another to force it on another unwillingly. She did not know which were real and which were fake. But she did know that the two most powerful examples of love she'd seen had come from Zahrah and Mitra—Christians.

Did that mean something?

From the corner of her eye, she watched Sergeant Brian. He stirred crazy things in her. Always had, which was why she'd rebuffed him from the beginning.

Her friend's words from earlier echoed in her mind. *"He is a good man."* And a good kisser. Heat spiked through her face again. Her mind replayed the way he'd taken charge, infused her with courage, which only made her angry, and then kissed her. Strong. Powerful. Hungry.

On her feet, she pressed the heel of her hand against her forehead as if she could push the memory straight *out* of her head. She just wanted to get out of here. Get away from him. From this storm that was devouring her life. Her hope.

"Okay. They're buried. Should be good for a while." He was next to her now, and when she glanced behind him, she could barely make out the mounds built up against the incline. He held up the leopard skin. Thankfully, he'd scrubbed away the blood. "It's wet, but maybe we can light a small fire to dry it out."

"You don't think they'll see the smoke?"

His intense gaze roamed their surroundings and the sky. "Maybe." He started walking, the pelt slung over his shoulder. "I'm just praying the wind and snow will blind them."

Praying? Did he really pray?

As they climbed, he hesitated before they entered the cave. Then glanced at her. "What we did—"

Fekiria glared at him then pushed past him into the cave. She would not talk about the mistake. She did not want to hear him apologize. Or say he shouldn't have done that. Or even bring it up because she had no idea what she felt or thought about it. Except for liking it. A lot. Too much.

"Wait," he hissed, his voice low.

Ignoring him, she made her way around the switchback. Ducked, though she didn't need to, and slipped along the edges. She quickly scanned the darkened interior. At the back, curled against a pitch-black wall, Aadela and Sheevah slept soundly.

Near them, Mitra opened her eyes and glanced up. Then frowned. "You okay?"

"Yes. Fine." She picked her way toward them. "Three men found Sergeant Brian, but we are okay."

He stepped into the cave and hovered in the corner, where he used something from his pack to start a small fire. Only then did she realize he had a bloody gash across his right cheek. Several other cuts and bruises peppered his face. Blood shadowed his jaw and mouth.

"So, nothing else happened?" Mitra asked, her voice strange.

Fekiria frowned. "What else would happen?"

Mitra looked to be hiding a smile. "If you want to lie to your friend, you should wipe the blood from your mouth." She laughed. "Or should I say, *his* blood from your lips?"

Hauling in a breath, Fekiria turned away. Pushed herself to a corner and sat alone as she swiped furiously at her face. Looking at her hand, she found the red traces. Her gaze betrayed her and skidded into his, but she jerked away. Closed her eyes. Sagged.

Sergeant Brian came over, sat next to her, and extended a small cloth. "I tried to warn you before you came inside."

She snatched the cloth and wiped away the evidence. "It was a mistake!" The cave's echo snatched her hissed words and trailed them around the smoky area. She hated herself more for saying it. She'd never lied to him before. But she couldn't do this. Couldn't undo all the words she'd spoken. All the things she said she believed.

"For a mistake, you were pretty passionate."

Tears swarmed her vision. She fought them. Fought as hard as she could. "Leave me alone."

"No."

Fekiria glowered.

He angled one arm over his knee. "Things are complicated. But don't give me that about a mistake, that you don't like me. I see the way you look at me. The way you watch me when you don't think I know." He leaned closer, and her breath went shallow. "I know, because I feel the same way. I do the same thing. I can't get enough of being around you. And it doesn't make a lick of sense."

She looked into his eyes. "No." Everything in her trembled with the admission. "It does not."

He nodded. "Good. We agree." He seemed to be memorizing her face. And she couldn't help but think he might kiss her again. Instead he rose to his feet. "Get some rest. We pull out in a few hours."

CHAPTER 35

24 February—0113 Hours

Like peace, sleep evaded Fekiria. Cold and restless on the floor of the cave, she curled close to the others wishing for a small corner of the thermal blanket. But guilt pressed against her, reminding her that Sergeant Brian stood at the opening watching over and protecting them.

Sergeant Brian. She'd kissed him, and she did not even know his full name. Honestly, she did not know much except he was a man of courage and honor. He had integrity and respected her as a person. She'd had admirers and offers of marriage, and men who saw a pretty girl and wanted to know her.

Like Captain Ripley.

An ache squeezed her chest. They'd killed him. Somehow that tragedy seemed like weeks ago. Yet it was only a few hours. How could that be? She felt like they'd endured a thousand troubles. She should be angrier. Grieve him more.

But he never made her feel the way Sergeant Brian did. He talked to her like a friend. Like someone who was his equal. Captain Ripley did the same, but his closeness did not set off sparks in her stomach. Did not make her heart race.

Even now, remembering the way Brian cupped her cheeks, told her firmly and forcefully that he wouldn't leave her, swam as real and tangible as if his hands touched her now. Embarrassed as heat filled her again, Fekiria curled tighter, her nose against Sheevah's back.

Sleep dragged her into its icy embrace. Pale moonlight bathed the landscape in a chilling tone. Howling crested the wind and snaked toward her, reaching, pulling. The mournful timbre gripped her tight, like unbreakable threads cocooning her in its haunting song. Wind swirled and spiraled, taking corporeal form before her. A man. In all white. Robed in winter but radiant as summer. "Go to the house," his words came as a strong whisper tickling her ears. Loud, yet not.

Cool, but strangely warm.

Something prickling cold seeped up from the ground, tugging at her attention. She did not want look away from the man. He could not be real, not formed of snow and whispering on the wind. Yet he stood there. "Who are you? Are you real?" she shouted over the storm raging around them. Though she raised her arm to shield her face against the storm, in the middle of that tempest, they stood oddly unaffected.

Cold snapped around her ankles. Pulling. Hard. Fekiria shifted, tried to kick her feet, to rid herself of whatever it was, but it wouldn't release. She glanced down, stunned to find the snow around her ankles was black. Ebony staining the pristine blanket. With a yelp, she tried to free herself. Instead of freedom, she watched in horror as the black crept up her legs. "Stop!" Her gaze hit the man, who stood placidly watching. "Do something!"

"It is your own doing. Go to the house."

"I can't go anywhere!" She gulped panicked breaths. Black slid up around her waist, creeping ever upward. Her breathing tightened. Chest constricted. "How do I stop it? Please stop it!"

"Just say it."

Fekiria frantically looked between the blackness overtaking her body and the snow-white man. "Please! Help me!" The black reached her throat, the heaviness unbearable. She screamed.

"Fekiria."

Darkness like night bled through her vision. *I'm dying!* "No!"

A firm shake against her shoulder. "Hey!"

Fekiria blinked, catching something in her hand. She jerked herself up, gripping tight to the lifeline. She saw in the semidarkness the hard lines of a handsome face. "Sergeant Brian," she breathed. In relief, she pulled herself into a sitting position, a hand automatically going to her throat. She rubbed her neck, reassuring herself the blackness wasn't real. "I—I was dreaming."

"Screaming is more like it." On a knee, he leaned closer. "And really? After that kiss, you're still calling me *Sergeant* Brian?"

She met his eyes, disconcerted and unwilling to be goaded into verbally sparring. "The dream. . ." Swallowing hard didn't shake the dread or near tangibility of the dream from her mind.

He lowered himself to the ground, concern stamped on his face. "You okay?"

"The dream," she repeated. Silly to even try to explain the concoction of elements a brain puts together during a dream. She shook her head. "It's nothing. Just. . ."

"Yesterday was enough to create some demons for dreams. A few angels, too." A twinkle in his eye told her he was thinking of their kiss.

Only then did she realize the darkness didn't hang as oppressively. "It's. . .lighter."

"Dawn, but the storm's shielding most of it." He thrust his jaw toward the others. "Let's get them up. Time to set out."

"Already?" She glanced toward the opening. How long had she slept? Disoriented, she tried to shake the cobwebs from her mind. "Did you sleep?"

"I'm going to get the little one swaddled up with part of the pelt. Can you get the others moving?" Without answering her, he moved to the other side of the huddle and crouched beside Aadela. He didn't wake the six-year-old but drew back the thermal blanket, lifted her leg, and to Fekiria's surprise, slipped on a makeshift pelt-boot. How had he made that?

As he shifted to place the other on, he met her gaze. Nodded for her to get the others moving.

Yes. The others. "Sheevah, Mitra, wake up."

Her friend turned to her, eyes not even an ounce sleepy. A sly smile filled her face as she sat up. And Fekiria knew in that moment her friend had heard Sergeant Brian's comment about the kiss. But she would not discuss it. Instead she turned her attention to waking Sheevah. "Time to go."

Sheevah whimpered as she rolled over, sleep clinging to her with an iron grip. "I'm so tired."

"We all are," Fekiria said. "But the sooner we get out of here, the sooner we can reach town again."

"Quiet!" Brian hissed, hand over Aadela, holding her in place as he stared toward the opening. With stealth movements reminiscent of a panther, he pushed to a standing position and freed his weapon. Slid through the semidarkness toward the mouth of the cave, every step deliberate. Silent.

Fekiria felt every move, every step against the thundering of her heart as she watched him. Anticipated the moment when he'd—

He jerked back.

So did Fekiria.

Brian pivoted toward them, a new storm on his face. "Up," he hissed. "Now. Go!"

She knew enough and trusted him enough not to ask questions. If he said go, they did. On her feet, Fekiria grabbed the thermal blanket. Folded it in half then again as she hurried to Aadela, who was still groggy and not sure about the new warmth tied to her legs. "We have to go," she said to the little one.

"I'm hungry," Aadela whimpered.

"We will eat soon. But first, we must hurry. Can you do that?" She nudged the little one toward the front. "Go stand by Sergeant Brian."

Aadela shuffled toward him as he knelt, stuffing gear and supplies into his pack. Groggy, the little one slumped against his back as if she'd known him her entire life. Brian jerked up and glanced at Aadela. His expression went from surprise to. . .confusion, it seemed. Fekiria couldn't help but feel a small bit of envy that Aadela could lean on him so openly. Letting anyone know what she felt for him would open her up to ridicule, condemnation. . .humiliation. Perhaps even death. All these years she'd spewed the "Americans are evil" venom, that now she'd infected her own world with it.

"It is of your own doing."

As if a lightning bolt shot through her, Fekiria jerked upright. Was that. . .was that what the man in the dream meant? A gasping whimper came from the side. She watched as Sheevah helped Mitra to her feet, her friend almost doubled over in pain.

Brian was already watching Mitra, his expression grim. He said nothing as he met Fekiria's gaze evenly. And she understood his silent message—Mitra had to walk on her own. They had no way to carry her.

"C'mon," Brian hissed to them, a hand on Aadela's shoulder as he stood near the opening again. "Keep her close," he said to Fekiria.

She slid her hand into Aadela's. She wanted to ask him, needed to know what was going on out there.

"Go out and to the right. Around the cleft. Understand?"

Fekiria nodded then gave the instructions to the others in Pashto.

Sergeant Brian—because he was the soldier once more—stepped into the switchback and crowded out the light. Seconds passed before her vision adjusted and light returned. Fekiria scooted along the space, stone touching her shoulder blades and chest as she sidestepped through.

She ushered Mitra through with the help of Sheevah, who seemed very distressed at seeing her teacher—who was more like a mother—in pain. "Stay close to each other," Fekiria whispered as she followed them, holding Aadela's hand.

In the open, she moved quickly but noticed the thick gray blanket stretched across the sky. Snow, deep and powdery, layered the mountain again. Wind swept the powdery landscape with a rough hand.

"Go!" Brian hissed and leaned into his weapon propped on a rocky outcropping, part of the lip that protected them in the cave. He never looked back. Just kept his gaze trained on whatever he'd spotted.

She turned to the right, finding a very narrow footpath—not eight inches wide—that snaked upward around the mountain like a spiral staircase. Though she'd hesitated and considered Brian, and though Mitra and Sheevah had a couple minutes' head start, Fekiria was already on top of them. Urgency and panic thrummed against her pulse. They were in danger and her friend could barely move.

"Here," Fekiria said to Sheevah. "Take Aadela. Keep going. Faster!" She hooked her arm around Mitra's waist.

Her friend grunted. "It is a storm. You would think the bad guys would stay where it is warm."

"Their veins are heated by bloodlust."

Rocks gave way beneath Mitra's feet, causing her to stumble. Fekiria tightened her arm around her friend's waist, holding her up. Gritting against the weight and the cold. Slowly—too slowly—they wrangled their way up the steepening path. Minutes in, she glanced back down the path, seeing nothing but snow and a hint of the path they'd trod.

Where was he? Why hadn't he caught up?

But she had to keep going. He told her to. She was responsible for the others now. He would want her to keep on.

But where was he? It took as many minutes to traverse a dozen paces. Each second felt like an eternity, her ears trained on the terrain behind them. Waiting for his arrival. For him to rush in and save them. He would. That was who he was. What he did.

Then where was he? She glanced behind them again.

"You kissed him," Mitra said amid a shallow breath.

An embarrassing flush heated her cheeks again and made Fekiria angry. "Hush. Save your strength." She noted the bandaged wound must be bleeding again.

"It is your own doing," Mitra mumbled.

Fekiria's heart spasmed. "What did you say?" Had she really said the same thing the snow-white man uttered?

"The pride and hatred keeps you from feeling what grows in your heart." Mitra panted hard. She stumbled, rocks and snow rushing from beneath her feet. She pitched forward with a yelp.

Fekiria focused on balancing them both on the treacherous path. But it seemed the incline increased every few feet.

"For so long, you've said you hated Americans. Now you feel that you *must* hate them." A shaky smile accompanied pain-hooded eyes. "Let it go and love him."

"Ha." Fekiria adjusted Mitra's arm around her shoulder, pushing more into her friend to support her. "Your pain is making you delirious. Quiet. Focus on walking."

But Fekiria couldn't help looking back for him again. She imagined the worst—like last night when he'd been ambushed.

—∞—

Camp Eggers, Afghanistan
24 February—0635 Hours

"Where are they?!" Dean slammed his hand against the table.

Falcon, Titanis, and Eagle stood quietly at the bank of monitors, having just returned from a failed search. Hours fighting the winds and elements that blinded them gave the pilots zero visibility and forced them to turn back. Night had set in with a vengeance, cloaking Hawk and the women in its fury. The deadly conditions made it impossible to attempt a rescue, but that there'd been no comunication with Hawk infuriated him. Worried him.

Dean paced, hands behind his head. "They've been out there for twelve hours—overnight in subzero!"

"It's impossible," Sal said with a grunt, rubbing his beard as he shook his head.

"No!" Dean stabbed a finger at him. "Not acceptable."

"I just meant—"

"I know what you meant. But negative doesn't help. We need positive solutions."

With a nod, Sal relented. "There's no way to know where they went or where to look."

"South." Eagle's left arm hung in a sling, leftover from the firefight he'd had with the Taliban who attacked them. "Hawk's intent was to get as far south as he could, away from the city and those hunting the women."

"But he went *northeast*. Into the mountains," Dean repeated what Eagle told them once they'd rendezvoused.

"Initially, yes." The man scratched his reddish blond scraggly beard. "It was the only escape. Those men were right there, gunning for us. There wasn't a thing I could do."

"Nobody's blaming you, man."

Eagle gave an acknowledging nod, but the guilt hung on him like a ragged scar.

"Blame doesn't help anyway," Titanis said. "What we need is a strategy. A way to find them."

"Think they're still alive?" Brie Hastings asked.

"Yes," Dean answered in unison with Sal then added, "Even if he was dead, we'd go out there and find him. No man left behind."

"Hooah," Eagle muttered.

"Can we tap satellite coms to search for unusual chatter?" Knuckling the table, Sal stared over the map. "They're up in the mountains. Not going to be a lot of chatter out there. Have the teams look for cryptic communication."

"Yes." Dean felt the heat of hope surge through him. He pointed to Hastings. "I want to know any phone signals. *Any* digital or electronic signals out there. Anything unusual. Even the usual. Dig, dig, and dig some more." Dean jerked back a chair and dropped into it. "As soon as the storm breaks, we head back out."

Titanis glanced at his watch and groaned. "Bad news."

"What?"

"The storm is not moving out like we thought. It's getting worse."

Dean swallowed the curse climbing his throat. Now they would be grounded. No help for Hawk.

—※—

Tera Pass, Afghanistan
24 February—0645 Hours

With the silencer screwed onto the end of his weapon, Brian stared through the long scope. Three more Taliban had tracked them and uncovered the hasty burial. He had to buy Fekiria and the others time to get away from here. Slow down these rabid dogs who seemed to have an unnatural ability to find him and the women. This was a serious case of *bad*.

If things weren't bad enough already, the darkening sky—which should be lightening—was the portent of doom. The freakin' point of no return in every horror story. So he had to nail this sucker between its eyes so they didn't end up as roadkill.

Controlling his breathing as he leaned against the rock face, Brian zeroed his sights on the lead guy. It'd taken a few minutes to rout out which of the three was leading. He'd already adjusted for wind and elements. He eased back the trigger and neutralized him.

Even as he realigned his sights, Brian felt the trace of Death's icy finger on his spine. And the rocket launcher whipped out by one of the other Taliban told him why.

Oh crap!

Brian turned and threw himself toward the path.

Rock and fire exploded around him. Hands gloved, bloodied, and freezing, he pushed. Smelled something. Felt heat at his ear. Heard licking, crackling flames at his cheek. *Fire!* He shrugged out of his pack and dropped it.

Crack! The ground beneath his feet rattled. Brian glanced down. Snow seemed to levitate. Oh no. . .no no no.

The shelf broke away. Gravity yanked him downward.

GLASS WALLS

The plan was in place. With the help of Takkar Corp., Daniel managed to get things set up in country to continue what he'd already acomplished against the Americans—the digital disruption of GPS signals. He'd misrouted, rerouted, and killed numerous radio communications, coordinates, and orders.

In exchange for help from a local tribal leader, he'd sent the team that had caused entirely too much trouble scattering in different directions. They would be ineffective. Useless. And perhaps even dead. His father's name would live forever.

"Sir."

Daniel did not like that tone. Urgent. Fearful. Filled with bad news. He remained at his bar and turned the glass in his hand without responding. They had made significant progress. He needed to cling to the success a little longer. A few more steps and they would have the operational security of the U.S. military completely crippled. They'd send the location of every black ops group—

"Sorry, sir, but—"

Calmly, Daniel slipped his hand inside his jacket and lifted the weapon holstered there. He shifted on the seat and aimed the gun at the messenger. And fired. *So much for not killing the messenger.*

Shuffling feet came running.

Mother.

Daniel stood and stalked to the hall before she could see. "Go back to your room, *Māma*." He did not want to call the doctor again, especially over something he had done to incite her nerves.

"What has happened?" she squeaked, her voice quavering. "It

sounded like a gun."

"Nothing," he said as he guided her by the shoulders back to her room. Already he could hear his assistant removing the body from the living area. "A book. I dropped a book on the wood floor."

"You clumsy boy." She went easily to her bed and drew the coverlet up over her thin legs. "Where is Kiew? I miss her smile. Such a sweet girl. You need to marry her and give me grandchildren."

"I am too busy." He held her face. "I am finishing what *Bàba* started, remember? His legacy."

She eased back, a smile on her face that had begun to look like wrinkled rice paper. She touched his cheek as she did every night when he helped her with her medicines and rituals. "You are such a good son. Gang would be so proud!"

That was why he could not fail. He *must not* fail. Exactly the reason he did not want to hear the news the messenger brought.

But even he knew not hearing did not make the news less real. It would only delay his stress a little while. He pressed a kiss to his mother's cheeks then flicked off the light. A stroll through the house brought him to Kiew's personal room. He stared in, thinking of her in there. Sitting on the chaise, a satin robe around her curves as she looked out over Shanghai.

"It helps me think," she'd said the first time he caught her there.

"But when you sit like that, then I cannot think." He'd traced the curve of her leg and thigh. And their night ended in each other's arms beneath exquisite Egyptian cotton sheets.

He longed for her touch, her laugh. To hear her voice. To have her help him think this through. She soothed the savage within him. To a degree. A man in his position must do things that others would hesitate to do. But he must teach them. Guide them. Be a leader to them. And leaders were not weak.

His phone rang as he stood in the hall, staring at her bed. Turning, he answered the call. "*Nǐ hǎo.*"

"*Wǎnshàng hǎo,* Jin."

The sound of her voice shifted the axis of his world. Just a simple "good evening" from Kiew, but the soft lilt of her words slid over him like warm honey. Still, he must be strong. And he knew she would not risk calling so late and waking his mother unless— "What is it?" He thought of the dead messenger.

"We had the team, but they escaped. One fled into the mountains. We are hunting him."

Clenching his eyes, he lowered his head. Turned to the rage that rumbled through him. He had ignored it too long. "Fix this!"

"We are working—"

"*Fix. It!*" he roared, his voice bouncing off the glass walls.

CHAPTER 36

Tera Pass, Afghanistan
24 February—0700 Hours

Fifteen minutes and he still hadn't shown.

The path had leveled out, but Fekiria wasn't willing to continue without knowing if Brian was okay. "It's taking too long."

"Go." Mitra reached for a cluster of large snow-covered rocks. "I'll sit." She drew in a breath and let it out in a gulp. "I need...the rest."

"Sheevah," Fekiria called to the teen a dozen paces ahead. She felt the ache of winter's breath stiffening her own bones as she waved the girl back. When the two returned, she said, "Stay with them. I'll be right back."

Fekiria set out, resolved and relieved to find out what happened to him. Each step made her heart pound harder. What if she had waited too long? Her fingers no longer ached against the cold—they were too numb—but she gripped the weapon as tight as she could. Or imagined she should. Her gaze skipped to her left. A brief opening in the clouds gave her a glimpse at the landscape. They were alone. Utterly alone and very high up in the mountain. Had they really climbed that high?

The shortness of breath.

The nausea...

"God, help us," she muttered. And in her heart, she reached for a thin thread of hope that Mitra and Zahrah's God would hear her. He seemed to hear them. Would He listen to her prayers?

As if an invisible hand blocked her, Fekiria stopped. Her attention lasered in like a targeting system on the space several meters away. A dark shape loomed there, taking stronger shape with each heartbeat. When her mind pieced together his long tunic, she choked back a scream.

Taliban!

A thousand questions pelted her as she spun around but nothing more powerful than the relief that he'd been looking the other way when she saw him.

Her foot twisted, but she threw herself up the spiral incline heedless of the pain tightening her ankle. Thick snow became a stark enemy, trying to push her back. Fekiria fought the elements, her fear, the questions—where was Sergeant Brian? Why were the Taliban ahead of him? Would they die here?—and plunged around another ledge.

The three waited, huddled against the cold and misery. "Get up! Go!" Fekiria growled, working every muscle to keep her voice down but urgent.

Sheevah punched to her feet, wide eyed and gripping Aadela, whose confusion washed over her face like a sheen of sweat.

"Run," Fekiria hissed as she rushed in and scooped her arms around Mitra, who felt rubbery in her grip. "Mitra, are you with me?"

Her friend's head lobbed, eyes popping open then drifting closed.

Fekiria shook her. "Mitra!" She strangled the sob in her throat. "Mitra, you must fight!" Afraid of the men pursuing them, the weapons they carried, she dragged her friend to her feet. Tugged her around the corner. Wedged herself in under Mitra's arm and wrapped her arm around her waist. Holding her left hand with her own, Fekiria forced herself to move. To put one foot in front of the other. The adrenaline shot through her, pushing her hard.

She wanted to cry. Wanted to shake her friend. Smack her into fight mode.

"Leave...me." Mitra's whispered words were almost lost in the wind and the huffing breaths.

Let them be lost. She could not let herself think of her friend as dying. That path was a dangerous, hopeless one. One they'd trip on and fall over the ledge to their deaths.

"Hadassah is waiting," Fekiria said. "You *must* fight this."

Mitra tensed. Her feet found traction in the crunching snow.

Crunching...snow...

Fekiria glanced back. Their footprints in the path created a homing beacon to their location. But there was nothing to be done for it. They had no time to hide their tracks.

"Here!" Sheevah waved to her from a thicket jutting up defiantly out of the snow and off the level area.

If they went there, they could be found.

But if they didn't, they *would* be found since Mitra could not move fast enough. Fekiria guided her friend into the area. "Sheevah, help," she said as she turned and shoved snow across the path and down. She swept her boots side to side, backstepping into the thicket. It was a vain hope to conceal their tracks.

Branches scraped her jacket noisily, and she could not help but wonder if the Taliban could hear that over the wind stalking the mountain. Eased to the ground by her friends, she brought out the weapon that Sergeant Brian had given her. She would not go down without a fight, without protecting Mitra, Aadela, and Sheevah.

Tiny arms wrapped around hers, binding Fekiria's weapon arm against her side and forcing her to look down. Aadela's pale face shone with the fear that gripped Fekiria's own heart. She swallowed, lifting an arm to place it around the six-year-old. "Shh," she whispered then readjusted so her aim was not hindered.

"Where is—?"

A shout came with a breeze that rustled the branches of the pine leaves, which teased the edges of Fekiria's cheek. She remained unmoving, muzzle pointed out. Three men came into view, their Kalashnikovs dangling carelessly. Anger and confusion gouged hard lines into the grim, weathered expressions. The tallest of the three tugged on his scraggly beard. One whose beard and hair were more gray than brown waved the youngest up the path, while the beard-tugger pointed to the path.

They know. Covering their path only created confusion, but it might buy them some time. It was a futile attempt—they were Taliban. Trained to track. Trained to kill. Merciless in both regards.

But not covering it would have drawn immediate attention.

Fekiria waited, watching and listening.

"They could not just vanish," Beard-tugger groused.

"Hiding tracks does not work." The older laughed. He turned a slow circle until his all-too-knowing eyes landed on the thicket. His eyes then narrowed as a sneer pushed his face into a menacing mask.

The thudding in her chest threatened to betray her. *Please, God!*

Aadela whimpered.

Sucking in a hard breath, Fekiria yanked the girl farther into her, pressing her face against her hip. She crushed her to herself, willing the whimper to die on the wind. To not betray them. Holding her breath gave Fekiria little confidence they wouldn't be found. Even the slightest movement of her head could betray them. The twig digging into the back of her head could shake loose some snow.

The man brought his weapon to bear. Muzzle pointed right at Fekiria.

A soft *thunk* sounded somewhere behind them. Both men yanked around.

Stealing a glance—without moving her head—Fekiria met Sheevah's glossy eyes. She tried to convey a "stay still, we'll be okay" look, but the girl remained terrified.

"Go. Check it out," Gray-beard ordered. Minutes hung like hours as the fighters waited.

"No tracks up the path," the younger said as he returned, his weapon now slung around his back. He feared little, this one.

Pine branches swayed against the tug of the wind, obstructing Fekiria's view again.

"What is Lateef doing?"

"Who knows?" The younger shrugged. Beside her, Mitra moaned.

Sheevah slapped a hand over her teacher's mouth and drew her close. Fekiria saw the grayness of death crouching at her friend's feet and prayed again they'd make it.

When she turned back, with a jerk Fekiria froze.

Beady black eyes peered through the branches.

CHAPTER 37

Tera Pass, Afghanistan
24 February—0715 Hours

A hand reached into the thicket.

Realizing she'd lowered the weapon terrified Fekiria. She snapped it up and fired. The sound ricocheted through the mountain like a giant thunderclap that pounded against her chest.

The man gasped and stumbled back.

But unlike Hollywood movies, the first shot didn't kill him. It only angered him. Solidified his determination to make her die an ugly death—she saw it in his eyes.

Large nostrils flared against the graying beard. He uttered an oath. Spat something about her being an American lover as he raised his weapon.

With a feral scream, Fekiria sprang from the thicket. Dove through the branches, carrying the man backward. They landed hard. His breath punched from him with a wheezing gasp. Before she could drive a punch into his face, she felt herself flipping.

Wrestling with him was another futile effort. He was bigger. Stronger.

Before she could fight it, Fekiria lay on her back with his hands around her throat. Squeezing tight. Tighter. Panic flooded her. She thrashed.

Like a cord snapped in her, she regained control.

Threaded her right arm up and under his. She threw all her weight to the right, breaking his hold. On all fours, she heaved raw, searing gulps of oxygen.

A scream from Aadela jerked Fekiria out of her air-deprived stupor. The young Talib was bent over in the thicket.

Reaching for him, Fekiria felt a noose wrap around her right leg. She clawed for purchase but found none. Just bone-numbing iciness.

Yanked backward, she collapsed against the frigid, wet snow. Funneling her energy once again into freeing herself, she stuck her left ankle behind her right. Used her hips to thrust herself around. The man was dragging her so quickly, her sudden twist caused him to stumble. His grip broke. Fekiria pushed up with her hands.

He didn't stay down long. With a growl, he lunged at her.

The screaming of the girls fueled her adrenaline. Told her she couldn't stop. She had to kill this man. Kill all of these men before they killed them.

She kicked him in the gut. He doubled over. Used his forward momentum to slam a hard right into her jaw. Sent her flying backward. Her spine hit something hard. Knocked the wind out of her. Before she could move—even think—he towered over her. Kalashnikov in hand. Sneer on his old, shriveled face.

Crack!

Thwump!

Warmth splattered her face.

Then Gray-beard tumbled forward.

Fekiria rolled out of the way. Exhaustion weighted her. Relief flooded her. She still struggled for air. She heaved. *Breathe. Breathe!*

Another scream—Sheevah's this time—yanked her head up.

The young Talib slumped to the side, a crimson stain widening like a sick, twisted halo around his head.

Fekiria flipped over to a sitting position, staring out at the trees. Probing the terrain. The vegetation. Who'd shot the two Taliban? *Please—please, be Brian.* Scrabbling backward toward the girls, she saw a figure emerge.

Brian trudged out from between two trees, face bloodied, clothes torn and ragged. In truth—*he* looked ragged. His right eye was swollen shut. Lip cut and bulging, he swiped his gloved hand across a large scrape on his forehead. Blood glistened around his leg. A bloodied scrap of material—from the hem of his shirt, she guessed by the untucked and torn tactical shirt—tied around his thigh warned of another injury. A large knot rose on his cheek.

Fekiria lurched toward him. "Brian!"

His arm came around her without hesitation. A brief tight hug flooded her with relief and courage. "Let's move." He panted through the words as he moved toward the others. "They weren't alone."

Beneath the thicket, she knelt. "What happened to you?"

"Later." He gathered up the weapons from the dead Taliban.

"There was another," Fekiria breathed, glancing around for the last fighter.

"Dead." Brian's voice matched the word. Weapons slung over his shoulder, he turned and reached for Aadela. A tear in his upper jacket sleeve revealed another angry gash. His jaw muscle popped as he gave a tight-lipped smile to the six-year-old. He was in a lot of pain. She could see it on his face. In the stiff way he moved.

"Here. I'll get her," Fekiria said.

Brian's gaze hit Mitra. "She's unconscious."

"No," came a very weak response from the woman. Her eyes fluttered. "I'm...here."

Brian muttered a curse. Sat back on his legs, his chin resting on his shoulder, and he puffed out a breath. With another sigh, he nodded as if agreeing with something. "Mitra, look at me."

Her head lobbed in his direction, eyes shuddering open.

"I have to carry you over my shoulder," he said. "It will hurt. Understand?"

Pale as the snow and covered with a similar sheen as the wintry elements, Mitra nodded. It looked like a drug-induced nod, but she understood. And whether she did or not, he had to carry her.

But...how would he? He was already limping and in a lot of pain.

As Brian hoisted Mitra away from the tree she'd been propped against, he screwed his face against the pain. With one more hoist, he hefted her into a secure spot across his broad shoulders.

Hand on her stomach, Fekiria swallowed the metallic taste that squirted through her mouth. That had to hurt. A lot. With the pain he was in and the pain Mitra probably no longer felt...

It was too much to think about, especially knowing there was nothing to do but continue on. Fekiria knelt and let Aadela climb onto her back. With Sheevah's help, she tied the extra pelt across the little one's back. She looked at Brian, and he gave her a weak nod.

He led them through the trees, off the path. They climbed at an angle across the rugged mountains. Leaden legs plunged into freezing snow. Fekiria pushed onward, refusing to quit. Refusing to fail. Refusing to let Brian down.

24 February—1045 Hours

He carried the weight of the world on his shoulders.

What's the point, God? Brian pushed the defeatist thought from his mind. If he followed that course of thought, he'd end up at the bottom of a ravine again. But he couldn't get away from the thoughts. He'd been tracking down a cyber terrorist. Now, he trudged across the back of a dragon buried in snow. What was this?

Wind pushed against him, threatening as real and effective as an armed enemy. The thick clouds hid them from the sun. Hours they'd hiked, and he wasn't sure they were getting anywhere. The rugged terrain was brutal enough, but he intentionally walked at an angle to avoid climbing up. They couldn't go higher or they'd face colder temperatures and stronger winds. Aadela, who'd been whimpering and crying the last few hours, had frostbite, and the woman on his back was as good as dead if they couldn't get real medical help soon. And Fekiria—the dogged determination. . .watching her fight that Taliban. Brian could not erase that image, of the man punching her, aiming his Kalashnikov at her. . . If he'd been two seconds later, he couldn't have taken the shot. Fekiria would be dead.

He missed a step. His leg buckled. On a knee, he stared up at the glaring white. His gaze rose toward the gradation of clouds. Light gray above them. And beyond that—a thick mattress of gray that warned him they had to find shelter. These girls would not survive another night in the elements. He wasn't sure he would.

"You okay?" Fekiria asked, her words gentle and warm as she came alongside.

Brian nodded, hated feeling weak. Hated that he wasn't 100 percent. "We need shelter." He pushed her attention to the clouds, away from him. "That's not good."

Fekiria looked at the sky then around them. "There's nothing up here. I've flown over it."

"If we don't. . ." No. He wouldn't say that. Wouldn't put those thoughts in their minds. He hated it—could see the hope in their eyes. The belief that he'd get them out of this. With the sun hidden behind the clouds, he was using that one rugged peak as his compass. He had no idea if it was the right way. He just had to keep moving.

"She's unconscious." Fekiria touched the woman draped over his back.

She'd passed out as soon as he lifted her onto his shoulders. He'd expected as much with her injuries and the pressure being carried would create, but they were negative on options.

"If we're caught out here when that storm hits. . . I'd guess we have an hour to find shelter again before this place is like night and brutal," Brian said as he struggled to his feet again. Shards of pain clawed through his thigh as he put weight on it. He nodded to the little angel on Fekiria's back. "She's not doing well."

Snow swirled and danced around them again, thick and fat. Both of them considered the second wind the storm seemed to have taken. "Just when I thought we'd get a break. . ."

Powerful fists of wind and icy rain shoved against him, forcing him to strain to stand still.

"We have to get out of here. Descend." But the freakin' Taliban had been driving them farther up into the freezing maw of the mountain.

He started walking. Talking did nothing but make them more aware that hope was getting buried beneath the blistering blizzard, just like them. Though he stumbled, he refused to slow. Got up again. Put one boot in front of the other.

Going on thirty hours without sleep and rigorous hiking was taking its toll. But he couldn't stop. Couldn't fail this. He'd made the decision to chase down Fekiria in the market. That led to this. Just like the other decisions that had gotten people killed.

God, just a little more. And a little more. Whatever it takes to get them down.

His feet tangled again. Brian went down—hard. Scored his knee.

"A break," Fekiria huffed. "Let's take a break."

No! It wasn't smart. It could expose them. Allow the Taliban to catch up. But instead of arguing, he nodded. Shifted to the side. He lowered the woman to a soft patch of pine needles at the base of a tree then dropped onto his backside. With gritted teeth, he stretched out his leg, slowly. Easing himself through the agony.

Brian closed his eyes.

A nudge at his shoulder snapped him upright. He caught the attacker by the hand.

"Brian!" Fekiria's wide green eyes were just inches from his face. "Easy, easy," she whispered. "You fell asleep." Her gaze fell to where his gloved hand, cut up and bloodied, grasped her jacketed arm.

"Sorry." He released her and roughed a hand over his face. "How long?"

Fekiria knelt at his side. "Just a few minutes." She studied him.

Brian saw it—the disappointment in him, that he'd failed them. That mingled with her fear. "We'll get out of here." He met her beautiful eyes again. "Alive."

With a weak sigh, she slumped against him, staring out through the branches, obviously not believing him. She leaned her head on his shoulder in the quiet roar of the storm. Brian had nothing left. He'd keep going. Until the storm froze him from the inside out. He'd never felt so powerless. There was no call to make that gave them hope. They wouldn't make it off this mountain without a miracle.

God. . .I got nothin' left. The woman leaning on him in more ways than one would die, and there was nothing he could do about it.

Fekiria sat up straight.

Adrenaline stabbed through his veins, heating them. Stinging. He grabbed his weapon, ready to fight.

"No," she said, putting her hand on his and meeting his gaze. "No, I think. . ." On her feet, she dusted off her backside and moved out of the trees. She walked up the slope a little.

Brian struggled to stand, hobbling to avoid the agony ripping through his leg. "Fekiria!"

His breath clogged his throat when he saw her running back to him. But then—she was smiling. Confusion raked through him.

She threw herself into his arms. "I found it!"

He frowned. "Found what?"

"The shanty." She pointed back toward a jagged rise. "Over that crest and down the other side there's a shanty." She shoved back her hood and the hair from her face. "I flew over it about a week ago. Thought it was odd."

Brian's heart felt like a flooded engine. Flooded with so much gas— this time, the hope of shelter—the gears wouldn't catch. "Seriously?" His gaze shot to the rise. "You sure?"

"I checked. It's there." She hurried to the girls, talking quickly in Pashto.

Hobbling up the rock and snow-packed incline, he begged God to give her that miracle. Give her a way out. Let her live. He eased up, lowering himself to the ground as he did. Low-crawling, he made the summit and peered over.

CHAPTER 38

North of Tera Pass, Afghanistan
24 February—1515 Hours

Agony had nothing on what Brian felt in his fingers and toes. Frostbite was a vicious predator. On the other side, the land sloped down fairly steep then leveled out and provided the perfect place for the medium-sized structure. Not exactly the size of a shanty. And it had mud-and-plaster walls.

"Do you see it?" Fekiria's excitement reached him as she made her way up.

"Yeah," Brian said, not mirroring her enthusiasm. Especially not with the smoke rising out of that pit and the truck parked at the side. He lowered his head...and his hopes. It was there. Shelter. Just like he'd asked for.

Just filled with Taliban.

Brian pounded the ground. Tried to restrain himself.

"What is wrong? What is it?"

He shoved off the ground, still working to harness his frustration. Teeth grinding, he threaded his fingers behind his head. Just one break. Why? Why was that too much to ask?

Fekiria was at his side. "Brian, what is wrong?"

He turned away from her, away from the fact he'd failed her. Let her down. Brought her up here to die.

She stepped into his path. Caught his arms. "Brian."

"What do you want from me, Fekiria?"

"What did you see?"

He tried to look away from her. To the side. But he could still see her. He dropped his gaze. Closed his eyes. Exhaled in discouragement.

Her gloved hand touched his face.

"Taliban," he grunted. "It's a freakin' Taliban stronghold. We're screwed. This whole thing is messed up. The girls are—"

"Hey!" Fekiria's expression ignited. "Listen to me."

The ferocity in her words surprised him. Stilled him.

"We need you. So you have to keep it together."

Brian turned away from her, rubbing his frozen hands over his face. He shifted back to tell her it was hopeless. To say they ran out of options about thirty klicks back. Hands on his tac belt, he lowered his head again. She was right. He knew that. But he was empty. Fed up. Through. He pivoted and walked a few more paces down the path they'd just come.

God, this would be a real good time—

"They're leaving!"

Brian spun on his heels. Jogged as much as he could with his injured leg to the lip of the overlook. There, he flattened himself against the edge. Eased up, watched as the trucks filled with men. Shouts and hustling. *In a hurry...*

The brakes of the truck groaned and popped as it lurched forward over the snow. With it went the despair that had threatened and overtaken Brian just minutes earlier.

"Did they all leave?" Fekiria lay to his left, close enough that she could whisper.

"Don't know." He didn't have nocs since losing his ruck. "We'll need to wait, make sure they're gone. See if anyone else comes out, maybe for firewood for the night."

Please...please, God. He'd never prayed this hard so much in his life. The girls had been through too much. They wouldn't make it one more night without this to feed them, fuel their bodies and spirits. Then again, they could get down there and find the place emptied of everything. He hoped for food but knew necessity demanded shelter from the storm.

He traced a path with his eyes along the outer rim of the ridgeline that created the bowl-like shape, with one side missing. The same side the trucks had disappeared down. "C'mon." He shouldered Mitra onto his back once more. "We'll climb down while we watch. Get a little closer."

It took them almost an hour to make the bottom of the valley—well, not really a valley. Just a depression. The thought of warmth and protection against the winds kicking up gave them the strength to make it down.

"Wait here," Brian said as they took cover behind a couple of trees.

He crouch-ran as best he could across the open, holding his weapon in both hands and ignoring the knifing pain in his thigh. What bothered him more was the numbness in his legs. He slipped up against the structure and shouldered his way around the corner. Weapon up. Eyes alert.

He listened, or tried to listen, over the howl of the winds. It rattled against his ears and made it impossible to know if anyone else was inside. The window was boarded up and gave no offer of help in determining occupancy. Door. He'd have to go through the door.

Brian took a breath. Stared at the rudimentary barrier against the wind. Hand on the catch, he lifted it. . .slowly.

Once he felt it release, he pushed in, sweeping the room with his weapon up and heart pounding. A simple two-room structure. Large and open, the main area provided little comfort but immediate warmth. He hustled along to the opening that led to a secondary room. Smaller. A pallet on the floor. Bedroom.

But safe.

A cabinet sat against the wall. Odd. Out of place. Brian eased over to it. Weapon at head level, he aimed and reached the door. Gloved fingers coiling around the handle, he saw something red. And black. His heart thudded. Hard. Harder. Brian stepped back, visually tracing the wires.

He cursed. They'd rigged the place. Touch something, lose a hand. Touch too much, lose your life.

Boards creaked.

Brian turned in time to see Aadela hobble across the room toward a table.

Every thump of her feet on the packed earth hammered against his heart. One step. Two.

His gaze swung to the small two-door cabinet in the corner. A pantry, he guessed. And he saw the wires trailing from it straight to his feet.

The blur of the little girl headed straight for it.

She'd be blown to pieces.

"No!" He rushed forward and scooped her up. He held her tight, but she squealed in frustration against him. He spun toward the door where Fekiria and the teen waited with Mitra. "It's rigged! Don't move."

Brian delivered Aadela to Fekiria then cleared the room. "Go ahead and sit down. There's blankets in the other room. Get warm." He knelt before the pantry, tracing the wires to a gray brick. After a short exhale, he went to work disarming the device. Once he pulled the det cord free, he coiled up the wires. Opened the doors slowly, hoping there weren't more surprises there. He shuffled over to the large metal cabinet and traced the wires to another brick tucked behind the cabinet. He neutralized that, too. Boxed up the equipment then opened the doors.

He stood, stunned. "No way," he muttered as he ran a hand over the equipment. He grabbed a couple of devices and then squatted and laughed. "Jackpot!"

"What is it?"

"Sat phone, laptop."

A scream pierced the cabin.

Brian jerked toward it, saw Fekiria removing the little girl's boots. "No!" He rushed toward them. "Keep the clothes on. Just put more on."

"But she— You said—"

"Nothing comes off until we get medical aid. Clear?" Aadela would be screaming a lot—all of them would as their limbs warmed back up and circulation returned.

Fekiria stared at up at him and nodded. "You think we can get help?"

He pointed to the table. "If they aren't already working, I can get them up and running. Then we can make contact with someone. Get an extraction."

"Up here? During the storm?"

Brian's excitement deflated a little. "No. But as soon as it breaks." He motioned her back to the others. "First things first. Can you see what food there is?"

She bristled. "What, I'm the cook because I'm a woman?"

Brian almost grinned. Not five minutes out of the storm and already her fire returned. "I'll cook. You want to do surgery on Mitra?"

She blanched, her lips forming a silent O.

Brian rustled through the cabinet and found pretty much nothing he needed—except a bottle of what he thought, and Fekiria confirmed, was the equivalent of ibuprofen. He told her to mash some up and give it to Aadela. She and Sheevah needed to take a few, too.

"Why?" Fekiria asked. "I'm okay."

"How do your hands feel?"

She hesitated.

"And your feet?" Brian didn't mean to be confrontational. "You can't feel them, can you?"

She blinked. "I. . .I—how do you know that?"

He tossed a few pills in his mouth. "Because you're not groaning or screaming in pain." He swallowed dry and went to the other room where Mitra was laid out, unconscious. He packed a blanket around her then drew her pallet toward the other room. There, he built a fire in the small pit and let the warmth fill the room.

Aadela eventually fell asleep, and that's when Brian knelt to work on Mitra. Hand against her carotid, he knew the odds of making it were against her. Her thready pulse made it unlikely she'd survive any attempts he made to remove bullets. And he couldn't sew her up, so. . .

—∽∼—

24 February—1730 Hours

Violent shivering wracked Fekiria hours into their stay in the shanty. She made a light soup with some leftover partially rotten vegetables. They were not so ruined they were unusable, so in the pot they went. After their bellies were filled, everyone lay down.

Everyone, that is, except Brian. He worked on. Exhausted. In pain. He worked.

As she lay before the fire, her back to the flames, agony tore at her limbs, fiery yet freezing. She curled on her side, holding her hands, keeping her feet toward the fire. She shared a blanket with Aadela, who whimpered in her sleep constantly. Sometimes, waking into full fits of screaming that broke Fekiria's heart as she held up her hands in obvious pain.

Wind howled and the storm raged through the night as Brian sat on the floor, not far from the fire either, with a powered-up laptop. He'd told her right away there was no signal. No way to communicate—yet.

But he worked. Fastidiously. Shaking out his hands. With the fire behind her, she was sure he couldn't see her watching him because he made no effort to hide the pain as he tucked his fingers under his armpits and doubled over, his face screwed tight. His teeth bared in what would be a growl—that is, if he allowed himself to make a noise. But he didn't. He soldiered on, as he liked to say.

He was handsome—even with the swollen eye, the cuts and bruises. He never gave up. Never left them. Strong and brave. A fighter. *A good man.*

She drifted in and out of sleep, awakened often by Aadela. Sheevah burrowed closer to them, smiling at her and muttering something about Aadela sleeping better if she couldn't see Mitra. Fekiria understood— her friend looked dead in the flickering firelight. Grateful for the girl's wisdom, she scooted over a little until they had Aadela sandwiched between them. The next time Fekiria awakened, both girls were sound asleep.

Brian cursed.

She looked up but he wasn't in the same spot. She heard the *clack* of him typing behind her and rolled onto her back. He was propped against the wall, his feet near her head, the glow of the laptop splashing a dull light against his beat-up face.

"What's wrong?" She tucked an arm behind her head to prop herself up.

Brian heaved a sigh. "Trouble."

Fekiria groaned.

"No kidding." He lifted the laptop, drew his feet closer to himself and put the computer near her face. He laid down on his stomach. "I think. . .I think the men who were here are the people who've been hitting my team."

Fekiria rolled onto her side, pushing her torso up. "Really?"

Another strong exhale. "Yeah." He jabbed a still-gloved finger toward the screen. "These codes. . .If I've figured it out right, they match the coordinates for our troops. It's all old data though. But still—"

"It's a lead."

Brian considered her. "You seem as excited as me."

"They took over my aircraft and tried to make me kill innocent people. Those are not the type of people who need to control Afghanistan, so yes—I am excited."

He bounced a finger toward the screen. "I'm running a program, searching the laptop for key phrases. If I can get this back to the base, they can dig into it better."

"Do you know who's behind it?"

His gaze bounced over the different applications running. "We only have theories, suspects, but no proof. Not sure I can—if I had equipment, I probably could figure something out—which is why I want to get this back to Command."

She noticed the disassembled phones on the floor. "They don't work?"

"Still working on them."

Fekiria couldn't help but smile. "I didn't realize you were so smart."

He scowled. "I'm not."

"How can you say that? The last twenty-eight hours, you've protected us, guided us. You knew how to skin that leopard. How to fashion extra protection for Aadela, how to perform surgery on—"

"Okay, okay." Brian shifted his attention back to the computer, his expression stern.

She'd faced her brother's anger. Her father's. And took it in stride. But seeing Brian's turned her stomach. "I did not mean to anger you."

Brian hung his head. "I know." He put a fist to his cracked, bloodied lips. "It's just. . . I don't like people thinking. . .*saying* I'm smart."

"Why? You are very smart."

"Smart isn't always a good thing."

Fekiria studied him. What was behind that statement?

"My dad," he said, as if it hurt to even speak the words. "My dad was this majorly smart guy—rated Mensa. He was too smart for his own good, felt he didn't owe anything to those who depended on him. His work, his wife, his family." Brian seemed to study the dirt floor. "When I was fifteen, he was arrested. Someone had told the police what he was doing behind closed doors."

"What was he doing?"

"Running a really big scam. Stealing money and funneling it to other agencies. He thought he was so smart he didn't have to answer to anyone else." He tried to wet his lip and shook his head. "He's in prison still. The whole thing really got to me. Changed my life."

Something in his expression shifted, went. . .vacant. Fekiria eased up, as if she could draw him out from the hole he'd vanished into. She could only imagine the humiliation his family must have faced when his dad went to prison.

"Why? Was it hard on you and your family after. . .?" Wondering about it and voicing it were two different things. She hurt for him—this clearly affected him. "Was it the shame?" She could relate to that, with all that had happened with her family.

A twitch in Brian's left cheek almost seemed like a smile. "No." He looked at the laptop, seemingly *through* it. "No, it changed my life because. . ." His hesitation dangled on the precipice of something haunting. Fekiria wouldn't push. If he wanted to share it, he would.

BORIS

Taking a bullet in the head would've been so much less painful than this whole interlude with the Chinese. Take down the American computers. Spy on them. Make them hurt.

Sounds easy, right?

That's what I thought, too. But now I'm staring at underground chatter in the hacker world and hearing something very disturbing. Osiris is taking credit for my work. The brainless, dimwitted Chinese hackers are taking credit for *my work*.

No. This is not happening.

I grab my phone. Almost press the keys through the device as I dial the number I'm not allowed to store in my phone but I've memorized.

"What do you want?" Her voice is sultry and hateful. Weird combo, but totally works.

"That is my code you've been using. My work. My genius—"

"If you call this number again, I will make sure your genius is available for everyone to see."

A threat? I laugh. "You can't kill me. You kill me and everyone will know."

"Yes, precisely," she says—and I swear it sounds like a cat purring. It's totally sick. And hot, which is twisted and wrong since she's totally threatening me. "You understand?"

I grit my teeth, forcing myself to be civil. "This isn't right."

"Do. You. Understand?" she asks, biting out each word.

"Your words are clear." I will not tell them I understand. Because this is wrong on every level and then some. And they've screwed me over so many times I can't see straight. Now. . .*now* they're taking credit for my handiwork.

Know what they say about payback, right?

I crack my knuckles and stretch my neck. This may be my last act of kindness, but it's going to be a doozie. Then Osiris will know not to mess with me. And I have the perfect counterpart to disguise as an accomplice. The Doris to my Boris.

But how...how can I do this? How to tip off the Americans without tipping *my* hand?

A line of code pops up on one of my monitors to the left. *"What the. . .?"* It's one of the hack-proof systems I provided. One that, of course, has a backdoor code. No decent programmer would hand over his tech without one. But—

I glance at the other computer. The video feeds from the chopper. From the other locations. Nobody should be on that laptop. They'd told me it wasn't working.

Streaming data sprints up the screen.

"Holy crud," I whisper, wheeling my chair to the keyboard. "Someone's hacking it."

It's a race. Whoever it is, he's almost in. And that *can't* happen. My fingers are racing against my brain. Where did this laptop come from?

Son of tortoises! It's him. It's Hawk. Gotta be. These systems were in the safe house.

And then, like a generator powering down, I realize. . .

This is perfect. Absolutely, singularly perfect.

So it's time to show them who is really in control. A few tips here and there—really, did they not figure out I'd tipped off the military elite months ago?—to remind my Chinese friends who had given them this feast on a platter.

While my good friend Hawk is hammering his way through the security measures, I'll just lay a golden egg.

A few keystrokes. . .

Right in his lap.

But just for good measure, to make sure nobody knows how many cards I have in play, I lift the phone. Dial.

Yeah, I know. She said not to call. But trust me, she's going to want to hear this.

"Are you stupid, calling me again?"

"Quite the contrary. I have information you will want." Oh wait. I can't tell her he has the laptop. Because they'll take it or kill it or him. "I know where he is."

Silence greeted me.

Ahhh, thought so, genius. "He's at Location Four."

And just like that, my systems are going berserk.

They're back-tracing me. Trying to figure out how I know where he is. I have to admit—my heart starts pounding. Did I go too far? Have they figured out what I'm doing?

"Good night, Mr. Kolceki."

That's it. They're coming after me. They're going to try to kill me. Trust me, I've heard that code enough times to know the real meaning.

Punching the leather seat, I curse. It shouldn't happen this way. "I gave you everything!"

CHAPTER 39

Above Tera Pass, Afghanistan
24 February—1920 Hours

Telling this sixteen-year-old secret. . .

It seemed stupid. Holding on to it. As if he did something wrong.

That was just it. Brian had betrayed his own father.

But Dad betrayed us with everything he did.

A soft pressure on his shoulder lured his mind from that dark alley in his past. Brian blinked and glanced to the side. Fekiria lay on her back, her gloved touch gentle. She was beautiful. One of the most beautiful women he'd ever known. And for all her "I hate Americans" talk, she sure showed him a lot of niceness.

If he told her the truth, she'd be the only one alive who would know. "I turned my father in."

She rolled onto her side and pushed up onto an elbow. Concern traced dark lines around her beautiful eyes. And he hated it. Hated that something he did put that look on her face.

Brian yanked his gaze back to the keyboard of the laptop.

"That was very brave."

Brian snorted. "Brave?" He shook his head. "I was fed up with him. Fed up with his lies. Hated that he was getting away with illegal money transactions and his criminal activity held the potential to destroy my mother. It had to stop."

"Yes, it did." She reached over and curled her gloved fingers around his. "You were sixteen?"

"Fifteen. Turned him in the week before my sixteenth birthday."

"How did you know—I mean, if the authorities hadn't figured it out?"

With a crooked smile, he met her beautiful green eyes again. "I'm smart, remember?" It was a lame answer, one that acquitted him of the guilt he felt. But...not really. "They knew. At least, I think they knew. My dad was smart—a Mensa, remember?—but I was smarter. Maybe not in quantifiable ways through Mensa measures, but through paying attention. I saw how things weren't adding up, the meetings he had with people. I couldn't cope with him lying through his teeth about the money he earned, money that would destroy all of us." But there was more. "I was sick of him telling me I wasn't smart enough."

Fekiria sat up now, their shoulders almost touching. "That must have been hard."

"No." He sniffed. "No, it wasn't hard at all. By that time, I hated him. I could never please him. And the way he treated my mom—she didn't have a high IQ, but she was a smart cookie."

Okay, enough with the confessional time. Brian glanced at her. "What about you?"

Her bright eyes widened. "What about me?"

"You don't exactly seem to have a good relationship with your family."

"The worst," she admitted with a smile. "Especially with my dad and oldest brother. They are both very old-fashioned. They both seem to like that women are under their fists."

Talking with her, the fire crackling behind him, Brian wanted to kiss her again. Wanted to take her into his arms. But...she was Muslim. "You aren't exactly the type to be suppressed."

She laughed. "No, I'm not. My mom just wanted me to be quiet so her house could be peaceful."

"That's a false peace."

She lifted her head, their eyes locking. "Yes. Yes, it is." Fekiria gave a fake smile then shrugged. "I just wanted them to accept me for who I was—a girl. I wanted to prove to them I could do anything they could do."

Brian smiled. "And you did—flying the bird."

She smiled back, sitting a little taller.

"Blowing up Americans." Did that give her pleasure?

Her smile fell. She looked away, but Brian leaned across her legs, planting a hand on the blanket on the other side. "Hey." Her chilled breath feathered against his cheek. "You still feel that way, think Americans are bad?"

Gaze skipping over his face, Fekiria didn't move. Didn't answer.

Brian felt himself being drawn in. He tilted his head. When she angled in, too, he resisted the urge to close the gap. "What am I to you, Fekiria?" He bent closer, just a fraction separating them. *Hold. . .*

"American?" He steeled his reaction when she swallowed. Parted her lips. "Christian?"

"Hero," she whispered.

With his gloved hand, Brian brushed aside a strand of hair dangling along her neck.

Fekiria's lips parted more, her chin drew up, and she pulled in a soft breath. All at his touch. He loved this, that the man she hated months ago was the same one dragging out a visceral response.

He leaned against her forehead. "We have things"—man, he wanted to kiss her again. But there were other—"things to sort out."

Her eyes shuttered. She leaned closer, her dry, partially cracked lips dusting his.

That was all it took. Brian cupped the back of her head and held her there, kissing her. Testing. He dragged himself a little closer, deepening the kiss. Her arms came up his back. A siren to his warrior.

Even with a touch of frostbite and cracked lips, she was soft. Curvy. Beautiful. She tasted sweet and—

A shriek startled them both.

Brian jerked back, his gaze skidding toward the little one. Aadela writhed in her sleep, kicking her feet. "Frostbite," he muttered, hauling his brain back to the situation. Out of the pool of heat and passion he'd been simmering in.

Fekiria sat up, her chin tucked and a blush in her cheeks. So she'd felt herself drowning in that pool, too. "I'll take care of her."

Brian caught her arm. "We should talk."

She nodded and moved toward the girl then curled around her. Holding her close. Brian wanted her curling up with him. Holding *him* close.

Head out of the clouds. Head out of the clouds, Bledsoe.

He glanced at the laptop—and stilled. The search program was spitting out information. Disassembling the encryption, files popped up. "Yes. . .yes!" He bent forward, opening the files—his awareness partially split by the gentle words Fekiria whispered to the little one.

A soft moan came from Mitra. Fekiria moved to her side, asking if her friend could hear her. Mitra whispered something, and Fekiria then shifted and dug into the woman's coat pocket. From there, she produced a tiny Bible. Fekiria's eyes shot to Brian's. Questions. Fears. She slipped back beneath the blanket, propped against her arm, and started reading out loud.

Okay, God. . .didn't see that coming.

Over the next hour, he read files as Fekiria read to her friend. It was nice, the lilt of her voice—it enabled him to drift past it and immerse himself in the files hidden in the laptop. Files that were clearly connected to the mess plaguing Raptor and the military establishment. His heart ricocheted around words like— "Zmaray," he muttered.

Was that the same one they'd faced off with eight months ago with the captain? The one who tortured the captain and had Double Z raped?

Then there was one that worried Brian: Osiris.

Why did that. . .? It felt familiar. Like he'd seen it—

051|215

Of course! Why hadn't he realized it before? 051|215 was hacker code for *Osiris*, the 0 being an *o*, the 5 an *s*, the bar and 2 together formed the *r*.

Where. . .where had he. . .? Slusarski! He'd seen it on the major's computer that day. Which meant Slusarski was complicit with Osiris— whatever that was. A person? A mission? Perhaps even the one feeding information to the enemy.

Then, by default, he could hold Slusarski responsible in the deaths of Parker and Davis.

But why? Why would an American soldier do this?

Ya know what? I don't care why! He just cared about stopping the piece of crap. The same way he'd stopped his father. The sick psychos had their own twisted reasoning that never made sense to the rest of the world.

That was beside the point. The point was—Brian was going to stop them. Somehow.

"So," he said, opening another file. "Show me how to stop you."

Another hour spent reading, both him and Fekiria with the Bible. Another hour poring over documents and coded files. "C'mon, c'mon," Brian mumbled as he clicked to another file. "Give me the lead to nail you between your black eyes."

And there it was.

Only. . .Brian couldn't move. Couldn't breathe. Not with his eyes glued to the last file. A message that had been hidden so deep in the system, nobody believed it would get found. That's the only explanation he could figure out for not having more security around it.

A mission parameter.

Names. And images. Names and images of the entire Raptor team, including him. Along with coordinates.

"A hit list," Brian breathed. "Oh crap. Oh crap oh crap oh crap."

"What?" Fekiria asked from the other side of the room, sitting beside her friend. "What's wrong?"

When was this date? When did they have those coordinates? He worked the file, checked the properties.

"Brian," came Fekiria's voice that held a tinge of panic.

He held up a finger then quickly returned to his task, unable to voice what was going through his head. If they had the team's location… if they had *his* location… He cursed.

"Brian."

Would they find them here? No…no, this was here before he was. So it had to be a bit outdated because he was climbing the mountain.

But the team hadn't been. They were most likely holed up at a…

"Base."

"Sergeant Brian!" Full-out panic shrieked through her voice.

"What?" He turned and found her staring down at her friend. Fekiria's eyes were wide, her face pale.

Mitra was staring up at the ceiling. Eyes unmoving. Chest—was her chest moving? He jumped up and hurried to her side. On a knee, he leaned close to see if he could feel her breath against his cheek. Nothing. He felt her carotid.

Nothing.

Brian stood, grabbed the edges of the pallet Mitra lay on, and dragged it through to the other room and out of the sight of the children, who were stirring. On his knees, he started chest compressions and breathing, all too aware of Fekiria watching with her arms wrapped around herself.

"C'mon, dang it," Brian muttered. "Don't die. Not on my watch."

CHAPTER 40

Above Tera Pass, Afghanistan
24 February—2240 Hours

Arms hugging herself, Fekiria watched. She couldn't breathe. Couldn't risk making a move. She clutched Mitra's Bible to her chest, holding tight as if that might make the words in the Bible heal her friend. Isa, the prophet the Christians held as Messiah, had healed people, right? Couldn't he heal Mitra? Save her from this wretched ordeal?

"Is she okay?" Sheevah asked, her voice small as she sat on the floor, huddled under the blanket with Aadela.

"Shh," Fekiria said, unwilling to trust herself to say anything else.

Brian lowered his head and knelt there for several long seconds.

What did that mean that he wasn't working anymore? "Why are you stopping? Save her!"

Pushing to his feet, he didn't turn or respond.

"What—?"

He stepped backward, tugged the thick blanket that hung in the doorway, and shut off the room. Turned. Eyes full of grief and defeat, he lifted his hands a little. "I'm sorry. . ."

Fekiria started to shake her head. Stopped. Then shook her head furiously. "No!" She rushed forward, but he caught her. Pulled her against his chest. "No, she can't be—" A sob wracked her. Her legs wobbled. "Noo!"

Brian's arms were around her, tight. Pressing her farther into his hold. Cradling her head. "Shh. Shhhhh."

But there were too many tears. Too much pain. Too much grief. Too much fear. Would they all die like Mitra? What of Hadassah, Mitra's daughter? Anguish twisted her lungs into a painful knot—Dassah was an orphan now!

"Be strong," Brian whispered against her ear. "The children still need you."

Swimming through that thick ocean of grief, she heard his words. Warm, challenging words. But it hurt—her friend had counted on her, trusted her.

"Fekiria."

Fought for the children—

The children.

His words, his meaning, finally made it through her muddied thoughts. Heard the gentle warning that the children were probably watching, probably growing more alarmed with her behavior. Easing back, she met his gaze as he cupped her face with his big hands.

"You with me, Kiria?"

She gave an acknowledging nod.

"I'm sorry. But we have to—"

"I'm fine." She stepped free. Gave him a stiff look, unsure what she felt or what she wanted other than to escape this nightmare. Things were fine—magnificent in his arms, kissing him, then atrocious with Mitra dying right in front of her. She shuffled around, rejoined the children, feeling more lost than she had in her life.

In her periphery, she noted Brian slump against the wall and rough a hand over his face. Guilt coiled around her grief-stricken heart, but she couldn't bring herself to talk to him. To look at him. She could barely process that her friend was gone, leaving her daughter alone in the world. Who would take care of Hadassah?

Who will take care of us?

"Is she dead?" Sheevah whispered as Fekiria curled up under the blanket and pulled Aadela into her arms.

"Quiet," Fekiria said firmly. "Rest. We must rest." If only she could.

Brian's heavy steps thudded back toward them, then the dirt scratched, and he was walking away. The thudding behind her sounded like he'd taken a seat at the small table. She remembered his cursing, how hard it'd been to pull his attention from whatever he discovered. His stricken, panicked expression. He'd come upon something very bad with that computer, hadn't he?

She repositioned herself so she could watch him. He hurriedly moved between the phones, trying different pieces with different handsets. After a few minutes of adjusting and working, he pressed a button. Tossed it down with a pinch of his lips. Tried another.

It seemed to go on forever. When he swept the pieces aside and roughed both hands over his face, Fekiria quietly rose. They were all dying up here. Little by little. Brian never gave up. He fought, he pushed, he encouraged them every step of the frozen journey. How did he do it?

It didn't matter. What did matter was that they needed each other. She couldn't turn her back on him—Mitra's death was no one's fault save the men responsible. She had to do what he did—fight on.

She nodded for Sheevah to stay with Aadela, who still held her aching fingers close to her chest, and joined Brian. "What's wrong?" She eased into the rickety chair opposite his.

Frustration coated every tense muscle in his face. "My team— they're targeting my team, and I'm st—" He pinched his lips tight. "I can't warn them."

Stuck here? Was that what he almost said? "An attack?" she asked, surprised. "You know of an attack?"

He turned the laptop toward her. Pointed to a line of code. "He knows who and where Raptor is. He's played roulette with our lives. Forced us to kill innocents and watch others die while we're handcuffed." His jaw muscle popped. "Now, I've got this"—he waved his hands toward the equipment then stabbed a finger toward the file on the computer—"and I can't do *crap* about it."

"It's a new threat? Something you can stop?"

"Doesn't matter. We're up here and they're down there. No signal or way to communicate." He sat back, tucking his hands behind his head. "They're sitting ducks."

"Then we need to leave."

"Can't." He tossed his hands in a futile gesture. "Even if we left right now. . ."

"It's a day's travel—"

"Not with the children." Brian looked down, swallowed. Glanced away. "The nearest base is at least a day's walk, for someone in perfect health. We're both battling frostbitten fingers and toes. Aadela is barking up a storm, which means she probably has pneumonia and prolonged exposure will kill her, too."

We're slowing him down. "Go without us."

Brian chortled. "Right. Leave you in the middle of this with no supplies and no way down?" He tucked his hands up under his arms. "No thanks. I'm not living with that on my conscience. We stick it out here and. . .pray God helps us."

"But your team—"

"They have techs. Entire teams working—"

"But not this!" She slapped the laptop. "How can you not do anything to save them?"

"Who do I save, Fekiria? You and the girls or the team?" He leaned forward, gray-green eyes sparked with anger. "Tell me—because I can't make this decision. I won't live with this. If I leave, you three don't have me. You don't have protection or supplies."

"You can't stay here." Desperation and frustration clashed like a tidal wave in her chest. "I can take care of us." Even saying it she couldn't convince herself. Or keep the weakness from her voice.

"I'm not leaving you—I promised I wouldn't, and I'm not breaking that promise." He grabbed the laptop and phones and moved away from her. Sat on the floor.

How could he do that? How could he make a decision to protect *her*, when she had shown him nothing but hatred, and not go after his team to protect them?

Things had changed. They'd kissed. He'd taken a turn for the worse—by caring for her. "Do not think a kiss means anything to me. I just needed to prove you were weak."

Without lifting his head, Brian glared up at her through a terse brow. Then went back to work.

She hurried to his side. "You must go. Save them!"

He ignored her. Kept working.

Fekiria turned and stomped to the small kitchen area. He was going to sacrifice his team? For them? She covered her mouth. It was too much. . .too much. . .watching Mitra die. Caring for Aadela and Sheevah. Knowing Brian would sacrifice his own life, his own friends, to save—*me*? Knowing they could all die up here.

She had been so horrible for so long. So unsure of what she wanted in life, from people, from herself. "I'm not worth it." But this—this she knew wasn't right.

He didn't answer.

"Your friends, maybe your entire Army, need you, Brian. They've been there, they've been your brothers—you said so yourself. I am nothing. Where is your loyalty to your country?"

"It's right here, commanding me to do exactly what I'm doing— protecting those who cannot protect themselves. I'm a sheepdog. It's what I do." He never stopped working.

A few minutes later, he smashed one of the phones against the floor several times.

"I cannot live with this decision."

"It's not yours to live with." He swept aside the smashed device and lifted another. Smashed it then gave a shout.

Fekiria drew up short. Fought tears. He had not lost control before. Not like this. He was sacrificing his team. For what? *For me?*

No. She had to find a way to convince him to go after his team.

Defeated, she sat in the wobbly chair at the table, glancing at the Bible she still somehow held. She turned the thin pages. Saw the marked pages, notes scribbled in her friend's delicate style. Was there hope in this world? Was there even the slimmest chance they would come out of this alive?

A deep, thick conviction coursed through Fekiria. One life—hers— against a team and possibly the American military?

A small scrap slid from between the crinkly pages. On it, Mitra had written out Psalm 57:1. *"Have mercy on me, my God, have mercy on me, for in you I take refuge. I will take refuge in the shadow of your wings until the disaster has passed."*

Something stirred within her breast as she read the words. It fueled her conviction that she could not let Brian stay here. He must save his team. She glanced toward the curtained window and knew it was still dark out. Night had fallen early, so dawn was still a good ways off. They should rest, then he could set out. Perhaps if she warmed some broth or made some tea—she'd seen some in the pantry, hadn't she? She'd get him to relax, get him to understand they would be fine. That their fate was not in his hands.

She could not live with their deaths on her conscience. But how could she convince him? He was a warrior. He felt she was his responsibility.

Her gaze again fell on the small, bloodied Bible. Dare she. . .?

God, if You are real. . .and true, show me how to convince him. And should he go, protect him. And us.

Was it selfish to ask for protection, too? She would be out there alone with two children. An image flickered in her mind. Of flying with Captain Ripley. Of flying over the Kush, over this very shanty. Then veering south. *The airport!*

Remembering that hardened her resolve. He wouldn't go out to save his men, so she would make him.

—※—

25 February—0115 Hours

Shivering and trembling worked against his efforts to get just one phone up and running. Do that, and he could warn Raptor, assuming he could get a signal—no guarantees up here in the rugged terrain—but he had to warn General Burnett or anyone else he could raise on the phone. Knowing he could never leave the three in this shanty, he would work through the night trying to save his friends. *Can't give up.* Couldn't surrender to the gnawing words eating at his confidence: they'd all die here.

His hand twitched, hard. The piece cracked.

Brian cursed. Threw it aside. Stood. Stomped back and forth. Went out into the storm. Let the biting cold chew on his face. On his sorry carcass. *Loser! Failure!*

If he was just smarter. . .

Dad's right.

He closed his eyes as the wind gripped his lapels and shook them hard. Then he looked to the heavens—or, rather, where they should be. Because only what seemed like a mile-thick cloud barricaded him into this nightmare. "God! Don't do this—don't let them die!"

He wasn't sure whose life he was pleading for more—the team or the girls. *If there's a way. . .please. . .please, show me.*

Light spilled out into the night, pulling him around. Fekiria stood there, huddled against the wind. In her gaze he saw the weight of the responsibility he bore to protect her and see them safely down the mountain. Even if it meant not saving the team. A piece of him died right there, in the snow, as he wrestled with the obvious choice.

Defeated, he trudged back and stepped into the surprising warmth that encircled him. Numb, he looked down into the tear- and dirt-stained face he'd come to love.

Heat spurted through his chest. No, he didn't mean that. It was just a figure of speech.

"Sit down," she said, pointing to the floor. "I warmed some broth. Eat. Rest. I can stand watch. You need to rest."

"I. . .can't."

"You must, or you are no good to anyone."

Though he took the cup of broth, he could not even think about resting. Not till they were all back safe and the team had captured that terrorist. Stopped Osiris. Whatever or whoever that was.

Fekiria sat next to him, placing a metal cup near his leg. "That's a bit of tea I found."

Brian didn't want her near him. "Don't try to change my mind."

Sitting back against the wall, she leaned against his shoulder. "You think I'm that good?"

"No, just trying to stop you from wasting your breath." He sipped the broth, savoring the warmth that tingled all the way down his esophagus. "When we get back, I'm drinking a gallon of hot coffee."

Fekiria laughed softly.

He gave her a look. Why was she all submissive and stuff now? All domestic goddess. . . "What're you up to?"

Those soul-probing eyes came to his, wide and startled. "Me?"

His suspicion grew.

She sighed and relaxed—did she realize she was pressed against him? He liked it. Liked having her close. Leaning on him. Not yelling and arguing with him. It was nice. *Too nice.*

Oh, who cared? He had no fight in him for small things. Not tonight. Not with Raptor out there like sitting ducks.

"When Zahrah started dating your captain," Fekiria said, her voice quiet and soft, "I was so angry with her. Of all the good Afghan men in the country, why did she have to choose an American invader?"

Brian snorted.

"I could not see any good in her dating an American. Families were slaughtered for having any association with Westerners." Her head rested against his shoulder.

Exhaustive weight pulled at his limbs. His mind. It felt so good to just sit. Listen to her talk. He liked her voice. Like the unique scent of her that—yeah, still made him hungry.

"We had an argument—I told her she had come to change my country, and I was angry. I wanted her to accept me and my people, who were hers, too." Fekiria yawned.

Good. She was getting tired. He looked at the phones. Once she fell asleep. . .he'd get back to work on them. He had a good brain, just had to tap the right neurons so he could figure out this tangled digital mess.

"But I realized I did not accept her. I wanted *her* to change." She sighed. "And you. . .I wanted you to change, to go away."

Brian felt a lazy smile tug up his lips. "You told me as much." That day. . .after the funeral. She'd given him an earful about how the soldiers were causing too much trouble. How they were drawing the attention of the Taliban. How they needed to go home, stop ruining lives.

"Is this your way of saying you're into me?" Brian had asked, flirting in *a way that only made her angrier.*

"You should leave our country. Leave us alone."

"Because you can't sleep at night without dreaming of me?" Getting a rise *out of her had made him want to keep teasing her. She had fire in those green eyes, a fire he liked.*

"Is this a joke to you? Men and women are being murdered because of you stupid Americans."

"The only thing that's a joke is you thinking that's true." He hadn't *meant to get terse, but he didn't deal well with people who spread lies like that.* "Even if you tell me to leave—"

"I just did!"

"I'm not leaving until my mission's done."

Then she punched him.

"You can't stay here. Save them."

She shoved him backward, and he landed with a splash in a large puddle. The guys laughed, until he turned and pushed Falcon. The team daddy plopped right into the same puddle. . .which was now oatmeal.

Raptor roared at the sight.

But then he saw the Humvee get stuck in it, too. Then the dog was drowning in it.

Brian lunged with a shout.

His forehead rammed into something.

He blinked and found himself staring down the barrel of a silenced weapon.

CHAPTER 41

Above Tera Pass, Afghanistan
25 February—0640 Hours

Lǎoshàng hǎo." A Chinese woman held a QSW-06 with a silencer to his temple. "What are you doing in this place?"

Hands out to show he wasn't a threat—yet—Brian surreptitiously surveyed his situation. Searched for the girls. Were they hurt? Dead? Tied up? Why hadn't they alerted to the threat?

"Well?"

"Shelter," he said, noticing the blankets that covered the children were gone. "Just needed shelter from the storm."

With the toe of her shiny boot, she kicked the phone pieces at him. "And this?" Young. But skilled. He didn't doubt that for a second.

"Trying to get a radio working so I could call for help. Got lost on a hike."

A man stood behind her, his AK-47 aimed at Brian.

Had they killed Fekiria and the girls? Brian's heart squeezed at the thought. But he saw no blood on the floor. He'd have heard a shot—well, maybe not with that silencer.

"Nobody else with you?" Her tone shaded toward incredulous.

Nobody else. That meant this chick hadn't found Fekiria. So where was she? And the girls? Brian lifted a shoulder. "Just me and my girlfriend." He flicked a hand toward the room where Mitra lay. "She. . .didn't make it." *Act sad, idiot.* He lowered his gaze. Swallowed. "P–please, don't kill me. I didn't know who owned this place. We just needed somewhere safe to stay through the night."

"Why aren't you on your American base?"

Brian lifted a shoulder. "Conscientious objector," he lied.

"Are you stupid taking a hike during a blizzard?"

"Just trying to get to somewhere safe."

"She is Afghan. You are American."

Brian met her gaze—the only visible part of her face. She was bundled up so tight—but not so much that he'd think she wasn't agile. He felt sure this chick could go all *Crouching Tiger, Hidden Dragon* on him given the chance or need. "That would be why we took to the mountains." This lie had to be solid. "Her parents weren't happy—"

"Get the laptop," she ordered the man. Then she rattled something off in Chinese—and though Brian couldn't be sure since he didn't speak Mandarin, it seemed the two argued. The big man kept his rifle aimed at Brian. The woman stepped between them, blocking Brian's view as her words flew fast and furious. They were distracted. That was the point.

Brian lunged. Threw himself into the woman, who flew backward, clipping her knees on the man bent over the laptop. Before she could react, he coldcocked her. She went out like a light. He heard the man dragging himself free. Brian saw her weapon and dove toward it.

Crack!

Searing pain blazed down his leg. He rolled toward the chair, taking any cover he could find, flimsy as it was. He crouched, wincing and holding his leg. The same stupid leg he'd injured taking out that Talib. Swinging around, he took aim. The man had reacquired as well. Brian eased the trigger back. Once. Twice.

The man stumbled. Managed to fire a shot. The bullet went wild. Glass shattered behind Brian. And still the man fought. Struggling, the man waved the gun in Brian's direction.

Brian fired another shot.

The man collapsed with a thud.

Hustling to the woman, Brian verified she was still out. Quickly, he confirmed Fekiria and the girls weren't in the room. . .dead. Relief spread through him at seeing only Mitra's body there. So how had these two gotten here?

When he heard the *thwump* of rotors, Brian started for the door. How had he not heard the rotors when these two landed? Adrenaline? Fear?

Wind curled in through the shattered window from the side, chilling him almost instantly. Frigid but no longer howling. *That's it. That's my out.*

But first. . .

At the man's side, he removed the jacket and gloves, snagging the watch with a compass, too. He stuffed them on and ignored the bloodied areas. Laptop pressed to his abdomen, Brian heard something crinkle. He hesitated, glancing down at his tac shirt. Something stuck out of his pocket. He lifted it and unfolded it. A well-worn card with the 71st Psalm on it.

As if the snow melted and spring had rushed in, Brian felt himself bathed in a warmth. At that instant, he felt as if Granddad were there. His mind jumped to the verse Granddad had sent him. Felt ashamed he hadn't thought of it before now. Life intervened, throwing him this way and that until he'd forgotten all about it. Eagle, who'd always been the zealot on Raptor, he seemed to be here, too—at least, in spirit. And it seemed God Himself stood there with him.

Where had the card come from?

He remembered Fekiria sitting at the table looking through Mitra's Bible with scraps of paper in her hand. He glanced down at the stylized lettering. Had she put the card in his pocket?

She was the only one who could have.

But. . .why?

Sort it later. Get out now.

Brian zipped up the thick parka, grateful for the immediate warmth. He secured his tactical belt around the waist, also giving support to the laptop. He slung the man's AK-47 over his shoulder and swung it onto his back, out of his way. With the QSW-06 in hand, he pushed to his feet. The prickling pain in his leg reminded him of the graze and cuts. He took a second to tie a length of fabric from his old jacket around it.

The woman moaned, pulling herself up.

Brian stepped back and rammed the butt of the weapon against her temple. Nothing to kill her. But he couldn't have her alerting the chopper to his escape. As he hopped up onto the small sink in the corner and reached for the window, his gaze brushed the solitary room that had become a morgue for Mitra.

I'm sorry. And with that apology, he climbed out the window and promised himself he would not let the same thing happen to Fekiria and the girls. First thing—verify she wasn't already captive on that chopper. He slunk along the back of the shanty in a couple feet of snow.

Fekiria was missing. Or had left on her own. To force him to save the team.

No. Brian hesitated at the corner of the shanty, rejecting the thought even as it took root in his heart. Yes, that was exactly what she'd done. Thought of the way Mitra's body had been covered. . .and yet not as "puffy" as she'd been the night before. *Her coat is gone.* Fekiria had taken the woman's coat. He'd told her he wouldn't leave her.

So she *left me.*

First things first.

Brian lowered himself to the snow, the laptop beneath the parka pressing against his abdomen. Weapon at the ready, he eased around the corner. He whispered thanks to God for having the storm ease up.

A pilot. No copilot. But he had a gunner in the door.

Gauging the distance to the trees and the proximity of the chopper, he knew he'd have to get rid of the bird or he'd be cut down before he got ten feet. Running flat out in a field was one thing. Running in two feet of snow was like slogging through oatmeal. Just like in his dream.

Once more he swept the terrain, searching for a sign of Fekiria and the girls. Where had they gone? Which direction? The rotor wash blew the snow around, burying any tracks.

There was no way to know which way she went. That meant he'd have to focus on getting to a position where he could radio for help. Aim toward the base northwest of the mountains. Brian glanced at the compass.

Yep. Time to make the chopper move.

On a knee, he holstered the silenced handgun then drew the AK-47 around. He took a bead on the gunner. And eased the trigger back.

Sparks flew.

The gunner dropped back.

A whine of engines and roar of the rotors yanked the bird up and away.

Brian sprinted—well, as much as he could with two feet of snow and a gimpy leg impeding his progress. But he moved. Threw himself. The whole thing was nightmarish. The roar of the bird as it circled. The knowing it would come back. The not knowing if he actually killed the gunner or just wounded him. The knowledge that Fekiria was out there, somewhere. Without protection. Without him.

Ten feet from the tree line, Brian heard the padded *thwat* of bullets hitting the trees and snow. With a huge thrust, he threw himself toward the natural cover. Almost immediately, it was easier to limp-run—the snow wasn't as deep, thanks to the protection of the trees and pine branches. Trees he was allergic to, but this time, he embraced their sinus-inflaming branches.

He reached for a tree to take cover.

Fire exploded through his shoulder. Pitched him forward. "Augh!" Brian grabbed a trunk to break his fall. Had to keep moving. Holding the slick warmth of his bloodied shoulder, he jogged up the slight incline. *Going the wrong way.*

No. He might not be on the right compass heading, but putting distance between himself and a gunner was right every day of the year. He heard the almost-silent swish of branches overhead as he moved.

The chopper would set back down. Verify their people were still alive. That'd buy him some time to get on the right course heading. For now, he'd run. And keep running till his legs fell off.

CHAPTER 42

Above Tera Pass, Afghanistan
25 February—0715 Hours

"My feet hurt," Aadela cried, arms dangling at her sides as she stood with her head tilted toward the sky.

Heart tangled in the little one's pain and her own—even with Mitra's gloves on, she couldn't feel her fingers again. It wasn't snowing, but it wasn't any warmer. The sun still hid behind the clouds, as if ashamed of Fekiria for leaving Brian.

They'd set out while it was dark, and she'd used the moon to guide them away from Brian's protection. Away from the guilt of knowing he'd never leave them to protect his American brothers. So she'd added chamomile tea she'd found in a canister to the broth and lulled him to sleep with long stories. It hadn't taken but a few minutes before he was snoring.

"Everything hurts," Sheevah muttered. "And nothing hurts because I can't feel my body!"

"I know, I know." Hours into their hike, she questioned the wisdom of what she'd done. "But we must keep moving. There is an airport just over the next rise." At least, Fekiria hoped that's where it was. She had learned land navigation, but right now, she wasn't even sure where they were.

And she felt alone, more alone than she'd felt in her life. Was leaving Brian like that the right thing? *It's too late to wonder that.*

"Why did we leave Sergeant Brian?" Sheevah asked as she hoisted Aadela up to place her on her back.

"No, she must walk," Fekiria said. "Put her down. We all must walk so our circulation continues through our feet."

"But they hurt," Aadela sobbed.

Had a knife been stabbed through her heart, Fekiria could not feel worse.

"I want to go back to Sergeant Brian," Aadela whined as she collapsed against the snow.

Fekiria lifted the girl to her feet. "You must be brave, Aadela. You want to see Sergeant Brian again, yes?" Aadela's watery brown eyes held hers. She nodded.

"And I do, too. But we have to get to the airstrip so we can get help for him." It wasn't a whole truth. Brian would probably reach his base before they made it to the airstrip, but if it would feed the children's courage, then it was worth the deception. "Can you do that? For him? I think he would be very glad for your help."

"I can't," Aadela sobbed. "I can't feel my feet."

Fekiria gulped the painful truth. She hadn't been able to feel hers either. They all suffered frostbite and would likely lose toes. "If we stay on the mountain, it will only get worse. And Sergeant Brian could die, too. We must be brave."

Aadela shuddered through a breath. "Brave soldiers, just like Sergeant Brian?"

"Just like."

CHAPTER 43

Camp Eggers, Afghanistan
25 February—0740 Hours

He's dead."

Dean rounded on Sal. "We have no proof, and even if we did, I won't be satisfied until his body is in a flag-draped coffin on its way back to the States." He shifted his gaze to Harrier, who had regrouped with the team late last night. He'd been different but said little. "Harrier— you want to tell us something?"

The medic considered them. Then shook his head. "Not the right time. Later."

"How about now?" Sal said, arms folded. "If you're distracted—"

"Not distracted." Harrier scratched the back of his head. "Married."

Stunned silence gaped.

"Judge was going to rule against me until Sienna offered to marry me. Only way I could keep the kids."

"Idiot," Sal said.

"Do you love her?"

Harrier snorted. "Yeah. . .actually, I do. Just didn't realize it."

With a curt nod, Dean studied him. "You have more reason to fight and live now. Is your head here with us?"

"One hundred percent, sir."

"Okay, then what do you think about his chance of survival up there?"

"If he's been in the elements the whole time. . ." Harrier shook his head. "Chances are slim to none."

"See?" Sal said.

"But if he managed to find shelter—"

"Where?"

"—then he has a chance." Harrier didn't flinch at the aggravation shot his way by Sal.

"If he's in that mountain, we won't find a body to bury."

"What is this?" Dean stared down the newly minted WO1. He shouldered his urge to yell and lowered his voice. "You've had this *Titanic*-sized chip on your shoulder since Mazar-e. What's going on?"

Sal's dark eyes flashed. "Nothing." He held his ground, but Dean could see the roiling anger and frustration.

"Say it. Say what's on your mind."

A twitch in the guy's cheek warned him of the breaking dam. "You don't want me to do that."

Dean held out his arms as they stood in the room. The others were headed back from chow. "We're alone. We've been friends a long time and been to hell and back in this war. I think I deserve some respect and honesty. This thing, whatever it is. . .it's getting in the way."

"Yeah, well, so's taking orders from a compromised team commander."

"Comp—" Dean swallowed the accusation. "After all this time, you're still trying to say *I'm* compromised?"

"You're dating the cousin of a very high-value target. She's roommates with Haidary's sister, and there have been times you've let her into the Command building."

"Hey." Dean held up a hand. "Are you now accusing my girlfriend of—?"

"Then you let Burnett walk Cassie into this thing, and if we weren't screwed before that, we are now." Falcon snapped out his hands in frustration. "She can't be trusted. She doesn't get what happens out here, and she will compromise—"

"Forget Walker!" Dean rested his hand on his belt. "You've been all bull-in-a-china-shop for the last ten months." He squinted an eye, thinking. "But whatever you have against Walker, Burnett brought her into this. And I won't believe for a minute that he's trying to get us killed."

"Me either, but her—trust her and you'll end up in a ditch dead."

"Captain!" Eagle shoved into the room, holding the door as the rest of the team flooded in. Titanis entered, ushering Hastings and none other than Cassie Walker into the fray.

Dean and Sal shared a glance.

"Um," Hastings said as she cast a frown between the two of them then to Lieutenant Walker, who tucked her chin but said nothing.

"They have something you mates are going to want to see," Titanis said as he took a seat.

"Please." Hastings motioned toward the door. "Come in."

Dean turned toward the door, his heart kick-starting at the man who entered. Tall, lanky, wearing a turban and a truckload of confidence and power. Dean straightened from the maps and discussion. Met the man's gaze. "Takkar."

With a slight incline of his head, Sajjan Takkar moved into the room. This man had his hands in so many international waters, Dean shouldn't be surprised at whatever he'd found. If anyone could tie together some threads of this nightmare, it would be this notorious spy. All the same, Dean didn't trust him. While he hadn't dealt a bad hand to the U.S. military, his loyalty couldn't be ascertained. But there was more trust than distrust. Dean had enough dealings with the man to surrender any suspicions.

Hastings walked around the table and stood beside Titanis, who seemed to straighten. "May I?" she asked the Aussie.

Titanis nodded, and if Dean didn't know the burly guy better, he'd say he grinned.

"About fifteen minutes ago, one of our techs searching for proof of life saw this." Hastings powered up a video player.

"Harbin Z-19," Eagle said as soon as the chopper came into view. "That's not ours."

"Chinese," Harrier put in. "Stealth reconnaissance/attack chopper."

Two individuals got out and trekked into a building covered in snow.

"They're in there for about ten minutes before"—Hastings fast-forwarded the footage—"this happens."

Suddenly, the chopper lifted and veered off. A minute later, someone stumbled out of the shanty, made it to the chopper just as the bird belched a rocket. The screen went bright white.

What was that about?

"What happened?" Sal asked. "They just leave their team?"

"No," Hastings said. "Look. Zoom in on the lower section of the screen." She spoke to Walker, who turned Falcon's military-grade laptop around then started tapping on the keys.

There, barely discernible against the black-and-white image, they made out a figure.

"Someone came out of the back of this structure and fired on the chopper."

As soon as the chopper lifted away, Dean saw movement. "Giving himself time to get to the trees." Firepower. Tactical. But he wasn't sprinting. Or fast. "It's Hawk."

"He's moving slow," Sal commented.

"Snowdrifts could be several feet deep," Titanis suggested.

"More likely, Hawk's injured. Thirty hours in the mountain. At least one firefight. . ." Sal motioned to the screen that was now blank.

"He's fighting for his life."

"And the obvious question," Eagle said, coming to his feet. "Where are the women and girls?"

A weight thumped against Dean's courage, the daunting realization that things were as bad as he had imagined.

"He'd never leave them willingly," Eagle said. "He and the younger woman—Double Z's cousin—seemed to have some chemistry. I just can't see him walking away from them."

"Unless they're dead," Sal said.

Realistic but haunting. "Okay, let's get up on that mountain." Dean turned to Hastings. "We're going to need a team and a Black Hawk."

"Riordan's team is on the tarmac waiting," Hastings said. "I've already communicated with Burnett."

"I think I have some *guests* who can help you out," Takkar said as he nodded to the door.

In walked none other than Candyman, his wife, and that ugly hound of hers, Beowulf.

"Tony!" After a shoulder-pat-hug, Dean stepped back. "How's life?"

"Great. Heard I'm just in time to save the day again," Tony said with his incessant grin.

Timbrel folded her arms across her chest, as tough and barricaded as ever. "Beowulf can track, if you need him."

It was one thing to be brothers for life as a Special Forces operator. It was another to be out of the field for a year and come back. "How's the leg?"

Tapping the titanium flag-painted prosthesis beneath his pant leg, Tony grinned. "As Iron Man's cousin, we're better than ever. Where we headed?"

"Hastings, where was that incident?"

"Twenty klicks south of Tera Pass."

Eagle shifted. "That's. . .that's got to be forty from the car accident." Blue eyes wide, he snorted. "I can't believe he made that much ground in that storm. It was a beast!"

"Yeah, well, that's Hawk for you."

"Especially if someone was shooting at him," Sal added.

"Let's move! Hawk needs us."

CHAPTER 44

Tera Pass, Afghanistan
25 February—0800 Hours

The world tilted and spun.

Stumbling, Brian jerked his head up. Dropped to his knees beside a tree. He dug his gloved fingers into the dirt. Lifted a handful and packed his shoulder wound. Gritting his teeth as he did, he reminded himself that Fekiria sacrificed her own life so he could do this. So he could get word to the others. So he could stop the attack.

And he'd be hanged if he would stop because of a little blood.

He pushed up but his knees buckled. Brian reached for a tree. Missed. Tumbled into the soft branches of a pine. Fell through them. Hit the ground. *Oof!* A fresh wave of jagged pain tore through his shoulder and spine. Brian growled through the agony, twisting to protect his shoulder, which only made the laptop strapped to his chest poke into his ribs.

He lay there, sprinklings of pine needles fluttering to his face. Lifted the sat phone he'd taken from the Chinese man he'd killed. Checked the bars. No signal.

He stuffed it back in his pocket, his mind on the fireball that had erupted as he made his dash over hill and dale. Had the woman he'd knocked out made it to the chopper before they torched the shanty?

And why hadn't she just shot him?

It just couldn't get worse, could it? Bleeding out on a mountain. Knowing the woman he tried to protect had left him and was probably dead. What was the point? *God, I got nothing. I'm done.*

Granddad had always said that when a bad situation presented itself, a person shouldn't fight it. They should learn from it, figure out what God wanted to change. Things couldn't get worse at the moment, and still, Brian found himself looking for the lesson. But everything felt trite. Fake. No, he wanted something real. Something true. He wanted a life. . .like Granddad's. God, a wife, peace of mind. . .

Crunch.

Brian froze. He darted his gaze around, not moving a muscle. Through the thick branches, he thought he saw a blur of black. He stared, waiting. Expecting.

But nothing came.

Must be going crazy.

Check that. He'd raced up a mountain, skinned a snow leopard, and played tag with an attack chopper. . .all for a woman. Yeah, beyond crazy. He was certifiable.

Somewhere nearby came chatter. He listened more carefully, steadying his own breathing against the howling wind, and heard the voices. Chinese.

Probably tracking the phone.

Brian shifted. This time the blur of black coalesced. Two men stood less than two yards from his position. Crap. Slowly, stealthily, he drew his legs under the tree.

Lesson of this mission—never think it can't get worse.

His mind drifted to the card in his chest pocket. The one with the prayer of protection. He remembered some of the words, but the more he thought of them, the more Fekiria's face flashed before his mind's eye. Tough. Smart. Beautiful. And didn't take junk from no one. Even him.

Which meant. . .she might still be alive.

Which meant, *he* needed to stay alive to find her.

Brian eased the silenced weapon from the holster. Aimed it at the man closing in on his position. *Steady. . .*

The man crunched closer.

What were the chances these two would miss him? Not see him and keep moving?

Right. Because they've just managed to find him each time out of profound luck that would what, suddenly fail?

Well, they say nothing is impossible with God. . .right, God?

A miracle would be *profoundly* awesome right now, what with the way his arm trembled and his leg throbbed with pain that doused him in sweat and blood. Distant shouts drew the man around.

No way. Brian strained, without moving his body, to see what was happening. The target closest to him started away.

Seriously? That worked? God worked the impossible? Yes and no. The man who backtracked was responding to voices. Voices of other targets. But at least for now, Brian only had one man to contend with.

The phone in Brian's pocket chirruped.

He froze. Snapped his gaze to the man.

Eyes stared back.

Son of a... With the slightest of moves, Brian lifted the silenced weapon. As the man raised his, Brian aimed. Fired once. Twice.

The man tumbled forward. Brian scrambled for the phone. Turned off the volume.

Hauling himself up took everything Brian had left. He pulled himself backward, dragging his weight in the snow to get free of the low-hanging limbs. On a knee, he double-checked the route the other man had taken. Though he'd returned, he was still alone and hadn't noticed his fallen comrade. It wouldn't stay that way forever. Meaning Brian had a minute or two at most.

Move, idiot!

He trudged on a parallel path with the spine of the nearest peak. The graze in his leg was numb. In fact, his feet were numb again. He pushed the realization from his mind. No more obstacles. No more excuses. Priority one was to get out of here. Notify the guys. Stop Osiris.

Right. Osiris.

Question remained—was Osiris a who or a what? A man or a plan? Either way, if Brian didn't keep putting one painful foot in front of the other, Raptor was dead. Weapon down and to the side, he traversed the terrain. Tricky because the snow concealed rocky traps that could sprain or snap his ankle.

He lifted the phone and saw it had a signal. "Yes." He pressed the number for the captain. Lifted it to his ear.

But there was nothing. No sound. No ringing. He glanced at the display and bit back a curse. Signal was gone.

Maybe if he could get a little higher. Planting his boot to the right he pushed up. His boot punched through the snow. A shelf broke away. Rocks tumbled down. Buried his foot and ankle. Brian wrestled to yank his leg free. But the rocks had a mind of their own. Each tug he gave seemed to harden the resolve of the rocks. A few seconds later, he couldn't get an inch of movement.

"What the freak?" Brian dug, tossing aside rocks.

Rocks spit at him. He jerked, a stinging warning against his cheek as he looked up. Two men stood there, aiming QBZ-95s at him.

Exposed. No weapon in hand thanks to nearly doing a face-plant on the side of the mountain, he had no recourse but surrender. "Son of a gun," Brian muttered, raising his hands.

The men slid-ran down the peak toward him.

And that worked its magic. The entire side of the hill gave way. Which tossed Brian down the crest but also freed his foot. And put distance between him and the Chinese men.

When the mini avalanche stopped, Brian spotted his weapon less than three feet away. He lunged and lifted it, coming to a knee, all too aware of the pain in his shoulder and now in his ankle, too. Pain later. Assassins first.

He traced the white and rocky chaos. Spotted one of the men pull himself upright. Setting up a good position, Brian knelt. Brought his AK-47 around.

A bullet seared his cheek.

Brian hissed and rolled to the side. "Augh!" His shoulder! More determined now that they'd nearly put lead in his brain, he dug in. Got his bearings. Remembered the shooter's position. He angled out. Peered down the scope. . .right into the face of the other shooter.

Who lifted his head. Lowered his weapon.

What the. . .?

Why would he pull off?

Crunch.

Brian swung around. Two things registered in that split second. The man looming over him with death in his eyes. And a distant thunder. Reinforcements? The chopper that had tried to pepper him full of high-caliber holes?

The man dived at Brian.

As his head connected with the rock, sprinkling spots across his vision, Brian focused on the sound of the chopper. That wasn't the same Chinese bird. Pinned against the rock, he struggled to keep his mind off the pain in his shoulder. But the weakness resulting from the wound threatened survival now.

Steeling himself, he slammed the fleshy part of his hand against the man's side.

With a wail, the man arched his back. Tumbled sideways.

Brian scrambled away. Groped for the handgun. *Where'd it go?*

The chopper raced nearer.

God, I can't die here. I gotta save Raptor and Fekiria.

He glanced to the side. Saw the QSW-06. Careful of his shoulder, he angled to the side, stretching to reach the weapon.

A massive eruption of pain exploded against his gut. Threw him backward.

CHAPTER 45

Tera Pass, Afghanistan
25 February—0815 Hours

Look." Sheevah pointed beyond Fekiria.

When she glanced that way, she didn't see what the teen meant at first. But then she saw it. A path, worn by feet or goats. "Get off the path!"

A chopper thundered over them, racing southward.

Toward the airport, she guessed. There was not much else for miles. A few small villages, but that little airport was the only hope she had for survival. Not that she expected to find a plane, but there would be radios. Maybe even people. She could signal for help.

Besides, it was the opposite direction Brian would have to take to reach the base. And she had to be certain he would not come upon them, or he'd stay with them. And they'd slow him. His friends and soldiers would die.

The chopper swung around. Came back.

"Hide against the rocks!" Fekiria pointed to the jagged outcropping of boulders that had tumbled down from the higher peaks. After grabbing Sheevah's hand, she ran, dragging the girls with her.

Pressed against the snow and icy boulders, she scooted in as close as she could and wrapped her arms around Sheevah as they burrowed down.

The deafening thunder pounded her ears. It grew louder. Fekiria could not help but wonder if they'd been seen, if someone was coming—

A peppering of noise made her still.

Was that. . .?

Bullets pelted the rock by her face. Fekiria grabbed Sheevah's head and pulled her down then covered the two girls with her own body.

Gunfire continued. Only. . . She trained her ear to the side—it sounded like. . .

Shouts. From behind them.

Fekiria glanced over her shoulder.

Saw a Pashtun farmer in the trees waving frantically at her. "Come. Hurry!"

Then she noticed the other Pashtuns with assault rifles firing at the chopper.

She drew Sheevah up and pointed to the men. "Go!" They hobbled and jumped over the rocks, climbing toward the trees. Whether friend or foe, at least this might be a chance to stay alive.

A boulder flicked shards at her.

Fekiria winced but kept moving, all too aware of the chopper spitting bullets at them. Arms folded around them, ushering them into relative darkness and a strange warmth. Not like a fire gives off but of a lesser cold. Because of the forest.

They hiked a worn path up and around the side of the mountain. Then down. Fekiria glanced back, her heart jamming into her throat at the half-dozen men trailing them with weapons. They led her and the girls into a small village of no more than a dozen plaster dwellings. Three women welcomed them by wrapping thick blankets around them and placing hot cups in their hands, urging them to drink.

Relief over the shelter and food warred with Fekiria's need to get help to Brian. But she sat and sipped the warmed broth, so much better than the one she'd made last night. Only as her limbs grew heavy did Fekiria think they might've put something in it. Something to kill them. Or knock them out. With a hard swallow, she set aside the cup.

The stocky woman kneeling in front of her lifted the cup back to her. "Drink. You need it."

Her head began to swim. "No, I need to call my captain. I'm in the ANA. My helicopter crashed." It wasn't entirely untrue, just the truth spread out a little. But she would never call the base. She would call her cousin, the only person she trusted right now.

The man who'd rescued them from the rocks handed her a phone.

Fekiria breathed a little easier, fighting the dizziness. Even as she dialed Zahrah's number, she noticed Aadela and Sheevah were sleeping soundly.

God, help me. They drugged us!

"Hello?"

"Zahrah," she said, her words slurred. "I—help me," she said in English. "I'm—"

"Fekiria?" Her cousin practically screamed. "Where are you?"

"A Pashtun village. In the mountains. . ." Her words sounded like they were echoing. She braced a hand over her forehead. "Brian. . ." It was so hard to talk. To think. "Help him. The house. . ." She licked her lips and tried to look at the woman, who blurred. "Where. . .?"

The woman gave her a sympathetic smile.

"Help me, Z. They drugged me. They're. . .kill. . .me."

THE OFFER

I think it is time for you to take a position here at Takkar Corp."

Daniel coiled the near insult beneath his dignity. "What do you propose?" It was odd, the dragon and the Sikh coming together once again, more than two decades after the original commitment had been set forth.

Sajjan turned his laptop around so it faced Daniel. Did the man think him a puppet? To be shifted at will? "I think it will please you."

Was he to trust this man? Daniel forced his eyes to the monitor. Surprise tugged up his eyebrows. A logo stared back. He shot the man a look. "What is this?"

"Long overdue." Takkar sat in the oversized leather chair, fingertips steepled. "Do you not think?"

The symbol entwined the Takkar lion with a dragon amid a flame.

"Why now?" If he did not work to tame the dragon within him, there would be flames. Heated, scorching ones cast at the man who had withheld what belonged to Daniel.

Sajjan met Daniel's gaze with a steady expression. "It has been awhile, yes, since you lived in Afghanistan?"

"Since we were children."

"Exactly." Sajjan lifted his head a little. "You have shown interest, and reports are positive with what you have achieved in Shanghai. You've done well."

"You patronize me?" Daniel came to his feet, ready to free himself of this insult. Of this man who held an illusory power, a power that had not been meant for him alone.

"Indeed not," Sajjan said. "I applaud you. What you have

347

accomplished in Shanghai is worthy of every praise I could give. Your interest in efforts here in Afghanistan speaks to me."

Was this a trap? Why had Sajjan suddenly decided to let him in? "I've asked for years to partner—"

"You asked, but you did not show me your interest." The man's face was a mask of civility and yet a stone mask impenetrable by emotions. "Words are cheap, Jin. You have come, shown me your interest, not just demanded a position and power, actively sought what your father sought and began."

Vindication swarmed through Daniel. Trembling with the satisfaction of hearing this man speak those words, Daniel worked to maintain his resolve. His determination that he would upend this man. This corporation.

"It is time to bring to fruition what our fathers dreamed here twenty years ago." Sajjan cocked his head. "Would you agree?"

"Yes."

"Then we will make it happen." Sajjan stood. "One week. Here at the tower, let's meet again with our lawyers and teams to make it official." He extended a broad hand.

Daniel wanted to grab the hand, twist it at the wrist, and push this man's face into the highly glossed floor. Instead he simply shook hands. "Next week." He needed to act grateful. "Thank you."

"There is no thanks needed. This belongs to you."

Yes, Daniel hissed inwardly. Offering only a nod, he walked himself to the door, not trusting himself to speak. Did this man seriously think it was his place to say what belonged to Daniel and what did not? What it was time to do and not to do?

Sajjan Takkar overstepped once again. And Daniel would make sure that next step was right off the roof of the thirty-something-story tower.

By the time he reached his hotel room, he shook with indignation. Slamming the door did little to appease the demons screaming within him. "*My father* built that corporation with as much blood as his!" He moved to the bar and spread his hands on the marble counter. Then fisted them. "How *dare* he—"

"Sir!"

Daniel spun, ready to skewer his man for interrupting. Instead, he went ice cold.

Two men hurried in with Kiew propped between them. Blood smeared across her face, almost shielding the swollen eye. The busted lip. "What is this?" he demanded to the two men. "You were to protect her!"

"The American soldier was in Location Four. We weren't expecting him."

Daniel spun back to Kiew. "He shot you?" She shook her head, looking at his guard. "No. We fought. . ."

"How did she get shot?" Daniel demanded of the guard.

Reluctance tied the man's tongue. "I. . .I manned the gun on the chopper. When I saw the American running, I tried to cut him down."

Fury tore through Daniel. "*You?* You shot her?" In a rage, he rushed them. Yanked the weapon from the man's holster. Fired into the man's chest. Aimed at the other.

"No!" Kiew whimpered as she stumbled into Daniel. She twisted and slid to the floor as a crimson stain blossomed over her abdomen.

The guard cursed.

"Get a doctor!" Daniel shoved the guard toward the door. He jerked and dropped at Kiew's side. As his beautiful Kiew lay there bleeding out, Daniel knew more than ever he would do anything to crush the American soldiers. "I will cut them down like dogs."

BORIS

An hour into the frantic thoughts of betrayal, I fire up the tin cabin's engine. Start driving. I'm not even a mile out when I realize I need gas. I mutter an oath. If I'd waited the two more hours like I'd planned, I'd be out of luck and petrol. Gas stations would be closed.

My little island unto itself lumbers up to a gas pump. Grabbing some cash from the console, I still can't shake the disbelief that they got so close to finding me again. With Zmaray, it was more an invasion of privacy. A breakdown of mutual respect.

This is more. Bigger. It's an outright threat that they'll kill me.

I'm no fool. I won't be that stupid. Just because I dig a fat bank account doesn't mean I'm willing to be someone's lackey. Doesn't work that way. A good business relationship has respect flowing both ways.

With a wave, I greet the store attendant. Shove a wad of bills into his hands then start pumping. He goes back inside. Through the grimy window, I watch him to make sure he's not making calls or talking to anyone. That's right. I'm paranoid now. And with good reason. But the owner stretches out on a bed, the blue hue of a TV glaring across his face.

Jamming the nozzle into the tank, I curse myself. How could I have been so stupid? What mistake did I make? I stare at the cyber beast, disbelieving. What was the weak link? How did I show my hand, reveal my identity?

I'll get away. Vanish. They'll never find me.

An icy wind blows up the back of my spine. The hairs on the back of my neck prickle in a very clichéd, overdone way. And I know. *Know—Something's wrong.*

I look up just in time to see the gas station owner staring out the window. At the same time, I hear an almost inaudible swish.

Something cracks. Pain explodes across the back of my skull. My

350

forehead slams into the extended-length van. "What the—?"

A hand lands on my shoulder, shoving me forward, back into the van. "Not a word."

Heart hammering, I obey. I'm not stupid—there's a gun to the back of my head, and the man seems much larger, so my hands go up. Like a good little boy.

How the heck did I end up here?

There's a pinch in my neck, and then the world swims out of view.

CHAPTER 46

Tera Pass, Afghanistan
25 February—0845 Hours

The percussive *thwump-thwump* of a chopper dragged Brian from the black void. He groaned, hearing his own heartbeat in his ears. As he bent to the side, around the laptop, he used the rocky, snowy terrain to pull himself to his knees. He glanced down, expecting to see a cannon-sized hole through his abdomen. Instead, a large hole in the military-grade casing of the laptop stared back.

Brian almost laughed—but another noise yanked him around. Sounded like...a dog. Up here? Goats, he would understand, but a dog? Middle Easterners viewed dogs as dirty or something, didn't they?

Wobbly legs made it hard to stand, but he wasn't going to die on his knees. But sure as the mountain tried to bury him in snow and Fekiria left him, a dog—a big ugly dog—came bounding over the rise barking his fool head off.

Leading them straight to me.

Brian took aim at the dog's brindle coat.

Wait...

His heart thudded when two men in tac gear appeared over the rise. Then three. Then four.

"You just standing around, waiting for a rescue?" came the voice of Captain Watters.

Potent relief blasted through Brian's veins as the brute of a dog slid to a stop at his feet. The brindled Bullmastiff's bark echoed through the mountains. "Yeah, well, never work harder than you have to." His knees gave out. Propped against a rock, he tried to avoid the tears. Tried to avoid the emotion drowning him.

But then he remembered— "The attack."

The captain jogged to him. "Easy, easy."

"The attack. Osiris. They're hitting the team. Tomor—what day is it?"

"Easy, Hawk. Easy." The captain's gaze swept over him, that thick brow knotting. "You're pretty messed up."

"Listen." He tapped the device strapped to his abdomen. "I've got it. I've got what we need to stop the attack. Stop Osiris."

Hands probed his shoulder.

Fire lit through Brian. His hand swung up on its own. "Augh!"

"Shoulder's tore up," Harrier said. "Frostbite. Fever. Sprained ankle. Bullet wound in his thigh."

Brian looked down, confused. Surprised. Disoriented.

"C'mon, Hawk. You've played hero long enough. Let's get you back to the base. You can tell us everything there."

Titanis slung his arm up under Brian's and lifted him to his feet. Brian was frozen and numb. Didn't care about pain. Just wanted to get home and— "Fekiria!" He twisted toward the captain. "Did you find her? Is she okay?"

The commander's eyes said everything.

That meant— "She's out here. Struck out before sunrise."

Captain Watters tugged him onward. "At the base, Brian. Tell us at the base. We need to get you warmed up."

"I'm not leaving without her—"

"If you die, you can't help us find her. If you die, you can't tell me what you know about that laptop," the captain shouted as the rotor wash of the helo drowned out any further argument.

It didn't touch down but hovered a foot above.

Brian hoisted himself on board then laid back. A medic went to work, tending the visible wounds, not removing his clothing. And that's what Brian dreaded—finding out what damage had been done to his hands and feet. To his shoulder.

To Fekiria.

God. . .bring her back to me.

CHAPTER 47

Camp Eggers, Afghanistan
25 February—1835 Hours

Hell hath no pain like frostbite.

Brian growled as the the pain dug through his skin and tissue layers. Forget the bullet they'd extracted from his shoulder and leg. Forget the sprained ankle. His fingers were swollen and borderline purple, as were his toes. His little toe was black. The doctor promised he'd be a freak show losing that one. If not more.

Forget all of that.

"I don't have time for this," Brian bit out, his irritation growing when he spotted Captain Watters and Falcon enter the room. Double Z waited in the hall.

"You're hypothermic," the nurse said. "You don't have a choice."

"A woman and two girls are out there dying because—"

"Hawk, stand down. That's the hypothermia talking—makes you combative. They're okay."

"No, *I* am combative"—he gritted his teeth and hissed as pain dug its way through his fingers—"when nobody listens to me."

"We're listening. Are you?" The captain leaned forward. "I said they're okay." He twisted his torso and looked at his girlfriend waiting outside. "Fekiria was found."

Brian stilled. Stared at his commanding officers. "You're not just saying that?"

The captain smiled. "Fekiria called Zahrah on a phone—some farmers found them in the mountain. Took them in. Let her use their phone. We sent a chopper out to pick them up."

"Seriously?" Brian felt like he could cry. "How are they? The littlest one, she was coughing—" He saw the look Captain Watters gave, and every ounce of his body froze again. "Tell me she's not dead."

"She's unconscious and critical." The captain rubbed a hand over his face. "It doesn't look good."

Brian tried to swallow but couldn't. His heart rate bleeped rapidly on the machine. "And. . .the others? Fekiria?"

"Same condition as you. Maybe a little worse."

Brian closed his eyes. Fekiria. . .he didn't want her to go through the pain he was experiencing. Frostbite was nothing to sneeze at. In fact, with the purple hue on his nose, he might not have a nose to sneeze with.

At least they were alive. At least they were alive. He repeated the words over and over, but it didn't make him feel better. "What about the laptop?"

Again, Captain Watters went all serious. "The bullet that saved your life might have destroyed it."

"But the hard drive?"

"Bullet went right through." The captain stood at his bedside. "Techs are flying the hard drive to a lab at CECOM to see if they can pull any data off it still."

Communications-Electronics Command would take time. Time they didn't have. A low growl turned into an all-out shout. Brian squeezed his eyes. Was it all a waste? "The attack."

"Burnett's on his way. We've got a team assembled to review what you've said."

"Slusarksi?"

"Missing."

"Son of a biscuit," Brian groused. "Are you freakin' kidding me?"

The captain laid a hand on his good shoulder. "Hey." Their eyes met. "You're alive. You saved three women. Now, tell me what you know."

"Ch–Chinese." Tremors violently shook his body, but he fought to speak around it. "There was a woman in the shanty. She was Asian. Chinese, I'm pretty sure. There were others there before Fekiria and I took shelter, but they left. Probably because of the storm. I guess. Anyway, I woke up to this Asian chick sticking a gun in my face."

Captain Watters eyed him, as if he didn't believe him. As if Brian was talking about dragons and fairies.

"What?"

"You're sure they were Chinese?"

"Dude, I might be losing fingers, but the frostbite didn't get my brain. I know a Chinese chick when I see one."

Falcon shrugged. "She could've been North Korean, Japanese. . ."

"She said *zǎoshàng hǎo*." Brian glared at Falcon. "That's Chinese for 'good morning.'"

"What else?"

Brian thought through the scenario. Thought through what happened. "She and the other guy in there started arguing. I have no idea over what, but I swear he was ready to put one between my eyes." Did she save his life? Intervene? Did any of that matter with what they planned? "The attack is huge. They have all our names and base locations. They're going to hit on the twenty-fourth."

His teammates shared a look.

"What?"

Falcon shrugged. "That was yesterday."

"But. . ." Brian blinked. Had he read it wrong? Decoded it poorly? That didn't make sense. "And their chopper, it was—"

"We have sat images of it. The techs are trying to enhance the images of her face so we can identify her."

A doctor came in but hesitated when he saw the captain and Falcon. The captain patted Brian's leg. "Warm up. We need you back."

Brian gave a nod as they left him. Any other day he might argue to Egypt and back, but right now, he wanted sleep. About a year's worth. Yet at the same time, he didn't feel they had time to sleep. But if he slept— "Hey." He leaned his head up, grimacing at the tug of pain in his shoulder. "Let me know when she gets here? That. . .that she's safe?"

Captain Watters gave a knowing smile. "Of course."

———✺———

Camp Eggers, Afghanistan
26 February—1320 Hours

Hands and feet bandaged, Fekiria sat up in the bed. "I didn't think we'd make it out alive." She looked to her right where Sheevah lay asleep, her hands and feet bandaged also, and her nose sported a large white salve.

"It's a miracle." Zahrah eased onto the bed beside her, brushing a strand of hair from Fekiria's face. "I still can't believe all you've told me."

She met her cousin's brown eyes. "God was watching over me, over all of us. That's what you were going to say, right?"

Zahrah seemed to wilt. "Please—let's not fight now."

"Psalm 57:1."

Her cousin blinked, her lips parting in question.

Fekiria had been truly hateful toward the two people who were probably the most precious to her in the world. "Mitra's Bible. . . She had me read to her the night she died, and I. . ." She looked to the small stand were the tattered book lay. "It helped me make the hardest decision."

Zahrah applied more medicinal cream to Fekiria's dry, cracked lips. "To leave Hawk."

She nodded. "I knew he would not try to save his friends."

"Loving a warrior is hard. Dying in the line of duty is an honor to them. They would rather take that road than to dishonor their sacred oath."

"When I first met him, I saw no difference between him and my father and brothers." Fekiria wished she could see him, to see if he held it against her.

"And now?" Zahrah's words were so soft and encouraging. Her cousin knew what happened on that mountain. Not just the logistics but the emotional element. Except the kisses. She hadn't told anyone about those. "A lot more than your pinky toe was lost on that mountain, wasn't it?"

"What do you mean?"

"I think you lost your anger and the hatred you felt toward Americans." Zahrah leaned a little closer. "And the hatred you harbored toward our God."

"We Afghans—most of us at least—are good people, Zahrah."

Her cousin smiled, so prettily and unmarred by the nasty black and purple scars of frostbite. "Of course *we* are." Zahrah laughed. "You forget, I am half Afghan."

"It's true. . .I do not feel the anger the way I once did," she said softly. "Can I see him?"

Zahrah's face brightened. "I thought you'd never ask." She slipped off the bed and went to a freestanding cabinet where she retrieved a bag. "Your clothes." From the bag, she drew out a pink silk hijab and held it up. "Yes?"

Hesitation had always been her enemy. "I may have lost my anger and gained curiosity about the Christian Messiah, but I have not lost who I am." She nodded. "Please."

Zahrah came to her side and brushed her hair back then expertly wrapped the hijab around her neck and face. With the hands still healing and bandaged, it was too hard and painful to do it herself. Her cousin helped her into a long tunic and pants then wheeled her down the hall.

"Knock knock," Zahrah said as they waited before a curtained area.

"I'm decent," came Brian's voice.

Zahrah tugged back the curtain.

Brian stood with his back to them—a tattoo, black and large, winged across his shoulders—and struggled into a shirt, which had caught on the bandage over his right pectoral. He was stuck for a moment, and Zahrah reached over and assisted.

"Thanks," he mumbled, then his gaze hit Fekiria. "Hey." His tone was soft and warm as he came and squatted beside the wheelchair, angling his leg out straight. A smile, thick with emotion, creased the corners of his eyes. "How are you doing? They wouldn't let me come down there—propriety and all."

Zahrah slipped past them as she promised to wait in the hall.

His hands were bandaged, too, but it didn't stop him from placing his hand over hers. "Heard you hooked up with some smelly farmer after you dumped me."

"So, you are not angry?"

He frowned. "You left me. Of course I'm mad." Then smiled again. "Kidding. Kiria, you're one of the bravest women I know. Can't say I was happy to find you gone. If I'd caught up with you, I might have buried you up there, but. . ."

"I had to," she said. "You wouldn't have gone, would you?"

"No," he whispered. "No way I could leave you."

Her heart thumped at his words. The soft, firm way he said them. The look in his eyes. "I knew you wouldn't, that's why I had to do it."

"You did the right thing." He smiled up at her. "And thanks for the Bible verse."

Did he understand what she meant with that verse? Not just sharing it with him, but. . .

Brian gave an affirming nod. "I don't have all the answers—that would be my granddad—and I'll be the first to admit that God doesn't make sense to me all the time, but I know. . .I *know* He watched over me, over you up there."

"I. . ." She felt like she had a terrible secret. A giddy, terrible secret. "I prayed to Him, asked Him to protect you."

Brian stared up at her for a long time. "You sure do know how to knock the wind out of a guy."

"Hawk! Let's go," came a loud voice. "AHOD."

Brian looked toward the curtain where a dark-haired, scowling soldier appeared, glanced at them for a second. "Captain wants you there." After another look between them, he started away. "I'll let him know you're on your way."

"Sorry," Brian said.

"Go," she said, feeling awkward and unsure. Zahrah and her American boyfriend were close to growing serious. She and Brian. . . was this a beginning?

"On one condition."

Giving him a warning look, she waited.

"Promise me you won't find some sheep farmer to hide out with while I'm gone."

"Goat farmers are better." She shrugged when he glowered. "They're nicer and have phones."

Brian leaned in, hands braced on the edges of her wheelchair. "No farmers, or I'm coming in with everything I've got to save you from your own foolishness."

EPILOGUE

Kandahar Airfield, Afghanistan
25 March—1640 Hours

Cassandra Walker strode down the hall lit only by the ambient light of the two or three offices with personnel working the night shift. Her heart thumped a little harder with each step closer she came to the briefing room. He would be there. Reviewing files. Reviewing reports.

General Burnett said an attack was imminent, but details were sketchy. She wouldn't be going with the team to recon, but she had to get Sal to talk to her. They had to clear the air.

A dozen paces from the door, she heard his voice.

Hauling in a breath, she stopped. Closed her eyes. Slumped against the thin wall. She had to get this under control. He still had too much effect on her. On her heart.

But she couldn't escape the memories. The semidarkened offices. His charm. He had that by the boatload, but he rarely showed it. Not while on duty.

Okay. Get it together, Cassie.

She pushed off the wall, drew in another long breath for courage, then turned the corner into the briefing area.

Sal stood with his back to her, tapping a file against the desk as he fingered another file sitting on a table to his left. Still had those broad shoulders. Trim waist.

Flashes of a shirtless Sal...taut muscles...warm kisses...passionate urging...

"What do you want?"

Cassie snapped straight. Blinked. She hadn't even noticed he'd turned around. Swallowing probably made this worse, but she was drowning in her body's betrayal. "We need to talk."

Sal snorted, turned, and lifted the files from the desk then came toward her. "No. We don't."

"Sal, please." She stepped into his path.

A mistake.

He was right there. Just inches between them. She couldn't breathe. Couldn't push the images that were as fresh right now as they were four years ago.

Brown eyes with gold glints held her fast. Held her hostage really. "Nothing needs to be said. You know what you did. So do I."

A piece of her died in his words. "I—"

"No." Fire ignited those gold flecks. His shoulders drew tight, and he hovered over her. Menacing. Powerful. "I don't want to hear it. I never want to hear anything from you again, Cassie."

It was still so hard to think straight in his presence. "You need to hear me out."

"The only thing I need to do is make sure I never see you again." Sal bumped her shoulder as he moved around her, that raw energy most didn't understand roiling in his wake.

And truthfully, she didn't understand why she was so drawn to it. Had been since they met back at Fort Belvoir. What terrified her was that she still responded to him the way she had as a love-struck, newly minted second lieutenant.

What would terrify her more was the day he learned of her new assignment.

—✕—

Kandahar Airfield, Afghanistan
25 March—1700 Hours

Sal balled up the churning anger and tossed it aside as he entered the Command building. He tugged off his cover and strode toward the rear room where Raptor had an AHOD. After their meeting earlier, they agreed to rest up, eat up, and meet back up to discuss plans.

He entered the room, eyeing Hawk, who sat at the table, his left hand sporting the angry purple welts of frostbite. His right was still partially bandaged. "Think you can handle this?" Sal asked as he slid the files onto the table.

"Yes, sir."

They hadn't gotten along in a while. The guy had too much machismo. Not enough wisdom.

Or maybe it was all the second-guessing since Vida.

"Good, we're all here," Dean said as he entered the room, trailed by Burnett. "Okay, listen up. The hard drive was messed up, but they've scrounged up enough to be verified. We have credible intel that an attack on the CECOM facility is imminent. We're going to head over there and do some recon."

Burnett sighed. "It's insane. They're running secondary and tertiary checks on everyone who's been in and out of that facility in the last few months, but—"

"They might get it sorted by next Christmas," Hawk offered.

"Exactly. There's too much and too few resources to do the legwork." Burnett's hands rested on his belt. "Now, we have information on Meng-Li." He nodded to the side. "We know he's here in Afghanistan."

"How are we knowing that?" Hawk asked as Hastings worked a laptop from her position next to Titanis.

"Because we have an asset with inside information that says he is. And Riordan's team has had eyes on him for the last twenty-four."

"Riordan?" Sal shifted. That was news to him. "Why are the SEALs involved this time?"

"Hooah," Hawk muttered.

"Because with Raptor being the primary target of Osiris, the SEALs can flop around incognito while attention is diverted," Burnett answered.

"We had a nasty run the last few months," Sal said, "but we've garnered enough intel to have us on an *assaulting-forward* trajectory. CECOM is only the beginning. Whatever they can accomplish here, they can repeat Stateside—imagine them getting hold of soldiers' families."

"We must ensure that does not happen." Burnett looked over his shoulder at the image on the wall then to Hastings. "Get Daniel Jin's mug up there."

"Yes, sir." Hastings worked her fingers quickly.

An image popped up on the wall. The slick Asian looked like he had as much money as fashion sense.

"Hold up." Hawk snapped to his feet, his face suddenly pale. "That woman—who is that woman?"

Hastings shook herself from the surprise of Hawk's question then glanced down at her laptop. "That. . .that's his paramour, we believe. She's his right hand. Her name is Kiew Tang."

"That's her," Hawk said, stabbing his blistered finger at the screen. "That's the woman from the shanty. She held the gun to my head."

Sal came around. Stared at the picture. "You sure?"

"Heck yeah! Think I'd forget someone pressing a silenced pistol into my forehead?"

Burnett nodded to Hastings, who lifted her laptop from the table and hurried from the room. "Good work, Bledsoe. We'll get eyes on—"

Crack! Thud!

The ground shook.

The team rose as one, hands going to their weapons. Eyes wide. Collective breath held.

"What was that?" Dean demanded as he went to the door.

A red-faced sergeant burst into the room. "CECOM just got hit! It's a ball of flames!"

ABOUT THE AUTHOR

Ronie Kendig is an award-winning, bestselling author who grew up an Army brat. After twenty-plus years of marriage, she and her hunky hero husband have a full life with four children, a Maltese Menace, and a retired military working dog in Northern Virginia. Author and speaker, Ronie loves engaging readers through her Rapid-Fire Fiction. Ronie can be found at www.roniekendig.com, on Facebook (www.facebook.com/rapidfirefiction), Twitter (@roniekendig), and Goodreads (www.goodreads.com/RonieK).

Also available from Shiloh Run Press

Hawk

Unabridged Audiobook

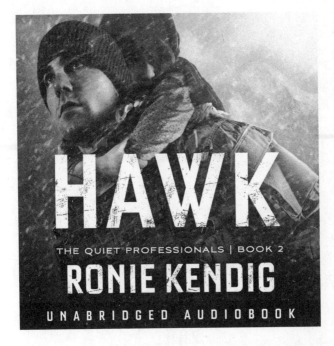

Available wherever audiobooks are sold.

THE QUIET PROFESSIONALS SERIES

RAPTOR 6
BOOK 1

Available Now

FALCON
BOOK 3

Coming Spring 2015